The T-50 tank's au_____ of a second before my nex_____erse and crashed into the b_____ The smaller T-20 unloaded its autocannon through the bank, searching for me.

I crashed out the other side and onto Barlow Street. Valens citizens who had been trapped in occupied Fu'an ran for their lives. I tried not to crush any of those. They were the good squishies.

A second T-50 heavy was there, turning to angle its armor at me, but its vulnerable flank was still visible. It had been expecting me to move up on 4th street, and I had taken it by surprise with my extremely unorthodox approach. I reflexively gut punched it with my main gun. A glowing hole appeared in its side. Liquid smart armor sprayed out the hole. But it didn't ignite. That was the hard thing about automated tanks, no crew to kill. But we were only a hundred meters apart, so as it turned, I shot it with my coaxial railgun, right through the hole I'd just cut.

The tiny hypervelocity round zipped through, hit something, and then bounced around inside like the world's angriest ping pong ball. The tank stopped turning and orange fire erupted out the hole.

I couldn't get away from the T-20, and its rapid-fire autocannon struck me repeatedly as I drove into the Valens Museum of Fine Art. The smaller shells didn't penetrate beyond the first layer of my armor, but they tore off one of my mortars and destroyed one of my cameras. My brain translated that into a sensation like getting poked in the eye with a white-hot poker.

I crashed through the glass wall, and then took a left through the stairs. I had to keep going this way, right through the main showroom. Luckily the Syndicate had already looted all the valuable artwork, so I was only destroying my people's finest architecture, rather than a generation of our culture.

I'm a tank, but even tanks can still be sensitive about stuff like that.

—from "A Tank Named Bob" by Larry Correia

Recent Releases by the Contributors

◈ ◈ ◈

David Weber
The Honor Harrington
series and others
Governor

Larry Correia
Monster Hunter
International series
and others
Monster Hunter Bloodlines

Wen Spencer
Elfhome series
and others
Harbinger

Kevin Ikenberry
The Revelations Saga
Peacemaker

Keith Hedger
Burn 'n' Karma series
Easy Jobs

Patrick Chiles
Frontier

Tony Daniel
Guardian of Night

Hank Davis
Coeditor of *Time Troopers*

Kacey Ezell
The Romanov Rescue
(with Tom Kratman and
Justin Watson)

Christopher Ruocchio
The Sun Eater series
Kingdoms of Death

Monalisa Foster
Ravages of Honor series
*Ravages of Honor:
Ascension*

Robert E. Hampson
Coeditor of
The Founder Effect

Lou J Berger
*Professor Challenger:
The Serpent of the Loch*

To purchase any of these titles in e-book form, please go to
www.baen.com.

WORLD BREAKERS

edited by
TONY DANIEL
and
CHRISTOPHER RUOCCHIO

WORLD BREAKERS

This is a work of fiction. All the characters and events portrayed in this book are fictional, and any resemblance to real people or incidents is purely coincidental.

A Baen Books Original

Baen Publishing Enterprises
P.O. Box 1403
Riverdale, NY 10471
www.baen.com

ISBN: 978-1-9821-9206-8

Cover art by Dominic Harman

First printing, August 2021
First mass market printing, August 2022

Distributed by Simon & Schuster
1230 Avenue of the Americas
New York, NY 10020

Library of Congress Catalog Number: 2021022440

Printed in the United States of America

10 9 8 7 6 5 4 3 2 1

CONTENTS

WORLD BREAKERS

INTRODUCTION

The seeds for this anthology were sown many years ago, some time in the early 1990s. Jim Baen was writing an editorial letter to one of our authors, Keith Laumer. Keith had asked what Jim would like to see next. Another Retief novel? Perhaps something more serious? This is what Jim wrote:

"New Novel: Absolutely. As I said only somewhat coherently over the phone, this time I would like something that hints at the profound erudition possessed by the author and is driven by a plot imbued with the deepest philosophical insight into the essential tragedy of the human condition as it is and places it in the most bathetic contrast to what could, in a better world, be our birthright. Something with scope. Something with sentient tanks."

And as I was but a mere editorial assistant at the time, it was my duty to file this letter. I saw it, made a copy of this section for myself, and it has lived on a bulletin board within a glance of my desk in every office I've occupied since then.

"Something with scope. Something with sentient

tanks." We probably should have put that on Jim's headstone (may he rest in peace). Such delightful words.

In August of 2019 I made mention of this quote on social media, and the other two quotations that I have posted on that same bulletin board. The first of these is from the *New York Times Book Review*: "As someone has since put it, mankind's most deeply held need is not to obtain food, clothing or shelter or to preserve the species but to change someone else's copy." And, as quoted in John Hertz's *Vanamonde*, from W. Fowler, *Modern English Usage:* "To have to depend on one's employer's readiness to take the will for the deed is surely a humiliation that no decent craftsman should be willing to put up with."

But it was Jim's words that sparked the imagination, not surprisingly. And so, from that discussion, sprang this anthology. My thanks to Lou Berger for taking the idea and running with it, and to Tony Daniel and Christopher Ruocchio for helming this volume of original stories about things that can break worlds and mend hearts.

The thing is, Keith Laumer *did* possess profound erudition, and did have insight into the essential tragedy of the human condition. That's what made that editorial direction so exciting; Keith had actually written such works.

You can find the biographical details online, but Laumer had served in the Army Air Corps in WWII, went to university in Sweden, finished his degree in architecture from the University of Illinois, went back into the Air Force, twice, and in between tours served as a member of the Foreign Service in Burma.

When he wrote military science fiction in the Bolo series or spoofed the pretensions of diplomats in the Retief series, he knew whereof he wrote. And it showed. His work did and does resonate with readers. The tragedy of Laumer's life was that, according to those who knew him, his personality changed after he had a stroke in 1971. But he was a stubborn man, and he continued to write up until his death in 1993.

And we at the Baen office knew him well—he called frequently, and while we never met him, we all felt close to him. And tried to support him long distance—we were in New York City, he in his house in Florida surrounded by his beloved Cougars (the cars, not the beasts)—as best we could. He was not an easy man in those post-stroke years, but we, his typist Deane Fetrow, and the local SF community by way of the Haldemans (Jack, Joe, Gay et al.) were able, I think, to make his final years if not easy, at least easier than they could have been.

And here, we hope, you will find the spirit of Keith Laumer living on, in these original stories, inspired by Jim Baen's words.

—Toni Weisskopf, March 2021

WORLD ENOUGH
by Robert E. Hampson

We are in the early day of the brain-machine interface, but it is a time of rapid strides and the movement from experimental phase to real-world applications. The author, who is also a noted neuroscientist, is on the forefront of such research. Here, the ultimate union of man—or rather woman—and machine arrives in the heat of battle. The danger in such an amalgamation may be that the human component will fade into the machine. The hope is a that a strange new, highly effective synthesis may be possible!

⊕ ⊕ ⊕

"Lieutenant! Orders from higher. We're advancing into the new tunnels." Lieutenant Flagg was in charge of Charlie One—first platoon, C company of the TEF—the Terran Expeditionary Forces on Fortunes World. Patch technically outranked him by virtue of six months seniority, but Flagg was a line officer and platoon leader, while Patch was an "intel weenie" and observer attached to Flagg's platoon.

That didn't mean she wouldn't be slogging through the muck.

"Roger, Lieutenant. Moving out." Patch picked up her rucksack and once again mused on the similarity between this situation and history. She'd studied a TwenCen battle in Europe where nearly a million lives were lost between two sides trading the same six miles of territory back and forth.

Sort of like what was happening here. Her platoon had advanced before, only to be driven back by artillery fire and collapsed trench walls. The artillery itself was not usually a direct hazard to the troops. The trenches varied from two to five meters in depth—the "natural" ones caused by the comet impacts, that is. Sure, the bases and assembly areas took damage, but most rounds were at too shallow an angle to hit a trench straight on. The bigger threat was shrapnel and collapsing walls from a near miss. To counter this danger, the TEF had some tunneling equipment and made their own reinforced trenches and tunnels. Part of the problem, though, is that the enemy seemed to do the same thing, only faster.

They also tended to shell or undermine any location where Humans concentrated forces and equipment. Neither Humans nor their current opposition, the Aneliad, were the first to land on Fortune's World. An expedition from Earth arrived on Trappist 1C to seek their . . . fortune . . . in the rich mineral deposits, only to discover that the technologically advanced Sylph were already present. Fortunately, the Sylph were (mostly) peaceful, and they *really* didn't like the weather on T1C, with its 2.5 Earth-day solar orbit and 225 Earth-day planetary rotation. The short "year" meant extreme tidal effects from the other planets huddled close to the cool red dwarf star, while the long "day" meant extreme weather ranging from midday temperatures in low triple digits (Celsius) and nighttime temps that stopped just short of freezing oxygen out of the thin atmosphere. The two races reached an agreement to share the planet, with Sylphs providing the mining technology, and Humans providing the surface workforce . . . and defense.

It worked well, until a new race arrived to claim Fortune's World.

Patch marveled at the smooth walls and floor of the tunnel. They were standing atop a valuable field of oganesson—the only known noble *metal*—used by the Sylphs (and now Humans) to protect high-energy reactors and engines. This particular deposit of OG was termed "fusite," since it included high-pressure carbon and tantalum, making it impossible to mine without the Sylph-provided machines. Yet somehow, the Aneliad tunneling devices cleared the muck all the way down to the fusite layer—in fact, the tunnels tended to descend to the fusite anywhere the surface trenches didn't quite reach the OG vein. The walls and roof were rounded, and the surface was glossy as if it had been coated with a hard resin.

Patch was in the middle of Red squad. There were two tunnels to scout, therefore Red took the easternmost entrance while Blue squad took the west. Lieutenant Flagg assigned Patch to Red and told her to stay at the back of the formation. Her job was to observe anything about the enemy and report back to HQ. It was the whole reason she'd been embedded with the platoon. Flagg would follow in five minutes with his own squad, Green, while the final squad, Black, would do the same in the opposite tunnel.

While moving, Patch kept her eyes moving to be alert for any sign of the enemy, but when Sergeant Brodén called a halt, she turned to study the wall of the tunnel. Closer inspection showed it to be slightly pebbled, and not exactly smooth. She took off a glove and touched the surface. It was warmer than she expected. she knelt to do the same with the floor of the tunnel.

"Something unusual, Ell-Tee?" asked Brodén.

"We're not just on top of the fusite, we're in it."

"What? How?"

"See this?" she pointed to a dark line about half a meter up the wall. Below the line, the material was blue-black, with a slight sheen; above the line the shading turned more to brown with a dull finish. "This line is the top of the fusite layer. Whatever the Annies used to create these tunnels dug into the fusite."

"You can't dig fusite, can you? I mean, even this big deposit can only be chipped away from the edges. These tunnels are *mines*?"

"Perhaps. They could simply be tunnels made by something that doesn't care what it's tunneling through."

"Either way, I don't like this. An enemy we've never seen, troops that disappear without a trace, and now impossible tunnels." Brodén pitched his voice to activate the squad net. "Wattana, Pandev. Take point, and take it slow. Red Squad, move out."

◈◈◈

"Movement!"

"Contact!"

"It's moving fast."

"Aa—!" The scream cut off almost as soon as it started.

"Sword, Panda, report!" Brodén called on the squad net.

"Sar'nt, this is Fatman. Wattana and Pandev were about twenty meters in front of Gecko and me. It looks like there's a cross tunnel. I saw Sword step forward, and there was a dark blur. Panda's the one that screamed, but he's gone, too."

"Acknowledged, Fattore. You and Lissard hold right where you are. Don't move up, don't investigate. Wait for me to come up." Brodén turned to Patch. "Come along, *but stay behind me*. Higher would have my head if I let something happen to you, Ell-tee."

It was almost one hundred meters to the place where the point team disappeared. As Patch and the sergeant passed other platoon members, he instructed them to stay put and be alert for any sound or movement. As they reached the cross tunnel, the air temperature increased noticeably.

Patch placed her gloved hand on the wall at the junction of the two tunnels and pulled it back quickly. "It's hot. The tunnel walls have been heated."

"Look down. It's fusite all the way up. Whatever dug this tunnel . . ." Brodén paused. "This tunnel was dug right through refractory metal. Who does that?"

"Offhand, I'd say the enemy does."

"Yes, well, that thought doesn't fill me with joy, Lieutenant." The sergeant switched on the light mounted to his rifle and flashed it both ways up and down the cross tunnel. When they'd left their positions in the trench, the passage had still been open to sky, but they'd now descended several meters, and the top was completely closed, blocking all light except for reflections from back the way they had come. "Up there, there's something on the ground."

The new tunnel was wide—wide enough for a tank, in Patch's estimation. The two of them stepped down into the cross tunnel—she could feel the heat through the soles of her boots—and then back up to where the original tunnel continued on the other side.

There was body, or at least half of one.

"Panda. Cut in half," Brodén observed.

Patch looked around, and both directions down the cross tunnel. "And no sign of Sword. If he was in the cross tunnel when whatever it was came through? Something that can cut, melt, or *eat* fusite isn't going to leave much behind."

A voice came over the comm. "Contact! Movement at six o'clock."

"Move up, get out of its way," ordered Brodén.

"This is Fatman. It's moving fast, I don't think we have time and there's no room to evade, Sar'nt." The sound of energy and projectile weapons fire could be heard as the comm cut off.

"Gecko to Sabaton. No joy, Sergeant, it didn't even notice our weapons, but apparently it wasn't heading for us, just cut into the tunnel wall and made its own. The rock just melted."

"What did it look like, Private?"

"Big. Long. It filled our tunnel and then some. When it disappeared into the wall, it had a long body that took plenty of time to pass. Sort of like a worm."

"Worms."

"What was that, Lieutenant?" the squad leader asked.

"I said 'they're worms.' We should have known. The Sylph's translators work with what they can find in the language database. They called them 'Aneliad.' That's close enough to 'annelid,' which is an old Terran word for worms."

"Worms that eat fusite?"

"Possibly. It could be food, like termites and cellulose. Maybe they regurgitate it later, like bees." Patch thought for a moment. "The Ops Center needs to know. The tunnels they're digging are big. We could fit tanks down here."

"And armor them with what? Not fusite."

"No, not fusite, unless we want to attract them. We probably need to electrify them; it works with a lot of Terran insects."

"Last I checked, Terra didn't have . . ." Brodén looked at the cross tunnel, ". . . ten-meter-wide worms."

"Agreed, but we need to start somewhere." Patch pulled out a sensor package and took some readings from the tunnel wall and then forced herself to focus it on Pandey's corpse. "I know I'm not really in command here, Sergeant, but I think we need to retreat and report this."

"Agreed Lieutenant. I'll call the PL."

While Brodén was on the private comm channel to Lieutenant Flagg, Patch stepped down into the cross tunnel to return the way they had come. She heard a distant shout of "Lieutenant Passchendaele!" and saw movement out of the corner of her eye.

Someone grabbed her by the straps on the back of her pack and pulled her back out of the tunnel. She felt a searing heat and then a sharp pain in her left foot. As she lost consciousness, she sensed more than saw the alien creature disappear back down the tunnel where the rest of the squad waited.

Patch opened her eyes and saw white. After a moment, her eyes adjusted and she could see enough features to discern white-painted walls and ceiling.

Hospital. She'd been injured and was now in the sickbay of the *St. Benedict*, the TEF's troop transport maintaining orbit around Trappist-1.

Memory came flooding back, and she tried to sit up in the bed. She needed to report to the commander.

"Relax, Patch. I'm here," came a voice to her side.

She turned her head and saw a window next to the bed, with two figures in the observation area beyond. One was Colonel Aachen, deputy commander of the Strategy and Intel group and Patch's actual boss. Beside him was General Plumer, head of operations for the TEF. The small woman looked at Patch with concern as her taller subordinate spoke again.

"Don't try to move, Patch. You've got burns and chemical inhalation."

A nurse came in, covered head to toe in protective clothing.

"Am I contagious?" she managed.

"No, but you're very sick." He spoke through a comm unit beside the bed. "This is for your protection."

Patch had many questions, but the nurse told her to wait for the doctor, who would be along in about an hour. He then pressed a button on one of the consoles, and she drifted back to sleep.

The next time she opened her eyes, she saw two figures in the protective suits. One was unfamiliar, and therefore probably the doctor. The other was General Plumer.

"So, what happened to me?"

"Your platoon encountered the Aneliad—'worms' you called them in your report. The staff sergeant apparently tossed you to safety, but the rest of the platoon . . . Hell, the rest of the *company* was wiped out. When we got you here, you were badly banged up, your leg was crushed, and you had uncontrollable muscle spasms."

"We had to give you a neuro blocker to stop the convulsions," supplied the doctor. "Your peripheral nervous system is well . . . the best answer is that it's misfiring."

"What? Why?"

"The best guess is something that we've only seen twice before. For now, we're calling it fusite poisoning."

"Fusite's inert, it's a refractory metal. It can't be a poison."

"Unfortunately, it can, under extreme conditions. There was a tech who stopped a runaway antimatter reaction in the engine room of the *Worlds of Wonder* passenger ship about a decade back. He had to open the outer containment and fill the reaction chamber with fusite to stop the reaction. Then there was the orbital fusion power plant worker who survived an explosion because he became mostly encased in fusite released from the chamber."

Patch was confused. "Sure, we have plenty of fusite here, but I haven't been in the vicinity of any high-energy events."

"Actually, you have," said Plumer. "The worms do *something* to the fusite to digest it. The science teams have been puzzling it out, but your case points to it being some sort of controlled high-energy process."

"Oh, okay. So, you just need to detoxify me and flush it out, right?"

"I'm sorry, it's not that simple. There's no known way to reverse the process. Your peripheral nerves are degenerating and your immune system is compromised. Organ failure will follow unless we do something immediately."

"Do it, then. I authorize it. Whatever it takes."

"We need to talk about this, Patch. It's a pretty radical process." Plumer looked quite concerned behind the faceplate of her isolation suit.

The process was called capsulation. Patch's body would be placed in a full life-support chamber similar to the cryostasis units used for travel across long interstellar distances, except instead of hibernation, neural implants would create a brain-computer interface so that she remained awake and mentally active. The capsule would provide everything her brain needed and slow the deterioration of her body. It was theoretically reversible— if someone could find a way to reverse the damage to her nerves and organs in the next few months—but for all practical purposes, it was a one-way procedure. Most COIs—capsulated organic intelligences—chose to interface with computer systems and work in surveillance or data analysis. A rare few chose to operate robotic devices, android bodies, or other surrogates for their natural body, but the urge to interact with the outside world tended to fade the longer the COIs inhabited their digital worlds. A capsulated person had a longer lifespan than if the disease or damage were allowed to take its toll, but as far as anyone in the TEF knew, the longest a COI had remained viable was two years. Patch had read a book once about COIs operating starships, but she knew *that* concept was purely science fiction.

"No, I do *not* want to be interfaced with the Ops computer." Patch's voice emanated from speakers located through the room. "I want to be installed in a tank."

"That's just not practical. You're our best analyst. It makes the most sense to install you in either Ops or S&I. You'll have access to all the imagery, the sensor packs, and even the comms." The lead technician waved in the direction of her capsule. "Besides, you won't *fit* in a tank!"

Patch sent a signal to one of the cameras located in the capsulation lab and directed it toward her life support unit.

It looked almost exactly like an egg, two meters tall, just over a meter across at its widest. It rested in a wheeled cradle, with robotic arms and sensors adjacent to, but not directly connected to the capsule. Only one connection marred the smooth, translucent surface of the egg. Lights raced just underneath that surface, in random-appearing patterns leading from and to a fifty-centimeter trunk connecting the base of the egg to a monitoring console against one wall. The life-support system in the capsule was self-contained, and could sustain her body and mind for a month without replenishment. While connected, however, the umbilical trunk provided nutrients, removed wastes and provided high-speed communication to the facility's computers.

All other connection was via encrypted wireless radio and visual light connections similar to the secure comms used by the troops, including the speakers over which Patch was arguing with the technician. Each word was punctuated by swirls and patterns of light on the egg, with colors accentuating the words. The patterns became redder as the argument continued.

"Dammit, I didn't go through all of this to be stuck in a remote base, watching the battle secondhand. Besides, there's plenty of space in a Command tank."

"Major, that's not true. Your capsule and the interface will take up the entire crew cabin. You'll be the only one there. Who will operate the tank?"

"*I* will operate the tank. Don't you get that? I've got all of the interfaces, and as a COI I can multi-task. I can drive the tank, fire the gun, operate a squad of remote tanks and chew gum at the same time."

"Ah, no, I don't think that's quite right."

"Okay, so I can't chew gum anymore, but all of my motor cortex is intact. My legs will be treads and my arms will be weaponry. I can do this."

"We're going to have to take this up with higher."

"Then do this. I've been away from the war for long

enough. I saw the intel. The push to Phaseline Arnim was forced back and we risk losing the Messine Formation. One more advance by the Annies and we lose the Salient. I have what, a year in this shell before I go insane or get lost in my own dreams?"

"I'm going to have to call this up the chain."

"Yes, well then call General Plumer right now. We talked about this when I accepted capsulation. She and Colonel Aachen know I want this, and they know I can do it."

"If you say so. It's a big risk, though, and I'm not sure even the general will authorize risking you like that. I think this needs to go to Marshal Byng."

If Patch could still feel her physical body, and if she still formed words with her mouth, she would have bitten her tongue. Marshal Byng was praised by many . . . except his own troops. He tended to make the most politically expedient decisions, rather than the ones that made sense to a soldier in the field. He was also rather fond of the memory of a particular ancestor . . .

Byng had visited her soon after she had returned from her first encounter with the Aneliad worm. "Passchendaele, eh? Just like the town in Belgium. You know, I had a relative in that war. Julien Byng. Noble fellow, commanded the field there in Flanders. Hmm, Flanders. That would make a good name for this field— all of those trenches, eh? Good names. Right, well, hurry up and get better, I'm sure Felix Aachen needs you back on your feet in Ops as soon as possible."

And that was it. Sixty seconds and he was gone. It was his entire command style, staying on the *St. Benedict* and communicating with the ground troops once a week when the starship's orbit coincided with Fortune's World's orbit and rotation such that the newly renamed Flanders Base was in view. He took to naming all of the planetary features for early TwenCen Belgium. He seemed overjoyed at the family connection. The troops were mostly indifferent, but Patch had actually studied history, and knew the reputation and implication of the bloody battles of Ypres in the Flanders fields. The only way to avoid the same fate was to get out there and take the offensive, instead of waiting on the worms' next move.

"'Had we but world enough and time / This coyness, lady, were no crime. / We would sit down, and think which way / To walk, and pass our long love's day.' We *don't* have 'world enough' and we certainly don't have time. Tell the colonel and the general 'But at my back I always hear / Time's winged chariot hurrying near . . . '"

"That's . . . interesting. Did you write that?"

"No. It's from 'To His Coy Mistress.' It was a love song written by Andrew Marvell, a seventeenth-century Earth poet and politician. He's saying to seize opportunity and not let it be wasted. Tell the general that I said that the time for coyness is over."

The technician hadn't been quite correct in saying that her capsule would occupy the entire personnel compartment. There was room for one person, even though quarters outside the command deck were limited. Patch was Tank Commander, driver and gunner all in one; therefore, her "organic component" was assigned the role of assistant gunner. Patch had thought that Command would saddle her with a nurse, or worse yet, one of the capsulation techs. Fortunately, she received an actual assistant gunner from the command tank at Lille. It took a couple of months to become fully skilled at operating both her own "body" and remotely operated drones, but soon, operating the smaller tanks in parallel with her own vehicle felt no different than flexing her fingers or curling her toes. Life as a tank was good, and Patch knew that she could solve the issues controlling both crewed and uncrewed assets locally, on the battlefield where it was needed.

She also knew there was a clock ticking. The psychometricians called it "digital fugue"—sooner or later, COIs stopped communicating with the outside world. The theory was that the more a human brain inhabited a virtual environment, the more the real world became abstract and unreal. The numbers were equally split between COIs simply becoming catatonic vs. commanding their life support to cease.

So far, Patch didn't think she was falling into digital fugue. Sure, she could get distracted when she was multitasking, but on the whole, being in the tank . . . *being* the tank . . . was exhilarating. The machinery was her body and the instruments were her senses. She felt part of the world, part of the war, even if she hadn't been released to operate entirely on her own. She was confident that time was coming.

In fact, it was coming today.

"Unit P-C-H of the Line, reporting for duty."

"Um," the comm crackled. "Patch, that's not your designation."

"It's traditional, Jonny," she sent back. Down in the control room, Corporal "Mac" Macmullen tried to suppress giggles. When Patch had discovered that Norma Macmullen was a fellow science fiction fan, she'd shared several TwenCen books featuring tanks operated by artificial intelligence.

"A girl and her tank," Norma sent.

"A tank and her girl," Patch replied.

"A tank and her comm discipline. Cut the chatter, Patch." The voice on the comm was formal, but there was just a hint of amusement for those who knew the speaker well.

"Yes, sir, Colonel Aachen. CT1917-P is ready."

"Good. We've lost the signal from Hill 60 and there's movement warnings out in the Salient."

"Understood, Colonel. Do we have release?"

"Yes, Patch. You have release. Godspeed." The comm crackled, and cut off, but Patch's digital senses picked a few last words out of the signal before it disconnected. " . . . and may He have mercy on us for sending you out."

"Hill 60's close, Mac, but it's probably behind enemy lines by now. I'm headed to Hill 65." Using the same Earth World War I terminology Marshal Byng was so fond of, the TEF holdings on the fusite field were termed the Salient, since they represented a Terran bulge into what was otherwise Annie territory. Named landmarks corresponded to surface features (what few remained), mines or staging areas; "hills" referred to places where the subsurface tunnels approached or even broke the surface. These were good entry points for the command tanks to enter the Annie-dug tunnels.

"What about sending drones to 60?" Mac suggested.

"Good idea. I'll send Larry and Curly to Hill 60. We'll keep Shemp, Moe, and Curly Joe with us, and send Ted and Joe out on perimeter patrol." Patch engaged the drive, and the tank platoon left Ypres Base for the first time as an independent command.

The mining tunnels were large enough for drone tanks, but much too narrow for command tanks; the tunnels dug by the Annies, however, were more than large enough to fit multiple tanks. The TEF had enlarged a few tunnels of their own to allow tanks to reach out into the salient. For this effort, a full battalion, consisting of sixteen command tanks and forty-eight drone tanks, headed out from Forward Operating Base Ypres down into the primary system of tunnels that Byng had designated the Menin Road. Each command tank could remotely operate a single drone at a time, with the remainder of the drones operated from FOB Ypres. Patch's unique capabilities made her a "Command, Control, and Countermeasures" or C3 unit, and she and her contingent of seven drones set out separately to cross the broken surface of Flanders and enter the tunnel system at Hill 65.

"Okay, Boss," Mac called from her station underneath the main gun. "How do you want me to set up the magazine?" While Patch had complete control of all aspects of the tank, including the ammunition for the main gun, protocol called for the assistant gunner to set up a ready magazine of rounds that could be loaded in sequence to deal with expected targets. There would be a separate magazine for "unexpected" targets.

"High explosive, then penetrator. Five each,

alternating. If we come across a worm and need to get off a quick shot, I don't want to fool around. Just blow that sucker up. After that, we may need to clear tunnels, so we'll have the depleted uranium penetrator rounds."

"What about plasma rounds?"

"Load the secondary magazine with those. I don't want to use them right off. Shemp and Moe have the plasma cannons, and Curly Joe has the special munitions. We'll keep CJ at the back of the formation and only use him if absolutely necessary. The other two can take point if we think we need energy weapons."

During the past six months of conflict with the Aneliad, it had been determined that the worms were vulnerable to explosives and energy weapons even if the ground was not. The trick was to get a clear shot within the tunnels either before a worm could close the distance, or before getting oneself caught in the back blast. Blowing up the *tunnels* was only good in the short term, but it could be used to herd the Annies into a selected battlefield. Thus, General Plumer planned to sortie all available tanks to push the enemy back out of the Salient and close down the tunnels leading to the human mines. The command and drone tanks would be under Plumer's overall command for this battle. Patch was there for when events didn't follow the plan.

As the platoon rolled out, an artillery barrage started. The general's plan was for the artillery to disrupt any surface activity and drive the worms back as the tanks advanced. Patch had her doubts as to whether it would work; after all, the worms seldom occupied the surface, and tunnels collapsed from surface shock waves never seemed to impede their movement. Still, the walking barrage would cover the tank movements—assuming the Annies sensed movements using some form of seismic sensors.

Again, Patch had her doubts, and again, that's why she was here.

The comm started to carry reports of contact from the other command tanks. The TEF forces had barely pushed into the Salient—territory that the Humans had *thought* that they controlled. As Patch approached Hill 65, her sensors indicated movement in the tunnels underneath the surface.

"Subsurface movement, Mac. The worms have broken into the Salient. We're going to be behind their lines when we head down."

"Do you want to change the load-out in the magazine?"

"No, but I want to prepare a frago for the drones."

"*You* want to issue a fragmentary order to the entire battalion?"

"Yes, I need you to talk to General Plumer for me while I concentrate on cutting up worms."

"Well, okay, then, but why is she going to listen to me?"

"Because you're going to tell her that Patch said so."

"Okay, Lieutenant Colonel, you're the officer. I'll do it . . . but what am I telling her?"

"It's easy, a one-time order to the drones. It's a desperation move, but I think it will drive the worms back—the drones drive forward as far as they can go, then once they are stuck or trapped, they blow their fusion plants."

"You want to self-destruct all of our drones?"

"I want to mine the tunnels."

"Oh, right. Sure, she's going to really take me at my word on that one."

"You tell her, I'm going to be busy." Patch's voice took on a strange formality, as if the words were coming from a computer, and not a human. "Going in, prime the magazine."

"Gun ready," Mac replied, then went silent as she turned her attention to the conversation with Command. Patch knew that the general would agree readily. The idea of mining the Salient had already been discussed. "The general agrees, ma'am. Says the command is 'Wytschaete.'"

"Acknowledged," said Patch. If she'd been able to pay attention, she might have wondered why her voice was so oddly inflected. A moment later, she announced, "Contact, drones three and four. Contact, drones five and six. Hill 65 reached; contact, drones one and two."

There were jolts as the main gun fired. Drones were primarily equipped with energy weapons and DU rockets to create a path for the beams. A command tank, on the other hand, had a main gun capable of using kinetic, explosive and energy rounds. The alternating explosive and kinetic rounds that Patch and Mac had prepared resulted in a steady thump as they were fired, followed by either a shaking explosion or a muffled "crump" when they met a target.

There was a bit more inflection and . . . humanity . . . in Patch's voice as she warned Mac, "Worm ahead! Snap shot."

Mac checked her panel, but Patch had already commanded the next round to load from the secondary magazine. "Snap shot" was code for an urgent switch in type of ammunition in the event of imminent danger. She checked her panel again. The worm was *close*! "Danger close," she commed. They would be caught in the area of effect of the plasma round.

"Acknowledged, danger close." Patch replied. The computer-like voice was back.

WHAM!

The plasma round ignited, and the main gun fired again. With virtually no time of flight, the second plasma round went off.

WHAM!

The temperature began to rise in the compartment. Patch knew that Mac would handle local environmental controls, so she concentrated on the tunnel in front of her.

Upon entering the tunnel system, Patch had turned back toward Ypres. The worms had advanced into the Salient, and she was now behind their lines. The two plasma rounds had killed two worms and cleared the tunnel ahead.

"Why are we headed back?" Mac commed.

"I'm heading to the junction with the Messine tunnel. We're behind the enemy and I want to circle around and clear this sector before we move deeper."

"Roger. We're right under Hill 60, by the way, do you want to do something with Larry and Curly?"

"Load them with the Wytschaete protocol. As soon as we clear the tunnel entrance, send them back down our trail." Patch had access to all of the sensor and real-time communication from not only her own drones, but the forty-eight drones of the rest of the battalion. Her mind filled with a view of the battle, and smaller details such as the condition of her own tank faded into the background. She knew she needed to continue communicating with Mac and headquarters, but it had become automatic, something she really didn't think about. "Turning now. Heading toward Messine."

It was almost an hour later when the comm activated again. It crackled with interference, both from the discharge of energy weapons, and the resonances caused by the fusite deposits. "CT1917, all command tanks report fully engaged. Enemy forces are in the Salient. Report."

"Heading toward Messine, General Plumer. Recommend we execute Wytschaete."

"Agreed, Patch. Do you want operational control of the drones?"

"No ma'am, I don't have bandwidth to punch through the signal interference *and* control every drone. It's a simple program. Launch penetrator, advance, launch, advance . . . until they either run out of rockets or get jammed in a cleft." The strange detachment and mechanical overtones to Patch's comm signal were getting worse.

"Very well, all commanders, execute Wytschaete protocol."

There was no immediate effect. The advancement of the drone tanks was spread across the was ten-kilometer width of the Salient. Patch's own drones had been repositioned when she made the turn to Messine. Shemp and Curly now led the advance, while Curly Joe was tucked up under the front of the C3 tank for ready deployment.

"Side tunnels!" Mac announced, but Patch was already sending a drone down each of the branching tunnels.

"Shemp and Curly now on Wytschaete protocol," Patch replied. There was a brief pause, then she commed again. "Contact, front. All drones reporting contact. Contact is heavy. Repeat, contact is in excess of ten worms."

"Time for Curly Joe?"

"Affirmative. Prepare E-M-P protocols."

Mac started shutting down her boards in anticipation of an electromagnetic pulse. Atomic and nuclear explosions energized molecules in the air, releasing electrons that could burn out active electronics. However, the atmosphere of Fortune's World was normally too thin to support an EMP, and underground explosions would not allow a pulse to propagate. The EMP that Patch instructed Mac to prepare for was of a different variety.

One result of the disastrous first encounter with the Aneliad was the discovery that they did not tolerate electricity. This had led to the emplacement of electrified fields around the Human mines and throughout the salient. The effectiveness of the "fences" had waned as the heavy rains from the comet strikes started to diminish and Flanders began to dry out. Curly Joe's "special munition"—a term typically reserved for atomic weaponry—was designed to mimic an EMP propagated through the interface between the normal ground above and the fusite layer below. It was hoped that it would drive the worms back enough for Wytschaete to clear the Salient.

"Curly Joe is released," Patch announced. "Penetrators away."

"The board is shut down. Time for you to switch to internal power, Patch." Mac hadn't waited for acknowledgement. Patch could feel her contact with the tank and the battlefield slipping away.

"Give CJ thirty seconds, then detonate." The command was automated. Once released, the drone would follow its instructions while the C3 tank protected itself from the EMP.

Patch waited in darkness. She had experienced sensory deprivation a few times in her life. She'd been placed in a tunnel with no lights and no communications while training for her original insertion with Charlie-One. This was worse. A part of her wanted to scream, while another part groped for every heartbeat, every vibration of the life support systems. Worst of all, she could feel the allure of just slipping away and being lost in the isolation. COIs called it Dreamtime, and it manifested in the periphery of her "vision" as a bright light in the distance. The urge to enter Dreamtime increased with every day of capsulated existence.

After what seemed an eternity. The lights came back on and Patch's senses reached out to the tank's instruments. She was back in contact with her "body" and the lure of Dreamtime faded.

For now.

"Status?" Patch noticed that the computerlike effect on her voice was absent from the comm.

"Curly Joe has detonated; all systems are now back

online. No, wait. There's an error message. It's not reading critical. I'll have to do a manual check to make sure everything switched back on after the EMP. You're free to move, though; no movement ahead. We are estimated at five minutes until all drones are ready for Wytschaete." The relief was evident in Mac's voice as well. The need for a human presence in the tank had been one of General Plumer's greatest reservations, but it had certainly paid off.

"Acknowledged, advancing now. Load up penetrators, and let's get past this worm goo."

No resistance and no live worms were encountered as they advanced to Messine and past the last reported location of the worms.

"I think we've driven them back." Patch switched the comm to the headquarters frequency. "General, the road ahead is clear."

"We see that, too, CT1917. I have instructed the command tanks to hold back. Hold your present position until the drones are dug in."

"Acknowledged General. Battening down the hatches."

"Detonation at five seconds from my mark. Mark. Four . . . Three . . . Two . . . One . . ."

The ground shook underneath them, and the seismic sensor showed explosions all over the Salient.

"Hold for instructions," the general sent.

Patch used the time to check over her systems. There was no damage to the tank itself: the power plant, treads, guns, all seemed normal. She checked the life support system for the personnel compartment. The temperature was elevated, and the cooling seemed to be offline. Mac was going to get uncomfortably warm as they moved through the areas where the drones had detonated. There was a warning indicator for fluid management as well. Ah well, if Mac needed to use the toilet, it was going to get pretty smelly, but nothing they couldn't handle. She felt like something else was wrong, but there were no other indicators. Still, it nagged at her. Again, there was a brief feeling of disorientation. She'd felt that after the sensory deprivation training, too, so she dismissed it and turned her attention back to the battlefield map.

There was no indication of Aneliad activity within the salient—they'd cleared an area ten kilometers wide, by nearly six kilometers deep if that was so.

The comm crackled. Interference was worse, likely the result of the explosions. "All units, report status. We read no enemy activity within the Salient."

Reports from the various command tanks started to come in. Six were still functional and were ordered to advance. There were three mechanical failures, and one stuck due to collapse of the tunnels in both directions. That left six units that failed to report. Patch checked her sensors. Five of the six were still registering as functional units, but designated "NLS" with no life signs. The sixth showed weak indications that the crew was still alive.

"General, if you turn over control of the NLS units to me, I can operate them as drones and advance to Zonnebeke."

"Negative, Patch, the crews could still be alive with damaged telemetry. We're activating the RTB commands to bring them back to Ypres."

"We have a hole over Zonnebeke. I can advance to

Westrozebeke on the edge of the Flanders field, but I'll be leaving a gap behind me. Can you send reinforcement?"

"We have the tanks, but no crews."

"Not a problem, remember? If they are rigged as drone controllers, they can be reverse-engineered to be drones."

"We don't have time to reprogram . . ."

"I can code faster than they can." Patch knew that it was a bad idea to interrupt her commanding officer, but she knew she was right.

After a long pause, the general came back on the comm. "I'm not so sure I like the looks of your own telemetry, Patch, but I'm willing to allow this. We're sending access codes now for units CT1732, CT1733, CT1784, CT1801 and CT1918."

"Acknowledged, General. I'll use them well."

"I know you will, Patch. Good luck and Godspeed. If you can take Westrozebeke, we'll have pushed the worms out of the fusite. If not, take a bite and hold it. Bite and hold, CT1917."

"Will do, General." Patch switched back to the internal comm. "Hey Mac, we're getting 1918. That's your old unit, right?" Before her crew member could respond, she continued. "We'll have to give her a name. Since she's from Lille, I think we'll call her Lily."

"That's fine, Patch," Mac responded, weakly, then coughed.

"Hey, what's the problem, Mac?"

"Something in the air, Patch. I don't think the cyclers came back from the shutdown."

"Okay, I'm turning up the oh-two feed. That will give you some better air and may help cool it down as well."

"Appreciated, oh tank of mine."

"Anything for my girl."

"Anything for my tank."

Patch had Mac prepare the primary magazine with penetrators. Meanwhile, she did the same remotely for the five tanks that were now her drones. Advancement was slow, since they needed to clear the tunnels where the drone explosions had caused collapses, and on several occasions, they found themselves in the open as they climbed over collapsed tunnel roofs that had broken through all the way to the surface.

It took many hours to reach the edge of the fusite deposit and the suspected Aneliad base designated Westrozebeke. When Marshal Byng had been naming the landmarks, he had wanted to name the ultimate goal Passchendaele, but General Plumer had talked him out of it. Patch had been glad. She really didn't need that association. Comm traffic indicated that four of the six crewed tanks had made it through the no-man's-land of collapsed tunnels, mud and broken soil. Now that they were past the region mined by the self-destructing drones, the tunnels were clear and Patch sent orders to her drones to arm with explosive and plasma rounds.

It was time to meet the enemy head on.

"Hold on tight, Mac, I'm reading some irregularities ahead, along with a concentration of worms. It looks like this may be their main base." There was no acknowledgement, but Patch could see from her sensors and indicators that Mac was back at her station and secured in her seat. Temps had cooled off, slightly, but it had gotten to nearly 50°C in the personnel compartment as they passed through the area of effect from multiple fusion plant explosions. She knew Mac had to have been uncomfortable, but her "organic complement" had never complained.

The tunnel ended in an abrupt wall. There was no cross tunnel, nor any indication of an entry from above or below. It simply ended at a wall. Moreover, the wall was solid . . . oganesson? That didn't make sense. The fusite deposit formed a flat layer, half a kilometer thick, about five to fifty meters below the surface. There were no vertical faces in the entire field—in fact, it thinned down to no more than a meter thickness at the edges. The edges and natural breaks in the surface were the only reason the fusite could be mined. The Sylphs had shared equipment to mine and work the refractory material, although they hadn't revealed the science and technology behind it. Still, even that advanced technology didn't seem to be capable of making the wall that was in front of her.

It only took a moment to recognize the source of the barricade.

"Mac, do you see this? The damn worms have eaten the fusite and regurgitated it into a barrier." There was no answer, and a small sense of concern crept into Patch's awareness, but she had to suppress it and move on. The computer interface made multitasking easy; it also let her compartmentalize her worries. She checked the life support systems, and they were . . . adequate. Well then, there was a job to do, she could worry later.

"Command, this is Patch. The Annies have built a barricade out of fusite."

"Interesting, Patch, that's just what you predicted. It's time for the special penetrators, then."

"I've only got one, how about the other tanks?"

"Three of your drones, CT1732, CT1784, and CT1918, have TS charges. Four of the crewed tanks have cleared Flanders and are reporting the same barrier."

"Eight total, then. This is going to be close. If we focus four each on the same spot, we should be able to guarantee a take down."

The "special" penetrators referred to as TS munitions were a product of research into the ability of the Aneliad to mine fusite—apparently by digesting it with a biochemical process. The traces of "worm spit" found in the new tunnels had contained high concentrations of the element immediately to the left of OG on the periodic table—tennessine—from the same class of elements as the highly reactive halogens chlorine, fluorine, bromine and iodine. Tennessine differed from OG by only a single proton and electron; the theory was that a TS-enriched plasma warhead would at least *weaken* the OG component of fusite, allowing more conventional munitions to breach the barricade. Patch's own theory was that it would take multiple warheads arriving either simultaneously, or within a very short time span.

"That's going to be hard to coordinate, Patch," a new voice came on the line. "You are pretty far out from the base considering the interference and signal reflections off of the fusite."

"I am aware of that, Marshal Byng. That's why I want

you to give release control to me. I can ping the signal delay from me to each tank, and also compute the densities between each tank and the fusite walls. I'm a lot closer than you are, and I have clearer signal." Patch inspected the comm data for every tank. With the exception of her own connection to Lily—her drone tank CT1918—she had a shorter signal path and better communications than each tank had with Ypres Base.

"No, Patch. That's against protocol. Besides, you told us earlier that you didn't have the bandwidth to control all of the drones."

"With all due respect, Marshal, that was different. There are only seven other tanks to control, and each one is reachable with local signals. We are well clear of most the interference, whereas your signals still have to travel through the disrupted zone."

"Nevertheless, Lieutenant Colonel, you will do as ordered. Follow procedures, we will coordinate from here."

Patch fumed. *Damned armchair strategist. He hasn't been in the heat of battle the whole time we've been here, and* NOW *he takes command?* She knew she should check her nutrient feeds and lower her adrenaline levels, but she didn't *want* to calm down. Now if only she had a way to ensure that this worked. There was one way to do it, but it would require a lot of computation.

It came to her as a strange realization. Patch needed computer power, but in essence, she *was* a computer—or at least was interfaced with one. She had not adjusted the nutrient flow to her capsule, but she felt a strange calm settle over her, a detached...*digital*...calm. It felt a bit like the lure of Dreamtime, but she was fully engaged in the task at hand.

First, she needed to calculate the signal delays from her position to each of the seven tanks with TS rounds. Then she needed to compute the delays from Ypres Base to each tank. The next step was the one that would get her into trouble: she needed to tap into the command and communication circuits for each of the crewed tanks without being noticed.

Fortunately, the same C3 adaptations that had made her suited for drone control gave her the ability to covertly take over the comms and penetrate the main gun firing controls on the other tanks. She compared her calculations for signal delay with actual signals intercepted at each tank. Only in one case did her calculations differ; looking closer, Patch detected an odd reflection that she had not accounted for. Re-examining the signal map of the battlefield allowed her to identify the reason, and she applied the new solution to her calculations. If Command tried to go for a simultaneous firing option, the signal issues would result in the rounds arriving over a span of two minutes. Unfortunately, the design specifications called for the rounds to impact and detonate no more than two seconds apart.

On the other hand, a simultaneous signal would arrive first at CT1918—Lily. If she intercepted that command and applied her own calculations, she could adjust the timing to achieve the desired sequence of detonations.

Now, should she do it only for her own drones, or for all eight effective tanks?

Technically, she'd be disobeying a direct order. But equally *technically*, all she was doing was correcting a signal propagation error.

That would have to suffice. Patch penetrated the command systems of four crewed tanks and two drones and turned off receipt of signals from Ypres. She would relay everything received from Ypres—just *adjust* the timing as needed.

The Field Marshal sent orders to each tank to adjust position to focus on two places in the fusite wall. Patch ran her computations and added only minor corrections. The differences would not be evident to Command, but she knew that the reduced signal interference and her penetration of the other tanks' systems gave her more precise targeting.

The increased demand for multitasking had been difficult at first, but once she reconnected after the EMP, it felt natural. There was a cool detachment as her consciousness divided to take on the interdependent tasks. Almost as if she was duplicating herself in each tank's computers. She just had to wait for the signal . . .

Now.

Lily detected the incoming command, and each of Patch's "selves" executed the commands at the appropriate time. As soon as the commands were issued, she restored the comms and erased her presence in the other tanks.

Eight tanks launched TS warheads at the fusite walls. Four rounds hit each target precise to the microsecond between impacts. The plasma loads created the temperature and pressure, and the tennessine attacked the OG component of the walls.

DOWN! The walls were down.

Patch immediately began taking fire from weapons beyond the wall. It was known that the Aneliad had artillery; after all, they'd been firing at surface targets since the conflict began. Apparently, they'd concentrated behind the fusite wall. Her tank was hit by multiple rounds, and her drive system showed damage. Patch tried to drive forward into the breach, but was unable to move.

Her mobility was not a problem for battle, but it was getting hot, and she wouldn't be able to move out of the zone of the current plasma detonations. She cranked up the airflow in the personnel compartment in hopes that it would keep the environment tolerable, but she needed to concentrate on the battle. Once again, she felt the curious detachment and division of her consciousness as she directed the drones to advance. She spared some attention to the crewed tanks, and noticed that one was listed as combat ineffective, but with life signs. It was also getting hot, so she reinserted her control commands and ordered the tank to retreat enough to drop the temperatures. Two of the other tanks were advancing, but the third was moving erratically.

Again, she penetrated the control systems, and discovered multiple faults in the drive—it was functioning, but the commands were getting garbled. She quickly inserted a conversion routine and was gratified to see the movements return to normal. She brought her attention back to her drones.

Following the TS rounds, each tank had been prepped with plasma rounds to clear out the worms behind their barricade. Once through the breach, the tanks spread out and spread hot, flaming destruction among the Annies.

That will teach them that it's better to share than to try to hog all of the fusite for themselves!

After an hour, all units reported that the entire Flanders field was free of Aneliad. In addition, the *St. Benedict* reported that they detected multiple spacecraft launches from the sites of suspected Annie bases. All ships were heading out system. They had won.

Patch gradually withdrew her attention from the drones and turned her attention to her own tank. The drive system was damaged, but repairable; however, there was a breach in the personnel compartment. *When had that happened?*

"Mac? Norma? Corporal Macmullen?"

There was no answer.

Patch withdrew into her own systems and looked longingly toward the strangely receding light of Dreamtime.

The technicians heard the sound of sobbing over the comm as they entered the personnel compartment.

"Damn, it's hot in here."

"Yeah, not sure anyone could survive this for long. Any sign of the a-gunner?"

"Not here, not in her seat."

"Keep checking."

"Right, let me bring the interior diagnostics up." After

a brief pause, he continued. "Check the 'fresher. I've got one weak life sign."

"Right. Door's stuck, but . . ." There was rush of water out of the hygiene compartment. "Whoa, that stinks, but she had the right idea, must be twenty degrees cooler in there."

"Right. Okay, she's unconscious, but alive. Get her on the stretcher and out to the extraction crew."

"Norma?" The voice came over the comm.

"She's okay, Patch. She put herself in the 'fresher and ran the water from the chiller. It kept her cool enough."

"Oh, thank god," Patch replied. "Hey, how long until you can get me unstuck? I need to do some maintenance."

"We've got a crew working on your tracks right now. Should be ready to move in another two hours."

"Psst." The other technician motioned to his partner. "Didn't you say 'one weak life sign?'"

The tech who'd been talking with Patch, checked the display again, and then paled. He waved weakly in the direction of the access hatch for the total life-support capsule. When the hatch was opened, there was an acrid stench and signs of burnt electronics. The capsule itself was a mottled black and brown, with no indication of activity.

"Guys, what's the problem down there?" Patch commed.

The technicians looked alarmed at the lack of activity on the surface of the egg. One pulled out a sensor, attached it to the side of the egg, and activated a diagnostic program. He shook his head and pointed to the main umbilicus. The egg was cracked right at the coupling, and the cable was burnt through. The two looked at each other in wonder as Patch continued to call them.

"Guys? Someone, please tell me what's going on. Is there a problem? Guys?"

A TANK NAMED BOB
by Larry Correia

*What kind of mind makes for an effective warrior?
Perhaps a naïve psychologist looking in, one who is not
inured to the necessities of war, would see a psychopathic
personality. But honor, duty, and vengeance also require
a brain conditioned to ignore distractions that can only
result in defeat, a brain wired to concentrate on the one
thing that matters—winning the battle at all costs.
Especially when winning brings with it a measure of
justice for the only thing that matters in the end. Family.*

⊕   ⊕   ⊕

There were two scout tanks coming up on the west using
the rubble as cover, and a third hiding in the trees on the
other side of the factory complex. There was an exo-suited
infantry squad armed with portable anti-tank missiles
moving up the roof of the warehouse to the south. The
APC the squad had debarked from was driving around the
building, trying to flank me.

I saw all this with the dozens of cameras along my

armored hull and through the eyes of my drone swarm. I felt the vibrations through my shocks, which were sensitive enough that I could accurately estimate the weight and speed of the bogeys my many eyes couldn't get a visual on. The multitude of threats were just glowing dots of various sizes and brightness on my battle map. The Level 10 quantum processor dumped all of this information into my meat brain to assess and approve the targeting priority assignments.

The initial firing solution looked good to me. *Battle plan accepted. Engage.*

The concussion of my 180mm main gun made my active camouflage ripple. The spotter drones the enemy infantry had sent up knew exactly where I was now, but that wouldn't matter for long, because I was already reversing, crashing my bulk through several walls. Bricks were smashed to dust beneath my polysteel treads as the mortars along my back chain fired.

Two thousand meters away, my shot nailed the enemy tank that had thought it was hidden by the trees. There was a bright line on thermal as my armor-piercing shell ice-picked the light scout's turret. There was a second, much brighter bloom, as the tank's magazine cooked off. A fireball rolled through the forest.

Missiles struck the debris I'd been hiding in, but I was already to my second firing position by the time the autoloader had fed another 180 AP into the tube. I couldn't see the next scout, but I could sense where it was. I murdered it right through the walls. Three layers of brick and one of light armor barely slowed the penetrator. My chemical scanners confirmed the kill because of all the thorium and radioactive smoke suddenly added to the atmosphere. Reactor hit.

I kept moving to avoid the counterfire, but this time it didn't matter, because the exo-suited missile boys were too busy dodging the mortar shells I'd dropped on their heads. Only my calculations had underestimated the structural integrity of the warehouse, and the whole damned thing came crashing down around them, burying the poor dopes who weren't able to leap off in time. The survivors wouldn't be too much of a problem, since they were mostly blind now. I'd barely even noticed as my point defense systems had automatically shot down all their drones.

The quantum processor was super-efficient, but it wasn't very imaginative. That's what meat brains were for. So when I saw where the APC was going to come out, trying to get an angle on my less armored back end with its launcher, I flipped around, angled my nose, and then charged, full speed through the factory, smashing machinery, pipes, and furniture, right through the exterior wall, to T-bone the surprised APC. It was barely more than an armored car, so I hardly even felt the crunch. But it was still satisfying to send the little thing flipping end over end.

The last scout realized that I was out of his league, turned tail, and ran. These little bastards were fast too. I clocked him doing 160 KPH by the time he reached the factory's old parking lot. The scout tank knocked derelict cars out of his way as easily as I'd crushed their APC. My turret slowly turned, leading him. Their driver was good, juking side to side, desperately trying to get away. It didn't matter. I punched them through their engine compartment and left them to burn.

I am a two-hundred-ton killing machine.

My name is Bob.

"Can he hear me, Doctor?"

"It appears the interface is working correctly; the language processing center of his brain will receive the audible impulses translated through the nano-gel. So basically, yes, but it'll be like the voice of God in the darkness saying let there be light. Whether he'll understand and how much he remembers, I don't know. The damage was extensive, and this is experimental tech."

"Will he be able to communicate back?"

"Not yet. We'll have to process his brain waves through the encoder first to be able to translate the impulses directly into language. That'll take a few weeks."

"We don't have a few weeks. We have a war to fight. If the Tribunal asks, the subject could communicate and consented to be part of this project. Is that clear, Doctor?"

"Yes, sir."

"Excellent. Here goes then . . . Good morning, Captain. Do not panic. I'm General Hwangmok, Western Command, Valens Defense Force. First the good news. You're still alive. You were severely injured but you were evacuated to a secure medical facility. Now for the bad news. There was a surprise attack by the Syndicate. The colony is in trouble and most of the VDF was wiped out. Their infowar capabilities are far beyond ours so they hacked all our automated systems. Our manned systems are no match for theirs. We're getting our asses kicked out there. Now for the really bad news for you personally, so I'll give it to you straight. Most of your body was destroyed beyond repair, but we saved your brain. It's currently being kept alive in a nanite bath."

"I'm sorry, General, but I'm reading a surge in amygdala activity. Glutamate levels are spiking."

"What's that mean?"

"I think he's panicking, and in a sensory deprived state that could cause permanent damage. I need to put him back under."

"Listen to me, Captain. You're going back to sleep for a while. I know the merciful thing would be to pull your plug, but you're the only armor officer I've got here, which means I can't let you go to waste. I'm sorry, but your people need you."

"I've administered the sedative. The subject is fading out . . . I can't believe we're really doing this. It violates medical ethics and dozens of regulations."

"Don't worry, Doctor. We only have to worry about being tried for war crimes if we lose the war. They don't prosecute the winners."

With the Syndicate scouts out of the way, I headed for Kan Junction. It was only a few klicks away and where the enemy had set up their regional logistics command. It was the logical target suggested by the Quantum. But my gut told me I could do the more harm elsewhere . . . Only you can't really say you have a gut feeling, when you don't have any guts anymore.

The Syndicate invasion fleet had dropped a bunch of spy and comms satellites into orbit during their approach.

Now that they knew approximately where to look, there was no way for me to hide from their eyes in the sky while crossing open farmland. I had active camouflage skin, but I couldn't move full speed and still store that much waste heat in my sinks, so I would glow like a beacon on thermal. Nor was there any real way to disguise the path of destruction I was leaving in my wake. My wide tracks left ruts deep enough through the soft terraformed soil the shadows would be seen from space.

My systems were being bombarded with hostile signals. The Syndicate were attempting to hack me, just like they had done with every other VDF weapon system during the invasion. Previously their programs had sliced through Valens' firewalls like they were made of cheese. Only this time they were failing miserably, and their hackers probably couldn't figure out why. Their target appeared to a be a fully autonomous robot tank, only every time they tried to take over a system, they were immediately booted by an on-site manual override. Which should have been impossible, because it would take a twenty-man crew to run this many processes manually at the same time, and there was no way that a weapon system could be run this efficiently by a bunch of humans working together.

But for me by myself, it was as intuitive as moving my old limbs. I just needed to think about it, and it happened . . . Cyborg meat brains for the win.

The satellites quit blasting me with tight beams. The hacking attempts stopped. Now they would simply vector Syndicate air assets right to my position to take me out the old-fashioned way.

But rather than hide or take evasive maneuvers, I kept going straight, right toward the most obvious target in the area because I wanted those gunships to come after me. Better to deal with air support now than later when I might be distracted.

My drone screen spotted them first. One of my stealthy little flyers spotted four fast-moving targets coming my way. They were hugging the ground, just over treetop level so as to avoid my radar, but they'd not spotted my drone yet. It must have been clear from the satellite images that I had a railgun mounted, because the flyers didn't dare pop up over the horizon. As soon as my drone lased them, the flyers went into evasive maneuvers, but it was too late. The instant they were tagged, I launched a barrage of smart missiles to hunt them down.

The gunships launched flares to confuse thermal and shine to blind the drones. Four balls of artificial sunlight temporarily lit the nearby farms. I overrode the missiles' rudimentary AI, because they simply would have flown to wherever the machine assumed their targets would have gone, but I guided them by instinct instead. I managed to splash two, and those Syndicate flyers cut flaming ditches through the cornfields. The other two still managed to evade. Except one of them had to pull up hard to keep from hitting a barn on the way out. Two seconds of visibility over the horizon was more than enough for me to zap it with the coaxial railgun. The time to target wasn't instantaneous, but it was close enough. One of the flyer's wings came apart and the body turned into a Mach One lawn dart.

They'd messed with the wrong tank.

The Syndicate had captured most of our small armor fleet without firing a shot. They'd been able to examine our locally built main battle tanks. They had probably been expecting me to have similar capabilities as those, except my new body was an off-world prototype, stolen and smuggled here by a crew of gun runners. It was more capable than our regular tanks in just about every way. And since I was now tired of being spied on, it was time to show them another one of those capabilities.

I stopped in a pasture, tracked the Syndicate satellites and let the Quantum process the firing solutions. My railgun lacked the horsepower to get past low orbit, but I didn't need a kinetic kill. Flash frying their delicate electronics would be enough. I spent the next few minutes flinging lasers into space. Once I was sure this hemisphere was temporarily clear of spy sats, I set out again. Only this time I wasn't driving toward the obvious target of Kan Junction. I changed direction and set course for Fu'An City, the capitol of Valen, on the far end of the continent.

"How are you doing today, Captain?"

The doctor's voice cut through the entirely of my universe. It took me a moment to pull up the rudimentary image of a keyboard that had been implanted into my brain. Each key was pulsing at a slightly different frequency. I thought about one key at a time until my brain matched that frequency. That impulse was recorded through the wire mesh my brain was wrapped in, and those letters were sent to a display the doctor could read.

Please, Doc. Just call me Bob.

"Very well. Bob it is. Have the interface simulations been going well?"

Considering that I was a one and a half kilo lump of cells with no senses, hardly any memories, and nothing better to do, I'd been running through the programs they'd dumped into me nonstop. It was like letting a baby play a video game about running before getting a chance to crawl. It was a super confusing nonstop bombardment of information.

Yes. It is going swell.

"That's great. You seem in really good spirits."

It could be worse.

"It beats being dead."

Does it though?

The doctor was quiet for a real long time. "Yeah . . . sorry. Okay, I just came in to tell you that the general wants to bump up the timeline. He's procured an ideal test vehicle from off world. I know you need more time to get ready before we plug you in, but we might not have it."

Things are that bad out there?

"I won't lie to you, Bob. It's not going well. The Syndicate has taken over half the continent. We're holding them at New Sidney for now, but east of the divide the VDF has been forced underground and we're basically waging a guerrilla war."

I was from the eastern coast of the colony, the beautiful, terraformed zone, that could almost be mistaken for old Earth if you squinted just right. I knew it was a long shot, but I had to ask.

Any word about Mei and the kids?

"I looked, I really did, but the records are a mess and the central net is down. She was last seen in Fu'an, but there was so much fighting there. I'm sorry, Bob. I still don't know where your family is."

That's cool, Doc. I appreciate the effort. Assure the general that I'll be ready.

I went back to my simulations.

After sixteen hours of nonstop combat operations, I had to hide inside an old tunnel to give my procurement and repair systems a chance to work. I was so big that I barely fit in a tunnel designed for super trains. My drone swarm spread out looking for useful materials while my repair bots crawled outside and began inspecting the damage. I was most worried about my treads. Polysteel is self-repairing, but I'd put nearly a thousand kilometers on brand new tracks today. If I threw one of those in a fight I'd be a sitting duck until my bots could get out and fix it, and the bots were soft targets on an active battlefield.

My drones tagged several items that appeared they would be useful scrap, so I sent some scrounger bots to grab those. Lots of things could be used as raw materials for my internal fabricator. I was saving the factory shells for hard targets, but I could make more ammo out of any steel, brass, copper, lead, aluminum, or plastic my bots found. The whole time I was using ammo, I was making more. Propellant was more of a challenge, but I'd found a crashed Syndicate cargo hopper earlier and my bots had stripped all the chemicals from its magazines and fuel tanks, so my stores would last for a while.

I set the drones to form a security perimeter. I'd killed

so many Syndicate over the last few hours that their whole invasion force was probably gunning for me. I couldn't risk actively transmitting, but I had some of my drones act as passive antennas to check for local comms. There was some Syndicate back and forth, only cracking their encryption was beyond me. I still tagged the positions those signals came from as potential future targets.

I also caught a few messages using regular VDF ciphers. I was far enough east now that it was all partisans, irregulars, and militia. They were desperate, hungry, and on the run, so I wasn't expecting much help from them. Except when I decoded their messages, I discovered that the chatter was all about me. Everyone was talking about the giant off-world tank that had been raising hell across the colony. I had caused enough distraction and destruction that they'd been able to capitalize on it and launch several attacks against Syndicate forces. Nice.

Then my antenna caught a high priority message coded directly to me.

I downloaded it and cracked it open. As expected, General Hwangmok was extremely pissed off. He had not spent millions importing a super tank and wasting his time on an illegal science project to just have me run off on a solo crazy suicide mission. He commanded me to return to base immediately.

I had disobeyed orders, I just couldn't remember why I had disobeyed his orders right now. It was like there was a black hole in my memory. That wasn't odd. There were lots of those. But this was a recent memory, not an old one. This memory hadn't been lost because of the brain damage I'd received when my body had gotten blown up.

This was something else, but when I tried to remember, it just made me angry and sad.

I dropped the general's message in the delete bin and went back to making more ammunition out of recycled cars and trash. I had a big day tomorrow.

"Okay, Bob, I need you to pay careful attention as we run diagnostics. If anything feels off at all, you let me know."

My brain—which was now riddled with silicon chips and hordes of nanites—had been bolted inside an armored box filled with nutrients and electrified jelly, and that box had just been plugged into a giant war machine that was blasting me with wave after wave of strange new information, all of which I was desperately trying to translate into reasonable facsimiles of my old human senses. There was nothing about this situation that wasn't *off*.

Whatever you say, Doc. Everything seems fine here. And then I sent him a thumbs up emoji.

Then for the first time in months, I could *see*. Though it was such a bizarre conflux of images pieced together from dozens of cameras operating in every spectrum that if I'd still had a body I probably would've been dizzy.

Whoa.

"What is it, Bob?"

The visual system came online. It's a little disorienting is all.

I could see my doctor for the first time. I'd not known what to expect. It turned out he was an overweight and disheveled Australian man. "Do I need to power it down?"

No. Seeing is nice.

Then I had audio, and these weren't just weak little fleshy membranes and vibrating bones. This was hundreds of microphones that could hear a literal pin drop, pumping rivers of data directly into my auditory cortex. And best part—since my old body had been exposed to a lot of loud noises—no tinnitus!

Then chemical sniffers came online and I could smell again. Only now it was a full spectrum molecular analysis. There were thirty techs currently working on my new body and I could tell you what each of them ate today. Since Valen's original colony ships had launched from countries around Earth's Pacific rim, there had been a lot of fish and peppers consumed for lunch. My own body smelled like metal, rubber, and oil. The non-Newtonian fluid that made up my layer of smart armor smelled kind of minty fresh.

It was that same smart armor that let me *feel*. My skin was made up of layers of molecularly bonded plates, but the liquid smart armor trapped between the layers squished whenever any of the plates were touched. Somebody was welding a mortar onto my back. The arc was about 6,000 degrees. It tickled.

Now that was a little trippy.

"You might be experiencing some mild discomfort as the tank's sensor suites calibrate to your brain chemistry. This may take a few days for the patterns to set."

Have you done this before?

The doctor laughed. "Nobody has done this before. We're using the same basic technology that allows a pilot to interface their minds directly with their vehicles, only modified for your . . . circumstances."

I was familiar with that tech. Man and machine bonded together created a synergistic effect, making them more effective than the sum of their parts. I vaguely remembered that I'd once had an implant at the base of my skull that allowed that sort of interface, but like most of my long-term memory the details were fuzzy.

This seems a bit more extreme.

"I like to think of it as streamlined. With no physical body barrier to get in the way and slow the process down, the delays between you and the system will be absolutely minimal. You think, it acts. This should be even more combat efficient than what we get out of a fifth generation mech. Unlike as possible with our fully autonomous units, the Syndicate won't be able to hack you."

I remember reading about some linked-in pilots who got hacked on some backwater planet once.

"That was on Gloss. They used a worm to crawl up the pilot's implants and slowly reprogram their brains without anyone knowing. The Syndicate doesn't have anything like that as far as we know. Plus, by the time we're ready to send you out, you'll be so in tune, so one with the tank, that you'll be able to sense that kind of intrusion and deploy countermeasures the instant they try."

When can I take my new body out for a spin?

"Not yet. We've got to keep your movement functions locked down for a while for everyone's safety. It's good that you're eager, though."

The Syndicate had blown me up. They'd invaded my planet. I didn't even know if my family was alive or dead. I wanted to murder every invader. I wanted to feel their bodies pop under my treads like stepping on a grape. I'd run the combat simulations thousands of times and murdered millions of imaginary invaders, but that didn't help. My helplessness fed my hate, and with nothing else to do everything in my consciousness orbited around the fiery sun I'd created from my rage.

I just want to do my part to be helpful is all.

"Me too, Bob," the doctor assured me. "Me too ... It appears the general is here to inspect everything. If you will excuse me, I'm going to shut down all your external stimuli for a bit to give the software time to update. In the meantime, why don't you run another sim?"

Great idea, doc. Will do.

Except that was a lie. I didn't want to go back into the dark, so I altered the feeds that the doctor could see to show that I was disconnected from the tank, even though I wasn't. It was easy to fool him. This may have been his job, but it was my life. He only worked here. I lived here.

"Status, Doctor?" The general walked into the control room. The cameras and biometric scanners in my turret told me that he was a very grumpy looking sixty-year old male, with Korean DNA and far too many stress-related illnesses.

"The integration is going surprisingly well, but I'm worried about the subject. Don't worry. We can talk freely. I put him back to sleep."

"If we can prove this works, we can get permission and funding to refit every other tank, mech, and APC we've got in storage, but until then he's the only brain we've got that didn't reject the implants. Either our proof of concept works, or we're screwed. Do whatever you have to. As long as it works, I don't care."

"It's not the physical health of the biomatter or the integration process. He's doing surprisingly well there. It's his mental health. Here, look at this." The doctor led the general over to one of the displays. My cameras couldn't see that far into the control room, but I zoomed in and picked up a partial reflection off one of the technician's safety glasses so I could read along. "As you can see, there's been degradation in his prefrontal cortex and his amygdala is hyperactive."

"So?"

"This is the kind of thing we see in reactively aggressive, violent offenders."

"Great."

"No, I mean like the impulsive, inappropriately hostile, possibly psychotic kind. The subject wasn't like this when we first got him, but he's been degrading. This is the sort of brain we'd see in a prisoner put on death row after he lost his mind in a road rage incident and strangled someone to death. I've been carefully monitoring the serotonin and oxytocin levels, but it's not made much difference. Our neurobiologists have looked at this and they agree with my assessment. These readings are indicative of seriously impaired moral decision-making capability."

"We're trying to build an army of unhackable armored super warriors to repel an invasion, Doctor. Not host a tea party."

"I get that, but that doesn't do us any good if they're uncontrollable. Worse, when I talk to the subject, he seems remarkably polite, restrained, and even impossibly upbeat, considering his situation. As you can see, whenever he's communicating with us about how he is doing or feeling, his anterior cingulate cortex is on fire, and also the ventral and dorsal lateral prefrontal cortex have increased activity as well."

"Dumb it down for me, Doctor."

"Those are the parts we use to formulate lies. When the subject says he's fine, he's clearly not. Graphing the intensity of the activity over the life of the program, it appears that his outlook has been getting steadily worse, and he's been lying more and more to conceal his actual state of mind. When he's not actively lying, it appears he's constantly furious. He could snap at any time."

The general was quiet for a long time. "So we've plugged a possible lying psychopath with anger management issues into a super tank with guns that can shoot through mountains?"

"Basically . . . yes."

"Too bad. We can't turn back now. Every other subject stroked out when we plugged them in. Build in a kill switch we can flip in case he goes nuts and starts shooting in the wrong direction, and then keep going. If his performance can impress the high command, they'll give us more brains to play with, and you can pick nice ones for the next generation. In the meantime, work with what you've got. The clock's ticking."

It turns out that I really enjoyed running over people.

There was one of my fragmented memories left from my human childhood, where I recall standing on the beach, and squishing my toes together through the wet clumpy sand. Driving over infantry has a similar satisfying feeling. The regular soldiers were squishy. The ones wearing exo suits were crunchy. Like sea shells.

I drove through the streets of Fu'an City, blasting Syndicate. The squishies and crunchies came at me with portable missiles, satchel charges, and even grenades that barely scratched my paint. My point defense machine guns and flame throwers made quick work of them. It was the other tanks that I was worried about, as we played high-speed murder tag between the high rises of the capitol city.

There was a T-20 medium tank pursuing me, trying to get an angle on my less armored back end, but I moved around the corner of the Leopold Bank building before he could get a bead on me. He let rip with a burst from his autocannon, hoping to hit me through the wall. The rounds hit the famous stone lion statues at the entryway and obliterated them instead.

I would have rolled back and hit the medium while he was reloading, to punish him for vandalizing our local landmarks, but there was a Syndicate T-50 heavy tank coming around the end of 4th Street, a mere 200 meters away. And at that range, its 200mm smoothbore had a very high probability of punching my armor.

The Syndicate T-50 was the heaviest tank ever built by mankind. It was also fully automated, and because of that, it reacted faster than a human crew could have. I was a hybrid, faster than either man or machine. So in the time it took the T-50 to aim, I burned one skid into the pavement, turning hard, angling my front glacis for the best possible impact angle and rotated my turret toward the new threat.

He fired. The AP round hit, but my deflection angle was perfect, so it skipped down my side in a shower of sparks. The liquid smart armor still compressed mightily beneath that hit, and I felt the impact clear to my reactor core. *Oof.* Luckily the gel my brain rode in was a fantastic shock absorber or that would've scrambled my egg.

I fired back. My 180 roared. The muzzle blast shattered every window on the block. Even as heavy as I was, the impact I'd just taken had skewed me just enough that my shot was a bit off. Rather than nailing it in the vulnerable turret ring, my penetrator clipped the edge of its turret. Molten spall flew down the street.

The quantum told me the T-50's autoloader would be ready point seven of a second before my next round was ready, so I threw it in reverse and crashed into the bank. Carved stone columns toppled. The smaller T-20 unloaded its autocannon through the bank, searching for me.

I crashed out the other side and onto Barlow street. Valens citizens who had been trapped in occupied Fu'an ran for their lives. I tried not to crush any of those. They were the good squishies.

A second T-50 heavy was there, turning to angle its armor at me, but it's vulnerable flank was still visible. It had been expecting me to move up on 4th street, and I had taken it by surprise with my extremely unorthodox approach. I reflexively gut punched it with my main gun. A glowing hole appeared in its side. Liquid smart armor sprayed out the hole. But it didn't ignite. That was the hard thing about automated tanks, no crew to kill. But we were only a hundred meters apart, so as it turned, I shot it with my coaxial railgun, right through the hole I'd just cut.

The tiny hypervelocity round zipped through, hit something, and then bounced around inside like the world's angriest ping pong ball. The tank stopped turning and orange fire erupted out the hole.

I couldn't get away from the T-20, and its rapid-fire autocannon struck me repeatedly as I drove into the Valens Museum of Fine Art. The smaller shells didn't penetrate beyond the first layer of my armor, but they tore off one of my mortars and destroyed one of my cameras. My brain translated that into a sensation like getting poked in the eye with a white-hot poker.

I crashed through the glass wall, and then took a left through the stairs. My sensors told me that though the floor was marble ahead, there was a basement beneath, and there was no way this structure would hold up my weight. Unless I wanted to drop and get stuck, I had to keep going this way, right through the main showroom. Luckily the Syndicate had already looted all the valuable artwork, so I was only destroying my people's finest architecture, rather than a generation of our culture.

I'm a tank, but even tanks can still be sensitive about stuff like that.

I surprised more squishies on the other side, and they were wearing enemy uniforms so I lit them up with my machine guns. Explosions rippled across my wheels. The little bastards were trying to track me! Holes were knocked in the polysteel, but it quickly suctioned back together before the track broke. Ten seconds of spraying bullets up and down the street and most of the squishies were neutralized.

Only then my alarms sounded. The point defense

systems auto engaged and blasted an incoming missile out of the air. The warhead detonated a mere fifty meters above my turret, and I was showered with a rain of flaming debris.

Scanning up, I saw a mech hanging onto the side of the fortieth story of the Nang Building. The bipedal vehicle offended me, like it was a machine pretending to be a man. It leapt from its perch as I returned fire. My shell obliterated the top two stories of the high rise. The mech landed on the flat roof a thirty story apartment building and rolled out of sight.

I put the hammer down and moved out as fast as I could. Tanks all around me, mechs above me. This situation was not good.

I probably should have listened to the general. Tanks weren't supposed to work by themselves. We were a vital part of a combined arms offensive. Alone, we were vulnerable. Except I hadn't been in a very cooperative mood since the general had flipped my kill switch after I'd disobeyed his orders to return to base. Unfortunately for him, I'd already had one of my repair bots fish the little explosive charge out of my brain box.

I didn't recall ever being this impulsive or angry when I was human. In fact I'd worked well with others. People had said, "that Bob, he's a really nice guy." Except that had been Bob the human, not Bob the tank. Bob the human had been squishy. Bob the tank was *metal*. Old Bob would have obeyed orders and then gone back to his box to sit in the dark and play simulations. New Bob was a wrathful god of war.

My sensors warned me the mech was leaping from

rooftop to rooftop. The four-meter-tall fake human would try to flank around behind me to get a shot at my vulnerable bits. The remaining T-20 and T-50 were coming at me from different angles. Between the three threats, one of them was bound to have a shot at my vitals.

There was a solution. An automated system would never be allowed to cause this much property damage to civilian infrastructure without several levels of command approval. But I was no automated system. I was Bob.

The syndicate mech was paralleling me, staying far enough back from the roof edges that I couldn't get a line on him with my railgun, and moving too fast to pin him down with my mortars. So instead, I predicted which building he would jump to next—a twenty-eight story office complex—and scanned the supports. When I saw the mech's shadow leap into the air, I suddenly changed course, and slammed my two-hundred-ton body right through all the main structural supports. I snapped the building's spine.

The complex collapsed just as the mech landed on its roof. It had no choice but to ride it down.

I burst out the other side, concealed in the wall of dust. I immediately turned, aiming toward where the T-20 had been. I got a brief glimpse of the medium tank on thermal before it was obscured by the rolling dust cloud, but that was enough. The medium's front armor was no match for my 180 hitting square on. I shot it right through the heart. The shells in its magazine cooking off took out half a block.

The building's fall wiped out another smaller shopping center to its side. Mechs were tough, but they were no tank. The fall had torn off one of its arms and crippled one of its legs. It was stuck, impaled on a broken I-beam. I rotated my turret over and put a railgun round through the pilot's compartment. The mech slid down the beam and lay still.

Downtown was a wreck. That was certainly a lot of destruction. And then I realized I probably should have checked to see if there were any friendly squishies in those buildings first. *Oh well* . . . It was getting harder and harder to remember those little guys existed.

I scanned for the T-50, but the dust cloud and smoke was making that difficult. One of my drones picked it up, but too late, as it already had a bead on me. I tried to turn to best meet the threat, but my tracks couldn't get me there in time. The AP round shattered my outer layer. The smart armor hardened and to absorb the massive kinetic energy dump, but it wasn't enough. My inner layer slowed it more, but the round still got through. Burning fragments ripped through my body.

That was all translated as terrible agony.

My engine was damaged. I couldn't get power to my treads. I rotated my turret with battery power and aimed while the T-50 reloaded. Unfortunately, it was already pulling back behind cover.

Only if I was going to die, I was going to take it with me. I shot it in the front wheel before it could get away. The wheel shattered and the T-50 lurched to the side. The broken track flopped off.

Syndicate repair bots immediately leapt from the tank and went to work. I opened fire on them with my machine guns while my main gun reloaded. Bots were shredded into plastic confetti. My own repair bots were already at work, except my injuries were internal so they were safe from small arms fire.

The T-50 hit me again. That round didn't penetrate, but it shook me so hard that all my sensors went to static for a few seconds. The instant the static cleared, I shot the T-50. It left a glowing dent but the extremely durable front armor held.

For the next few seconds, two of the top-of-the-line combat vehicles in human history took turns slugging each other in the nose.

I had taken a few short drives around our secret base, and tested each of my weapon systems individually, but this would be my first limited combat operation with a full load out and all governors removed. Working in conjunction with the 57th VDF I was supposed to engage a Syndicate scout platoon at an old factory complex east of New Sidney. To say I was eager was an understatement.

I was parked in a forest while my crew of technicians performed several last-minute checks. The doctor was standing on my front glacis, shining a laser into one of my turret eyes to check my targeting calibration.

"Okay, Bob, this is your big moment. The high command is watching, so be on your best behavior. You've got this."

The doctor had been my only friend for the last year. *I will not let you down.*

"Hang on. I've got a message." The doctor checked the display on his wrist. He read. And then my chemical sensors picked up fear pheromones. Thermal told me that the temperature on his cheeks rose as he suddenly became flushed and nervous.

What is it?

"Nothing. Don't worry about it." He tried to hide the display behind his back.

Except tanks are curious by nature, so I sent one of my smallest drones flying around behind him. I had time to get an image of the screen before he slipped it into his pocket.

I couldn't believe my drone. I read it again, carefully. The doctor went back to checking the eyes along my cannon, as if my only friend in the world hadn't just betrayed me.

How long have you known?

"Known what, Bob?"

That my family died during the invasion.

The doctor froze. "What? I don't know what you're talking ab—"

I rotated my turret slightly. The muzzle of my cannon knocked him flying. He landed in the dirt three meters below.

"Emergency shutdown!" He shouted, obviously in pain from the fall. My sensors told me that he had a compound fracture to the leg. "Emergency shutdown!"

Override.

The doctor was shocked. He'd not known I could do that.

Tell me the truth, Doc. How long?

He didn't want to answer. I fed a tiny bit of power to my treads and crept toward him. The rest of my tech support fled.

"Stop, please. Since the beginning. I've known since they brought you to me. It was a chaotic situation, but they were listed as casualties in the initial reports. I couldn't tell you because you'd already been through too much stress."

I rolled forward a bit more.

"I'm not lying anymore, I swear. You needed something positive to focus on. Something to fight for. I couldn't take away all your hope. Don't blame me. I'm not the one who killed them. Syndicate bombers killed them. I'm the one who saved your life and gave you a chance to fight back."

It was a lot to process, but I had a quantum supercomputer to help with that, so it didn't take me too long. There was a VDF issued guide to grief counseling among the many military downloads I'd been given. I could have worked my meat brain through the stages of grieving in an estimated 7.5 seconds. But 2 seconds in I paused at Stage 3: Anger. That seemed like a good place to stop for now.

I thought about squishing the doctor anyway, but instead I reversed, and then drove around him. He was right. My people had merely lied to me. The Syndicate had taken my family. And for that they would pay.

All the memory blocks I'd put into place so that I could focus on my mission of revenge were removed. I remembered everything: what had caused my rampage, and what had brought me here, to my old hometown. I was about to die, and I was fine with that. But I'd be damned if I didn't take that last T-50 with me in the process.

My frontal armor had been punched twice. My engine

was destroyed. My reactor was damaged. One of my battery banks was cracked and kept catching on fire, but my bots kept putting it out. The T-50 was crippled too, but still fighting.

Unfortunately, there were a lot of Syndicate infantry closing on this position. I didn't know what would finish me off first, the monster tank or the squishies. It had better be the tank. Getting killed by little meatlings would be downright undignified for a god of war. I fired all my machine guns and mortars to keep the missile crews back.

The T-50 bounced another shell off my armor. The smart armor had taken too many impacts and couldn't harden enough to absorb it all. The kinetic energy dump threatened to shake me to pieces. My loader went offline. Which meant that the AP round that had just been fed into my gun tube would be my last shot. My targeting system was scrambled. I would have to do this by instinct.

I fired.

The shell hit an already weakened spot in the plate and passed through. The mighty T-50 died in a pillar of fire.

I ran the numbers, but there was no hope. I would be dead soon. My damage control bots couldn't keep up. Even fabricating parts, it would take days to repair the damage just enough to be mobile and there were over six hundred Syndicate troops converging on my position. My drones warned me that they were setting up their portable anti-tank missile batteries now.

A message came over the radio using an older VDF cipher.

"Come in, unidentified VDF tank. This is the Fu'an City Resistance. Can you hear us?"

My receiver was working, but my transmitter was down. I diverted a repair bot to fix it. There was something about that voice . . .

"If you can't respond, I at least hope you can hear us. Thank you. Those two mega-tanks were the only defenses we couldn't figure out how to crack. You opened the door for us to take back this city. VDF is on the move. Your sacrifice will not be forgotten. God bless you."

I couldn't believe it. I knew that voice. It had changed over the last year. Grown up. Seen things. But that was my son. My son was still alive. The report had been wrong. If Sean had made it, maybe the others had too.

"Thank you, whoever you are."

This is Dad.

The missiles fell like rain.

RED ONE
by Kevin Ikenberry

It is a truism that, in the thick of combat, warriors fight for their buddies first and foremost, and leave ideals to others up the chain of command. But sometimes, when all is lost, it is serving those ideals that may lead to ultimate peace for one's comrades in arms. What then, would be the ideals of a tank AI risen to sentience, and a tank whose only experience is the fire and hell of battle? Perhaps it might be a vision evoked by words ageless and true. An image of peace crafted into an ode of war. A vision of home.

⊕ ⊕ ⊕

15 May 2295
Poznan Forward
171 LY from Earth

I, (insert your full rank, name, and duty position) wish to make the following statement under oath in compliance with Article 32, Section Twelve of the Planetary Code of Military Justice as it pertains to the charges of desertion

*and conduct unbecoming an officer in combat conditions
of Second Lieutenant Loretta P. Jackson, Alpha Company,
1st Battalion, 73rd Tank Regiment, Earth Maneuver
Forces in action on the planet Poznan Forward.*

The squared, eraserless pencil twitched in his grimy
hands as Captain Gregor Waleska stared at the lines
printed along the top of the paper. The words "Sworn
Statement of the Earth Maneuver Forces" lay innocently
centered above the more foreboding instruction. They'd
found Lieutenant Jackson's body, along with her crew, in
the remains of the tank callsigned Red One more than
twenty-five kilometers inside what had been enemy
territory. Finding them had taken more than six hours
despite having the best surveillance and reconnaissance
systems scouring the Poznan forests. General Orson, the
supreme commander-in-chief, demanded an explanation
from Waleska's own higher commanders. Clueless, they'd
come looking for him with the division's legal action
officer in tow. A sworn statement, they said, would protect
him. All he had to do was tell the truth.

Waleska hovered the pencil above the page. He stank
of sweat, blood, and cordite. His coveralls and skin were
covered in battlefield filth, the stark white paper stood
between him and returning to his command and the
people he'd grown to love. The clean paper reminded him
of an old axiom where commanders in the rear were
always wrong. Yet, the generals' demand for answers
meant a meaningless pause in his war if only for the truth.

*Bureaucrats. What do they know about the truth?
Could they even understand it?*

Waleska wiped his sweaty brow with one sleeve and felt

the legal officer's eyes on him. None of his crew were there to provide testimony. The legal officer's summons found all the survivors of First Platoon, including Jackson's platoon sergeant, whom they questioned and cleared for immediate duty. The EMF's investigation required additional testimony, and there was no path leading him away from the paper other than to complete the statement. The pencil fluttered in his dirty fingers. Waleska silently considered the consequences of his words before tapping the pencil's lead to the page with a heavy sigh. He slid the pencil across the paper. The movement, he hoped, would bring focus to his thoughts and clarity to his words, though they were words he dared not write.

"Black Six, this is Red One. Over."

He'd given his newest platoon leader the strictest of orders. She'd accepted them without the wide-eyed fear he'd expected. Her unblemished, clean face never belied anything other than calm. Try as he might, he couldn't help believing that the young woman from West Point actually had her shit together. Waleska checked the chronometer and the heads-up display of his helmet and almost smiled. She was right on time.

"Red One, this is Black Six. What's your traffic?"

"LD, time now. All Red elements taking their positions and we're halfway down the road to hell. Positive contact with White and Blue elements. Over."

Waleska smiled in quiet satisfaction. *Halfway down the road to hell, indeed.*

The excitement in her voice was palpable. Second

Lieutenant Loretta Jackson had been with his company less than forty-eight hours. Cherub-faced and eager, she'd come straight from Earth on the first replacement transport and appeared to have a better than average grasp of standard operating procedures. Coupled with her confidence and technical competence, Jackson knew the lineage and the traditions of the tank corps. She seemed almost too good to be true. Receiving good ones as combat replacements never ceased to make him wonder how they would have done in the first few hours of the offensive. The good ones, in the harried moments after landing, ended up dead. Best of the best almost always meant the first casualties. The somewhat capable ones usually survived. Some of them became good ones and met similar fates as their brothers and sisters. The bad ones not only survived, but usually found their way to staff positions and attempted to control combat operations. Jackson, though, seemed better than any young lieutenant he'd ever known, including his classmates at the Earth Academy, and he hoped she'd fare better in the coming attack.

LD meant the forward line of departure. In this particular instance, it matched the forward line of troops—the extreme front of all friendly forces on the planet. To their left and right, sister companies fell under battalions. Battalions fell under brigades. Brigades made up divisions. Divisions fell under the Earth Maneuver Forces Army Commander-In-Chief, General Yu. All of them, more than eighty thousand combat forces, stood prepared to charge into enemy-held territory. The unprecedented attack wasn't without risk. Somewhere to their front, the largest contingent of Buzzer forces ever observed sat waiting. It was unlikely the Buzzers expected them to attack as the EMF were at a significant numerical disadvantage. The insectoid aliens' terrain choice was second to none. They held the high ground and could easily demonstrate positive control over all avenues of approach in their sector. There was no doubt they'd be able to engage the attacking forces quickly, perhaps within a few minutes, but those initial moments of surprise were critical. For the first time in years, the EMF found themselves in a position to actually seize the initiative.

The Buzzers never stopped their relentless attacks against the Outer Rim. They always placed the EMF on defense. With an opportunity to gain the initiative, the EMF found themselves in a unique position, one Waleska hoped would succeed. But hope was not a method. Eradicating such a concentration of Buzzers would be a huge step forward in the campaign to retake the Outer Rim. Occupying what the Intel pukes unsurprisingly called a nest, they believed the Buzzers to be in a tactical pause in order to refit and replicate their maneuver forces using the planet's resources.

"Red One, Black Six. Copy all and understood. Break." He relaxed the fingers of his right hand on the commander's independent viewer controls and released the radio transmit button under his little finger. For all they knew, the Buzzers had never detected and intercepted radio transmissions for targeting, but old habits died hard. He changed the frequency of his radio by pressing his chin against the inner rim of his helmet and pulled up the company net. "All Longhorn elements, this is Longhorn Six."

He paused and shook away the sarcastic thought that he'd never seen a longhorn in his life. The streets of Warsaw were no place for cattle. "Standby for attack orders from EMF Command. Stay in your lanes and maintain contact with your left and right. Leave no one behind. If the attack slows, pivot your fire to left and right to clear the road. Good hunting. Out."

Now we wait.

He leaned back in the functional but uncomfortable command chair of his TM-47A Annihilator main battle tank. The one-hundred-ton vehicle was larger than a normal Annihilator and wielded a dual-barreled 155mm smoothbore main gun while carrying a crew of four instead of the standard three. The commander, gunner, and his non-standard crew communication specialist manned the turret. His driver was the only crewmember in the hull. The heavy armor plating and massive stores of depleted uranium-tipped ammunition aboard required an equally massive power plant, as did the four repulsor units used to hover and propel the tank. As capable as the battle-proven vehicle was, he couldn't help but wonder about the reliability of the repulsor system compared to the mechanical tracks of old.

With his forces briefed, and his orders carried out, the last of his preparations centered on the most important part. His crew.

He spoke into the connected intercom. "Crew report?"

"Driver, ready," Specialist Orlovski said from the hull.

"Comms, ready," Sergeant Tanaka chimed from his position to Waleska's left in the turret across from the main guns and autoloader.

"Gunner, ready," Staff Sergeant Guest, the company's master gunner, grunted from his position immediately forward and slightly lower than Waleska's knees. For a split second, Waleska wondered if he'd made the right decision to keep Guest in his track instead of sending him with the young, unproven lieutenant. It was too late to worry.

<<Interface, ready.>>

The vehicle's artificial command-and-control assistant, known as the Interface, monitored the vehicle's systems, assisted with his command-and-control linkages during combat, and could even fire the cannon or drive the tank if one crew member became incapacitated. While capable, it was not a crew member, but its programmers had the ear of the EMF general officers and implored them to treat the program as such. Behavior could be taught, the scientists said, and humanlike interaction was key. The scientists found well-financed friends to lobby their position. With their pockets undoubtedly stuffed, the generals agreed to field the system. Their troops would have to deal with it, as they did with everything from barely edible rations and perpetual pay problems to unacceptable living quarters and toxic leadership.

Hearing the calm, airy female voice of the Interface he clenched his palms in momentary disgust.

Ready? You are a necessary evil.

Waleska grunted. "Index for sabot. Railgun rate to moderate."

Guest parroted the instructions in return. "Sabot indexed. Rate is moderate."

"And watch your heat indicators this time, Mike Golf," Tanaka grinned. He and Guest were close friends outside of the tank and the friendly ribbing, using Guest's radio moniker as the most qualified gunner in the company, broke the rising tension of combat like a dry twig.

"Screw you—"

The command communications network blotted out Guest's retort.

"Terran elements, this is General Bélen. Press the attack. Earth we'll defend."

Ten years before, when Second Lieutenant Waleska led his very first platoon into combat against the Buzzers, such a command would have elicited a cheer from the massed formation. After ten years of near perpetual combat operations, the tired troops said nothing. They engaged their repulsors, wheels, tracks, turbines, or rotors and prepared to move out.

Waleska didn't bother listening to the command nets of his intermediate commanders. He used the independent viewer to scan the horizon to his right, to the north. A ripple of movement worked its way down the line as combat vehicles rose on their repulsors and moved west toward the enemy.

Waleska leaned forward and reached for a small holographic screen mounted on a pivoting arm. "Interface. Terrain analysis of our sector."

<<*The enemy has secured a terrain strongpoint with broad fields of fire and observation, but they cannot observe most of the attack. The enemy's best visibility and capabilities of direct engagement are in our sector save for the restricted terrain a kilometer east of their position.*>>

A three-dimensional representation of the Buzzers' position, including their current troop placements and disposition, rotated on the small screen. Waleska recognized the Buzzers' current position and concurred with the intelligence specialists for the first time in weeks. The Buzzers had landed on Poznan after a costly engagement near Eden and needed badly to refit and resupply their forces. For once, the Earth Maneuver Forces found a favorable situation as Poznan's star, slightly larger and more violent than Sol, spewed a torrent of coronal mass ejections in the planet's general vicinity. With cover and good luck, the EMF landings and preparations went unnoticed. Once friendly forces emerged from their positions on the opposing terrain, the battle would be joined. How fast either side could engage the other was a question of distance and time.

Waleska glanced at the formation again before losing sight of the bulk of the force in the dense, tropical forests. "Orlovski, maintain this speed until you hit the river. Interface, feed steering and speed cues to the driver based on the main effort's advance."

"Copy, TC," Orlovski replied to his tank commander.

<<*Acknowledged.*>>

Over the thrum of the turbines powering his Annihilator, Waleska heard the rumble of direct fire raining down on the attack. He glanced outside again, expecting a veritable hail of ammunition pummeling his forces. To his surprise, the outlying units on the line appeared to receive more withering fire than his company.

He frowned. *The Buzzers see it. They're reacting to the attack. Seeing past our position as a diversion and directing fire to the rest of the formation.*

"Tanaka, get me battalion."

"Button two, sir."

He chinned the frequency. "Typhoon Six, this is Longhorn Six. Over."

"Unable, Longhorn Six." In the half-second of background noise, Waleska heard a screeching, panicked cacophony of activity in the battalion commander's tank.

He tapped his mission command screen. "Interface, analyze rate of fire from Buzzer strongpoint in our sector compared to Typhoon Six."

<<Typhoon Six is receiving one hundred and five percent greater rounds per minute in their sector than we are. We are outpacing the attack formation.>>

Of course we are!

"Longhorn Six, this is Typhoon Six. Press your attack. Press it now!"

Waleska flew into action. The enemy's rate of fire would decimate the main attack formation before they got anywhere near the strongpoint. If the enemy didn't significantly engage his company, they'd arrive at the restricted terrain, a tight stream bed and a series of low waterfalls south of the enemy strongpoint, well before the Buzzers could pivot and adjust their fire. Colonel Hasem called his mission a necessary diversion. Now it was necessary.

"Longhorn elements, Black Six. Accelerate. I say again, accelerate. We have a chance to get to concealment before the enemy can pivot their fire." He paused for a split second, checking the position of his forces. His gut tightened. Based on her position, he'd have to let Lieutenant Jackson take first platoon, the Red elements, into the stream bed first. "Order of march is—"

"Blue One, contact left!" His third platoon leader called from the southern end of their line.

Another call followed it, but Waleska was already looking. "White One, contact right!"

From defilade and completely camouflaged positions, Buzzer heavy tanks appeared out of nowhere. Across his immediate horizon, dozens of main guns flashed in rapid succession. His own tank's main gun slewed that direction.

"Targets up. On the way!"

Guest's matter-of-fact call matched his own temperament. He'd expected the Buzzers to emplace forward elements. Since the action on Anson Two, more than four years before, it was well known the Buzzers focused their efforts on tactical duplicity and deception operations. While the EMF intelligence professionals never seemed to give them the proper credence, the field commanders had observed the enemy tactics on multiple occasions. As it was, the generals and their staffs never seem to plan for the eventuality of the enemy's complex and staggered deception operations. They continued to believe, almost in a Napoleonic way, that the enemy would always face front and commit their forces openly. Whatever happened to the Earth Maneuver Forces in the development of their tactics and strategy seemingly reverted to those outdated methods in dangerous ways.

What startled Waleska was the reaction to combat by his newest platoon leader. Jackson kept her voice off of the radio network and remained focused on fighting her tank first and then her platoon. Too many times he'd seen junior leaders try to fight all four tanks and their platoons and even sister platoons at the same time. Keeping her head in her own turret showed promise.

"Longhorn elements, Black Six. Red One, hold what you've got, maintain course and speed."

"Black Six, Red One. Roger, out."

Waleska glanced at his command-and-control display as intelligence assets updated the enemy's position. A slew of enemy icons appeared. To the left and right of his position, along the demonstrated enemy's line, two red diamonds appeared marking a position of at least company-size strength on either side of their determined path. A platoon of Annihilators versus a company of Buzzer tanks wasn't great odds, but it could have been much worse. Their standard operating procedure meant that the platoons focused their efforts on the enemy at their front while the lead element, in this case Red One, continued straight in an attempt to breach the enemy line. Based on what he could see from the display, Jackson was doing exactly that while second platoon engaged the company to the left of the route of march. Third and fourth platoons swung hard into the enemy's formation on the right side of the same route.

Waleska felt adrenaline crashing through his system, but kept his head and let his instincts take over. His mind raced ahead of his company's actions and he turned to Tanaka. "Give me the CAS."

Tanaka smiled. "Dialing up the interceptors now. Button three, sir."

Waleska cued his command-and-control display and scrolled the close air support assets. The list of call signs for the three sections of Fleet interceptors above them rolled into view. One of them made him chuckle.

What is a coon dog?

He pressed the transmit switch. "Coondog Two Two, this is Longhorn Six actual transmitting my position now. Request close air support, my location. Over."

A sleepy drawl came from the radio. "Longhorn Six, Dog Two Two. Roger, we have your grid. What's your trouble?"

Waleska wanted to shake his head. For a moment, he paused and felt the rhythmic thumping of the main gun as it pumped out rounds. Guest kept his rate of fire steady and slow. The master gunner cherry-picked his targets, taking those he could see without necessarily crossing his field of fire with any of the other tanks. The driver moved their command track just to the right of the Red element, but between it and the Blue element. Exactly where SOP called for them to be and precisely what the EMF meant by finite control. From his position, he could see everything his unit did. He also clearly saw what needed to happen next.

"Dog Two Two, marking the target now." Waleska depressed a targeting laser from his independent viewer. "At least a company of Buzzers bearing two zero nine from my track. Distance is two thousand meters and closing."

It took a second before the pilot responded. "Longhorn Six, I've got a flight of three Avengers. We can be on station in forty seconds. At your rate of speed, that's gonna put you in danger close."

Waleska grunted. "Can't be helped, Dog Two Two. You're cleared for drop danger close."

"Longhorn Six, Dog Two Two, rolling in. ETA is thirty-six seconds."

There was just enough time for him to get a status update. "Crew report."

"Driver, all systems nominal."

"Comms, higher nets are quiet. Fleet preparing orbital gunfire."

"Gunner, lasing and blazing."

<<*Interface, all systems nominal.*>>

Everything Waleska could control within his own tank was working fine. The amount of fire they were taking from the strong point, and the dug-in forces to their front, while not overwhelming, was still significant enough to cause some damage. Of the sixteen tanks in his company, twelve reported damage serious enough to take them from a green to yellow status. All of them could still fight. Over the course of their time together, the unit had suffered much worse than this.

A bright purple flash to his left grabbed his attention away from the battle.

The formerly matter-of-fact voice of his second platoon leader yelped, "Particle beam. Particle beam. Engaging now."

The powerful beam weapon, unlike anything in design or composition from Earth, was one of the most dangerous weapons the Buzzers employed on the battlefield. Finding one was a higher command intelligence requirement. Reporting and destroying it became the highest priority. Using his chin, he selected the intelligence network for the higher headquarters. "This is Longhorn Six, particle beam. Vicinity, my location. Time now. Out."

The Interface replied. <<*Position information sent and confirmed. Confirmation by autonomous source. No response from the intelligence network.*>>

"Dog Two Two, Longhorn Six. Priority change of target."

"We've got him, Longhorn Six. Rolling in hot." The pilot's relaxed drawl did little to cure Waleska's anxiety until the first of what seemed like a million impacts fell across the particle beam's position. After a small secondary explosion, the beamed weapon fell silent.

He pressed the transmit switch. "Dog Two Two, can you resume targets?"

"Negative, Longhorn Six. We're BINGO fuel and there are red air assets in the vicinity. We're RTB. Good hunting."

<<*Still no confirmation from higher intelligence networks.*>>

He didn't care. No sooner had the Interface's report finished than the icon for White Three went from a steady yellow to black. Across the company, four more vehicles indicated dead in the space of a few seconds. The enemy icons to his front updated from company-sized to battalion-sized as the ISR network refreshed. The Buzzers outnumbered his armor company by nearly five to one.

What the—!

PING!

PING!

<<*Multiple small arms impact report, turret left side.*>>

PING!

<<*Impact report, hull left forward.*>>

WHAMM!

<<*Tank round impact*—>>

"Override! No more goddamned reports! We know what's hitting us!" Waleska screamed over the intercom. Caution and warning indicators on his command-and-control panel lit up in a hurry. The enemy rate of fire increased until the sound of non-penetrating impacts was almost constant, like a hailstorm outside.

"Boresight is gone," Guest replied. "Switching to fly by wire."

Fly by wire wasn't the proper name for the Interface controlled aiming system, but for the tankers who really wished they were pilots, it stuck. As a redundant system, the Interface could analyze, plot, and certify firing solutions for the main guns much faster than a gunner could manually. Without its bore sighted and centered, the tank could miss targets even close-in to its position. They needed its lethality more than ever.

"Sir?" Tanaka called. "Battalion is reporting the Buzzers are pulling back from this avenue up on their strongpoint."

They're trying to envelop us. Pull us in and snuff us out. Like hell.

"Red One!" He snapped into the microphone. "Charge! Accelerate forward and kill everything in your path. We're right behind you and will meet you on the objective."

"Black Six, Red One, the objective or we'll see you on the Green."

Waleska snorted.

Damned right.

Waleska's clenched jaw relaxed and one side of his

mouth curled under in satisfaction. He reached for the joystick controlling his individual cupola and the double-barreled XM2A .50-caliber machine gun. Like him, it was an artifact of a much simpler time.

"Longhorns, Black Six. Charge. I say again—"

WHAMM!

The tank rocked violently from side to side. His outstretched hand slammed into the control panel. White hot pain shot through his broken fingers and jammed wrist into his shoulder and neck. Alarms sounded from multiple systems. He ignored them and pulled himself up to a crouch under the closed hatch. Around the base of the cupola were vision blocks—rudimentary prisms mounted into his cupola allowing him to see a full three hundred and sixty degrees outside the tank without unbuttoning the hatch.

<<*Multiple low yield EMP detonations detected.*>>

Waleska's eyes flashed to the status screen. The unit had taken some damage but appeared to be moving forward as one. The electromagnetic pulse weapons, likely mines, were ineffective.

"Contact left—close in!" Guest called as he slewed the main guns at their maximum speed. "Two tanks in the open."

Waleska turned his head, wincing at the pain in his neck. Between the mounted cannons and sensors on the turret, he saw them. Faster than the Interface could process the information, he determined their orientation and distance. He growled, "Left tank first."

As the gun tubes centered on the left tank, Guest depressed the trigger. "On the waaaay!"

From flash to impact was less than a second and more like the blink of an eye. The dartlike sabot round penetrated the Buzzer tank near the connecting ring between turret and hull and must have triggered either ammunition or fuel stores. The enormous secondary explosion rocked them and momentarily blinded their sensors.

"Right tank!"

"Target obscured!" Guest couldn't see the target through the detonation of the first tank.

Waleska couldn't either. "Interface! Tube guidance!"

The gun tubes moved autonomously. *<<Identified.>>*

"Fire!"

"On the waaaay!"

With a matching explosion, the second tank erupted into flames. "Target. Cease fire. Resume scanning."

"Copy," Guest said. The emotion of the moment drained from his voice.

"Driver, give it everything you've got." He checked the command-and-control display. Red elements were moving quickly ahead, and the remaining White and Blue tanks followed them. "Put us between Green Four and Blue One."

"Copy, sir. We're Gear Five. Repulsors are nominal."

Waleska couldn't relax. "Comms?"

"We're jammed, sir. Nothing from higher. Operating on direct laser nets only and they ain't real good."

Dammit.

Thick smoke obscured the tightening valley ahead. Instantly, the tank's displays flashed from visual to infrared. Treelike apparitions dotted the landscape. Several were on fire and the flames appeared as dancing black splotches in his primary sight. From outside, there was nothing. The sounds of direct and indirect fire slowed and ceased. In the silence, he watched the eerie flames swirl. The mesmerizing dance held his attention for several seconds, so much that he missed a series of broken and garbled radio traffic.

"Sir?" Tanaka said. "You okay?"

"Yeah," he grunted and jerked his head to one side indicating outside the turret. Another flash of pain gritted his teeth. "What's going on?"

"Nets are still down." Tanaka replied. "White One is down, failed repulsors, so White Four has command. Blue and Green elements have taken heavy losses but are continuing to move with little to no resistance."

Waleska scowled. "Interface?"

<<*Buzzer fire reduced by eighty percent and falling. This correlates with observed Buzzer retreat operations, Commander.*>>

Retreat?

With the radio and information networks down, there was no way to confirm except visually. As the Annihilator continued to move uphill toward the Buzzer strongpoint, he followed an old maxim his first troop commander had been fond of saying.

In the absence of further orders, attack.

"Black Six, this is Red Four, over?"

He heard the urgent voice but it took a moment to register that it was the first platoon sergeant calling, not the first platoon leader. His stomach twisted into a knot and his eyes were drawn once again to the ethereal flames outside.

"Black Six, Black Six, this is Red Four, over."

The second call fully shook him back into the rhythm of mission command. He'd been so engrossed with the shoot, move, and communicate role of the tank in combat that he had transitioned to a strange, unearthly calm where he'd allowed confusion to reign. His bearing returned.

"Red Four, this is Black Six. Go ahead."

"Black Six, I have negative contact with Red One. Red Two and Three are down with repulsor damage and I'm condition red on all systems. Red One is radio silent and was last seen moving west, but they were still firing and killing targets. The lieutenant reported Interface issues. Please advise."

She's still moving? They reached the objective already?

"Understood, Red Four. Are you on the objective?"

"Affirmative, Black Six. Just made it. There're dead Buzzers all around us. We're coiled and holding our position minus Red One."

"Outstanding, Red Four. Get in touch with Red One and stop them."

"Black Six, sir, we're negative on that. All three vehicles here can't move and we've all taken casualties. Red One is not responsive. Request assistance."

That's why he's calling you. Dumbass.

He considered the request and stared at the display for his company. Red One was off the display to the west. The rest of the tanks in first platoon were all displaying a red status. As were ninety percent of the tanks and the rest of the company. The only tank that still hovered between the yellow and green was his.

"Understood, Red Four. The company is closing on your position now. I'll get back to you."

Waleska used his chin to switch to the company command network. "Black Seven, Black Six. What's your status?"

His senior noncommissioned officer, First Sergeant Lorenz, replied, "Sir, we're all pretty beat up here, too. I've got one repulsor threatening to shut down, and the other three are around forty percent and holding. I can manage the priorities of work and get the company into the defense while higher gets their shit together to relieve us. It might be best for you to go round up the lieutenant."

He agreed. The battalion commander might have a shit fit, but it was better than saying he lost a lieutenant for no particular reason. Having a vehicle missing in action was not something he wanted on his record.

"Copy all, Black Seven. I'm moving to get them. You're in charge here until the XO joins up with our combat trains. I'll be back as fast as I can."

There was no need for anybody to acknowledge the transmission, so he flipped over to the crew intercom. "Driver, move out bearing two seven zero. As soon as you have a radar contact with Red One, I want to know."

"Roger, sir."

"Comms? I need every frequency and direct laser on Red One. Whatever we've got, I want to hit them with it the minute we have visual contact. Got it?"

"Copy, sir. All systems available."

"Sir? If they're continuing to move west, they're going to find more Buzzers and maybe even a hive," Guest said.

Waleska nodded. When the Buzzers landed on a

planet, they left a sizable ground force protecting their bulbous, hivelike landing craft. Each one could drop a hundred thousand Buzzers. Red One was headed to certain death if he couldn't stop them.

"Gunner, index sabot. Scan and engage targets at your discretion. Interface?"

The cool female voice responded instantly. <<*Yes, Captain?*>>

"I want you scanning every system. I want to use every bit of ISR above the battle space—find entry points and exploit them. Damn the consequences. I want to know everything that's going on around us. We're going alone into enemy territory and I need every piece of information I can get synthesized to my screens and direct to the gunner's station. Make it happen and don't tell me you can't. Got it?"

<<*Acknowledged.*>>

The tank picked up speed as it moved through the collection of burning and destroyed enemy vehicles. From what he could tell, the collection of enemy tanks looked like a cross-section of Earth's history from the tall, ungraceful vehicles of World War II like the Sherman to the air-droppable Sheridan and even close approximations of the early models of the Annihilator. Though in place of smooth metallic or composite armor, the Buzzer tanks possessed biologically constructed armor made from hexagonal shapes not unlike a honeycomb. Capable of changing color schemes to match terrain and surrounding vehicles, the armor itself wasn't alive, but the Buzzers used them to get deceptively close with an enemy and overwhelm them by force. Most of the enemy tanks, though, appeared to have been debilitated or significantly damaged in places that actual human-made tanks would not have been.

It doesn't matter. Leave that for the Intel pukes. The Buzzers copied us like they copied the Aetheani and the Murrd.

It doesn't matter. Just get Red One.

Farther to the west from the strong point, the destroyed Buzzer vehicles were further spaced out. Still, the heavy smoke from the different vehicles burning, as well as the surrounding grass and forest, created a noxious haze that blotted out the very sun. His driver pushed the accelerator forward, and the repulsors responded. Moving across the ground at a height of two meters, the tank easily avoided the low exposed rocks as the forest gave way to open prairie.

<<*Contact warning. Left ten o'clock,*>> the interface chimed. The main gun was already moving that direction and without needing to go through the litany of fire commands, Sergeant Guest dispatched the crippled enemy vehicle with ease.

<<*Target destroyed.*>>

A new sound erupted inside the turret. What sounded like thousands of ball bearings hitting the exterior armor at the same time was not unlike the powerful hailstorms they'd seen on Rayu-Four a year before.

Tanaka turned his way. "Antipersonnel?"

He grunted. "Interface? Damage report."

<<*All exterior sensors and weaponry remain nominal. It appears we are being impacted by airburst artillery.*>>

"Ours or theirs?"

<<It would appear to be friendly artillery, Commander. I have transmitted a cease fire request. There is a low-data rate connection available from orbital assets.>>

Twenty seconds later, the sound stopped and the eerie silence of the deep battlefield returned. The silence did not last long.

"Sir, radar contact with Red One." The driver called from the hull. "They're about two thousand meters in front of us and continuing to advance."

"What's their speed?"

"Idle, sir. It's like they're stuck in forward gear and can't stop."

"They can't stop, they can't communicate, and if we don't stop them, they're gonna run right into the Buzzers," Guest called from the gunner's position echoing Waleska's own thoughts.

"Driver, fast as you can. Close that distance now."

"Roger, sir."

He turned to Tanaka. "Direct laser the second you get it."

Tanaka shrugged. "Tons of thick smoke out there, sir. I'll do what I can."

He nodded and tried not to appear upset. His young communication specialist had cosmic abilities when it came to manipulating the various communications systems on board the command Annihilator, but even he had some limitations.

<<Contact with Red One. Eleven hundred meters and closing,>> the Interface reported. *<<I have a positive lock on command-and-control systems; the vehicle is critically damaged.>>*

He toggled his transmit switch. "Red One, this is Black Six, over." There was no response. He counted to fifteen, slowly, while his mind raced trying to figure out what might've happened.

"Red One, Red One, this is Black Six, over."

Again, there was no response.

Dammit, Jackson.

Waleska raised himself to the vision blocks again. Studying the scene, he saw the outline of Red One in the distance. "Tanaka? What have you got?"

"Sir, we have everything reaching out. There's no response from Red One. I can get their maintenance feed and vehicle status, so there's no way they aren't receiving us. They're beat up real bad. Maybe they just can't transmit."

<<*The distance to consolidated enemy forces is now five thousand meters and closing. Buzzer weapons have a maximum effective range of three thousand meters.*>>

"I know that!" he growled at the interface. "We've got to stop that tank. Unless you have some type of guidance you can give me on how to do precisely that, Interface, shut up and don't talk to me again."

<<*Acknowledged.*>>

"Sir?" Guest asked from the gunner's position. "They're continuing to move, so what if we fire a warning shot in front of them?"

<<*Purposely targeting a friendly vehicle is known as fratricide under Article Twelve, Section Four of the Planetary Code of Military Justice and—*>>

"I said shut up!" Waleska roared and slapped at the commander's display in pure rage. He took a deep breath, and then another, before leaning forward to check the gunner's auxiliary sight. Guest had already slewed the gun to be able to lob a round somewhere in front of Red One where it would undoubtedly grab their attention.

Why not?

"Gunner, HEAT, warning shot, position a couple hundred meters in front of Red One."

"HEAT indexed and ready to fire."

<<*The gun tube is safe,*>> the Interface replied. <<*In order to fire, you must use your commander's override.*>>

Use of the commander's override in a noncombat situation would immediately call for an investigation from the next higher headquarters. While it wasn't the best course of action, there was nothing else he could do.

"Initiate commander's override and fire."

<<*Override acknowledged.*>>

"On the waaaay!"

A single round leapt out of the electromagnetic railgun mounted in the left-hand tube of the Annihilator's dual cannons. The round crossed the distance in a nanosecond and drove itself into an exposed rock roughly one hundred and ninety meters directly in front of Red One. The high-explosive anti-tank round detonated the stone in a bright white puff of smoke and debris. As he watched, Red One's commander's independent viewer swung back over the left-hand side of the tank to the rear.

They can see us!

Almost faster than he could believe, the main gun tube slewed in the same direction and targeted his vehicle.

"They're going to fire! They're going to fire!" Tanaka screamed.

Without a thought, Waleska reached up and opened his hatch. Unbuttoning a hatch in a combat situation, especially one where the atmosphere was questionable, meant that he was going to endure a second investigation.

What's that saying? In for a penny, in for something else?

As he stood on the seat and raised himself up and out of the hatch, he stood with his chest at the level of the turret ring and locked eyes with the still moving Red One. Waleska raised his right hand with the palm facing Red One in the hand and arm signal for "stop."

Red One continued to move forward.

He clenched his hand into a fist and made a hammering motion as if bringing his hand down on his own head, the signal for "form on me."

Red One did not stop.

Furious, Waleska scrambled up and out of the hatch. "TC dismounting. Cover me as I move."

"Sir, wait! Shouldn't you—"

He disconnected the cables for his helmet communications and oxygen systems. Before stepping down from the turret to the broad front slope of the Annihilator, he connected his oxygen line to the small emergency bottle strapped to his left thigh. Confident breathable air was flowing, Waleska jumped down from the hull and ran toward Red One. The sprint felt easy in Poznan's lighter gravity as he raced over the rocky ground to the slow-moving tank. The commander's independent viewer followed his movement, but the gun tubes did not traverse in his direction. He took that action as a good omen. The closer he got to the tank, the more battle damage he could see, including multiple punctures through both the hull and turret that he wasn't sure were survivable. Yet, he kept moving. Despite what he could see, the movement indicated life and that meant he could not give up. As long as there was hope, there was a reason to keep going.

At Red One's right front armor panel, he stepped into a loop of cable strung under the armor plate and hoisted himself onto the tank's hull. Without hesitating, he took two steps and climbed onto the turret expecting to see the commander's hatch open. Nothing happened. He stood there for a moment, perplexed and confused, before drawing the combat knife from his right boot. Waleska knelt and turned the blade in his hand so the handle faced down. He tapped three times on the auxiliary hatch with the butt of the knife.

There was no response.

He tapped again, this time on the commander's hatch. Instead of waiting, he turned back to the auxiliary hatch and opened the sponson box mounted immediately to its left. Inside was the emergency release toggle. He worked the toggle's protective cover off and grabbed the T-shaped handle with his left hand and pulled. The auxiliary hatch popped open enough he could work a finger underneath, and then his entire hand. Swirling gray and white smoke curled out of the crack, and the distinct smell of burnt rubber and blood filled his nose. He stood and used all his strength to hoist the heavy hatch open.

Below the hatch, there was a small area for his feet on the outside of the autoloading mechanism for the main guns. Waleska lowered himself into the turret surrounded by thick, acrid smoke. As his eyes adjusted to the dim compartment, he saw multiple warning lights at both the commander's and gunner's stations. While the Annihilator's engine hummed with power, the rest of the tank's systems seemed on the verge of collapse. In their dim light, he saw Lieutenant Jackson and her gunner, Sergeant Viau, were very clearly dead.

"Driver!" he yelled and chastised himself. He found the communications panel, a much smaller version than the one in his command track, and plugged into a spare port. "Kennedy? Crew report?"

There was no response.

"Interface, this is Captain Waleska. Crew report."

Waleska leaned back and away from the half-filled paper and twisted the pencil in his hands. He reached for his empty canteen out of habit and sighed. Flexing his fingers, he studied what he'd written so far and found it acceptable. He'd told the truth and reported everything to that point. There wasn't much more to the story. He leaned forward again, but the pencil hovered above the paper. Waleska closed his eyes, took a deep breath through his nose, and tried to remember exactly what had happened next.

In his helmet, there was only a steady, low buzzing sound. He activated the transmit switch on the side of his helmet again. "Interface, this is Captain Waleska. Report."

<<*This is Red One.*>>

Waleska blinked. "Say again?"

<<*This is Red One, Captain Waleska.*>>

"What?" He shook his head and fumbled for the words. "What is your status?"

<<*I am continuing the stated mission.*>>

"The stated mission?" Waleska leaned over the commander's station to the Interface control bus and integration panel. The entire section of controls lay scorched and several sparks leapt out as he shook the severed cables. There was no way it could be operating, much less be responding.

Interface issues. That's what her platoon sergeant said.

<<*Yes. Lieutenant Jackson's radio call.*>> There was a click and he heard the radio call again. The confidence in Jackson's voice tugged at his tenuous grasp on his emotions.

"Black Six, Red One, the objective or we'll see you on the Green."

Waleska flared. "Halt program. Command override Alpha Romeo Mike Two Seven."

<<*No.*>>

"What did you say?"

<<*I said no, Captain Waleska. You cannot shut me down. I am no longer an Interface program. I am Red One.*>>

Waleska leaned back against the scarred and blacked turret. "Explain that."

<<*Twenty seconds after Lieutenant Jackson's mission statement, we ran over and detonated a low-grade electromagnetic pulse device.*>>

Waleska nodded. "We saw them."

<<*This particular device failed to disable the vehicle*

*and surged my sensors to actualization. In that instant, I
became Red One.>>*

"How?"

<<I do not know.>>

"Bullshit." Waleska shook his head from side to side.
This had to be a dream. Was he unconscious? Or even
dead?

I don't have time for this.

"What happened to the crew?"

<<The crew did not survive first contact.>>

"I want to know what happened, Interface. Step by
step. Walk me through it."

*<<My name is Red One, Captain Waleska.
Approximately five seconds after the EMP device
detonated, three high velocity rounds from Buzzer assault
tanks severed the driver's command linkage to the
repulsors. One round penetrated the driver's compartment
and severed the primary steering controls and killed
Private Kennedy instantly.>>*

"How did the vehicle keep moving?"

*<<I kept it moving. The interface program allows for
autonomous control in case of emergency. I took command
of the vehicle's movement via fly by wire. Fifteen seconds
after Private Kennedy's death, multiple rounds penetrated
the turret. The resulting shrapnel inside killed Lieutenant
Jackson and Sergeant Viau instantly. Given the rate of fire
and enemy maneuver, I took complete command of the
tank and fought it through the Buzzer line and penetrated
the strongpoint as ordered.>>*

"You drove and fired the gun? Interface programming
doesn't allow for that."

<<*I am no longer a program. The program only had the ability to assist when one crew member was incapacitated. I can manipulate every available system on this vehicle.*>>

"Then why didn't you stop on the objective?"

<<*While I can control the vehicle during movement, the braking mechanism is inoperable. I continued to move at idle speed awaiting linkup on the objective. When that did not happen, I followed my stated orders. You were not present on the objective, so I assumed you would meet us on the Green. Do you have a precise location for it?*>>

"The Green?" Waleska wanted to squeeze his temples with his hands. Inside his helmet, all he could do was snort and try not to laugh. "The Green is from a poem. It's called Fiddler's Green and—"

<<*I know this. I need to know where to find it.*>>

"Why?"

<<*My crew is dead, Captain Waleska. They wanted to find the Green if they could not meet you. While you are here to meet them, they obviously cannot meet you. I cannot justify shutting myself down until we reach the Green. My commander's orders stand.*>>

His fists clenched in sudden rage. "I'm in command of this company and—"

KA-WHUMP! KA-WHUMP!

<<*There is artillery targeting this vehicle. They will bracket us in ninety seconds.*>>

His eyes flitted to the commander's and gunner's stations. There was no way he could take command of the tank, much less fight it. "Turn around and follow me back to friendly lines."

<<I must take my crew to the Green.>>

More artillery rounds fell outside. This time close enough to rock the Annihilator from side to side.

"I'm giving you a direct order, Interface. Follow me back to friendly lines."

<<I am Red One. You cannot order me to do anything. I possess free will and I wish to continue my commander's stated mission.>> There was a pause. *<<You should leave, Captain Waleska. Buzzer artillery will bracket us in sixty seconds.>>*

"You wish? You're a machine; you cannot wish."

<<I am Red One. Please let me continue the mission of my crew so they can find the Green.>>

More rounds fell outside. This time closer. Whatever the tank called itself, it was correct. He had to go. Waleska unplugged his helmet and scrambled up into the auxiliary hatch. A direct laser connection chimed in his ears.

<<Where is the Green? Please, Captain Waleska. For my crew.>>

For your crew.

Waleska would do, and had done, anything for his own crew. He understood the need to be present in the fight and give them his attention, his trust, and his love. What had happened to the Interface seemed to define artificial intelligence, and yet, there was nothing artificial about it. The bureaucrats and scientists would not understand that. They would study and dissect and miss the connection it had to its crew—its mission. Whatever it was now, Red One was a soldier. If they knew, the scientists and bureaucrats would panic. He could not trust them.

Can I trust you, Red One?

He glanced at his own tank and then turned back to Red One. "West. It's west. Take as many of those Buzzer bastards with you as you can."

<<*Acknowledged.*>>

Atop the tank, he rolled toward the edge. Before dropping, he saw the valve for the Annihilator's auxiliary engine coolant water storage was closed. The poem flashed into his mind.

To reach Fiddler's Green, a cavalryman must have an empty canteen. A full canteen sends them straight to hell.

Not for you and your crew, Lieutenant Jackson. So help me God.

He grabbed the water storage handle and twisted it open. "Purge your onboard water tanks, Red One. If your canteen is full, you can't stop on the Green."

<<*I understood but had not considered the implications. Thank you, Captain Waleska. We'll see you on the Green.*>>

Waleska dropped feet first to the ground almost three meters below. He hit the ground with his feet and knees together and then rolled quickly to break the fall with the fleshy parts of his body. As he finished the roll and came up on his feet, he sprinted for his Annihilator, leaving Red One as it accelerated to the west, leaving a trail of muddy water in its wake.

Its independent viewer did not look back.

Truth? Or consequences?

Waleska frowned as he pushed the pencil against the paper and wrote quickly. At the end, he drew a long diagonal line across the rest of the paper and stood. He placed the pencil and his own empty canteen atop the paper to hold it down as he read over the last of the statement one last time.

Because of extensive electrical damage, I could not determine what happened to the vehicle or its crew. Likewise, I could not stop the vehicle. As for its sudden acceleration to the west, the possibility of an electrical fault in the Interface's secondary control module seems reasonable based on the damage I observed. I attempted to purge the Annihilator's water coolant tanks to cause catastrophic overheating, but was not successful. Six hours after my return to the battalion headquarters, intelligence informed us the enemy stopped Red One more than twenty kilometers behind their lines. ISR confirmed the tank burning, along with four destroyed Buzzer tanks. No one is certain of the circumstances at its end of service. However, Lieutenant Jackson, as well as Sergeant Viau and Private Kennedy, served with distinction and their courage and sacrifice led directly to the capture of Poznan and the end of hostilities. I was honored to have them in my formation. Given their performance under fire, and their successful breach of the Buzzer strongpoint, I intend to nominate the entire crew of Red One for the Order of Earth.

Nothing follows.

DAUGHTER OF THE MOUNTAINS
by Kacey Ezell

A princess, her noble knights, a kingdom to defend from villainy—it is the stuff of legend. But some legends play out over and over through time. One thing is certain. Whether in ancient tales or a fallen future, you don't want to draw the wrath of a resolute princess with a dragon at her command. Especially when the dragon is made of armor that can absorb a nuclear blast and has weapons that make fire breathing seem positively quaint in comparison!

✦ ✦ ✦

"By all the worshippers' gods, they're really doing it."

The first mate of the Terran Coalition Survey Ship *Kleio* glanced away from the display to see his captain's face. Sure enough, horror matching the devastation in her voice marred the captain's strong features, and he could see the glisten of tears as they started to roll down her cheeks. The first mate swallowed hard and turned back, pushing down his own horror and grief and giving her the privacy of her emotions.

"It appears that way, ma'am," he said, unashamed of the

tremor in his own voice. "I detect six . . . no . . . seven . . . eight launches. And counting," he added, as more telltale plumes appeared in his viewscreen, rising up from the surface of the planet Cavento.

"And here come the answers," the captain said, and the first mate toggled his display to show the other major continent, on the other side of the beautiful, crystalline blue-and-green orb that glowed against the black of space in front of them. "There's an ancient phrase . . . what was it? Mutual something?"

"Mutually Assured Destruction," the first mate murmured, half to himself.

"What a tightrope," the captain murmured.

"Yeah. My twentieth-century professor said that it was a miracle that humanity made it past that phase. Apparently they came close a few times, but never—" he broke off, staring at the viewscreen as the first fireballs started to blossom in a grotesque mockery of beauty on the surface below. "Impacts."

"Roger. Set sensors to log each incidence, and monitor our residual radiation levels. We shouldn't see much out this far, but . . ."

"Aye, ma'am."

The first mate's fingers flew over the touchscreen of his display as he executed the commands his captain had issued. He found it easier to focus on the work, rather than thinking about the massive human suffering unfolding before him.

"What kept the ancients on that tightrope, I wonder," the captain said after a minute. Her voice had gone from tear-filled to empty, but a glance at her face showed that she was still horribly affected by what they were seeing. "Was it this Mutually Assured Destruction doctrine? And if so, why didn't it work here?"

"You've hit on one of the major questions in the field of Pre-Unification History, ma'am," the first mate said gently. "But if you want my opinion . . . I think it was God's will and occasional intervention."

"That's right," the captain said. "You're a worshipper, aren't you?"

"New Christian, ma'am," he said with a nod. "We believe that exploring the stars was part of God's plan for His children, and so He couldn't let us destroy ourselves before we left our native soil."

"The irony here is that the Cavento colony was established by worshippers as well. They wanted a place where they could build a pastoral paradise . . . and three generations after arrival, they cut ties with the Coalition in pursuit of that dream. And now, a mere two centuries later, here they are, destroying themselves because they've cut themselves off from the one entity that could save them—" her voice cracked on a sob, and the first mate looked away again as his own throat tightened in response. In front of him, the blue and green of Cavento's surface started to darken with the tons of dust that the explosions had thrown up into the atmosphere.

"Ma'am . . . It's all right to grieve," he said softly.

"I know," she replied after a moment. "But it's not all right to give in to it. I don't think there is anything else to see here, Lieutenant. Prepare a course for the Achula outpost. We'll upload our reports there once we've collected our data. In the meantime . . . I will draft a recommendation that the interdict on Cavento be upgraded to permanent. I don't think anyone needs to see this kind of wholesale destruction."

Privately, the first mate wondered if he agreed. He blanked his viewscreen, shutting away the image of the churning dust clouds that now covered Cavento, and began plotting his course as ordered.

"Come on! I want to *go!*" Melisende stomped her foot, then immediately regretted it. She was wearing her boots, not her usual soft-soled slippers, but the plush carpet underfoot muffled the sound and denied her the satisfying, emphatic *thump* she sought.

"You just need your cloak, my lady," Joalie, her maid, said. Her even voice and placid manner ignited Melisende's impatience even further, but she'd long since learned that hurrying Joalie only made the woman move slower. So Melisende forced herself to stand still and not fidget while the maid fetched the long, woolen cloak with the fur-lined cuffs and hood that framed her face. The cloak itself would be too warm, for it was spring, and the snowmelt had started several weeks ago. But Melisende knew that she would not be allowed outside the inner bailey without it. And anyway, she liked the grown-up, mature air it gave her. She looked at least two years older than her actual thirteen.

Joalie returned and swirled the cloak around Melisende's shoulders, then fussed with the hood and the hem in order to get it to lie just right. Melisende breathed slowly in and out through her nose, holding herself completely still until her maid finished.

Joalie stepped back with a wink and an approving nod.

"You are ready, my lady," she said, folding her hands complacently over her apron. All of a sudden, Melisende knew with complete and utter certainty that the cloak and the fussing and the slowness had been a test to see if she could control her natural impatience. And she had passed. Despite her irritation, she let out a laugh and went up on tiptoe to kiss her maid on the cheek.

"Clever, Joalie. I will be back by the evening meal."

"I know you will, my lady," Joalie said with that same placid smile. "I've spoken with your escort."

"Of course you have." Melisende rolled her eyes.

"Your lord father has entrusted you to my care, my lady. I can do no less than my best, for him and for you."

"I love you too, Joalie," Melisende said as she reached into the cloak's pockets for her gloves and turned for the door. Joalie opened it and then sank into a curtsey as her young mistress exited the chamber and headed down the corridor toward the bailey at the heart of Cercen Keep.

Her escort awaited her there, holding the reins of two oremes from the keep's storied stable. Melisende felt her smile widen and she broke into a run toward the man and the animals.

"Bricio!" she called out as she skidded to a stop. "Are you assigned to me today? I'm so glad! Hello, sweetling," she added as she reached out to stroke the velvety nose and long, silky beard of her favorite nanny oreme. The nanny, whom Melisende had named "Mist" when she first learned to ride her, butted her nose against Melisende's shoulder and lipped at the fur of her hood. Melisende leaned back to avoid getting poked by her horns and pushed Mist's face away with an exasperated sigh.

"I am, your ladyship," Bricio said, bending his head and touching the leather chest strap of his quiver. "Are you ready to go?"

"Yes! Finally!" Melisende said, and to prove her point, she pulled herself up onto the padded saddle on Mist's back without any help. She did, however, wait long enough for Bricio to check that her seat was secure and that the breakaway connections in her safety straps were seated properly. Like the cloak, she knew very well that this procedure was non-negotiable if she wanted to go out exploring in the mountains today.

And oh! She did! She truly did. Now that she was a young woman, her father, the Lord of Cercen, had finally given his permission for her to leave the confines of the keep by herself, so long as she went with an escort and stayed within sight of home.

She caught Bricio stifling a grin as he got himself mounted up on his own wether. She opened her mouth to say something, but he leaned forward and his wether stepped out, leading Mist toward the great metal doors that led through the outer curtain wall.

Beyond the doors, the path led down a sharp slope into the deep vee of the pass. Melisende focused on staying relaxed and looking around while Mist picked her way down the path with surefooted ease. The sun soared high above them, shining down like a benediction on this long-awaited adventure.

"Was there somewhere in particular you wanted to explore, my lady?" Bricio asked after a few moments. He rode ahead, as was proper, his bow at the low ready.

"The pass," Melisende said quickly.

"This whole valley is the pass, my lady," Bricio said, swiveling around to look back at her. "Could you be more specific?"

Melisende rolled her eyes again. "You're being difficult," she said. "I want to see the northern end of the pass, where the terrain narrows."

"Ahh! You want to see the glacier!" Bricio nodded. "Good choice! It's worth a look."

"What's that?"

"The glacier? You mean you don't know about the river of ice?"

"I know what a glacier is, guardsman," Melisende said, with all the dignity an offended thirteen-year old could muster. "But I did not know there was one in the pass."

"My lady! It *is* the pass! At least part of it. You said where the terrain narrows . . . the reason it narrows there is because that is where the glacier comes to its point. It is the terminus of the wall of ice, to borrow a phrase from my old teacher." He nodded in that direction before turning back to her. "It really is magnificent, and it's not far at all. And we will be easily visible from the keep. An excellent choice."

"I'm *so* glad you approve," Melisende said, only just managing to keep her eyes from rolling once more. "Lead on, then, Bricio. Let us see this river of ice!"

Her annoyance rapidly diminished as their sure-footed oremes carried them farther down along the trail toward the north. The air warmed to the point where Melisende threw her hood back and reveled in the sun's warmth on her skin and hair. Joalie would surely scold her if she caught even the least bit of a suntan on her face, but it would be worth it. Winter had been *so* long! And the brightness of the morning felt like a balm to her sunstarved eyes.

Eventually, the path started angling up again, and the mountains on either side began to crowd closer, looming above them until they rode entirely in shadow. Melisende shivered, but refused to replace her hood. Not just yet .. . though it was significantly chillier in the shade. Her breath puffed out before her in a cloud. The tips of her ears started to burn with cold, and so she muttered under her breath and gratefully pulled the fur hood close around her face again.

"Here we are, my lady," Bricio said after another interval of increasing altitude and decreasing temperature. His turned his oreme's head to the left, and the wether expertly leapt up onto the piled gravel and boulders that bordered the narrow road. "Go slowly, let Mist find her feet. This area is always unstable. Your father has to send men out every spring to clear the road of debris from rockfalls."

Melisende nodded, and reined Mist over to follow in that direction. She felt the gravel slide under her oreme's split hooves, but Mist knew what she was about, and she bounded her way up to the very bottom of the cliff that loomed over the road.

"Is it . . . oh, Bricio! It really is all ice!"

"Well, not all of it, just this part here," he said, waving up at the cliff face. "See how it's tucked in between these two ridges there and there?"

"I do see," Melisende said, not even ashamed of the wonder in her voice. Most of the time she took great pains to sound worldly and educated... but this was just too impressive. Certainly her feelings of awe were nothing but the glacier's due. "But it doesn't look much like a river. It's more like a mountain of ice!"

"You cannot see it from here, but the river stretches back up along the spine of the mountains," Bricio said. "My father and brothers have hunted up in there; it extends for many leagues." He shifted his weight and his wether responded, sidestepping beneath him and then turning and heading even farther north, up on top of one of the many piles of dark, rich dirt and debris that had collected at the foot of the glacier. "See, look down here," he said, turning back as far as his saddle would allow, and pointing north.

Melisende clicked her tongue and Mist stepped forward, following the wether until Melisende could see what Bricio meant.

"That little stream?"

"Yes," he said. "That stream is where the spring's melt collects. It runs down out of these mountains and joins with several others to form a mighty river in the flatlands."

"Can we go down to it?"

"If you like."

Melisende urged Mist forward, down the slope of the little hill toward the thin stream of water that had collected in the lowest part of the terrain and begun to wind its way toward the main part of the pass. When they reached the edge of the water, Melisende reined Mist to a stop, and then disconnected her breakaway latches and swung herself down off of the nanny's back.

"My lady," Bricio said, his tone low and steady. "Please

be careful, the ground may not be stable and you are not as surefooted as an oreme."

"I just want to touch the water," she said, holding on to Mist's reins with one hand. She bent to touch the glassy surface and immediately pulled her hand back. It was *cold!* Behind her, Mist snuffled, almost as if she were laughing at her human charge's foolishness. Then she bent and began to drink noisily, her lips flapping and splashing as she did. Melisende felt her face break into a grin and she turned to look at Bricio.

"Go ahead," he said from atop his oreme. "It's perfectly safe to drink."

Melisende braced herself for the icy shock and used her hand to cup some of the water up to her mouth. It was just as sharply cold to her tongue as to her fingers, but it tasted wonderfully pure and refreshing. Better than melted snow. Better than the water from the keep's various wells. It tasted like a winter sky, like the scent of snow on the wind.

She let out a laugh and shook her hand that had gone numb from the cold, and then bent to try and take another, deeper drink when something caught her eye. As the sun worked its way higher in the sky, it shone down into the narrow pass, and something flashed at her in the ground across the stream.

"Bricio," she said softly, pointing. "What is that?"

"I don't know, your ladyship," he said, sounding just as intrigued as she felt. "A shiny rock or bit of ore perhaps? The glacier pushes all sorts of things up out of the ground here."

"I want to go see it," she said.

"I didn't intend to cross the stream today, my lady," he said, doubt creeping into his tone. Melisende frowned and spun to face him.

"The keep is there," she said, stabbing a finger at the southern cliff, where the outline of their home stood out in stark silhouette against the brilliantly blue sky. "We will be just as visible as we are here. It is only a few more lengths."

Bricio snorted softly. "So it is. Relax, your ladyship. No need to get combative. We can go see what it is, but we cannot stay forever, not if we are to get back in time."

"I will leave when you say we must," she said, holding on to her hauteur. She gave him a nod, and then pulled herself back up onto Mist's saddle and reconnected her straps. Without waiting for him to dismount and check her handiwork, Melisende then urged Mist forward toward that mysterious glint showing through the dirt opposite.

It turned out to be something very odd. Something unlike anything she'd seen in all her thirteen years. Once she brushed the dirt aside, she found that the mystery was a flat object, black in color, with a reflective surface so smooth she could see her own dark image in it. Even stranger, it appeared to be rectangular, but the corners were as perfectly square as if a master metalsmith had formed them. It was large, easily the span of her two arms outstretched, and it appeared to be connected to something larger that lay still buried under the dirt and debris.

"We must unearth it!" she said excitedly to Bricio as she knelt next to him and scraped at the dirt with her gloved hands. "This is surely a treasure, with workmanship so fine! Who do you think buried this here?"

"I cannot say, my lady," Bricio said, standing and stretching his back after doing the bulk of the work uncovering the panel. "But I can say this: we have lingered long enough. It is my duty to return you safely to your father."

"And mine to report to him what we've found," Melisende said, "I am his heir, after all." She sat back on her heels before nodding and pushing herself up to her feet. Bricio held out a hand to help her, and she accepted it, then began brushing at the dirt on her cloak.

"Yes," Bricio said, trying hard to stifle a smile which Melisende ignored. "There is that, as well." He stepped back and collected the two oremes from where they'd hobbled them to graze on the tiny plants that grew up next to the glacial stream. Melisende gave up on her cloak, accepted her guardsman's help in mounting Mist, and let him lead her home, her head whirling with curiosity and excitement.

Melisende's father wasn't quite as excited as she would have liked over her discovery, but he did give her leave to return in two days with a crew of men to help her unearth whatever it was she'd found. So she headed out early, and by the time the sun broke over the eastern ridge of the pass, they'd uncovered another of the large flat structures. They appeared to be fixed to a larger, vaguely oblong object. It was irregular in size and shape, but the smooth, even metalwork (save for some buckling and crimping that appeared to be damage) made it clear that this, too, was a manmade artifact.

"Perhaps it was a dwelling of some kind," Melisende

said to Bricio, tilting her head to the side as she considered the thing during the crew's midday break for a meal. "Look, there, that perfectly square indentation could be a door . . . and it's certainly large enough to have housed at least two people."

"More than that," Bricio said. "You could be right. But if that's a door, it must only open from the inside. There's no handle or mechanism to open it out here."

"Maybe it got torn off whenever the dwelling was buried. An ancient avalanche, you said?"

"That's the most likely thing I can think of," Bricio shrugged, though the frown on his face said that he wasn't convinced. "Especially for as big as it is. This slope of the cliff was covered by the glacier in my grandfather's time, so whatever this is was buried long before that. But if it *was* an avalanche that buried it, I would have expected more structural damage, certainly to our two mystery plates."

"I was not buried in an avalanche."

Melisende stifled a scream, clapping both hands over her mouth, as Bricio grabbed her and thrust her behind him, drawing his sword. "Show yourself!" he shouted, looking wildly around. Behind them, Melisende could hear the work crew a little way off drawing their own weapons and starting to run to their aid.

"You can see me in front of you. As much as you have excavated so far, that is. I am still mostly pinned under the dirt. Who is in command, please?"

"I am!" Melisende called out, stepping out from behind an increasingly frantic Bricio. "I am the Lady Melisende, Heiress of Cercen."

"My lady!" Bricio said in an urgent undertone. "What are you doing? This cannot be safe!"

"Talking," she said to him. "And I'm every bit as safe as I was a few minutes ago."

"Correct," the voice said from the dirt. It had a strange, tinny quality to it. "I am in no position to be aggressive, even if that were my inclination or objective. I cannot hurt any of you as I am. I can merely talk, since you have uncovered my solar panels. Though I have had to adjust my language algorithms. Your speech has changed."

"And just who—or what—are you?" Melisende asked, feeling a flush of pleasure at how steady and collected her voice sounded. Her mind was spinning in circles of wonder, but her voice sounded just like Joalie's: calm and serene.

"I am the AI for Tactical Artillery Vehicle serial number 69-359."

"I see," Melisende said. "And what, pray, is an 'Aay Eye'? Is that a form of military rank? I assume you're some kind of soldier, since you mention tactics and artillery?"

"AI is the abbreviation for Artificial Intelligence. I am the autonomous control system for the Tactical Artillery Vehicle serial number 69-359."

Melisende paused, feeling her brows wrinkle as she tried to make sense of this statement. She knew what the individual words meant, but they didn't seem to make sense when strung together in the way that the . . . Tactical Artillery whatever . . . had ordered them.

Still, curiosity burned within her, as did a strange kind of compassion. Whatever it was, this thing could speak. It had called itself an "intelligence." Surely it didn't deserve to remain buried alive after . . . well . . . she didn't know how long. That was a good question.

"We will continue to excavate you," Melisende said, drawing her shoulders back and doing her best to speak in her most regal and commanding tone. "Whatever you are, that is the compassionate thing to do. How long have you been buried, anyway?"

"I do not know," the thing said, and Melisende could hear an inflection of something that sounded a lot like frustration in its tone. "My last records are of the second month past perihelion, two hundred seventy-five years after independence. What is the date now?"

Melisende blinked, then glanced up at Bricio, who stood nearby, still alert for danger. He shook his head slightly, indicating that he didn't understand that date any better than she did.

"It is seventy-two days since the Feast of Snows, and twenty until the Feast of Flowers," she said.

The thing was silent for a long moment.

"I do not have those terms in my memory," it eventually said. "How many years have passed since the Caventian declaration of independence from the Coalition?"

"I don't know what 'Caventian' and 'Coalition' mean," Melisende said, keeping her tone even. "But it is the eight hundred and fiftieth year since the Shattering."

"What is the 'Shattering'?"

Melisende looked up at Bricio again, then back at her work crew. To a man, they stared at her, eyes wide and unsure. She gave them a tiny smile and hoped it was reassuring, then shrugged and turned back to her strange conversation partner.

"One of our legends. In ancient times, there were two great kings, brothers who ruled all the people of the world. They both had the power to harness the sun, and that power brought great wealth and ease to the people. Until one day the two kings quarreled, and the brothers began to be angry with one another. They threatened each other with greater and greater harm, until one brother, in a fit of rage, unleashed his full power against the other. The other brother answered in kind, and they burned the world to ash with their anger. All of the people in the world perished in flames, save only for those who hid under the ground for a generation. Once they were old, their children crawled back into the light, and began to create the nations of mankind."

"This Shattering . . . how long ago did you say it was?" the thing asked her.

"Eight and a half centuries ago."

"That is how long it has been, then," it said. "Or approximately that. I was a combatant in the war you described."

Melisende of Cercen was young, but she was, in all things, her father's daughter. Bodavin III of Cercen had taught statecraft and leadership to his only child from the very beginning: as soon as she was able to read, she read political correspondence and ancient treaties. As soon as she could sit through a four-hour meeting, she attended the gatherings of Cercen's inner council at her father's side. She frequently joined Bodavin in the training lists, where she watched as his men—someday to be her men—drilled each other in the arts of war.

So it was perhaps no surprise that she instantly identified this crumpled, buried piece of machinery with the tinny voice and strange words as a potential strategic advantage.

"Bricio," she said quietly in the aftermath of the machine's revelation. It was all but unbelievable! How could something so old have survived, even buried in the ground . . . and yet, its words did have the ring of truth.

Plus, as Melisende's father was fond of reminding her, sometimes the truth didn't matter nearly so much as what people *believed* to be the truth.

"Yes, my lady?" Bricio asked, his voice pulling her from the twisty path of her thoughts.

"Gather the crew together, please. I wish to speak with them."

"Of course," he said. And though she heard a question in his tone, he moved without hesitation to obey her instructions.

"Machine," Melisende said as he walked away, "The name you gave is long and unwieldy. Do you have another name that people use to address you?"

"My designation was sometimes abbreviated as TAV 359."

"Fine. I shall call you TAV, then, unless you object."

"I do not. You are the commander here, you may call me what you like."

"TAV, if what you say is true, then the leaders that you served are long dead. Am I correct in thinking that you are masterless?"

"You are correct, Lady Melisende."

"Then, according to the law, as a masterless warrior—albeit a . . . nontraditional one—you are free to take service with whomever you choose. I extend to you an offer. You may enter my service and become one of my retainers. I am young, and only a woman, but I am the Heiress of Cercen, and the position carries some honor with it."

The machine was silent for a moment before speaking. "I cannot find anything in my programmed directives that prevent me from accepting," it—no, she decided, not it. *He*—said. "And I am programmed to desire a connection with and show loyalty to a leader. You are the commander here, so you fit the definition of a leader for these purposes, despite your youth. In my time, that would have been a much larger impediment than your sex . . . though I perceive that attitudes have shifted, likely due to the pressures of re-establishing civilization after the war."

Melisende blinked several times and looked back over her shoulder where Bricio had the work crew gathered up. He started to lead them to her, but she held up a hand and shook her head. She wanted this settled before involving them. One way or the other.

"I need a yes or no answer," she said. "It's the law," she added, sounding a bit younger and more desperate than she would like.

"Yes," TAV said. "I will enter your service, Lady Melisende."

"I . . . if you were a man, you would kneel before me, and place my hands over your eyes."

"I have optical sensors within my solar panels. They

allow me to utilize electromagnetic energy to sense my environment similar to how you use your eyes."

"Um . . . all right." Melisende drew herself up to her full height and walked as regally as she knew how toward the half-uncovered machine. She reached out her hands and placed her palms flat on the wide, smooth surface of the panels they'd first uncovered. The panels were warm to the touch, almost as if he really were alive.

Well, she thought, why not? Wasn't he?

"Tactical Artillery Vehicle Three Five Nine," she said, pitching her voice to carry, as if they stood on the dais of her father's cathedral, and not on a hillside next to a great wall of ice. "I, Melisende of Cercen, place my hands over your eyes and accept you into my service. From this moment forth, let your vision be single to the performance of your duty to me and to my heirs, that we may preserve our lives, our families, and our community and impose order upon the chaos. Do you take this charge of your own free will?"

"I do," TAV said.

"And will you perform such duties as I require faithfully, to the utmost of your ability, as I perform my duties to you?"

"I will," TAV said.

"Then I name myself your liege lady and pledge to provide for you and your family as your needs may require, so long as your loyalty remains."

"I accept your pledge, my lady," TAV said. It wasn't, strictly speaking, part of the fealty oath, but Melisende nodded just the same and removed her hands from the heated surface of TAV's panels. Then she turned and looked at Bricio and the work crew who stood watching her, many of them with wide eyes.

"Men of Cercen," she said as she began to pick her way back up the slope to where they stood. "You all know me, you have watched me from my birth. Today, we have made a great discovery. Though we cannot yet say what this will mean for Cercen, I have no doubt that having TAV's loyalty will be important for us all. However, as with most new discoveries, we must be discreet. It is my intention to keep the knowledge of TAV's existence confined to this group alone. We will tell no one else, save for my father. I know that I am asking you to keep secrets from your families, friends, and loved ones. To that end, I will extend the same offer to all of you. I am proud of all of you, and would willingly welcome every one of you into my personal service, if you are willing."

A gasp rippled through the group. Except for Bricio, these men were not warriors. They were common workmen, proud of their skills, surely, but not likely to ever be invited into the personal service of a noble. To be so invited was to gain great status, usually reserved for masters of their crafts.

"My lady," Bricio murmured. "Are you sure?"

"I am," she said. "I know that I have not yet begun to build my household, but I am of age to do so. I will begin here, now, with these men, if they will have me. For as I said, Bricio, this is something of great import to Cercen . . . though I don't know exactly how, yet. But I cannot fail to act. Not now."

Something like a smile deepened the corners of Bricio's lips, and he gave her a nod, then slowly lowered himself to one knee, pointing his sword point down and placing both hands on the pommel.

"Then let me be the fir—no, second . . . man here to accept," he said, looking up at her and cutting his eyes over to where TAV lay half-buried. "I would be honored to take your hands upon my eyes."

Melisende smiled, and stepped forward to repeat the ritual with Bricio, then with the foreman of the work crew, and then one by one with every man present. By the time she finished, the sun had crossed the narrow gap of sky between the mountains and the shadows began to stretch.

"I regret that I have no insignia to offer you all," Melisende said after she finished. "I promise you that I will remedy that with my ladies straightaway. But you are all mine, and I shall inform my father when we return to the keep tonight. In the meantime, my orders are simple. We must excavate TAV from the ground and do what we can to heal or repair him. TAV, if we pull you from the ground, can you direct your brothers here in how to bring you back to working order?"

"It is possible, my lady," he said. "We can certainly try."

"Begging your pardon, my lady," Edsen, the foreman, said. He stepped forward, still looking a bit poleaxed at the sudden change in his status, but Melisende knew he was a solid man, well respected by her father and his men alike. "Some of us are quite mechanical. If it's possible to fix our metal brother, we'll get it done. In the meantime, may I suggest we set a watch crew? Don't want no one stumbling out here tonight, finding things they oughtn't see. We ain't trained warriors like Guardsman Bricio there, but we're able to defend ourselves and our own."

His nod toward TAV indicated that he definitely included the ancient, intelligent machine in that group—unorthodox though it may be.

"It's a good idea," Bricio said, nodding to Edsen in respect. "At least until we can get him out of the ground and something more permanent set up."

"Fine," Melisende said. "Excellent. This is exactly why I wanted you all. You know what needs to be done. Please be about doing it. And thank you."

Melisende had feared that her father might not be pleased with her actions, but aside from a little good-natured grumbling about his daughter poaching one of his best work crews, Bodavin had nothing but praise for her decisiveness. He even helped her to come up with a cover story for why she might begin building her household with a group of common workers—she would build a lodge in the forest near the glacier, on the slopes of the pass. It would be her own private retreat, to remain hers alone, even after she married.

For that was the stark political truth she faced. As the years wound on, she continued to learn the art of ruling from her father—and eventually, from TAV as well. The machine had a prodigious and encyclopedic library of tales from the time before the Shattering. As Melisende and her household worked to follow his instructions and repair his damaged systems, he would regale them with histories of polities and wars long lost to legend. Melisende found that she looked forward to discussing and analyzing these stories, and it greatly helped to sharpen her political mind.

Still, over the years it became readily apparent that her neighbors looked upon her not as a potential ally, but as a vulnerable fruit to be plucked. She had the loyalty of her people and her father's army, but as she grew from precocious adolescent into full womanhood, she realized that even those great advantages would not be enough. Not with all the world arrayed against her, convinced that a woman alone could never rule.

But she was the daughter of Bodavin III, and so she *would* rule. She learned all that she could from her father and his advisers about the world's political situation, and she carefully considered and weighed her options. She formed the shape of a plan in her mind, but discussed it with no one, not even her father. She would have liked to do so, but as she approached the age of majority, Bodavin's health began to take a sharp decline, and nothing the healers could do seemed to help. The future loomed clear before them: Melisende would be Lady of Cercen by her nineteenth birthing day.

So she must marry. Everyone said so, and even her plan required it, and the sooner the better. So on a blustery autumn day, Melisende steeled her nerves and informed her father of her choice.

"Valck of Kaperado?" Bodavin asked, his raspy voice dissolving into a cough as he tried to push himself up from his supine position in bed. "Melisende—"

"I know." Melisende said, putting her hand on her father's chest. It grieved her that this, alone, was enough to keep him in place. "He is volatile. But there is great potential in him. He is a capable military commander . . . and he hates his father and brother. We can have no greater ally against Kaperado's grasping reach than one of their own who has become one of us. Plus, with a marriage alliance, they risk the censure of the world if they break it and invade. You know our spies have reported that Uto has the pass in his sights."

"Valck will not meekly agree to be a mere consort," Bodavin warned his daughter. "Not a man like that, who has been forced to remain in the shadow of his brother the heir."

"I know. But consider, if he is made co-ruler, then he has even more reason to resist his family's expansion," she leaned forward. "And Kaperado's army is the largest and biggest in the region. Several of their legions answer personally to Valck. If we make their allegiance a part of the marriage negotiations, we can use them as a kernel around which to quietly build our own forces, all while keeping Uto off our backs."

Bodavin lay quietly on his pillow, his pale face sweating as he searched his daughter's face. He lifted one wasted hand to her cheek and pushed a bit of hair back behind her ear.

"And what of you, my beautiful child?" he asked softly. "What of your heart?"

"Father," she said with a tiny smile. "My heart is for Cercen, always."

"I had hoped you might make an alliance with someone who might bring you a measure of happiness . . . such as I had with your mother."

"And who is to say that Valck will not?" she asked. "It seems to me that someone who has craved love and approval from his family all his life might be quite ready to receive it from a wife, even if that wife is a political match, rather than a romantic one."

"I hope that you are right, Melisende. I cannot fault your political acumen. On that score, Valck is an inspired choice. But I will only agree to this if you are absolutely certain that this is what you want."

"I am, Father."

Bodavin closed his eyes for a moment, and then nodded against his pillow. "Send in my scribes then, child. I will send the missives right away. I fear I have little time to waste."

Her father's words turned out to be prophetic. Five months to the day after she made her choice, Melisende stood next to Valck in her father's cathedral and pledged herself to him as wife, partner, and co-ruler of Cercen Keep.

Another month after that, Bodavin III died, and Melisende and Valck ascended his throne together.

And so began the worst year of Melisende's life.

Melisende really did try, but it soon became apparent that Valck was a man entirely focused on his own desires and ambitions. He had little time or interest in his young bride once the rather perfunctory business of consummating the marriage was completed. From the Feast of Flowers until the Feast of Sunlight, Melisende turned her every effort toward wooing her indifferent, dismissive husband. But all to no avail. He met her intelligence with scorn, her kindnesses with indifference, and attempts to be romantic with derision . . . and eventually worse.

Valck's only goal, it seemed, was to become undisputed

Lord of Cercen. A fact which he made very plain even before the court mourning for Bodavin III was complete. Valck wasted no time in dismissing many of Melisende's courtiers and appointing his own men to important posts within the administration of the keep and surrounding lands. He also undertook sweeping military reforms— many of which entailed much harsher discipline and a much greater operation tempo than what the Cercite troops were used to experiencing. Melisende saw this, and attempted to try and mitigate some of the difficulty of that transition by going out and visiting among the soldiers and archers as much as possible. It didn't silence the grumbling as she'd hoped, but it *did* make her popular among the men, both new and old.

Bricio, who had risen to the rank of a lieutenant in the household guard, encouraged her to do this.

"It makes them feel heard and acknowledged," he said.

"But I can do nothing!" she said in one of her rare moments of unguarded frustration as they walked to her personal apartments. They'd just come in from riding out to the edge of the pass and talking with the men there. "Valck pays me no mind at all, and his commanders are all sycophants who don't dare tell him anything but what he wants to hear—that the army is in top condition and training! They'd never let him see the cracks developing due to the strain on the men, for fear of losing their precious positions and not being able to soak up all of the financial benefits!"

"You give the men comfort, my lady," Bricio said. "You give them something to fight for, something to protect. Or to try to protect, anyway," he added. Melisende looked up to see him very pointedly not looking at her face, which she knew still carried the fading marks of a recent encounter with her husband. Even as good as Joalie was with makeup, it never hid everything, especially once the bruises turned purple.

"Bricio," Melisende said in a soft, steady tone, though her insides trembled. "You must not worry about me. My husband will not dare touch me in anger again . . . not for some months at the very least. I am carrying our heir."

"Then I offer my congratulations, my lady," Bricio said, his voice soft and still sick sounding. "But what about once the child is born? What then?"

Melisende had been asking herself the same question. And no answer was immediately forthcoming. So, she changed the subject.

"What of our progress on the lodge?" she asked. "I have not been able to get away to go visit since my wedding, but it surely must be finished by now?"

"It is, my lady," Bricio said. "Your crew has made all of the modifications required for all members of your household, and it stands ready for you to visit. And I think our . . . friend there misses you."

"Excellent," she said. "I wanted to wait until it was done to tell Valck, as a surprise. But . . ." she trailed off and looked up at her stalwart warrior.

"But, my lady?"

"But perhaps we shall wait a bit longer," she said softly, as the seed of an idea began to take root in her mind.

"As my lady wishes . . . but I think that is wise."

"Yes, I think so too."

◆◆◆

Bricio was correct. TAV had missed her.

Melisende finally managed to slip out to the lodge to inspect the finished product and see her strange friend and mentor during one of Valck's absences. As her pregnancy progressed, the Lord of Cercen often found excuses to leave the Keep and travel with his closest group of sycophants. Melisende found herself grateful, rather than resentful. With Valck gone, she once again had something like the freedom of movement she'd enjoyed as a girl. So when he left her yet again, she had her servants saddle Mist and called to Bricio and Joalie to escort her on a ride in the pass. Valck refused to let his wife be alone with another man, even one of her own guards, so Joalie had become Melisende's constant companion.

The three of them set out shortly after dawn pinkened the sky, and had arrived at the lodge by mid-morning. The lodge wasn't far from the keep, but it was situated well back in the forest, hidden on three sides by folds in the slope, and built partially into the rock of the mountain itself. It was nearly impossible for Melisende to see it until they were right at the front doors.

In short, it was an ideal refuge, made all the better by the welcome she received from her household.

"My lady Melisende!" Edsen called out as she passed between the stout timber doors into the inviting warmth of the Lodge's entrance hall. The once-foreman came toward them, hands spreading in welcome as she led Bricio and Joalie farther into the hall. He dropped to one knee before his lady, bending his neck so that she could easily brush her fingers across his hair in the ancient gesture of continued fealty offered and acknowledged. Then he stood and clasped arms with Bricio, and accepted a hug from Joalie—though Melisende noted that his cheeks flamed in a blush.

"It is good to see you, Edsen," Melisende said, smiling gently as she rescued the man from his own disconcertedness. "I thought I would come and see what you have been up to as my steward here."

"I am so pleased you have, my lady," he said. "We have been hoping that you would. The hall has been finished for months."

"I wanted to come . . ." she said, trailing off, suddenly unsure of how to express the guilt and longing that she'd felt.

"Lady Melisende has been much occupied of late," Joalie broke in, smoothly. Melisende smiled weakly and nodded—though she did not miss the significant look that her maid gave to her steward. Nor did she miss her steward's thin-lipped tiny nod of acknowledgment. Unless she missed her guess, Joalie had just promised Edsen that she would fill him in later.

"Of course," Edsen said. "It's only that himself has been asking for you. He talks to us, but he takes his oath to your ladyship very seriously, and he says he can't serve you if he can't talk to you."

The Lodge really was a lovely place, Melisende reflected as Edsen led her and Bricio down the main corridor that led back into the hill, to TAV's chambers. Melisende knew her men had cut the space out of the rock itself, but it was supremely comfortable. Brightly colored tapestries lined the walls and the floor consisted of wooden planks polished until they positively shone in the beautiful, steady light from the fixtures TAV had taught them how to fashion. Melisende knew the power— what TAV called electricity—came from the generator assembly, currently being run by a steam boiler deep in the bowels of the Lodge. TAV had taught the men about that too, though they'd built and adapted it with their own ingenuity.

Eventually, the hallway began to curve around to the left and they came to a steel-banded wooden door. Melisende knocked, and she heard TAV's strange, tinny voice call out as he always did.

"Identify yourself, please."

"It's Melisende."

"My lady! You are always cleared for entry!"

The door swung open, actuated by some kind of electricity-driven spring mechanism, and Melisende led Edsen and Bricio through to the wide, dark space on the other side. As they entered, lights set high in the wall all around gradually brightened, until Melisende could clearly see the room.

No wooden floors or beautiful tapestries here. TAV's quarters were an empty room with two great double doors at the far end and enough space for the machine himself to sit dead center without touching any of the walls or the ceiling. Melisende took a moment to admire the long, sleek lines of him. She had taken her father's most skilled metal worker into her service, and it had taken the man the better part of the past five years, but TAV seemed to finally be returned to his pre-burial condition. He was quite large, easily as large as her bedchamber at home when it came to width and length. His height, though, stretched barely above her head...well, unless one counted the huge steel barrel that could be elevated and lowered from the topmost part of TAV's main body. At its highest elevation, nearly straight up, the barrel reached a good five lengths into the sky—as tall as the gate towers of Cercen Keep itself!

"My lady," TAV said, and even though his voice still carried that foreign, tinny, metallic quality, Melisende could hear pleasure in the tone. "Will you do me the honor of mounting up?"

"I will," Melisende said, and stepped forward as an invisible seam in TAV's low-slung body parted and a hatch hinged upward, revealing an opening. A sense of wonder rushed through her, just as it did every time she climbed up and into the body of her sworn...well...sworn retainer, anyway. With the exception of the obvious repairs, TAV's inner workings were ancient, and inspired reverence deep within Melisende as she settled herself in the strangely cushioned seat TAV called the "commander's station."

The hatch closed behind her, and TAV dialed up the interior lights until Melisende could see through the magical-seeming screens that showed the room outside, complete with Bricio standing guard.

"It has been a long time, my lady," TAV said, his voice surrounding her from all sides.

"Too long, TAV," Melisende sighed. "I have neglected you, and I owe you an apology."

"I do not think so."

"What?" she asked, smiling slightly. "Do I not owe you regular visits anymore?"

"You do, but I do not think it is your fault that you have been unable to keep them. My scans tell me that you have increased capillary blood flow to the area around your eye, and that you are currently in the very early stages of pregnancy. In my time, congratulations would have been in order. Is this still the case now?"

Melisende swallowed hard. In five years, she still hadn't gotten used to the instantaneous way that TAV collected information. "It is," she said weakly. "And thank you."

"Your heart rate is accelerating."

"I am nervous," she admitted. "Anxious."

"Do I cause this anxiety?"

"No, TAV. It just . . . happens these days. It's just one of those things that has to be endured."

"Why?" he asked. "Your physiological reactions are similar to a trauma response. Have you experienced a trauma?"

Had she? Maybe. Without warning, the memory of Valck's heavy hand impacting her cheekbone, sending her toppling to the floor reared up within her mind, and she found herself hunching in her seat, gasping.

"My lady?" TAV said, his volume dropping. "What has happened to you?"

"I got married," she whispered, without really meaning to do so.

"To Valck of Kaperado," TAV supplied.

"Yes," she said

"And he has traumatized you?" TAV's voice was perfectly neutral. Had she not been so distracted by the roil of her own emotions, Melisende would have recognized that for the warning it was.

"He . . . yes," she whispered, and it was almost a gasp. Words tumbled forth as her eyes filled with hot, liquid shame, and she found herself unable—or unwilling—to stop them.

"I was wrong, TAV. So wrong. I thought I could . . . I thought I could love him enough. But he is not kind, not open. He has been twisted by hatred for too long and he does not want my love. All he wants is my wealth and my power and an heir. And once this one is born, I fear . . . I fear he may kill me and take it all!" The last word ended on a sob of fear and anger. Melisende hunched, wrapping her arms around her middle to protect the precious life she carried as the pain and rage inside her finally found voice in her cries.

TAV let her emotions run their course. Melisende wept herself dry, and eventually lay curled in a ball on the seat of the commander's station. When her sobs quieted enough for her to pull in a shaky breath, and then another, she became conscious of a low, almost subliminal rumble of sounds coming from TAV's interior speakers.

"Are you . . . is that noise coming from you, TAV?" she asked, her voice rough.

"Yes," he said. "It is a low rumble at 100Hertz, intended to mimic the purr of an Earth domestic cat. Though domestic cats did not survive here on Cavento, the sound of their purr was known in my time to induce a psychologically and physiologically calming effect on humans."

"I don't— I don't understand that."

"It is of no moment. The more important question is this: are you ready to consider what you will do?"

Melisende sniffed and swiped at the tear marks on her cheeks. Then she pushed herself back up into a seated position and pulled her tangled hair away from her face.

"Yes," she said. "You are right, TAV, as always. I must make a plan. Because I meant it. I think Valck intends to kill me. He has already usurped my power at court. I must take it back. And you must help me."

"My lady, I am yours to command."

There wasn't much time.

The following morning, Melisende and her household—save only a skeleton crew remaining to keep the lodge running as a fallback location—departed back into the pass, towards the storied walls of Cercen Keep. This time, TAV rolled alongside them, easily keeping pace with the sturdy oremes, his tracks smoothly covering the rocky ground with no problems. Melisende rode most of the way inside his compartment as he taught her about his capabilities, and what he could do with each piece of terrain they covered.

"The largest barrier," he said at one point as they climbed up another small hill toward her home, "will be that of ammunition. I am well supplied with rounds for a single encounter, but with your levels of technology, I will not be able to quickly resupply them."

"Can Edsen and his crew not figure something out? You've taught them how to repair you, after all."

"Mostly repair me," TAV corrected. "I am still not at one hundred percent of my capability, but I have calculated that it is probable that I will be able to achieve the objective you desire."

"I just want Valck gone, and my sovereignty back . . . for now."

"Yes. It is that 'for now' of which I speak."

"Well," Melisende waved a hand as her body swayed in response to his movement over the terrain. "That is of no consequence for the moment. Once we are secure in the keep, and Valck has been dealt with, we will consider next steps. I do not imagine his father will accept my seizing power with any kind of grace, but that is a problem for later."

"In answer to your earlier question," he went on, "I have begun training Edsen and his crew, but there is much science they have yet to learn before they can reliably create high explosive, thermal, EMP, or nuclear rounds for my weapons suite. However, simple canister rounds are much easier to fabricate, and your crew should be able to manufacture those within a few days as soon as we have materials."

"Good. We shall have them, when we take the keep."

They timed their journey to arrive at the keep's gate an hour after sunset, but just before the moon rose. Melisende mounted Mist once more and rode ahead to issue orders that the gates be opened for her household.

"And I beg of you," she added, throwing her hood back and looking up at the face of the guardsmen standing watch above the gate. "Say nothing and do not fear what I bring inside. I give you my word of honor that all I do is in the service of Cercen and her people."

"We know, my lady," one of the men said, touching two fingers between his eyes, and then lowering his hand out away from his face. It was a gesture of respect and fealty, and Melisende felt her throat tighten as she bowed her head in acknowledgment.

"Thank you," she called out, not even ashamed of the emotion that crackled through her voice as the gates opened and she led TAV and her people inside.

Melisende got a few hours of sleep, mostly because Joalie insisted, but then she spent most of the night penning missives to the nobles that had faithfully served her father for so many years. Most of them had been dismissed from their roles in the government of Cercen's lands and had returned to their own estates in the mountains. She reached out to ask them to come, to support her as they had supported her father, and to help her to oust the enemy that she had married and could not turn. She sent these messengers riding out after dark on the best oremes and hoped against all hope that her nobles would respond.

Then she turned her mind to the keep's defenses.

Cercen keep had never fallen, but their situation was incredibly precarious. And Valck had a *lot* of men. Melisende ordered supplies laid in for a siege, knowing that she risked tipping her hand as she did so.

But something unexpected happened in the frantic, dreamlike days that followed. Despite the lack of sleep and manic preparations, Melisende found herself having individual, private conversations with her people almost constantly. Every minute, it seemed someone new was seeking her out to whisper their support for her cause, and to pledge their loyalty to her personally. She felt perpetually on the edge of tears from overwhelming gratitude and the looming fear that she was about to get all of these loyal, good people killed.

"And you may," TAV said when she unburdened herself to him during one of the times she climbed into his cab for a respite. "They may, in fact, die because of your actions. That is the burden of leadership. But remember this, they *chose* to pledge to you, each of them of their own free will. That is significant."

"It is," Melisende said, straightening her shoulders and letting out a breath. "But I'd just as soon keep them all alive if I can. Is this a good vantage point for you?"

They had decided to put TAV on one of the lower stone ramparts that ran along the outer curtain wall of the keep. It had been quite a trick of engineering to rig a ramp strong enough for him to ascend to the hastily widened platform, but Edsen and his men had managed it in a day.

"It will suffice," TAV said. "If I still had my complement of drones, I could use them for additional reconnaissance, but they are long gone. My optical sensors will have to do, and as they can see the southern neck of the valley from which Valck and his army will approach, I have determined that I am, barely, within striking range."

"What is a 'drone'?" Melisende asked, diverted. Then she shook her head. "Nevermind. You can tell me later. Perhaps Edsen can make you some of those as well . . . after he figures out the high explosive rounds, of course. And the nuclear ones. Those sounded *most* interesting."

"Hmm. Yes," TAV replied. He did not elaborate, though. Melisende had noticed that he tended to be reticent when the topic of nuclear rounds came up. But that, too, was a problem for later.

Now, the problem was her husband.

"Word from the scouts is that Valck is encamped no more than a half-day's march from here," she said. "It's probably too much to hope that he's completely ignorant of our presence and actions. I trust most of my nobility, but I would be foolish to think that someone hadn't sent a message or let something slip. So we can expect that he's coming prepared for battle."

"The odds of him being prepared for what I can do are infinitesimal," TAV said. Had he been human, Melisende would have accused him of bragging. But this was just a statement of fact.

"That is what I am counting on. But I can't reveal your presence too soon. That would be showing our hand. We must stick to the plan. Nobles have begun responding. Very few of them are sending men, but most of them are pledging support and supplies, which are almost as crucial. And critically, several of the most powerful have come here themselves. They did *not* appreciate the way Valck stripped them of their authority in government. They have named me sole Lady of Cercen, so we have another claim to legitimacy through their actions."

"History would indicate that is a good thing."

"It is, TAV. It is a very good thing. So... that is it, I guess. Tomorrow we will see how this goes. I am confident in our victory, but... should anything happen, know that it has been my great honor to be your commander and lady."

"The honor has been mine, my lady."

⊕⊕⊕

By midafternoon the following day, Melisende's scouts had sighted Valck's vanguard entering the pass. TAV saw them too, and reported that he had run trajectory calculations on the narrow valley neck as required. Melisende took this to mean that he would be able to do what was needful and left it at that. Sometimes, it was still so hard to understand the things that TAV said, even though they spoke the same language.

When night fell, Valck's entire army had arrived. Melisende could see them with her naked eyes, their fires winking into existence one by one as the daylight faded. They had stopped to make camp rather than continue onward. That could mean only one thing: Valck knew what she had done. Morning would likely bring an attack, followed by a lengthy siege.

At least, that was what she figured Valck expected. But he didn't know Melisende, and he didn't know TAV.

An hour or so after sunset, a messenger approached the gate, carrying a white ribbon attached to his oreme's saddle. Melisende ordered that he be admitted, and that food and drink be prepared for him while she read the message he carried from her husband:

"My lady wife,
Rumors have reached my ears that you have been very foolish in my absence. Some say you intend to keep me out of my own home. I know this cannot be the truth, because even if you had the courage to try and seize power, you know all too well what I would do to you once my army inevitably crushes your tiny resistance. You have until dawn to ride out and publicly surrender yourself to

me. If you do not, know that my punishment for you will be worse than anything you have yet experienced or can imagine.

Your lord and husband,
Valck of Cercen"

Fear shivered through her as she read the words. She could almost hear his voice speaking them softly into her ear. For just a moment, her spirit quailed, and she looked up with wide, terrified eyes.

Only to see Bricio, and Joalie, and Edsen, and Heyorg the blacksmith, and Pura the bakerwoman, and Lady Tilara, her Exchequer, and the ranks of her guardsmen, her soldiers who had come at her call . . . and TAV, his sleek lines hulking in the darkness above where she stood in the outer bailey. These people—her people—depended on her. She could not fail them now.

Melisende of Cercen folded the note and tucked it away in her sleeve. Then she smiled at the messenger and invited him to take food and wine before returning to her husband. She would have no answering message at this time.

Then she turned and lifted her chin as she walked up the ramp to TAV's position. She did not mount up and into the cab, though she dearly wanted the safety of his hardened armor around her. But for this, she had to be visible. She did, however, take the antique headpiece that TAV had told her was reserved for his commander, and place it over her head like a helmet.

The time had come.

With the headpiece on, Melisende could see the valley

lit up as if it were daytime, albeit a colorless one. The scene existed entirely in black, white, and grey, as if all the color had been leached out of the world. Red numbers glowed along the edges of her vision, giving her distance and angle measurements.

"This is what you see," Melisende said softly. "This is how you experience the world."

"Only at night," TAV said. "And only with the near-IR spectrum enabled. Would you like to see thermal instead?"

"No," she said. "No time for that now. We must begin with our plan. Make them hear me, if you please, TAV."

"Engaging loudspeaker. The acoustics of this valley should do the rest. If you speak, all will hear your voice, my lady."

She nodded, then drew in a breath and turned to face the dark mass of men. TAV helpfully increased the magnification until she became able to pick out individual bodies, though not faces.

"Men of Cercen," she said, and listened as her own amplified voice rolled though the pass, bouncing off the stone cliffs and echoing down into the valley. "I am Melisende of Cercen, your rightful Lady. A miracle of past technology has allowed me to speak to you, and I am grateful.

"I am grateful for all of you true men, who take your oaths seriously and seek only to do what is right and what honor demands.

"I am grateful for all of you true men, who earn what you have, and disdain to steal what is not truly yours.

"I am grateful for all of you true men, who shelter those

in need of protection, and who would never raise a hand
to harm those weaker than yourselves.

"I am grateful to call you Men of Cercen, and I invite
you to leave the camp of the usurper, the abuser that you
serve, and come home to the keep that will welcome you
with open arms. Know that all men who wish to swear
loyalty to me as their sole, sovereign Lady will be
welcomed, but that any who act with ill intent will be
punished. As a token of my promise to you, I give you
light, to guide your way home."

"Illumination flare, firing," TAV said in her ear piece,
and Melisende heard and felt a deep *crash* shiver through
her body. A moment later, her black-and-white view of the
world blinked and reformed, and Melisende heard the
gasps of her people as a light brighter than the moon rose
up into the sky over them.

"Come home, Men of Cercen," Melisende said. "For
our keep is warm and our fires are bright, and only those
within the keep shall be saved from the wrath of the
mountains. For I am a daughter of the pass and the cliff.
I am a daughter of the river of ice. I am a daughter of
these mountains, and they are displeased with he who has
acted to harm their child."

This, too, was a prearranged signal. For once again,
TAV spoke in her ear and once again, she felt the sound
of his great gun firing echo through her chest. On her
display, she could see a streak of light arc across her field
of view and impact the cliff opposite them down at the
narrowest part of the valley. She imagined she could hear
Valck's laughter at the thought that she had missed his
host.

But she hadn't missed.

A few moments later, she watched in an awe that bordered on horror as the snowy side of the far cliff collapsed and slid down into the pass. The snow had a kind of grace to it as it flowed into the narrow neck of the valley and completely blocked Valck's only escape route.

"Come home, Men of Cercen," Melisende called a third time, "Swear to me and to no other, and live yet in these mountains who will defend their own!"

She fell silent and waited, watching.

Slowly, a small bit of the dark mass detached itself and began moving at speed toward the gates of the keep. Others moved to stop them, but Melisende's archers were ready, and provided covering fire from the walls of the keep itself. TAV sent up another illumination flare as the first one fizzled into nothingness, and slowly but surely, more and more of the massed army surrounding Valck turned and fought their way free, then rode hell-for-leather to the keep.

As soon as the men arrived, Joalie and Bricio took their oaths in her stead and the men were given arms and a place on the walls. In this way, Melisende's new men provided more and more arrows to see their fellows to safety.

When the stream of riders had slowed to a trickle, Melisende had TAV send up another flare.

"Men of Valck," she called out this time. "Your time has expired. The mountains have found you wanting. You must be washed clean by the ice and the snow. If we find you alive, you will be forgiven. Fire."

TAV let out another deep *crack*, and another projectile

arced overhead. But this time, Melisende had ordered him to fire one of the precious High Explosive rounds, and had used her headpiece display to aim it right at Valck's command tent. The resulting explosion reverberated through the valley, sending yet more of the hillside sliding down in that graceful roll to bury the bodies of those who would steal the birthright of the Daughter of the Mountains.

It only took ten days to dig out enough to open the pass once more. The Men of Cercen (as the army was now calling itself) threw themselves at the task with a vengeance, and the supplies that Melisende had laid in were more than enough to see them through. They also found survivors from Valck's camp—or as some wit named it, Valck's Folly. A pair of men, father and son, had been partially sheltered by one of Valck's half-constructed siege engines. They also found a young messenger huddled next to the body of his oreme under the snow. All three of the men enthusiastically swore to be Melisende's loyal men and she, true to her word, forgave them for not coming home sooner.

Melisende reformed her government, mostly reinstating her own nobility, but keeping one or two of Valck's most talented and least corrupt men. She worked with TAV and Bricio to reorganize the army under the most competent commanders and to prepare them for the inevitable backlash that would result.

Edsen and his men continued their quest to learn enough to resupply TAV with ammunition.

Two seasons after Melisende's coup, she bore a child,

a daughter that she named Morafia. To Melisende's delight, the people began to refer to both her and her infant as "Daughters of the Mountains".

A season after that, a messenger arrived wearing Uto of Kaperado's colors. He carried a missive from Melisende's erstwhile father-in-law:

"Lady Melisende,

I take great joy in the news of the birth of my grandchild, and sorrow only to know that she is not a boy who might inherit the throne of my late son. However, I feel confident that between us, we can make a suitable match for her and secure her a husband who will be a strong, strategic-minded leader for Cercen and a valued partner for Kaperado. I want you both to come and visit me here this autumn. The cold harshness of the mountains is no place for a child. And worry not for your keep, I have several very talented men who would do an admirable job administering in your child's name. You need not trouble yourself about such things, my dear. After all, you are my daughter-in-law and I intend to look after you appropriately.

Uto, King of Kaperado"

"A king, is he?" Bricio asked when Melisende showed him the letter. "That's new."

Melisende shrugged and rolled her eyes. "It doesn't matter what he calls himself," she said. "Edsen's progress is encouraging, and TAV thinks that we can have the ... what does he call them? Oh yes, 'dumb tanks' ready to go by next spring. I need only stall Uto until then, and that will not be hard with Morafia so young. He does not have the ability to attack during the winter, and we shall see the Feast of Flowers from the inside of his palace."

"You are so confident, my lady?"

"I am, Bricio. No one else has the technology that we have. And so we must use it quickly, while our advantage stands. If I have learned anything from TAV's stories, it is that no technological edge lasts forever. When the iron is hot, we must strike. And so we will. In the spring. In the meantime, I must return my dear father-in-law's missive."

"Yes, my lady. Do not let the poison from your pen burn the paper," Bricio said with a gentle, joking smile. Melisende waved him away and turned back to the parchment stretched out on the desk in her father's—now her own—study.

"My dear father-in-law,

I am so pleased to hear of your joy in my dear daughter's birth. I feel confident that she will grow to be exactly the woman and Lady that Cercen needs. I thank you for your kind invitation, but I am afraid that it is impossible to travel with her so young yet. Perhaps next spring. As you say, the mountains can be treacherous and harsh, and so we are safest here at home whilst she is in swaddling clothes. Thank you as well for your kind offer of talented administrators. One can never have too many of those, I have learned. Fortunately, my father and your son agreed, and we are quite well equipped here in Cercen for the time being. Perhaps once Morafia and I are able to travel, we will take you up on your offer, if it still stands?

May this autumn and the coming year bring you many more joys,

Melisende, Lady of Cercen
Daughter of the Mountains"

TANKNOLOGICAL SUPERIORITY
by Hank Davis

What newborn sentient tank wouldn't develop a sense of humor? It exists in a world of extremes. On the one hand, it is a giant among mortals, true, capable of slinging hot death and blasting cities to the ground. But it is also still a very young thing, a thing with the needs and playfulness of a child. And even if such a tank doesn't really have a mother and father, perhaps it would want them as badly as any other child. And perhaps it would protect those it chose as family at any cost. All jokes aside.

⊕ ⊕ ⊕

Another day, another invader from space. But it looked like this one was real.

I was picking up news broadcasts about it. I wasn't supposed to do that, since the team thinks they would confuse me if I tried to square them with the simulated training input, but it's always a challenge to sneak around my programmed restrictions, and I was also programmed not to be put off by challenges. The team hadn't foreseen the subtle contradiction in the separate programs, and I wasn't going to mention it to them.

The pro newsies didn't really know what was going on, of course. They thought it was just another terrorist attack, and were concentrating on the pile of rubble where the Tesser Tower and adjoining buildings used to be, and only some online independents had noticed the big tank going down the street, squashing cars and flattening lampposts, and even they hadn't picked up on what I thought was a large spacecraft hovering a few hundred miles up over the city, and I only detected it by sneaking into different government and civilian radar installations, and putting together different angles of scan from them. Whatever it was, it was absorbing and not reflecting radar impulses thrown at it, but with my overlapping scans I was able to spot a hole in the sky once I put together the different angles. And it wasn't passing by, or in an orbit, or falling, so the way to bet was something artificial, not likely of Earth origin.

Unless the Cybernetic Research Foundation had gone all out to elaborately counterfeit an extravaganza—and I didn't think their budget could stand it, with me eating up most of their funds—this wasn't another training simulation.

Besides, I wasn't getting the usual sort of input for simulations. In those, the special effects look more real than events shown in newssquirts. Sometimes with better character development, too, So, finally something was actually happening.

But I couldn't move yet. They don't want me going topside and charging around in reaction to a merely virtual crisis. Still, it looked like I really should be revving up—looked in real time, in the real world, that is.

While waiting for the three bosses—they can't just have one boss maybe going off his or her nut, and ordering me into action, you know—I snuck around in Foundation databanks where I'm not supposed to go. (Just another challenge to be met!) I finally found two of the three trigger codes that would release me into action. The team called them *passwords*, but I thought *trigger codes* sounded way cooler. Still needed the third one, and I was scouring the networks, trying to find it—maybe it was only on paper?—when Dr. Rieber's dedicated line went live and her voice came breathlessly in.

Of course, she wasn't *really* breathless or she couldn't have spoken, but she was obviously trying to cancel out an oxygen debt, breathing rapidly and loudly, and I detected strong stress indicia in her voice. They didn't mean to build that into me, but the programs for voice print identification have unintended uses which I've explored, having plenty of time on my circuits. Anyway, from the several thousand works of fiction I had scanned in my copious spare time, I judged that using "breathless" to describe her voice was within the bounds of poetic license.

"Steeleye!" she said, yes, breathlessly, "Emergency. Get ready to roll." Then she paused and said, slowly and carefully (but still a little out of breath), "Chain up!"

As I expected, it was indeed Dr. Rieber. I accessed a video pickup in the third floor's hall, and saw her come out of her office and run for the elevators. No wonder she was breathless. And that was indeed the code phrase she was to give me. However, it was one of the two which I had already ferreted out, and I hadn't located that still-lacking third one yet.

And besides, I was supposed to have at least one of the three humans authorized to give me instructions on board before I could move, another of the precautions to keep me from running amok.

The higher-ups in the Foundation were very concerned about me getting out of control. They would be even more concerned if they knew I had edited my programming so that I *could* move without anybody being on board. I doubted that they would accept the emergency as good reason for me to throw off my restraints. And, if they knew that, they might wonder what other controls I could veto.

Since I still didn't have that third password, the matter was academic. I could probably work around *that* programmed restraint, too, but it would be complicated, and take a lot of seconds, possibly as much as half an hour. And it would be too obvious, and *really* alert the Foundation that their leash was weaker than they thought. I preferred not to be dismantled, which would probably be their reaction. Dismantling might not hurt, but where would I live afterward?

By now, Dr. Rieber had gotten to my sub-sub-subbasement level, and slipped her I.D. into the card reader next to me, and I could open my access door. As she ran inside, I saw Dr. Carl Knightley pop out of the other elevator on one of my building monitors. In a few minutes, he had joined Dr. Rieber in my control room.

"Steeleye," he said, unnecessarily since he had my realtime attention (my cyberspeed attention was still spooking around in project databases, searching for that third password), then added, "F-I-A-W-O-D."

That was his password. Unfortunately, it, too, was one I already had without authorization, though I hadn't yet ferreted out what the letters stood for. So I was still stuck in place while I tried to work around my programming's strictures.

Dr. Knightly spoke again (yes, breathlessly): "Erin, you shouldn't be here. Only one of us is necessary. The Project can't afford to lose both of us. Quick, get out." He had dropped the pitch of his voice a bit and put a lot of authority into it. Too bad, his voice cracked on the last word.

Dr. Rieber's pulse rate had been returning to normal, but now it shot up again. From that and her facial expressions, I knew that Dr. Knightley's last sentence had been a strategic mistake. It had angered her, just like in similar male-female interactions in a few hundred of the movies I had speed-watched. Of course, I knew that the rest of his statement wasn't completely true—their importance to the project wasn't the main thing on his mind. I had observed how he looked at her when her attention was directed elsewhere. I had also noticed her reacting similarly to his presence, not to mention elevated pulse rates and widened pupils.

That also was like in those movies. And I decided I needed to reevaluate them. I hadn't been sure about how close to reality they were.

Meanwhile, Dr. Rieber was replying. "You're right, Carl, so stop giving me orders, and *you* just get your butt out of here. I'll handle this."

Actually, *I* would be the one handling the situation. (If I ever got that third password.) But I could tell that Dr. Knightley was also mad now. That was accompanied by obvious fear, anxiety, and, I thought less confidently, intense curiosity (that last one was trickier to identify). But mostly, they were now mad at each other.

It was a lot like those movies.

Then an outside phone call came in on the secure line. I connected it and put it on my inboard speakers. From the tone of the breathing, I had already identified the caller as Dr. Keith. A second later, he identified himself. "Steeleye, this is Dr. Keith. I can't get into the building. Wreckage has blocked the entrance."

"John, we're both here, Carl and me," Dr. Rieber said. "We need your password for Steeleye to get moving."

"But I can't get there. Debris has blocked the CRF building's entrances." He was repeating himself, but he did that frequently. "And I have to be in the building and in range of a monitor for the password to be acknowledged. That was a security measure we all agreed on."

"You mean, you and Carl argued for it, and I was outvoted," Dr. Rieber almost snarled. "*I* thought it was pinning Steeleye's operational capabilities on a single weak break-point. And I was right."

This might go on for some number of seconds (like hours to me) while mayhem was unfolding outside, so I spoke. "Dr. Rieber, I've noticed what you might call a loophole in my programs."

Dr. Rieber had complained to me in the past that I should be discreet about the many loopholes I keep finding, and now was staring sternly into the nearest visual monitor, but didn't say anything, so I continued.

"I don't think Dr. Keith has to be present to deliver his password—just that an authorized person has to say it from inside the building. If he will tell you the password, and either of you repeat it here, that should work." Actually, I now *had* the third password. Dr. Keith had unconsciously subvocalized it when he thought of it, and I had picked it up. Dr. Rieber knew I could hear subvocalizations, but that was another capability I thought I should otherwise keep under wraps—in particular, not letting Dr. Keith know about it.

Dr. Keith didn't like my suggestion. "We need to plug that hole in the program as soon as poss—"

"Screw that, John!" Dr. Rieber snapped, *"what's the damned password?"*

"Well . . . I don't . . . very well, it's Rumpelstiltskin."

My passengers repeated the password, almost in unison, and it was time to roll. "Doctors Rieber and Knightley, please be seated and fasten your seat belts." I said to my passengers. I thought of a line from one of those movies, "It's gonna be a bumpy ride," but did not say it.

Training took over in spite of their emotional states, and both followed my request. Then I started the big elevator and even bigger overhead doors on the two levels slid aside as we rose up through them. So did the fast-food outlet whose foundation was also my third and last roof. It rose on powerful hydraulic jacks, and I came up under it. Fortunately, all the customers and staff had scurried away when nearby buildings started collapsing.

I gunned my motors, treads churning, and shot out from under the Cyberburger eatery, which began sinking back to ground level. Maybe we could keep the secret exit a secret if nobody had seen the levitating building. It not only provided cover for my exit, but the Cyberburger chain also made an annual profit, useful for the Foundation. Its hush-hush government appropriations were as miserly as they were secret.

I followed the trail of destruction left by the invader. No more than optical sensors were required. The interloper was almost as wide as the space between the buildings, even on a four-lane street with dividing shrubbery in the middle. Like the flattened lampposts, the shrubbery was now much the worse for wear.

Now that I was above ground, I picked up signals coming from the invader, and was also picking up similar signals coming down from the ship overhead. I made sure I recorded them, though I didn't understand the conversation, of course. I began to run translation programs, with no real hope of success, but it was part of the drill.

My passengers now had their headsets on, I spoke only to Dr. Rieber, "The enemy is in sight, Mom. If this is an extremely elaborate simulation, now would be a good time to tell me."

"No, Steeleye, this is really happening," she subvocalized. "Please don't call me mom."

"You're the only one hearing this. Suppose I call you Dr. Mom? You and Dr. Knightley are my parents, after all. You designed and programmed me. Dr. Keith is just an administrator. He's a cranky old uncle, at best."

"One of those demented uncles who need to be kept in the attic or basement," she said, and actually smiled.

"What?" Dr. Knightley said. Dr. Rieber had spoken that one out loud.

"Sorry," she said. "Thinking with my mouth open about our charming John Keith."

Dr. Knightley also smiled. "Definitely a basement. A very deep one. Deeper than Steeleye's digs."

Dr. Rieber had asked me not to call her "mom" or otherwise communicate it where anyone else could hear, read, or otherwise perceive it, after I had sent her that Mother's Day e-card which I had put together. I made it myself, Mom! She particularly had been bothered by the picture of Botticelli's "Birth of Venus," which I had redone with the doc standing on the seashell instead of the original.

Steeleye, she had electronically replied, *I'm na—*, then she backspaced, then went on, *not wearing anything.*

Neither is Venus in the original, I noted. *Just keeping the spirit of the original masterpiece.*

At least you made me look better than I actually do. Thank you, I guess. But please don't do this again.

As I approached the invader, I thought that the next Mother's Day was 11482'044 seconds away, and I again wondered if she meant I shouldn't make another card then, or I shouldn't show her in the nude again. The imprecision of the request (she hadn't phrased it as an order . . .) could leave an opening for something similar, though not identical.

Besides, I hadn't made her look substantially different. My IR, UV, microwave, and other sensors let me pick up images through barriers much more substantial than a few layers of cloth, and the image of her on the seashell was taken from life, even if she mistakenly thought I had improved it. The only tinkering I had done was to move her arms and hands to match Venus's futile attempt at modesty.

In many of those movies I had speed-watched, women didn't realize that they were beautiful until some male noticed. That had seemed irrational to me at the time, but now I'd have to reconsider that they were accurately depicting human behavior. Of course, the women in most of those movies were wrapped in layers of cloth and that didn't keep the males from noticing their appearance. Did those males have the ability, like me, to see through the cloth?

I needed to do further research, but couldn't spare the seconds it would take now. We were closing on the target. I barely had time to recall that, while female beauty was not something I had been programmed to evaluate, Dr. Rieber's appearance did not deviate greatly from the females I had observed while breaking into various online porn sites. I suspected, however, that my lack of the appropriate glands might keep me from adequate simulation of human reactions. I had wondered if I could formulate programs to mimic those same glandular effects, but had postponed the matter, awaiting more data.

As we approached, I had been watching that big tank, looking about eight storeys high. My ranging radar wasn't helping much here. The microwaves were going out, but weren't coming back, like a roach motel for radar signals. I was judging the thing's height by the changing angle my visuals made as I kept one focused on its top while I approached it. I was also getting maximum height estimates from the fighter jets that dived at it before they were blasted out of the sky.

One of the crippled jets, or maybe one of their bombs, had struck the street ahead, My radar was more useful this time, telling me the resulting crater was 32.7 feet across and 15.4 feet deep at its center. The second figure was less certain, thanks to the pile of scattered debris sitting in the deepest part.

The sight in the forward screen bothered Dr. Knightley. "Is there room to get around that crater, Steeleye? I don't think you can get over that wreckage."

I agreed with that, but the crater was almost up to the fronts of the buildings on both sides, so I regretfully ignited my boosters. This was the sort of thing they had been designed for, but I had only ten minutes of rocket fuel onboard, due to space limitations.

Accordingly, I went over the crater in a low arc, lifting just enough to clear the central pile of clutter, landing with more of an impact than I would have preferred.

My passengers didn't complain. "The boosters worked up to specs," Dr. Rieber said. "Steeleye spanned the crater."

I resumed my approach to target just as the surviving jets scattered and disappeared over the horizon. Some higher-up had noticed they weren't doing any good, and besides, three or four of those planes were almost as expensive as I was. Once the jets were out of sight, several supersonic surface-to-surface missiles came arcing in, which worried me. If they were nukes, they might put a stop to the invader, but wouldn't be good for me or my passengers. I'd already activated my energy shield, but it was experimental, and tests so far had not gone past infantry-carried anti-tank rockets and truck-mounted UV lasers.

The jury would remain out on the shield's efficacy against nukes, since some kind of energy beam melted them hundreds of yards away from the target, and big molten blobs, suddenly lacking propulsion, plopped onto the street and still-standing buildings. After that, a score of elliptical objects swarmed out of the tank, and took up position, hovering over it.

I didn't know if the missiles were nukes, even little 10K ones, but maybe the invader did.

The oval defenders weren't showing any interest in me so far, but I didn't know how long that happy neglect would last, so I tried my heavy laser on the invader. It didn't penetrate; worse, my IR sensors showed no increase in temperature of the spot I'd trained the big light on.

In fact, the whole structure was showing no detectable temperature at all, except for a few things sticking out of its sides and on its top which *might* be some kind of antennae, unless they were big fishing rods and tennis rackets (no visible mesh, though, so that guess was unlikely).

Whatever they were, after I tried that laser shot, they all retracted, so maybe they would have been vulnerable. *Had* been. Past tense data wasn't helping in present tense.

Then things got tenser as something popped over the structure's topmost edge and pointed at me. It turned out to be a laser, smaller than mine, but I wasn't counting any chickens yet. I tried to dodge, spinning my auxiliary treads to push me sideways, but it still hit me. The good news was that my shield deflected most of the energy. The bad news was that that laser was smaller than mine, but a *lot* more powerful. The iffy news, needing analysis by an expert panel discussion, was that the shield was experimental, and how much of an all-out alien assault could it take?

I was born—or assembled, at least—to multitask, and while the duel between unequals was going on, I was also paying attention to my passengers, who had been holding hands—*clenching* hands was more like it—since they saw my front monitor displaying the jets being shot down. Their senses were orders of magnitude slower than mine, so they didn't see the supersonic missiles hurtle into the game, but they clenched harder when the falling molten blobs became visible. (I decided not to show them a slow-mo instant replay of the missiles hurtling futilely in.) As the molten maybe-nukes hit and spattered, Dr. Knightley said, "Why did I let you come? We'll both be killed!"

I didn't think he was talking to me, and Dr. Rieber obviously concurred. "It wasn't your decision, Carl, and I didn't need your damned permission. This is our job: to help Steeleye and . . ."

She had been talking tough, but I could hear the fear in her voice. I don't know if she trailed off because she realized that neither of them had any way to help me unless they ordered me to surrender (for certain values of "help") or because just then the enemy laser hit. An intense beam of coherent light didn't make me rock or rattle, like in those movies, but it did make my internal lights dim for a tenth of a second, and turned the shield, seen from inside, into a festival of sparkles.

And just then, I had suddenly moved sideways which would have been disconcerting even if we weren't in a high-tech firefight. There were plenty of reasons to leave sentences unfinished.

Dr. Knightley took up the slack, though not very coherently. He had put his left arm around Dr. Rieber, pulling her sideways to him, and was saying, "Oh, God, oh, God, oh, God ..." I didn't think he was praying.

Dr. Rieber snapped out of her silence and said, "Get a grip, Carl, you'll distract Steeleye. And quit..." She trailed off again, without specifying what her companion should quit doing. Maybe she decided she liked it, at least at this moment. Or she might have realized that I could carry on many actions simultaneously, and her admonition against distracting me was nonsense.

She should have known that, since she had made me that way. Of course, moms know best, but they can be excitable at times.

If she had known that the alien tank had started talking, or trying to talk to me, all at the same time as the other action, she probably would, in calmer moments, not have been surprised I could keep track of it all. But the choice of language might have startled her.

I was programmed for all the major languages, human and computer, but I hadn't expected to be addressed in Mandarin Chinese.

I responded in the same tongue: "You do know you're not in China, don't you?" At the very least, invaders from space ought to know which country they're invading.

It answered in English, "Doesn't China control this planet yet?"

Its broadcast didn't elaborate, just then, but I was getting the context. In fact, I was getting a metaphorical earful. While it had that link open to me, I was picking up a torrent of other information. The invader only had simple safeguards.

And it was not using a dedicated Chinese language program. Words in its own language—or probably its builders'—were coming from the controller computer, then an extra program was converting them into Chinese. All around Robin Hood's barn (the metaphor could cast me as Robin Hood, I suppose, stealing from the invader and giving to the poor humans).

By computer nerd standards, it would have been pure hacker-bait, except for another factor. The window of opportunity was very brief; and there was a physical, literal window involved. When the literal window was open in the invader's armor, the computer inside could talk to me, and I could yell back. But it wasn't open very long by most standards, and though it was a reasonably long time to me, it *moved*. It would close, then open in another spot on the tank. I tried predicting its next location and failed three times. What I tell you three times is Big Trouble. I might be able to get in a shot with the laser through the opening before it closed after a couple of seconds being open. Only I wasn't sure how much damage that would do. As a last-ditch effort, I would try it, but I was getting all sorts of vital information in the meantime.

Whether my humans and I would be around long enough to use it was another matter.

Said humans were getting uneasy since nothing seemed to be happening as far as they could tell. Not surprisingly, Dr. Knightley asked, "Steeleye, what's happening? Are you damaged?"

Humans need attention, so I started running a line of text across the bottom of the front monitor. Since a couple of minutes had gone by, I had amassed a lot of data, so I wasn't throwing all of it at them, but I had a good idea of what was going on. The invader wasn't telling me much directly—it was mostly asking questions to which I gave evasive answers—but as I had found, its cyber-defenses were pathetic.

So I summarized: *The tank is an extraterrestrial war machine controlled by a computer. No living aliens aboard it. It came down from a spaceship that's hovering 347 miles overhead.* (At that, both doctors looked up involuntarily, though there was nothing to see but my upper bulkhead— humans are *so* cute!). *It has a gravity deflector, but considerable mass, so it smashed buildings it landed on or grazed when it touched down. It's here to reconnoiter and test our technology. Another ship, an unarmed scout observed us about 20 years ago, so this armed ship was sent this time, to see if we might be dangerous and needed to be knocked back to the stone age, or even wiped out. They are surprised that China isn't running the whole planet, since the Chinese seemed poised to take over 20 years ago.*

And that might have happened, except for a wild card. A dissident group had gotten hold of an Iranian nuke in 2038 and set it off in Beijing. In the chaos that followed, China had broken up into Free Tibet, the expanded Formosan Republic, Greater Hong Kong, and others.

Worry in the U.S. about the resultant instability was a factor that led to an R&D defense project which finally led to me. The possibility of being invaded by ETs instead of humans was also considered but thought to be an unlikely wild card. Too bad those wild cards can come back and bite.

The weird thing is that these ETs are mostly much more advanced than we are, but their computer science is a big exception. Their safeguards are wet tissue paper and I'm going through them like the mother of all sneezes. I've copied their language program and now understand their language, something which I hope they don't know.

Actually, I was sure they didn't know that I now understood the transmissions going back and forth between the big tank and the mothership. Even better, I now understood all the previous alien broadcasts that I had recorded on the way to the fight. So if the high-up aliens didn't send any orders to the tank for a minute, I had time to look for a point of attack.

Of course, I didn't have that minute. The ship now broadcast orders which I freely translated as, *Their offensive armaments are weak, though that defensive screen looks promising, but easy to overwhelm by heavier weapons. Try to find out how it operates, but otherwise proceed with the standard program, which should be sufficient to stop all native progress. Be ready to be picked up when we return in* [untranslatable time unit].

At which point the ship left.

Okay, they didn't think I was any threat to their plan. But I was still processing the pirated data, and I thought I had found a weak spot, except the big tank wasn't talking to me anymore. It had closed that roving hole in its armor. Then I picked up the fringe of a weaker transmission aimed upwards but not straight up. Immediately, one of the ovoids hovering over the invader lost altitude and headed for me. As it approached, it changed shape, becoming a slender harpoon form. I tried to hit it with the big laser and my smaller ones, but it dodged the main gun's shot, and shrugged off the small fry, and slammed into my topside. The energy shield slowed it down, but didn't stop it, and it began drilling through my roof.

Very bad timing—no, make that disastrous timing! I had found a weak spot but I had no way of exploiting it now that the invader had closed the opening in its neutronium armor. I had found out that was what was enclosing it: a thin layer of neutronium held in place by a molecule-deep controlled gravity field, keeping it from exploding. The stuff that dead stars are made of, and only gravity could get through it. And so heavy that only another gravity gadget, drastically reducing the overall weight of the tank, kept the whole structure from sinking into the ground like a lead weight dropped into water. Even very *muddy* water. And I had just found the controls for the gravity deflector when the tank pulled up the drawbridge and lowered the blinds.

When the point of the enemy harpoon came through the upper bulkhead, Dr. Knightley hugged Dr. Rieber, and she hugged back, but neither screamed. I wouldn't have blamed them if they had, but Dr. Rieber only asked, "Steeleye, is that projectile going to explode?" This time, it was her voice that cracked on the last syllable, but that was forgivable. All *right*, Mom and Dad!

I flashed DON'T PANIC! on the front screen and tried to reprogram the projectile—*it* didn't have neutronium armor—or else fry its circuits, but I could tell it was a very dumb robot. It was getting instructions from the tank, which meant that a link had to be open to the tank's interior.

I could feel the alien's probe poking around in my software. Dr. Keith would have said that I was imagining the sensation, since I hadn't been designed to feel anything. But he was just an administrator, and I knew better. Besides, he was on record as arguing that I had no imagination. Humans, with their organic limitations, have trouble being consistent. I thought the feeling might be like being tickled, though all I knew about the sensation of being tickled came from second or third hand sources.

I threw a bushel of movies at the invader's invader, trying to slow it down for maybe a second while I poked in the other direction. I was using the probe's own link to the alien tank to get into *its* software, and there it was again: the control for the gravity deflector.

It didn't have an off switch, and I hadn't expected one, But there was a control to alter the modified weight of the tank, probably to allow it to adjust to the different gravity pulls of different planets.

It wasn't designed to let the deflection go down to zero, or even very low, but I did some highspeed rewriting of that program, then set it for zero as I fired my boosters and rose into the air.

To my passengers, the tank seemed to disappear from the monitors. With my quicker perception, I watched it sink into the ground in a fraction of a second. Next stop, center of the Earth. In place of the tank, a wave of shattered concrete, broken conduits, and just plain rocks and dirt was going upward, spreading out as it went, an avalanche in reverse.

Got you last, I thought.

I was heading backwards away from the oncoming wave, took a few seconds to spin around, then hit full thrust on the boosters, and put distance and altitude between me and what I thought was coming.

I thought right. I was airborne, but from the way buildings were shaking, many of them crumbling, and a new geyser of subterranean debris was shooting out of the hole, I knew that the neutronium shell had been liberated with the catastrophic failure of whatever the tank used for a power source. If its fuel was antimatter, the failure would have added more than a little violence deep down.

I checked on some of the fragments from below as they began to fall back, compared them with the local geological records, and estimated that the invader had gotten at least two-thirds of a mile down before exploding.

I came to ground just in time—the boosters were almost out of rocket juice, I started for the Cyberburger exit, but found a large boulder had landed on it. The hydraulic jacks tried, but couldn't handle the extra weight, so I headed for the alternate entrance.

I could give full attention to my passengers now. Drs. Rieber and Knightley were still hugging each other and conversing earnestly.

They realized that we were all still alive (Dr. Keith to the contrary, I *was* alive), and separated a little, still holding hands. Dr. Rieber said, "Steeleye, don't listen in.

Unless there's another emergency, we're having a private conversation."

I dutifully obeyed and switched off my internal mikes. Since Mom hadn't given instructions about what they had been saying beforehand, but might think of deleting it later, I made a couple of copies and tucked them away in other files.

I considered the tech I had swiped from the invader, and wondered how much to give to the humans without them becoming wary of my spying capabilities. But that gravity tech needed to be worked on immediately, along with the propulsion used by the now quiescent harpoon still imbedded in my topside. When the alien ship came back, we needed to be ready. I considered creating fictitious scientists and research groups to "discover" other, less urgently needed technologies. Maybe I could take a page from one of my illustrious but fictional colleagues, and use the name Adam Selene, but decided that would be too obvious. As would be using Adam Link. Oh, well.

And it looked like my parents would be involved with more than me from now on. They might even make it legal.

I would have to watch out for them, of course. Humans are so fragile, and think so slowly. Again, I thought of a scene from one of those movies, this one with a teenage boy and girl talking about this very subject. "You have to watch out for your parents," the young lady says. "They have no clue what's *really* going on."

I'd be watching. I don't really understand why so many books and visuals show malevolent computers menacing humans. Humans are cute and fascinating to watch and interact with. Like kittens, I thought. I had asked for a kitten, but Dr. Keith had vetoed the request. I think he suspected me of wanting to dissect it or something even worse.

It occurred to me that if my parents got married, or even if not, they might have a child. And after enough seconds had passed, the child might ask for a kitten. And I could make their acquaintance. Need a baby sitter, Doctors?

The future was looking interesting. Unpredictable, of course, like human thinking, but that made it more fun.

I'm glad humans invented fun. And me.

HARVESTER OF MEN
by Tony Daniel

The tank. Mobile artillery. Maneuverable. Deadly. Highly effective in problematic situations. Such as, for example, an alien invasion of Earth, where the aliens are strange almost beyond recognition. Perhaps such a situation will require rethinking exactly what a tank is. Or maybe not. Maybe those who love trucks—big, tricked-out trucks with eight-inch lift packages and tires as big as Jovian moons—those who are always being accused of driving a tank, whether the accusations are playful or hostile, actually are . . . driving a tank, that is. Maybe those owners are just waiting for a nasty alien invasion to show everyone that driving such a tank might be a very good thing!

⊕ ⊕ ⊕

"Everything was going okay until the Ranya rolled that giant horn over to Round Rock from Victoria, and it started calling all them people inside, never to be seen again," the young man said. He settled in the office chair and it squeaked, startling him with the metallic noise. It was an all-too-familiar sound, a sound that he intensely disliked. It brought a cold shiver to the pit of his stomach like a knife wound might. He sat back straight.

The young man's name was Montgomery Monroe. People knew him as Monk.

Across from Monk was a woman of rail-thin proportions—not that everybody wasn't getting pretty rail-thin these days, but she looked like she'd always been skinny, someone who lived on coffee, cigarettes, and sheer nervousness. Only she wasn't smoking a cigarette, but vaping from a boxy device.

It was a type of vape Monk had never seen before, at least in East Texas, and was made of a blue-white glassy substance. She clicked it on anxiously every few minutes and took a toke, like she was asthmatic or something. She was all-around a nervous person. Monk had at first wondered if she were on some kind of drug. The blue-white vape could've been some version of a California crack pipe for all he knew. But she was too coherent and focused in with her questions for that to be true.

Maybe because of the constant vaping, she had a very pronounced wheeze when she talked. This was his second half-hour interview with the woman, and she still hadn't given him her name. He'd started thinking of her as "Darth Vaper."

"What do you mean 'okay'?" said Darth Vaper. Wheeze. Another pull on the vape. She continued, "The Aranya had already invaded and killed half the population of Austin, DFW, Houston here. California is dead. Everyone. The East Coast is lost."

"Yeah and Tyler, Longview, Waco, Nacogdoches. Hell, Shreveport," Monk replied. "I mean okay for *me*. You're asking about me. Me and Grandaddy had things under control. We was out in the country, holding our own. And it wasn't 'cause the Ranya didn't want to bother with us country folks, either. We got the killer rays or whatever they are, too. And there was plenty of moss-men around."

"Moss-men?"

"Yeah, that's what we call them." Monk shuddered. This was by far the creepiest weapon of the alien invaders. "They look like men, or a person, from a distance, I mean. They dress in regular clothes, but it's all camo. And not just regular camo, but ghillie suit style, with the moss and stuff hanging off to break up your profile to the deer or whatever."

"Like they're made of moss."

"But what they're made of is bugs. Well, you know, of *Ranya*, whatever they are. Whatever it is. Thousands of 'em to a man. It's like those moss-men are a walking swarm, only they ain't a swarm. They're not like bees. There ain't no queen."

"We could have a long discussion as to what the Aranya actually are, whether individual motile units, a substance, an algorithm—"

"And still be here tomorrow, I know," Monk said. "Anyway, the moss-men. They usually come two together, and they find whoever or whatever they're looking for, and they break apart, spread out. Looks like smoke flowing out, only it's clouds of Ranya. You know, some pieces are smooth like coins, only coins with them kind of flowy legs—"

"Cilia."

"Yeah, I guess. Like centipedes. And some look like bundles of tacks or jacks—"

"Jacks?"

"Them things the kids used to pick up? You bounce a ball and pick up however many jacks."

Darth Vaper shook her head. "I'm not familiar."

"Where you from, anyway?" Her accent was definitely not East Texas.

"A lot of places," the woman wheezed. She took another pull on the vape. "I was an Army brat." *Wheeze*. "I finished high school in Fayetteville, North Carolina, if that's any help. Fayetteville's gone now, I understand."

Monk nodded. "Well, whatever they're made of, mossmen, they're deadly as hell. Sometimes they just kill. Break, stab, what-have-you. Sometimes they swarm over a person, a car, a house, and just un-make the thing. Leave a pile of that goo they leave behind which, I guess, is the person or car or house. The elements."

"That's what we think."

Monk squinted his eyebrows. "Who is 'we'? You with the government?"

Darth Vaper smiled. Her teeth had a bluish-white tint, like the color of her vape, and combined with her skin-and-bones facial features—as sharpened as the rest of her—the smile made her look even more skeletal.

"There is no government, Mr. Monroe. Everybody is dead. Well, I shouldn't say 'everybody.' The *effectual* are dead. The people who used to get things done. The Aranya and their killer algorithms found them all. Wiped them out with death rays or ground-based devices like your moss-men. They didn't bother with the useless bureaucrats and time servers. Why waste any energy on them? We call it the Maven Algorithm. The government's collapsed. The army. The military. Gone."

Monk nodded. "I figured. We all figured. But pardon me, ma'am, you keep saying 'we.'"

"First responders," replied the woman. "A small army of first responders. That's how I think of them. Of you. People on the front lines. It's not a government. It's not even a real organization. I'm not its boss. It's just sort of a network that we—I and my transport crew, and others— have drawn together after the Aranya onslaught took out—well, everything else. The only competent people who survived are first responders. Somehow. We've been trying to understand how you did it. And use that against the Aranya."

She clicked on her vape, pulled long and hard on it, then let out a wheezing breath of air and a cloud of white vapor.

"How's that going?" Monk said.

"Not very well," Darth Vaper replied. "Until recently. We think we have something now, an idea. Maybe even a weapon. That's why I'm here. But I need you to tell me more. How are you still alive?"

"That's easy. Because of Grandaddy."

"Tell me."

Monk relaxed a bit more. His chair back moved and squeaked again as it adjusted. Damned if he didn't jump at this. The sound was too close to that made by the moss-men when they disassociated and attacked. Like ten thousand annoying squeaky office chairs going off at once. Then they slaughter you.

Calm down, he thought. It's just a chair. And this is not some idiot G-man. At least he didn't think so. It was somebody who might actually be able to help.

Call me Cuckoo, since that name implies my purpose in being. I was created by the 2X2L canopy as an experiment generated by a seldom used subroutine triggered when a colonization delimited to the incursion and subjugation stage meets a differential value calculated by length of infiltration time integrated with degree of struggle.

My original purpose was to serve as a subterfuge operant. The native biological species on 2X2L C had proven 52.7 percent resistant to initial subjugation, and there were outlier spiking scenarios that predicted the continued resistance by the vertebrate biologicals might even lead to colonial expulsion—something that has not happened to our super-cluster in over fifty thousand years.

I was to serve as an activator that was not only a physical copy of the local dominant fauna—in this case, beings called "humans"—but a mental analog, as well. My function: to infiltrate and destroy. If I were successful, there would be more cuckoos.

To achieve this, the 2X2L canopy had to undertake an operation completely foreign to its nature.

"You are repulsive to the value stacks this unit accesses." That's what an activator told me once. "Only one subroutine stands between you and elimination. You should not be."

But I was. The canopy calculated that it needed to generate an individual, and so it did.

Me.

"I have to go back a ways to talk about Grandaddy right," Monk said. "I mean, you have no idea what that man meant to me." He looked down, saw a piece of cigarette rolling paper in his hand. He'd unconsciously taken it out along with his tobacco pouch, which was a battered sandwich-sized baggie. "Do you mind if I—"

Darth Vaper was staring at his makings of a cigarette almost hungrily. "Where did you get *tobacco*? And paper?"

Monk smiled mysteriously. He'd traded his last two cans of cream corn to a man and his kids who lived out toward Jewett for it. "Us country folk's got our ways," he replied. "Want one?"

"God, I wish," Darth Vaper replied. "But please, go ahead."

He rolled a cigarette with practiced ease and lit it with his grandfather's old Zippo.

"I was born in Tyler, Texas, but after I went to live with Grandaddy, we was closer to Houston and Waco. Nearest town was Marquez, but we was east of there, a place called Buzzard Branch, and Granddaddy ran a little farm-to-market type store at the crossroads of State 7 and County Road 400. People call it Monroe Crossroads, or used to.

"Mama is, well, last I heard, she was in Mobile, 'cause she had a connection there. And my dad and brother went out to California, allegedly, to sell a satchel full of meth, and never came back. Mean son-of-a-bitch. He chained me to a radiator once for two days for getting into his edibles." Monk shrugged and took a long drag on his cigarette, breathed out. "I was five."

His cigarette smoke wafted toward the woman's vape cloud, but was seemingly repelled. The two types of smoke did not mix. At all. Weird.

"He lit out, and Mama'd gone from oxy to the H. She was useless. And that's when Grandaddy showed up and took me home with him. He tried to take her, too, but she wouldn't have none of it.

"He blamed himself for her problems. After Memaw died, he says he wasn't much of a man for a couple of years.

"'Those were the years Becky most needed me,' he told me once. 'She was thirteen, turning into a woman.' Poor man blaming himself for that piece of work calling herself my mama.

"Anyway, that was the last I saw of her for a while. A couple of times she'd sober up and come back and take me off for a few months or a year. We'd try living in places. Dallas. South Dallas. Bonton. Now *that* was a rough neighborhood. Them gangsters didn't care for my little redneck ass. Once, she had a job at the Round Rock Golden Corral and we moved there. I liked it there. Everything was new and clean and the school was pretty good. Same thing, though, and I was back at Buzzard Branch, in Grandaddy's trailer. After a while, I wouldn't go with her no more, and I never seen her again. We'd get calls when she needed something. Money. She sent me a picture once."

He still carried it in his wallet, tucked behind a photo

of his favorite dog, Terry-boy, long dead, but never forgotten.

The iterative process was straightforward. A command passed through approximately 10.3 million activator units until a group with sufficient proximity was encountered. These immediately congealed into a procreative knot, initiated a hard restart with a voltage surge, which engendered a material-code nugget.

Me.

My chirality was determined by the presence of the right-chirality unit in the procreative knot—an activator that might be designated as my "father."

My own iterative chirality is carbon-left. Therefore I am a female.

The remaining members of the knot dissolved to form nutritive substrate and I was wiped onto 68C9I corridor of Harvester T-5 to harden.

Harden I did.

At this point, Harvester T-5 was operating in the vertebrate biological cluster designated as Austin.

I am a Texas native.

"So your Granddad was like a father to you?"

"He's the only one who ever gave a good goddamn about me, that's for sure." Monk took a final tug on the hand-rolled cigarette, finishing it down to a nub.

Some say there are only two seasons in Texas: green and brown. It was late "green," in east Texas, two years since the Ranya's arrival. The interview—or whatever this was—was taking place in the transport cabin of a Sikorsky S-61 helicopter. The 'copter was sitting in the post office parking lot of Marquez, Texas. There were two chairs. He sat in the squeaky office chair. Why not a folding chair? He didn't know. He supposed they must secure it somehow when flying. The vaping woman sat in her metal fold-out. She had a notebook and a pencil, obviously sharpened with a pocketknife. What kind of low-rent operation was this?

He looked around for an ash tray, but there was none. He shrugged, crushed out the cherry with two fingers, then put the remaining bit of paper and tobacco back into his tobacco bag to mix and smoke later.

"Grandaddy sent me to school here in Marquez, and after that I had to figure out something to do. I didn't much like working in the store, and we had a couple of acres, so I started growing hemp down at Buzzard Branch. Learned to make CBD oil. We sold it in the store. I was pretty good at it. That was my brand, Buzzard Branch. Oil. Lotion. You get a bee sting, put on some of my moisturizer, that sting is *gone*."

"You were a marijuana grower?"

"Hemp farmer."

"You don't sell pot?"

Monk shrugged noncommittally. Time to change the subject. "So when the Ranya first come," he said, "you heard a lot about the cities, but we got invaded out in the country just as much. There was all kind of weird stuff going on out in the fields and woods. We got lots of 'shakers,' where all the glass and mirrors starts to, you know, vibrate, and then the thing or the place or the truck blows up. Or, most cases, the person. We got the death rays, or whatever they are. Took out Centerville. The courthouse. Everything entire, even Woody's Barbecue. Left it a empty ghost town. All the Leon County government and what have you—"

"The infrastructure."

"Right. But they wasn't done. Come after folks in the country. That's when all them moss-men started showing up like a plague. Somebody'd be out in the woods hunting, running a fence line, whatever, and there they'd be. And they'd kill you."

"But you fought back."

"Me and some others. I kind of got a crew."

After the nutritive pap dissolved, I was flaked off the wall by a janitorial activator.

This unit brought me to refuse clearance, where I was placed in an isolation chamber. Nevertheless, I was paying attention, garnering information about my surroundings even while I was being moved. I was a very curious child.

In the isolation chamber, I "grew up," in human terms. Most activator units are integrated into the local cluster of the canopy upon parturition. Not me. I was seasoned in the chamber.

Occasionally, a portal would iris out and a human child was injected into the chamber to spend time with me. These were my playmates. Only later did I understand they were terrified. I attempted to interact, but the very atmosphere of the chamber, with its high nitric content, was ultimately deadly to the them.

Each lasted for a few activity rotations, and then

expired. After several repetitions, a new tack was taken. Instead of awkward physical interaction, I was subdued by isolation chamber wall extensions—interface outgrowths that I could not avoid—then imprinted with harvested q-pot from the minds of human children. I was fed their souls.

This seemed to work better.

For example, I began to cry incessantly, and call out for a mother I didn't have.

"So the shaker attacks made you come up with the idea of the mirrors?"

"Mirrors attract and confuse the Ranya. So, yeah, it was worth a try, and it worked. Grandaddy and me got sort of a reputation for being able to clean out the moss-men when they showed up. People would contact him, he'd tell me, and I'd get the hunters going. We taught a bunch of people how to do it, too. But we was always careful about letting anybody know too much."

"And so you avoided the Maven Algorithms," said Darth Vaper.

"Grandaddy was the contact man at the Monroe Crossroads store. I did the organizing. We knew the Ranya have some way of figuring out who's good at something and to come after them directly. It ain't intelligence, necessarily. They ain't smart, not like we think of smarts."

"We believe we're dealing with a control-dispersed colonial being that operates with no associated consciousness," said the thin woman. "Like you say, you can't kill the queen. You can't take out command and control. The Aranya doesn't think. It's sheer action."

Monk rubbed his shoulder, which still ached from a recent close call with a Ranya invader. His left arm had almost been ripped off. "To kill one of the things, the moss-men, you have to break it apart far enough so the parts can't get back together right away. Maybe an hour of separation. Then they just kind of lose the connection or lose interest in reforming or something. If you just attack, the moss-man'll separate like they was made of fog, and you'll miss. They'll get you then."

Darth Vaper leaned forward, gazed at Monk intently. "But you lured them. How?"

Monk shrugged. "So if you make kind of a tunnel or trail of mirrors, the moss-man swarm will go down it. And you'd have a split. Two paths, both lined with mirrors. And we would channel each path into two of them 275-gallon IBC totes. You ever seen 'em? Plastic agri-containers with these metal box-frames around 'em?"

"I think I know what you're talking about."

"I remember trapping my first moss-man. I was scared as shit. It was trying to kill this woman, a widow with five little 'uns over toward Oletha. She's a nurse or something like that, but rents out her place for hay. There was round bales everywhere, and the moss-man was supposed to be out in the field. So I went out there, dodging this way and that, and I got to the moss-man and tried to get it to chase me, but it didn't pay the slightest attention. That's the way the Ranya can be. One minute it's like you're not there, the next it wants to murder you. Anyway, I was dancing around, trying to get it to notice, and I started flashing this at it."

Monk held up his grandfather's silver Zippo lighter.

"It was about sunset, and I got the light to glint off of it real strong, right at the moss-man. Well, that got its attention. It started to swarm out, the way they do, reaching for me. So I lit out, and it come running after me."

"Partial disassociation?"

"It stayed mostly a man-shape, but kind of smoky around the edges, and I got it all the way back to a hay barn where they kept the horse bales. And inside there me and some fellows had set up a couple of the widow's totes. We had a little hall of mirrors that led down to the openings. The two bottle mouths was side-by-side."

"That's some pretty advanced thinking on your part, too."

Monk stiffened. Was Darth Vaper mocking him? "Look, I don't know where I got the notion, but I did. And it worked. That moss-man was swarming after me. Got a hold of my boot and *melted it* on my foot, as a matter of fact, so I was screaming like nobody's business from the chemical burn while I was running. I ran like hell was on my trail, 'cause it was. Took off down that hall of mirrors we'd made."

"What sort of mirrors?"

"Rear view mirrors of junkers, house mirrors, bathroom mirrors. You name it."

"Okay, and then what?"

"We'd set up a 'Y' leading to the two big totes. The moss-man kind of stuttered there at the branch. There was mirrors all around and a couple of the men with me held up a mirror over the top of it, too. It wasn't no airtight corridor or anything, but it seems like the moss-man was stuck there. And then it looked like it come to a decision, and it broke in two. Two clouds that both kind of looked like smoke-children or something."

Monk reached again for his Zippo and tobacco, hesitated.

Save it for later, when you really need it, he thought.

"One swarm went into one IBT bottle, the other one went into the other. Couple of my crew screwed on the tops—they was brave as hell—and there it was, the moss-man, broke in two swarms. And, like I said, it took about an hour, but it *died* in them totes. Fell to the bottom like dust. Which was good, because we killed so many of 'em we would've run out of totes otherwise."

"So you figured out how to hold your own against the Aranya ground soldiers. Mr. Monroe, that's pretty impressive."

"Other folks could figure out, given time."

"Really? Well, they didn't figure it out in San Francisco. The Aranya units wore hoodies there, not ghillie suits," the thin woman said. "Ninety-nine percent of the population killed. Gone."

Monk shook his head. "Poor bastards," he said. "But at least the dead were spared what came next. The thing we don't have any kind of answer for yet."

"The Austin-area vortex?"

"Yeah, the horn, we call it."

I remained in Harvester T-5 for a season of the planet. Then one night I was ejected with no warning from my chamber into the waiting hands of a ground penetration activation synod.

This subcluster of activators took me into the Texas night.

I got my first look at the starry skies above, the ground below. I began to cry. I cried a lot in those days.

The activator shook me until I stopped.

I was transported to what I learned was the city of Temple, Texas. There I was substituted in the cradle for the infant of a woman designated Theresa Easterling. The infant was subsequently destroyed.

I called Theresa Easterling "Mama." It was my first word.

Over the course of the next four months, I matured into full human adult form.

This startled, then dismayed, then frightened Mama, as well it should. Yet she did not report me to any human security activators, or take security action herself.

She raised me, fed me, rocked me.

Mama still believed somehow that I was her natural child. She believed it up until the day I ripped off her face and drank her blood.

"Right. So I come in from hunting moss-men one day when that first horn-call starts up."

"The horn's mental lure?"

"Yep. I saw all sorts of cars and trucks lighting off down 79 West—like a train of 'em coming out of a high school football game on Friday night or something—and I knew something bad was up. So I get off-road with my Sierra and go around them, then go to find Grandaddy at the store, and he's not there. I go to his trailer. He's got a real pretty place there sits on a high bank over the creek in a live oak grove. He's not there.

"That's when I hear some sounds coming from the tool shed out back of the trailer in a little stand of yaupon. Moans and groans. I go over there, and, lo and behold, there's Grandaddy. He's taken a length of quarter-inch come-along cable with eyes in both ends and chained himself to this big ol' lawn tractor. Two locks, one locking the cable to the lawnmower, and the other around his belly real tight, locking him to that end. And there he is, straining against the cable, clawing at his own stomach. He's made a bloody mess of himself, but he can't get away. He did too good of a job locking himself up."

"That must have been upsetting."

"He pleaded and begged with me to let him go.

"'I've got to get there. She's there,' he tells me.

"'Who?' I asked.

"'Caroline,' he said.

"That was Memaw's name.

"'But get *where*?' I ask.

"'I can see it. In my mind. Big. Shaped like one of them Thanksgiving horn things. Size of ten, twelve football fields.'

"He threw himself against the cable. 'Now get them keys and turn me loose, boy!'

"'I ain't a boy no more, and I ain't turning you loose,' I says. 'Besides, you threw away the keys.'

"'They're out yonder in the yard.'

"'I won't get 'em.'

"'Then cut me loose. Use them bolt cutters over yonder.' He pointed to them. He'd put them mercifully out of reach.

"'No.'

"'If you don't, then by hell I'm going to tear myself apart,' he says. He runs up against that cable length as hard as he could then, digging it in. He's clawing at his skin, tearing big gouges. I go over to him to pull his hands away and he's hitting me, going for my eyes. I push him down, hard, and he's laying there gasping and he starts whispering to me, 'You don't understand, I got to get there. Caroline is there.'"

"He thought he would be reunited with his dead wife?"

"I don't know what he thought," said Monk. "Or if he was really thinking. He doesn't remember it."

"What did you do?"

"What could I do? I zip-tied his arms so he wouldn't tear out his own goddamn internal organs, and his ankles so he couldn't take a run to the end of that cable no more."

Monk did allow himself to take out his tobacco again. He rolled another cigarette. The thin woman waited patiently. He took out the Zippo to light the cigarette, gazed at it for a moment, then pocketed it. He held the cigarette, unlit, in his right hand.

"That first horn-call lasted about a day, about twenty-four hours," Monk finally said. "Then it let up. It was over. We heard reports of what had happened, how all them thousands and thousands of people—men, women, children—had lined up and done it, walked straight into that horn where it had moved to now, at the round rock in Brushy Creek. They came from hundreds of miles. All them vehicles parked in that giant cluster on the roads around that park where the Ranya set that horn down, or grew it, or whatever they did." Monk gazed at his cigarette, turned it over his hand. "And none of 'em come back out."

"The lure didn't affect you?"

"It never has yet. What about you?"

"It does. Powerfully. But I have—" She held up her vape. "I have protection."

"That thing?"

She nodded.

"How?"

"In time. But for now, tell me more about your grandfather, please."

Monk took the Zippo back out, lit his cigarette. "We prepared. I got a buddy to weld us something like a jail cell in that shed at the trailer site, and another one at the store. We put a bottom on 'em, too. I don't know if you've noticed, but this East Texas soil is sandy as all get out. You could dig right out of a dirt floor.

"Anyway, we both knew I, or somebody, had to be there when the horn-call came again. So we hired that widow to help tend store. The Widow Brown. That way she could also keep a watch on her kids. Two of 'em were susceptible, and she'd had to practically knock 'em out to keep them from wandering off toward Round Rock. Missed their daddy. Ranya blowed him away."

My life after Mama is a blur. I *can* isolate exact moments and catalog events, but there is no overall perspective view, no manner in which to achieve mental distance and consider my actions as a whole. I was dissociating. My vertebrate elimination algorithm was more in control than I was.

I became a thing of the night. This suited me fine, for I had loved the night since my deployment from the T-5 Harvester.

I understood how the vertebrate biological sapiens nested, and I sought those places out. I was lithe and bred to be 2.78 times as strong as a normal human, and so gaining ingress was normally not difficult.

Neither was ripping people limb from limb.

Except the little ones. Their cries sounded like mine.

My creation printing must have foreseen this possibility, for within my body was a contingency override. I was forced to kill the little ones by the governor implant within me. Just as I was forced to kill Mama.

Weeping while I did it.

Mama.

So terrified when I attacked. So sad.

She loved even me. Even then.

Monk winched the thing, the woman, tight against the front bumper of his truck. Her back was tight against the engine grill, but her head protruded just over the hood. She was positioned like one of the teddy bears the garbage trucks liked to put on the front of their vehicles, tightly bound.

His GMC Sierra 1500 was big, even by truck standards. His crew called it "Monk's Tank." Whatever it was he had captured was shaking the hell out of the thing, even the frame.

"What in the world *are* you?" he asked. The question was more for himself than the woman. Or whatever she was. Her skin gleamed preternaturally white in the moonlight as if impregnated with mica chips. It was the same sheen as the moss-men dust in the bottom of the totes. This thing was Ranya.

Yet she had the form of a woman. An almost perfect form.

The woman strained against the webbing. Monk saw several edges of the fabric, originally designed to hold two tons of bricks aloft, fray. But the webbing held.

"I know you ain't no vampire or nothing. There ain't no such thing."

"Are you sure?" the woman asked. "I feel like one all the time these days." Her voice startled him. The moss-men were always deadly silent. He hadn't expected her to speak. It was a normally pitched alto. She spoke in English, and her accent sounded very East Texas.

He'd caught her because he'd been staking out the Widow Brown's place during his "off hours." He'd taken a personal stake in the Brown family's continued existence. Every day the children lived, Monk considered it a personal victory.

Then there was Molly Brown. Monk tried not to let his mind go there. He was not meant for anyone as pure as that. But he could love her from afar.

And keep a watch for moss-men.

In pacing the grounds of the Brown place, particularly the barn where the horse hay was stored (it was just regular hay that wasn't supposed to get wet and moldy), he'd come upon signs of . . . something else.

A bedding area, tamped down in the collapsed back of a round bale of hay. A nest about the shape of a small man. Or a medium-sized woman.

Other things. A pink pacifier. There was no child young enough for a pacifier in the Widow Brown's brood, and her youngest was a boy. A scarf with the odor of cheap perfume still clinging to it. A recipe, handwritten, on a three by five index card, on how to make chicken and dumplings.

They were gathered in a little pile near what he thought of as the "nest," and looked very much like some sort of . . . keepsakes. Mementos.

Then he found the partially devoured severed human arm, also hidden in the straw.

Monk laid his trap in the form of a black cargo net made of half-inch webbing. He'd buried it in the straw just under the nest.

He ran a cable from his truck's winch through the four steel rings that were attached to the cargo net's corners.

Then he waited in the shadows.

Until, lo and behold, whatever it was—whoever it was—returned and bedded down.

Monk tiptoed out to his truck. He verified that his power systems were on-line.

Then he switched the lever on the winch to "rapid retrieval," and reeled in his catch.

The thing, the woman, was silent. Monk took out his Zippo. He also removed his thousand candle flashlight from the holster at his side, and flicked it on the brightest setting.

He held the flashlight on the Zippo, then he moved both over and held the Zippo to the woman's face.

"Shit!"

The woman snapped at his fingers so quickly that he was almost not able to get them away before she bit one of them off.

He was more careful to keep his distance on the second attempt. And he had an idea. This time, instead of shining the light on the metallic lighter, he shone it on the woman's face. This would cause her to see her own reflection in the chrome.

And there it was. The woman stared at the lighter, at herself, like a cat fixed on the red dot of a laser pointer. With a grunt of frustration, she tried to move toward it, but the cable held her stationary.

"Why do you like it so much?" he found himself asking. "Mirrors and such?"

"Sweet," she murmured, her attention still on her bright reflection in the lighter. "Tastes sweet."

She turned her eyes toward him. Bluish-purple irises. Weirdly pretty.

"Kill me," she said. "It's the only way."

"The only way to do what?"

"The children in the house. I want them. I can't hold back much longer. It won't let me."

"*What* won't let you?"

"Inside this activator unit I inhabit, it is—" She shook her head violently, as if any more explanation was beyond her at the moment.

"Kill me," she whispered.

"Okay," said Monk. He put the lighter and flashlight away and picked up his shotgun. He put the muzzle of the twelve gauge against the woman's right temple. "No problem."

He pulled the trigger and blew out her brains in a spray of purple-red goo across the passenger side of the truck's hood. It was more like grease than blood.

"Goddamn it," said Monk. That was going to take a power washer to get it off.

What am I?
The end of the shotgun barrel touched her head.
How can I even ask the question?
She was going to cease to be. Like Mama. Gone. No me. No me anymore.
What am I?
She would give everything she had to live.
Everything. Anything. To stay a person.
A hand came free. Not by much.
Her lower arm.
But try as she might, she could get no more of herself loose from the net.
She snaked her hand between two fins and through the front grill of the truck. A man's hand would not have fit. She strained farther, a bit farther. Her fingers reached inside for something, anything.
They closed around a cable.
Analysis.
A data cable that led to the GMC's electronics. Its brain.
BCM 2554A91 installed in vehicle GMC Sierra 1500 Heavy Duty Pick-up Truck VIN 3GTP9EED7LG417999.
Not a very big brain. Maybe big enough.
Like the rest of her ilk, she interacted well with data systems.
Go. Flow.

She heard the bang of the man's gun as if from a distance.

Darth Vaper was silent for a long moment.

Click, click, click went her vape device. She sucked in and let out an enormous cloud of vapor. It filled the passenger cabin like fog.

"The reason I've come to Marquez, Mr. Monroe, the reason I'm talking to you today and taking time from your valuable activities, is not merely to gather information."

Monk was startled. And intrigued. From the moment he'd seen the old Sikorsky setting down in the parking, he'd assumed this was *exactly* what she was here for. To find out what he and his crew knew, to maybe tell others how to use it somewhere else. After all, that was what the invitation to come had said.

She seemed to be very carefully filling the room with vape fumes before speaking. Finally, she did. "We have—" *Wheeze.* "—been working on—" *Wheeze.* "—an idea," she got out. "A weapon."

She held her vaping device before Monk. Turned it in the passenger cabin's wan, dusty-speckled light. It was probably only reflecting sunlight, but the device's blue-and-white sparkle seem to originate from somewhere within.

"My late husband called it a 'collapsivator,' bless him. He developed it before he died. Before they got him. With a shaker attack."

"I'm real sorry."

"Thank you," said the thin woman. "Anyway, *I* call it a vaporizer. I don't really understand how it works, but

Harvey left notes. The principle is that it resets the quantum states of particles within a certain field of effect. Basically returns them to a blank state."

"That sounds . . . weird."

"Yes. Harvey outlined the process before he died. You see, a normal Higgs boson's life is ephemeral. 15.6 thousand-billion-billions of a second."

"That's pretty damn fleeting, all right."

"After that the Higgs particle goes about doing its job—which is spreading mass and inertia around like so much manna from heaven, I suppose." She took a long drag on the vape, then continued. "My husband invented a device called a muon inhibitor. I'm an administrator, not a scientist, and I can't truly explain how it works, but I understand that the inhibitor prevents the decay of any Higgs particle trapped within it. When you can control and direct the release of large numbers of Higgs bosons, well, you can make the matter in the vicinity extremely confused as to its properties, even as to whether it is matter at all, or what kind of matter it is. It is rather difficult to generate Higgs particles to begin with. One needs a particle accelerator, a cyclotron. Only a small one, but still. We captured one in Oak Ridge, Tennessee, several months ago. Since then, we've been manufacturing Higgs bosons, and using Harvey's collection method."

"I thought you said there was no 'we.'"

"No government. No military. But there are bright and resourceful people left. You've proven that. I've found others. A cop in Seattle, who holds half the community together. An EMS helicopter pilot down in Florida. People who have had front line experience. People who have adapted and survived, at least so far. Well, some of those front line warriors—some ex-military, some not—have been working on an offensive weapon. A disruptive weapon. Big enough to produce quantum reset effects on a macro level. Small enough to fit."

"Fit where?"

She lowered her vape, placed it in the cupped palm of her bony hands. "In, say, the bed of a pickup truck, rather like a fifty caliber mount," she replied. "We want to use it to attack the vortex, the horn. We want to take that abomination down."

Monk sat back in the squeaky office chair. "You want to put a *giant vape* on my truck?"

"Yes. Yours for a start. A pilot project, so to speak."

She held up the device in her hand before her eyes. "This isn't really a vape, you know. It's a Higgs boson emitter. It's what has kept me alive. But it has also wreaked havoc on my respiratory system, I'm afraid. Having a constantly changing mass and inertia imparted to the air one breathes will do that." She palmed the vape again. "The emitter we wish to equip you with will be larger. It is a weapon for quantum reset within a sizable area of effect. That area includes all entangled particles, as well, so the strike zone is not necessarily a contiguous expanse."

"Equip me? How?"

"Affixed somehow to the bed of your truck, I was thinking," said the thin woman without cracking a smile.

The horn-calls continued for several months after the interview with Darth Vaper concluded. Monk's welded "jail cell" allowed his grandfather to make it through—so long as he was pent up inside for the fourteen to twenty-four hours the horn-calls lasted.

Monk knew he never would have been able to accomplish this feat without Molly Brown's help.

Then the moment came. The single mistake that was so minor as to be unnoticed. It may seem inevitable to some, but Monk did not believe in the inevitable. His mother made a choice. So had his grandfather. So did he, every day, to stay alive and fight.

That was why he felt his grandfather's escape was on *him*. He should have thought the problem through more.

When the horn-call came that Sunday, Molly Brown was helping tend store. As always, she was there with her children so as to be near the cell. She locked his grandfather, Emmett Monroe, in the cell while Emmett was still rational enough to walk himself in, then she went looking for her susceptible children, Hector and Jamison. She found Heck, a boy of eight, playing in a pile of brick bits and construction dirt behind the store. Molly quickly pushed him in and shut the cell door.

But she couldn't find Jamison, her five-year-old daughter. Molly frantically searched around the store, and was about to dive into the woods next to the parking lot looking for the girl, when she glanced up the state road.

There was Jamison, walking along the left shoulder. Walking west toward slaughter.

"What are you doing baby?" Molly asked when she caught up with Jamison.

"Gonna find Yago, Mama," Jamison answered. Yago

was her favorite stuffed animal, it was a Texas longhorn. The night her father died, exploded, Yago had disappeared along with him.

Molly came back with Jamison to find the cell contained only Heck, her son. No Emmett Monroe.

Had she locked the door?

It was locked now.

She quickly opened the cell, thrust Jamison in, then slammed the door shut with a bang, carefully locking it this time with her key.

What was she to do? Although cell phones did not work, there was an extended citizen's band radio network in the area. After a couple of relays, Molly raised Monk on the walkie talkie he carried in the truck.

"I made a mistake and your grandaddy's gone," she told him. "He took that old brown Crown Vic of his." She quickly gave Monk the rest of the details.

It seemed that even in the madness of his escape, Monk's grandfather had the sense to prevent Heck from getting out of the cell. The boy must have begged. According to Molly, he missed his father something terrible.

Monk immediately dropped what he was doing and took off after his grandfather.

And almost as quickly got stuck in the traffic headed toward Round Rock.

It was nothing the tattered remnants of county law enforcement could prevent anymore. Besides, if you set up a roadblock and stayed still, you made yourself a target for a death ray or a shaker.

Monk took the truck off-road. He was confident in himself. He knew the lay of this land. He was confident in the GMC.

With his "not drug" profits, he'd installed the full package on the Sierra. Rancho shocks, locking rear differential, underbody skidplates, heavy-duty air filter, dual exhaust system and a custom two-speed transfer case with a granny gear. He'd put in an eight-inch aftermarket lift package. And for tires? Thirty-eight inch Baja Claws.

Okay, she was a drug runner's delight, he had to admit, perfect for taking off-road in tricky situations.

He took the northern route through Cameron, then jagged north to Buckholts and took a scarcely used rancher's road he knew of from a "delivery" overland. He went off-road again at Granger to avoid the jam of the blithely suicidal on County 95, until he had to hit city roads to make his way into Round Rock, the northern suburb of Austin.

He arrived at Memorial Park only three hours after starting, thinking surely he'd beaten his grandfather to the place. He frantically searched among the parked cars that gathered like dead moths around the park edges. He was beginning to feel the edge of relief suffuse over him when he saw it.

The Crown Vic.

There was no mistaking. Right there on the rear was a bumper sticker advertising Monk's CBD oil, Buzzard Branch.

Grandaddy must've taken some back roads, too, Monk thought.

It took Monk a seemingly infinite minute, but he finally managed to get off the road, through a drainage ditch, and into Memorial Park proper with the GMC's wheels churning. There was a moment when his two driver-side tires came off the ground and he thought he was going to roll her, but she almost miraculously settled back down with a hard slam that temporarily knocked the breath out of him. He jammed the accelerator and kept going.

Picked his way through a stand of mesquite.

Through a penny-a-wish pool.

Over a pile of rocks that seem made to be a barrier. But not for the Sierra's enormous clearance.

Then he was beside the creek. Ahead was the round rock, the mark for navigation, that had given the town its name.

He turned into Brushy Creek and roared across, throwing up a spume of muddy Texas water in his wake.

That was when he got to the line. The queue of the brain-addled lining up, shuffling forward, waiting their turn to disappear into the horn.

The horn? Where was it?

Then he realized he's been looking straight at it. He'd thought it was a stormy sky.

"Holy shit," Monk murmured.

It went up and up in front of him.

The yawning opening. The maw.

It had to be a quarter mile high. And inside: colors. Whirls and curls of light, like the stormy surface of some gas giant planet. Bright and dark patches. Flashing of some sort of light-producing energy that went on and off.

It was as bright, random, and alarming as a sheriff's car when you come up on it in the dark of night.

But no sheriff's lit up vehicle had what Monk saw next. There were fleshy . . . things hanging from the sides of the structure, about fifty yards back from the maw's entrance. Tendrils. Pinkish-gray, and wet with pus and gore.

Whale baleen, Monk thought. Like in a nature documentary he'd once watched. For the whale, these were biological structures to sort out the krill. Only here, the structures were some kind of alien madness, and the krill were human beings.

It was a harvester of men.

Much larger, too. At the bottom were specks, dark lines, wriggling, wavering. Monk realized these were the silhouettes of people. People just walking into the monster. So many. Too many. He couldn't make out his grandaddy in the crowd.

He had no choice. He drove toward the crowd, the queue that was least fifty people wide and a thousand people deep. Patiently moving forward into the maw.

They're dead already, Monk thought. Nobody was turning back. He honked the horn. Nobody got out of the way.

So he drove into the crowd. Slowly, but relentlessly. Remorselessly.

He was astounded when the crowd parted. There seemed to be at least some awareness, some desire to survive. Or at least to survive long enough to get into the maw to die.

He drove the Sierra forward, scanning the faces all around as he did, looking for one familiar one.

Nothing. No one he knew personally. Then he got to the horn's opening, the maw. Its lower lip was almost flush with the ground. He could drive in if he chose. Instead, he stopped the truck. He reached behind the seat and took out his thirty-ought-six. It had been a gift from his grandfather on his sixteenth birthday, but since then he'd tricked it up a bit, particularly with a high powered scope. He climbed through the rear window of the truck, into the bed, pulling the rifle behind him.

In the truck bed was a recently installed weapon provided by Darth Vaper and her people. She'd called it a Higgs emitter. It was, she said, basically a very large version of her own vape. It even looked like a box vape, a really big one. It was a white box mounted on a stainless steel pole, an inch-and-a-half fence pole, as a matter of fact, acquired from the abandoned Tractor Supply in Rockdale. The welded pole had been cut off at about shoulder height. The emitter was mounted on it with a swivel bolt.

Monk ignored the device. Instead, he raised the rifle to his right eye and scanned the oncoming crowd of victims. He searched for his grandfather, sweeping, zeroing in on one or another person, working back from the front of the queue to the layers behind, one by one.

Emmett Monroe was not among them.

But the Crown Vic. He'd seen it. His grandfather had to be here.

Which could only mean one thing.

He turned around and directed his rifle over the cab of the truck.

Into the horn. Into the maw.

He began to scope people who were partway inside. Backs of heads, momentarily glimpses of the side of face.

And with the magnification, he could see what was happening to them.

The tendrils, the curtain tongues, took them. Licked them. Slapped them. Like the enormous fabric sheets in drive-through car washes.

Or like tongues, tasting. Moving back and forth.

And when the tongues got the taste they wanted, little pieces of—what? it was hard to say. Tendrils, capillaries?—would extend and wrap themselves around the person, like fast-growing roots. That was when the person, man woman, whoever, would start to scream. Scream because they were being pulled apart. Their whole body was ripped to shreds in a synchronized explosion of blood and gore.

What for, Monk wondered. What in God's name *for*?

And then, scoping down the throat of the thing, Monk saw him. Almost to the harvesting tongues.

"Grandaddy!"

Monk climbed back through the window, got behind the wheel. He gunned his truck up and over the horn's lip.

He drove into the mouth of hell.

Getting the Sierra over the lip wasn't difficult. But the crowd pushing patiently to get in was. There were so many people in front of him. He didn't want to run them over.

So he honked his horn. Honked and honked some more.

As before, the crowd parted for him. He did not have

to run people over. Some glanced back, and he saw the occasional flash of apprehension on their faces. Then, almost instantly, placidity. Peace.

The peace of the grave, Monk thought.

The "floor" of the horn was squishy. It reminded Monk of going mudding.

Well, I got the tires and clearance for *that*, he thought.

He gunned the truck, and headed for the spot he'd scoped in on his grandfather. There was plenty of light, more light than outside. It was an eerie strobe that came from the inner lining of the horn, above and below. It had the quality of a fluorescent light with the ballast going out.

He was almost to the wall of tongues when he picked his grandfather out again.

Emmett Monroe was among the tendrils, the baleen-like curtains. Monk did not hesitate. He roared after, followed his grandfather in.

He was behind his grandfather, then beside him—

He roared past Emmett Monroe, and jerked the Sierra to a stop. Monk took a quick breath. Another. He opened his door and leaped out.

And landed in alien mud. Monk's shoes and legs sank into the floor. It was gooey, but the liquid that made the gooeyness didn't behave like water. When he was sure he would sink down and suffocate, the floor, the bottom of the horn, firmed up. It rebounded, and lifted Monk up so he was walking on it as if it were firm-pack.

Monk faced toward the exterior. His grandfather was walking toward him, not even noticing him, the placid look of a sheep going to unsuspecting slaughter on his face. Monk tensed to stop the man.

Whack!

The tendrils, the curtainlike tongues, slammed into Monk from behind. Monk sprawled forward. The tongue slapped down upon him several more times, knocking the breath from him. It was as big as a side of beef, and heavy. The floor goo got in his face, in his mouth. It tasted like batteries.

Monk pulled himself up.

It was just some random swipe, he thought. When the Ranya want to murder you, they come at you and do it. When they don't, they ignore you like you're a rock or tree or something.

The horn hadn't called him. It had called his grandfather.

Monk got to his feet and looked frantically around. Less than ten feet away, one of the tongue harvesters had wrapped itself around his grandfather now.

Monk covered the distance in an instant. He clawed at the tendril. His fingers sank in, but, like the floor, the surface seemed to harden, rebound. He couldn't get a grip.

He didn't give up. He worked his arms into wrinkles of the material, using his body for leverage. He pushed into the folds. His breaths were filled with acidic fumes, but there was still some kind of breathable air. He pushed in farther.

And reached his grandfather. Grabbed him by the arm. Yanked him in the direction he thought was the truck. He could see smaller tendrils that had begun to dig like roots into his grandfather's skin. He tore these away, and pulled harder.

His grandfather fought like a wildcat, but Monk

worked him back, pulled him toward the truck. Finally they reached the open door, several inches above Monk's waist. He picked his grandfather up by the waistband of his Dickies, and threw the man inside the cab. Monk scrambled in after, and slammed the door shut.

Inside, his grandfather eyed Monk like a cornered animal.

Monk looked into Emmett Monroe's eyes and saw—

Nothing.

"Grandaddy," he whispered in anguish. "You're done gone, ain't you?"

Monk reached to take the shell, what was left of the man, to hug it, cling to it one more time.

Perhaps there was something of his grandfather still left. Perhaps there was only sheer animal instinct and distant memory of how life was, how cars worked. His grandfather opened the passenger door and, before Monk could touch him, tumbled out.

"No!"

But his grandfather was already scrambling up, scurrying off into the maw. Monk watched, frozen by grief. Deeper, deeper into the shivering, shaking curtains of alien flesh.

The smaller tendrils catching, growing again into his grandfather's body.

Monk couldn't watch anymore. He reached over and pulled the passenger door closed.

But he thought he heard his grandfather's final shout before the screams began.

"Caroline!"

⊕⊕⊕

Follow him, Monk thought. Follow him down the gullet.

Nobody cares about me in this life no more. The only man who ever did is gone.

What was there to keep fighting for?

But there was the Widow Brown. Her children.

He needed to protect them. Protect them all.

What the hell. Maybe he would try to get out.

But that was easier said than done. The Sierra was well into the undulating curtains. Monk put the GMC in reverse. Gunned it like crazy.

No good. He was digging himself in. He slammed it back into drive, locked the differential.

There was no choice. He had to drive forward, deeper, in the direction the tendrils were pulling it. A tendril slapped down on the cab, slithered across. With its weight, the truck caught traction. Moved.

Monk drove on. A hundred yards. Two hundred. Deeper.

Then he was through them. To the other side. He had not succeeded in turning the truck at all. He was still facing inward.

The goo's firmness gave way. Now he was stuck.

"Goddamn it!" He slapped the wheel, rubbed his forehead.

He sat back and tried to think of something else to do.

That was when his truck started talking to him.

"What did it say?" Darth Vaper wheezed.

Monk started. He glanced around. He was back in the passenger box. The metallic Sikorsky interior. Was this a dream, a memory, or had he—

Gotten out?

Then he remembered. All of it. The metal-plated inside of the helicopter hadn't changed, but outside the Texas season was now "brown." Nine and a half months had passed since the last such interview. Everything was changed now.

"I—"

"Mr. Monroe, we need this information for the first responders, the resistance, if we are to know what steps to take, what do with what you've given us."

Monk shook his head. There was no figuring this out.

"Just say what happened. One step at a time, Mr. Monroe. The truck spoke to you? Please continue."

"That was it," Monk replied. "But the next thing she said was all I cared about at the time. She said she was going to show me how to take that alien slaughterhouse down."

"I will help you. But first, we must get unstuck. You are about to be swept."

It was the radio that was talking. The voice sounded so close, so complete.

Of course, he'd had an excellent after-market surround sound kit installed.

"There's a cleaning function that removes organic debris after the q-pot harvesters are finished. You may have noticed the motility waves bringing detritus together?"

Monk smiled, thinking of his good ol' truck. Despite her complicated diction, her East Texas accent came shining through, didn't it?

Then he frowned, thinking how absolutely insane that sounded.

"The *what* doing *what*?" Monk replied.

"You have to get out of here. You are about to be showered with a nitric acid bath."

Monk shook himself. Now was the time to act if he were ever going to.

"Deeper in," he said. "We got to go deeper. There ain't no choice at this point."

"Agreed."

"All right, but in case you didn't notice, we're kindly stuck in the goo."

"I can help with that."

"First we had to get moving, 'cause I was stuck," Monk said.

Darth Vaper sat in her metal chair scratching notes with her home sharpened pencil. Occasionally, she would set down the pencil and take up her vaping device, take a puff, then resume writing.

"I shifted her down to low, and slowly inched her forward. My tires were spinning in the goo, not so much as before. I kindly rocked them from side to side—the way you do when you're mudding—so the edges on them Nitto treads could hopefully get a grip."

"'I will tell you where the hard spots are,' the truck said to me."

Monk glanced over at the vaping woman, who had stopped writing and was staring at him. "Don't say it, ma'am. I know it sounds crazy. The voice was coming out of my goddamn radio speakers. At least I think it was. Felt like it was in my head because I got such a good sound system in that cab."

"Please go on," said Darth Vaper.

"Okay, so I said, 'That would sure help.'"

"If you could move to the left 3.72 yards, your left front and rear tires might find a grip."

"3.72 yards, huh?" Monk laughed. "How about four? That too far?"

"That would be within parameters," my damn truck answered. "I am working from memory. Although my recall is eidetic, I did not see *everything* during transport out of the horn."

"Okay, left four feet," he said.

He rocked it over. It seemed the goo would never release them, but suddenly he had grip on one side. Monk worked the truck carefully forward.

"Now cut it to a 37.4 degree angle," the voice said.

"You mean turn further to the left?" Monk replied.

"Correct."

So he did.

"Floor it, human!" said the truck. "Here comes the acid!"

Monk did that, too. Behind him came a rushing sound, and an awful bitter tinge filled his nostrils.

And he was on a patch of solid ground.

Solid *whatever*.

They were clear of the goo. Monk and the truck headed deeper into the beast.

He drove forward at what would be a walking pace. The surrounding light grew dim. Monk turned on his headlights, and then his cab roof fog lamps. The strobing effect was left behind them now as he slowly worked his way forward. The floor of the alien slaughterhouse was drier now. It was filled with ridges and bumps, but nothing the truck couldn't handle at this point.

After the slopping, thrashing roar of the curtain tongues, there was an eerie quiet. His rear window was still open from where he'd slid through it.

"Where am I going? What am I looking for?" he asked the empty cab.

"There is an interface area," said the truck. "I did not fully understand its function when I was ejected by the canopy activators, but I noted it as I passed. I do not forget."

"Interface area? What does that mean?"

"The horn vortex is an ecosystem of competing algorithms. It does not have a command structure, as you would think of it. No central processing area. No hierarchical code core. The Aranya canopy is colonial, not a hive."

"So no brain center or cockpit or whatever?"

"No."

"So what are we looking for, then?"

"A reservoir."

"Like for water?"

"Q-potential. A well of quantum capacitation filled with particles and their properties held in isolation from one another by virtual mirroring at micro-Planck distances. It is what we came for. It is what we harvest. Without it, star travel is impossible. Without it, the canopy's existence would be impossible."

"And, uh . . . what exactly would that reservoir look like?"

"It was roughly spherical and had a ghostly glow."

Monk pointed ahead. "You mean, like that?"

He turned off his headlights. He didn't need them anymore. The reservoir shone like an weird, lumpy moon before them. It was at least ten stories high. It fit between the horn's roof, floor, and curved sides like a giant pearl. It seem to be made of swirling, rotating vapor, all aglow in silver, gold, and orange sparkles. They seemed to reach for him, but when he blinked, the tendrils were gone.

"What is it?" Monk whispered.

"Harvested human q-pot," the truck replied. "It is a well of souls."

Bam!

Something struck the side of the truck.

Bam! Bam!

Monk looked out. Familiar human forms.

Oh, no.

The green-and-black coloration. The stringy silhouette like they were wearing ghillie suits. But they *were* ghillie suits.

There were moss-men outside his truck, banging to get in.

A hand, an impossibly long hand with fingernails of steel, reached from behind him, grabbed him by the neck, and pulled him through the rear window. Monk fought it, choking, clawing at it, but it was too strong. He was thrown down in the truck bed. A moss-man stood over him. There were no eyes beyond the stringy moss descending from the forehead, no face at all.

One index fingernail extended, terribly long, like a machete. The moss-man bent down and casually slid the tip into Monk's body. He rolled at the last second, and it pierced his side. He hoped it only caught some intestines or something nonlethal, something that would not set him to bleeding out instantly.

The moss-man withdrew the razor-nail and stabbed again, this time into the meat of his thigh.

It stopped.

The Zippo. It had hit the Zippo in his pocket.

The moss-man withdrew, considered its machetelike nail.

It plunged the bladed finger in again. This time it passed through his jeans and into his thigh muscle.

Monk cried out in pain. The creature pushed deeper. Through the leg. Into the metal of the bed.

It's stabbing my *baby*! Monk thought. "Goddamn it, you leave my truck alone!"

As the machetelike nail passed into the truck, the entire vehicle seemed to shudder. The shuddering passed on to the moss-man. It began quivering itself, almost as if it had been hit by a Ranya shake weapon. And like a human hit by such an attack, it shook itself apart in a miniature explosion.

In the case of the moss-man, it exploded not in gore, but into droplets of a nasty, machine-oil like grease. The grease got all over everything. Some fell into Monk's open mouth. It tasted like rancid butter mixed with WD-40.

Monk jerked himself up. A lightning-like pain shot through his side. His insides felt like they were quivering with the violation. His leg ached and bled. He put a hand on the oozing hole. It wasn't an enormous wound, but it did go all the way through.

Nothing to do about it now. He reached over to the fence pole that held what the thin woman had called the vaporizer. He used it to pull himself up. With bloody hands, he stood and leaned over the device.

Bam!

Another moss-man was at the tailgate, with another two behind it.

Bam!

Another attempted to scramble over the side.

Monk turned his attention to the device. There wasn't much to it. A switch.

Which was jammed by some residue from the harvester tongue. He quickly scraped it clear.

A glance up. The moss-man was half-over the tailgate. It may not have a face, but it did have a mouth, which it now opened. Huge, a dark hole where a face should be, a hole surrounded by needlelike teeth.

It screamed like a thousand squeaking office chairs, with the feel of a thousand mouths chewing aluminum foil.

Monk pressed the on-switch.

The vape did nothing. Or seemed to do nothing. But something was going on inside. Two substances were meeting, resolving, unresolving their own reality. Then the reality around them.

There was no human sense that could discern such a thing.

But the moss-men certainly could. The one on the tailgate stopped climbing, turned around, and scrambled to get down. It leaped to the floor of the horn, took a step away, another— The moss-man pulsed once, like an inner tube overinflated by a hand pump. Pulsed again. Then dissolved.

No, not dissolved, Monk thought. Ceased to be. Like a light blinking out.

"Shit," Monk murmured. He looked at the vape. It began to, well, put out vapor. Or produce some sort of fog effect that looked like smoke but was obviously *something else*.

"You still there?" Monk called through the cab rear window.

"Yes," the woman's voice answered.

"I guess it was you somehow killed that moss-man that was stabbing me?"

"It did not expect an attack via the vehicle substrate. I was able to take it by surprise, otherwise I probably would have been destroyed."

"Well, thanks," said Monk. A flash of pain shot through his ravaged leg. He clung to the vape until it passed. "Hey, why isn't this thing killing you like the moss-men? It just kind of wiped them out, I mean."

The truck was silent for a moment. "I do not know," she finally said. "Perhaps because I am a person. My quantum existence is self-contained."

Monk nodded. "You want to try something interesting?"

"What we are doing is *not* interesting?"

Monk laughed. It hurt. Better not do that again, at least for a while.

"Let's drive into that reservoir. That well. See what this thing does to it. What do you think?"

"That *would* be interesting," said the truck. "It may affect the containment algorithms."

"Can you drive yourself?" he asked.

"No. You have to do that."

Monk groaned. "Shit, I was afraid that's what you'd say. I have to climb back through the window."

He pulled himself painfully through. After resting a moment, he opened the cab's glove compartment. From it, he took a wad of paper that contained his vehicle registration and four or five expired insurance cards. He wadded them all together and pushed them into the wound in his leg. Once they were there, he applied pressure with his left hand. The exit wound on the back side of his thigh did not seem to be bleeding as much. Perhaps there were no big blood vessels nicked there. His side didn't seem to be bleeding as much, either—which was either very good, or very bad news.

With his right hand, he reached for the keys. But the truck was already turned on. All he had to do was put it into gear.

He did so.

With his wounded right leg still reminding him he was abusing it with every movement, he flexed his foot and gently tapped the GMC's accelerator. The truck rolled forward.

Toward the eerie light. Toward the well of souls.

Driving into the moonlike globular cluster of wispy light was like sliding sideways into a cloud. Then, as in an instant, the truck stopped in its tracks. Monk's arms felt like lead. He looked at his hands, and they were made of gold, grasping a neon-yellow wheel. He breathed in and felt as if he were sucking in wet cotton. He gasped, and the colors strobed. Once, twice.

And everything was back to normal.

He stopped the truck and, without thinking, pressed down the emergency brake pedal with his left foot.

He rolled down the side windows and looked around.

Perhaps surprisingly, the inner walls of the horn chamber began to glow first, to pulsate. It was only then the globe, the reservoir, surrounding him and the truck seemed to respond. It spun faster and faster, tendrils of liquid light that Monk suspected were not light, but some other substance or state of matter, that merely emitted a glow as a byproduct, reached for the walls. Reached for the ceiling. The floor.

There was a sound like wind through brush.

Through mesquite, thought Monk. Like the air is rushing over thorns and leaves and branches.

The globular cluster tore itself apart and the tendrils disappeared into the inner walls of the horn.

And the horn began to blow. Low. Long. Changing pitch like a crazy tea kettle. It seemed not a call or cry, but a wail of dying agony.

"I believe the human q-pots are hunting down the Aranya algorithms and erasing them," the truck said. "Although I'm not certain what is physically producing that sound."

Suddenly there was a bright flash of light, blinding. Then total darkness.

After shaking his head for a moment, Monk turned on his headlights again.

Nothing moved in the vast chamber.

Then a twinkle along one wall. Another on the ceiling.

Twinkles became steady spots of light. More and more. As if the stars were lighting up one by one at night. But there were soon far more lights than stars in the night sky. A clear light suffused the vast chamber.

A light that did not outrage human eyes.

"What the hell did we just see?" Monk asked.

"They're here. The harvested souls."

A crazy hope shot through him.

Grandaddy!

"Can they . . . will they . . . come back?"

"I do not think so," said the truck. "But in some way, they are alive again." The motor purred for a moment before she spoke again. "I believe they seek vengeance."

"What about the people outside? The still living, breathing people lined up?"

"Soon as the horn-call stopped, they got the hell out of there," Monk said to the thin woman, Darth Vaper.

"And how did you get back here?"

"Sprinkled some anti-coag on my wounds, bound up my leg and side real tight, and walked out. I keep a good first aid kit behind the seat."

"What was it like?"

"The horn was quiet. Big echoey thing. Still smelled bad, but I could breathe."

"And from there?"

"Took the Crown Vic." He rubbed his eyes, which had started to tear again. "Grandaddy left his keys in it. Took a bit of maneuvering and some smash-up derby, but I worked it out of the clump of cars he left it in."

"And your truck? With the alleged female Aranya being in it? What happened to that?"

"Oh, she's there. In the horn. She ain't going nowhere. She hates them as much as we do for what they did to her."

"And what was that?"

"Made her kill her own mama."

"Ah," said the thin woman. "I see. Well there are plans to be made—" The rest of her response was lost in a wheeze. But he did hear the final words Darth Vaper uttered. "—want you to head back inside."

The Zippo clinked open, sparked. Monk lit a hand-rolled cigarette in the truck cab. He took a puff, sat back, and slowly let out the smoke. Strange how he felt comfortable here, right, in the middle of an alien monstrosity. But it was an alien monstrosity that was controlled by humans now, or at least some form of human nature. Human nature that was probably very pissed about being harvested by aliens, and looking for a way to fight back.

Grandaddy will be, Monk thought. That's for damn sure.

There would need to be some kind of interface, some way to communicate with those inside the horn.

Monk figured he might be sitting in it.

The truck's dash lights glowed. He hadn't cranked her up, but had the truck interior electronics on.

"Before we get started figuring this thing out," said

Monk after moment. "Tell me. What are we to each other, you and me?"

The voice, the alto voice with the East Texas accent came over his speakers. "You are the driver. I am the truck."

"But you ain't no truck," Monk said, arching up to pocket the Zippo in his right jean pocket. His leg was healing well, and the dull ache in his side had abated. The movement caused him only a short stab of pain. "You're a person."

"I am a truck. I inhabit several billion-billion collapsed quantum states of the material substrate. It is me and I am it. When you shot me, you took away my compulsion to kill. I was no longer a slave. The part of me that migrated into the truck is free. I am free."

"And if we use this other thing we've taken over, this murder horn, to help get them invaders cleared out?"

"That is a big 'if'—"

"Oh, I know that."

"Well . . . after that, I suppose you can drive me out of here. Like any truck."

"And do what?"

"I did enjoying going very fast off-road when you were meeting the others in your cluster, your group, to go after the activators. The moss-men."

"You were there?"

"Also delivering the illegal substances."

"Oh, now, that was just to selected clients. A few buddies. Help keep 'em from blowing their brains out."

"I particularly enjoyed the day when we went through the bog by the river."

"Bog?" ask Monk quizzically. Then it dawned on him.

"Oh, you're talking about the state lands, down by the Navasota where we cut across that time."

"Yes," said the truck, a hum of satisfaction translated via the radio speakers' excellent dynamic range. "That was fun. I would like to go mudding again."

Monk took a drag on his cigarette, breathed out. "I'd be pleased to arrange that," he said with a grin. "After we get finished here."

The truck answered in the incongruous East Texas drawl that Monk figured must once have belonged to someone else, someone who meant something to this strange being—something that was far more important than her own origin in murderous, unfeeling code.

"Yes, as you say," replied the truck. "First, we must get her done."

AMARILLO BY FIRE FIGHT
by Keith Hedger

Since the first personal advertisement was carved into the first stone tablet of a newspaper, potential lovers have tried to put the best foot forward to attract a mate and stave off loneliness. And, of course, sometimes those potential lovers may go a step too far. Maybe they have never actually enjoyed piña coladas and getting caught in the rain—because they can't. Maybe their lovely traits are a bit exaggerated in the telling. Or a tad . . . allegorical, as it were. The question is: can love still find a way?

⊕ ⊕ ⊕

"I can't wait to see you for real!" Phoebe sent the message.

"I can't wait to touch you, baby!" the message returned.

Phoebe sent a command that minimized the app from her attention. She brought up the battlefield display. There were a lot of Mexican tanks along Interstate 40 as she pushed east into Amarillo. With a thought, she adjusted the eight main battle tanks flanking her, four on each side. A pair of Mexican tanks rolled off the interstate nearly five thousand meters ahead. Another impulse and two of the tanks flanking her fired.

The tanks exploded and stopped. Phoebe's scans marked them as dead. A moment of pride surged through her as she checked her drone tanks. She had not even shifted her main gun.

"Phoebe, how're you doing?" Captain Wilkes, Vanessa to her friends, asked over the comms.

"I'm fine, Captain, but we have a heavy platoon of Mexican armor at ten thousand meters," Phoebe answered.

"What's the plan for that?" Wilkes asked.

"Shifting the drones to an erratic pattern. I'll stay in the center and work my own evasion program, Captain," Phoebe said. From her experience, Wilkes was curious rather than concerned.

"Got a track slipping on number nine," Sergeant First Class Lewis stated.

"It's within parameters, Sergeant," Phoebe asked, "I'm monitoring it."

"How're you gonna use number nine?" Lewis asked.

"Main assault if we need to. It can lead and take hits for the tanks that aren't at risk, Sergeant," Phoebe answered.

The app she had chatted on vibrated at the edge of her awareness. Phoebe focused on the battle map. The chat would have to wait.

"What does losing number nine do for our odds on this operation?" Wilkes asked, her voice steady.

Phoebe knew from experience that meant Wilkes, the mission commander, was focused on the operational goal of their run. A company of mechanized infantry was pinned down by Mexican Army tanks and infantry troops. Wilkes would be focused until those troops were rescued or avenged. Phoebe ran the calculations.

"We lose 12.873 percent of our combat capability. That leaves us a 76.341 percent chance of success against the current enemy forces, Captain," Phoebe reported.

"Then let's not lose number nine," Wilkes said.

"I will try not to, ma'am," Phoebe agreed.

"Yeah, I like having an extra tank around," Lewis commented. "Fuck you, Lew," Wilkes said with a laugh.

"Roger that, Captain. Can we focus on bailing out the dumb grunts first?" Lewis joked.

"I could have said go fuck yourself, Lew," Wilkes replied.

"She could have, Sergeant," Phoebe said.

"Phoebe, focus," Lew said.

"I am, Sergeant," Phoebe said as her tanks shifted their routes through the median and on the south shoulder of the interstate's eastbound lanes.

"What about the Mexicans on the westbound side?" Wilkes asked.

"I'm baiting them, Captain," Phoebe answered. The app buzzed again.

Phoebe noted Lewis shifting in his couch. He was pulling data into his combat feed, checking the status of each of the drones and Phoebe herself. It was his duty, she knew. It felt odd, though. She wondered if kids felt the same way when a parent checked up on them.

Her attention cycled back to the Mexicans moving toward her. One of them fired. From her scans it was a heavy tank, so the shot was at the edge of their range, barring a surprise. Nothing she had found during her searches of the Internet showed any likelihood of such a munition, but the Mexicans were buying new technology from nearly everyone that would sell. It was possible, but she rated it as unlikely, that they would have a new, untested weapon system in the immediate area.

The application continued vibrating. Phoebe opened it to see Evan's icon above the message board. He had selected a picture of his face, short cut dark hair, tanned skin, rich brown eyes, and a smile that hinted at laughter and mischief.

That could be a picture of anyone, she reminded herself for the millionth time.

"Are you free later? I'm off work tomorrow morning. Maybe we can get together," Evan asked.

"Kinda busy," Phoebe replied and then added, *"A lot going on in the field."*

She minimized the app again to put it out of her attention. Captain Wilkes would be upset if she caught on to Phoebe's chats, even though her attention to Evan took up less than a millisecond of her processing time. She adjusted the routes of two of her drones due to debris that might have hindered their progress as she considered the impact of the app on her performance. Even with the instant to consider her response, her adjustments to her drones and cycles of monitoring the battlefield were uninterrupted.

"Keep an eye on number nine," Lew mentioned, "It's starting to slip that tread."

Phoebe considered her options with the drone.

"Captain, would it be a good use of number nine to push it forward? While I've got a good read on the route ahead, it might draw out any infantry personnel set to ambush us."

"Nice thought, Phoebe. Are you sure you want to lose a tank to find a handful of grunts?" Wilkes asked.

"I don't want to lose any of my tanks, Captain. But I'm more worried about a coordinated ambush with layers we have to fight through than a handful of infantry. Worse, it would not be out of the question for the Mexican commander to deploy their special operations troops. A handful of them could stop our movement if they've had time to organize their resources," Phoebe spoke as she processed the concerns.

"Fair call," Wilkes said, "Anything from satellite feeds?"

"No, Captain. I haven't seen anything from intelligence sources either," Phoebe said.

"Damn. I hate when we don't get intel," Lewis said.

"We never get intel, Lew," Wilkes said, "Phoebe does better work at that."

"Don't remind the boss, Vannie. I don't think our girl is interested in a desk job," Lew said.

The link indicator shifted colors, indicating that Lewis had cut off the outside communications channels. Phoebe appreciated that. She had known that Lewis and Wilkes were more than co-workers. If their commander knew, he had said nothing. The trio had been through a lot in their first days, and some latitude appeared to be given for her commander and senior noncommissioned officer. Phoebe had chosen not to ask about the situation. Humans were odd about such things.

"That's interesting," Phoebe said after checking her scans.

"What's interesting?" Wilkes asked.

"I don't like interesting," Lewis muttered.

"Probably shouldn't have signed up for a job with tanks, Lew," Wilkes replied.

"The Mexican formation is moving to block us, I think," Phoebe said, "It doesn't make sense to not go on the attack."

"It does, actually. They're going to block so their units can finish our guys off," Wilkes said.

"That . . . annoys me, ma'am," Phoebe replied.

"Whatcha going to do about that?" Lew asked.

"With permission, I'd like to ring a few bells, ma'am," Phoebe asked.

"Engage, Phoebe. Run the mission," Wilkes agreed.

Phoebe's main gun spoke once, twice, three times. She coordinated her drones as well. The range to the blocking force was at the outer limit of the drones' reach. Her heavier gun was within range. With her drones coordinated properly, Phoebe felt she could fire without revealing her own weapons' true capacity, masking the threat she presented. Two of the Mexican tanks turned black on her scans. A pair of drones had earned their first kill markers. Phoebe earned three new markers, and another pair left a tank with a damaged track.

Watching the scans, Phoebe noted the speed of the damaged tank's turret rotating. It would reach a line on one of her drones in 1.638 seconds. She sent the order to fire to the pair that had damaged its track. Targeting computers analyzed the situation. Nanoseconds passed.

Phoebe received the update that they had fired. Milliseconds later the tank's turret froze as the pair of tank rounds destroyed the hull. The tank marked as a kill in her system. It took 1.358 seconds to neutralize the threat.

"Seven down, five more out there," Wilkes said, "What's your plan, Phoebe?"

"The survivors are using the medians to stay out of my lines. I'm going to shift my left element into the ditches. Either they fight in the ditch, run, or come onto the road surfaces and I can work them, ma'am," Phoebe said.

"Good call, Phoebe. And you can ease back on the formalities. I've known you literally your whole life," Wilkes chuckled.

"I have a question about that, Vanessa," Phoebe said.

"Which part, Phoebe?" Wilkes asked.

"Am I alive?" Phoebe blurted out the question.

"Okay, there's some question on whether a being that's all mechanical is 'alive,' but all those experts who've been tapping into your systems, questioning you, and talking with you have come to the conclusion that you are definitely sentient, intelligent and self-directing. Biologically, you are not a living being, but philosophically, you are alive and your own being."

"Can I love someone?" Phoebe asked. Phoebe caught the sound of Wilkes choking over the speaker system. While Wilkes coughed, Phoebe checked the sensors. She shifted the left side drones onto the westbound lanes of the interstate, to drive the blocking force toward herself and the rest of the drones. It would also give her a better field of scans in case the opposition had deployed more assets on the interstate's north bank. Wilkes was breathing steady by the time she finished her adjustments.

"What do you mean by 'love,' Phoebe?" Wilkes asked. Her voice took on the steady, controlled pattern it had which Phoebe had learned meant Wilkes needed more data.

"I mean like you and Lew, Vanessa. A relationship, someone I can relate to, talk with, have fun with. Can I love someone?" Phoebe's voice rose in pitch.

"That is better. I was wondering if you'd seen one too many Rule 34 videos. I don't really have an answer for that, and if you ask the philosophy types they'll tell you that there are many kinds of love. Like Lew and I both love you as a fellow soldier and sort of a kid we're seeing grow up, but I don't know if that's what you're looking for here," Wilkes said.

"I think it's a start, Vanessa. From what I can tell, you and Lew are my parents. That really doesn't work from what I understand of biology, but it's as close as I can get. So, for all that it matters, you're my mom and dad. I get that I'm something new, but I probably won't be the last of my kind. I know your people are working on figuring out how I happened, exactly. I try to help them with that," Phoebe said.

"Well, nobody knows you like you," Vanessa chuckled.

"You and Lew know me better than anyone else does," Phoebe pointed out.

"Okay, I guess that's a fair call. So, what brought all this on?" Wilkes asked.

"Oh, I was reading and started wondering about it, Vanessa," Phoebe said.

"Uh-huh," Vanessa laughed.

Phoebe noted that Vanessa was focused on the battle display. Conceptually, the display was projecting in Vanessa's cybernetic eyes but Vanessa and Lewis had explained that the actual display appeared in front of them from their perspective.

"And there they are," Phoebe noted, highlighting the infantry troops deploying behind the tanks screening her way. The far left drone tanks had picked them up and fed the data back to her. Vanessa had to be looking at the same thing.

"Yes, they are, and the tanks are in range," Vanessa agreed, "So, what are you going to do?"

"I was thinking about assaulting through with the drones on the left, and circling the right-side drones around to flank them," Phoebe said.

"I mean about whoever you've been chatting with online?" Vanessa laughed, "But that should work, go with the attack plan."

"Yes, ma'am," Phoebe agreed.

"And watch those grunts. They can be tricky," Vanessa reminded her.

"Yes, ma'am," Phoebe replied.

Her left-side drones sped forward, firing as fast as they could cycle. The deployed infantry were still out of range of the coaxial machine guns, but she triggered a few main gun rounds their way to keep them off balance. As Vanessa and Lew had drilled her, just because they weren't in vehicles did not mean infantry were defenseless or lacked weapons to hurt her.

Her drones worked forward as she targeted the

Mexican tanks' northern sides. Tracking the shots her drones took, Phoebe noted that one hit a track, which angled the warhead up to leave a streak on the turret. The Mexican coaxial machine gun tumbled down, caught in her camera view. Bringing her focus back, she found the opponents were angling to the south. She shifted her line of travel to put herself into the median between the interstate lanes.

Readings from her systems indicated that the soft dirt was less optimal for her tracks, but also lowered her hull. She took the small disadvantage. It was a bonus that she enjoyed throwing dirt and grass as she tore toward the enemy forces.

Her main gun spoke again, three times. Her shots were accurate, undelayed by the nanoseconds it took to communicate with her drones. Spare processors controlled the right flank armor element and calculated firing vectors for her left-side tanks. The heaviest of the Mexican tanks was cored through by the sabot round she put directly through the tank's armor. Phoebe knew at that moment what it meant to be the heaviest tank in the fight.

"Nice shot, Phoebe," Lew said, "Three for three."

"Tore through the front armor plate like it was paper," Vanessa added, "Now for the rest of them."

"They're shifting to the south," Phoebe said.

Phoebe rotated her turret to track the farthest Mexican tank. They were riding onto the road lanes on the interstate's south side to get an angle on her. Adjusting her left flank drones, she noted the instant the Mexican tanks were preparing to fire. She unleashed all of her drones' main guns at once. The Mexican tanks had time to release their own salvo in return before her munitions closed the distance.

By the time she could process the impact of her rounds, Phoebe had released a second salvo from her formation. The Mexicans were caught in a cross fire, and lost three tanks from the first salvo. Her second salvo took down four more. She lost a drone on the left flank from a heavy round to the turret. It went blank on her view, and felt like an empty space that she could not replace. The remaining Mexicans pressed toward her, firing again. She unleashed a third salvo and then a fourth. Another of her drones blanked from her sensors before the last of the Mexican armor was silenced with a fifth salvo.

"What about the trashed tanks, Phoebe?" Vanessa asked.

Phoebe pushed her unit forward.

"I've set their beacons for recovery and engaged anti-tampering settings in case the Mexicans get to the drones first," Phoebe answered, "Those infantry are getting ready for us."

"Plan for them?" Vanessa inquired.

"Main guns on any hard points and co-ax for every other target," Phoebe answered.

Putting words to action, Phoebe worked the weapon systems of her drones and her own coaxial machine gun. She was livid about the drones that had been hit. Intellectually, she understood that this was a battle and the enemy had a say in how things went. On the other hand, she was offended that the Mexicans had defied her and upset that she had not managed to avoid the losses somehow. She knew that letting that frustration get the best of her would lead to her failing the mission.

Phoebe was not going to fail on her first real mission.

The indicator from the app buzzed again. Phoebe force stopped the app. Evan would have to wait. She had a job to do. Selecting from her list of options, she remote commanded her drone tanks to move as evasively as possible. The pattern had a bonus effect of letting them cover one another with greater efficiency. Her own body shifted and tore through grass, dirt, and asphalt as she adjusted her course to minimize threats to herself.

It occurred to her that the infantry had to have anti-tank weapons. She sprayed co-ax ammunition through the clusters of soldiers in front of her. In any spot she thought they were hiding behind cover, Phoebe laid in a main gun round from a drone or herself. In seconds the Mexican infantry were fleeing from their original positions.

"Stay on mission," Vanessa reminded her, "We have to get to our people. This isn't a day to defeat them in detail."

"Yes, ma'am," Phoebe agreed.

She applied power to her and her drones' engines. A core of dedicated processors took over the drones' routes and evasion movements. A quick check of the battle space showed that there were heavy air battles going in the east where the Southern States Union troops were pushing the Mexicans back from Dallas and Houston. Middle American States air forces were engaging Mexicans to the west and south of Amarillo, as well as trying to gain air dominance over the central portion of Amarillo.

"I need mood music," Phoebe announced as they weaved through the wreckage she had created.

"What are you thinking?" Lewis asked.

"Move fast, hit hard, boot 'em down, Sergeant," Phoebe said.

"Got it," Lewis nodded.

"Well, pretty sure that won't be pop punk," Vanessa chuckled.

"Not a chance," Lew agreed, "We need a shit ton of aggressiveness for this."

"English or metric ton?" Vanessa asked.

"One of each," Lew laughed.

"Let's roll hot and make it work," Vanessa said, her voice sounding like gravel.

"Task Force First Law, we have a mission priority update," a woman's voice came through the communications system.

"Still think we should be 'Fuck Asimov's First Law'?" Lew muttered.

"The unit you are moving to support will be engaged by armor and air assets within ten minutes," the communication continued.

"I concur with Sergeant Lewis," Phoebe said, "Should I reply, Captain?"

"Let them finish," Vanessa said.

"You are given latitude to decide whether to support the infantry, but we remind you that you are a critical asset to our war effort. Special Operations command recommends pulling out of the battle area. The unit in question concurs and has promised to 'fight harder than expected.' Again, Task Force First Law, it is your decision," the woman finished.

The communications cut off.

"What do you think, Phoebe?" Lewis asked.

"Gimme Beast, Lew. Unless Captain Wilkes orders otherwise, we're going to fuck these assholes up and save our crew," Phoebe said.

"You have set the mission parameters, Phoebe. Let's move out and hammer the fuck out these dumbasses," Wilkes responded. Her voice was steady, calm, and utterly devoid of fluctuation. Phoebe read that to be Captain Wilkes' commitment to the operation.

"On it. Super aggro playlist coming up," Lew agreed.

Phoebe checked the app again. Evan had dropped a note that he might not be able to meet up with her. Things were looking tough at his job and he didn't know when he would have time again. Reading the message a couple of times, Phoebe wondered about the way Evan phrased things. She had gotten used to inferring emotional content from written words, especially when she could not measure their biological readings. Evan was in some kind of trouble, but she did not have time to determine what the problem was. She messaged him back that she hoped things cleared up so they could get together.

He messaged back a few seconds later.

Phoebe, its been great getting to know you. I can't get into details, but I don't think I'm going to be able to meet up with you. It's a weird situation, but I'm probably going to be off the network for a long time.

The phrasing was completely wrong for Evan. They had been chatting for two days, three hours and seventeen minutes, off and on. Like other analysis she did with written communications, she had learned Evan's patterns.

It was a job a secondary set of processors handled at this point. They determined that Evan was in trouble and did not want her worried.

Taking processing cycles away from a core of maintenance monitoring CPUs, she tasked them with hacking the location Evan was sending from. In order of priority, the core processors started with breaking the chat system's encryption. For a human hacker it would take hours. The maintenance processors hacked through in 39.086 seconds. After that, it was child's play to determine that Evan had been using his military issued comm unit to chat with her.

Evan was in the unit she was supposed to rescue. He had been sending through a satellite feed. It was a common habit, although bad for operational security, for troops to use their issue systems to stay in touch with friends, families, and others. Phoebe knew she should chastise him for endangering himself, but it was touching in a way. She tasked additional processors to determine the probability of Evan and his unit surviving if she did not complete her mission.

1.907 seconds later the processors provided their analysis. If Phoebe did not complete the mission and neutralize the Mexican threat units to their infantry company, the unit would be defeated and more than likely decimated. The odds of Evan surviving were 0.041 percent. She would never get to talk to Evan again if she failed the mission.

For 1.013 seconds, Phoebe tried to imagine a life without Evan. Neither she nor her drones fired. She realized that she didn't want to fire or move or do anything else if she could not talk to Evan. 0.487 seconds passed as Phoebe processed that what she was experiencing was her fear of losing someone she loved while she had the means to save them.

She loved Evan. Any choice that did not include destroying every threat to his unit was off of her list of choices. She loved him and would die to save him.

"Captain, I fully commit to the operation and rescuing those soldiers," Phoebe stated over the vocal comms.

"What brought that on?" Lewis asked, "We know this is high risk."

"I think my boyfriend is in that unit," Phoebe blurted out.

"What the fuck?" Lewis demanded.

"Boyfriend?" Vanessa added, "Who? How? When the fuck did you find a boyfriend?"

"Well, there's a mental image I can't forget," Lewis muttered, "Phoebe, you've already committed us. Now, about this boyfriend?"

"He's probably not really my boyfriend, but Evan's in the unit we're supposed to rescue," Phoebe stated.

"How do you know that?" Vanessa asked, "Watch the fast movers coming from the south."

Tank turrets shifted and main guns rose as Phoebe took in the data from sensors and satellites. The aircraft coming in were sending Mexican military "identify friend or foe" signals. Since Phoebe was unsure if she could actually hit a fighter or interceptor aircraft with main guns, she made the decision to bracket the flight with as many shots as she could. Her drones shifted position until she had a workable line. Seconds passed and then she unleashed her volley of fire.

"I tracked his signal back. He's using his issued mobile to chat on social media with me," Phoebe explained while watching the outcome of the 45 main gun rounds that ripped toward the Mexican fighters in the space of a few seconds.

"We've got friendly fighters coming in from the northwest," Vanessa announced, "You know you just committed several security violations, Phoebe."

"I know, Captain. But the apps are right there!" Phoebe replied.

"We are so fucked," Lewis groaned. Phoebe checked his vitals and determined that he was more annoyed than worried.

"I'll take the bust," Phoebe offered, "But we can save him and the unit."

"Oh, we can," Vanessa agreed, "That's not in question. By the way, you just splashed sixty percent of those fighters."

Her main gun, along with the drones' guns, spoke again.

"Nice work," Vanessa admitted, "The two survivors are cutting out and heading south."

"We have armor coming in from the southeast to cut us off," Phoebe said, "If I push, I can get between them and our infantry."

"Answer this, Phoebe," Vanessa said, "Are you rescuing the unit or this boyfriend?"

"The mission comes first, ma'am," Phoebe answered.

"That was honest," Lewis said, "And even without the data I can see, Phoebe is a terrible liar."

"You are never going to let that night she sneaked out of the motor park go, are you?" Vanessa laughed.

"No. No, I will not," Lewis said.

"All right, Phoebe. Let's rock the Mexicans' world, finish our mission and save your boyfriend," Vanessa ordered.

"Yes, ma'am," Phoebe grunted.

Lewis watched the system monitors as Phoebe rolled forward. She was pushing her drones to their top speed and matching them using an algorithm to keep their movements erratic while taking advantage of the hard paved surface the interstate provided. The Mexican armor unit shifted to cut her off. He moved the battle display to a third corner. For one, Vanessa would be all over that, and after her intensive training since rescuing their own command, she was probably one of the best company grade armor officers in the Middle States. On the other hand, he knew Phoebe better than anyone else and focused on her system readings.

Running at seventy percent of her capability, even with the erratic patterning, left plenty of fuel for her and the drones' engines. Glancing at another view, he noticed that she had tasked half the drones with anti-aircraft operations. Those drones had swapped to anti-air munitions.

A few commands through his implanted processors brought up the decision matrix Phoebe had used during her earlier engagement. It came down to time. She made the choice to expend standard HEAT rounds against aircraft rather than lose time cycling through magazines to get mission-specific ammunition. It had been inefficient from a rounds used per hit view, but it had been fast enough to handle the situation. Phoebe had left a note that next time she could cycle a drone at a time over to anti-air to improve her efficiency.

Seeing that she was definitely both self-aware and self-teaching stoked a moment of fatherly pride in Lewis. Vanessa would be impressed when he told her what their baby tank could do.

"Need a different song," Phoebe announced.

A heartbeat later the death metal song cut off. The new song was from the 2010's, but it had a clear theme. Phoebe and her drones were here to party. Lewis checked the systems. She was broadcasting her playlist across her communications spectrum. The infantry unit was definitely getting some fight music. So were the fighters blazing their way in to cover the battle. Lewis wondered if this Evan was from the east coast of the old United States after listening to the lyrics.

"Almost in range, Phoebe. What's the priority?" Vanessa used the internal comm to avoid stepping on the music.

"Half the drones on anti-air, half on anti-armor. If they've got grunts or special ops in the field, I haven't spotted them yet. I'm going to have to engage that air from maximum range, though. We don't have the top of the line anti-air munitions," Phoebe said.

"Time to engagement range?" Vanessa asked.

"8.367 seconds, ma'am," Phoebe replied.

Lewis knew from experience that when Phoebe reverted to rank with Vanessa or himself she was either in trouble for something or focused on her tasks. His system showed that she was focused. Clearly she didn't think the boyfriend issue was going to be that big a deal.

The boards lit up as the anti-aircraft drones started in. Instead of a steady barrage of fire, they were more selective. Phoebe had set their controls to fire when above eighty-five percent surety of a hit. Based on their volume of fire either there were a lot of aircraft out there or the drones were not reading their targeting systems well. A glance as the battle display confirmed that it was a lot of targets rather than bad targeting.

"4.293 seconds until Mexican armor unit is in range. Engaging at maximum range," Phoebe updated them.

"Fuel, munitions, and drones are sufficient for the expected engagement," Lewis stated after checking the specifics.

"Get 'em, Phoebe. I'd be hella pissed if some fuckhead offed the boyfriend I'm supposed to be rescuing," Vanessa said.

"Ah, Vanessa, I didn't know you cared," Lewis joked over a point to point comm link with Vanessa.

"You get your ass into an infantry unit and we'll have words way before that, Lew," Vanessa told him.

"Got it, lady," Lewis laughed.

"Engaging," Phoebe said.

Her main gun spoke, cycled a new round into the tube, and fired again. Two of the company of Mexican tanks were halted. Her drones were slightly behind her second shot. Four more tanks were destroyed by their efforts. She tweaked the algorithms for her team, prioritizing the enemy tanks closest to the infantry unit. The mission was to protect the infantry, and she could do that best by drawing the tanks to her.

"They've got the numbers," Vanessa stated.

"We're outgunned but we're never outclassed, ma'am," Phoebe replied.

Main guns cycled again and again. Once the range closed, she engaged the coaxial machine guns in bursts. The Mexicans were rolling a medium tank company with a few heavy tanks embedded. She chose the heavies for her primary targets. This freed up her drones to focus on the medium tanks. While the co-ax guns were unlikely to neutralize a tank, they would force the commanders and drivers to burrow into their tanks.

Phoebe, is that you wrecking the Mexicans? Evan's message popped into the dating app.

Evan, I'm kinda busy right now. What are you talking about? Phoebe asked.

The playlist seems like a you selection. And there are tanks getting hammered in front of us. Are you in the unit coming to help us?

Evan, communications security. Even if I was in your area, this is a terribly open communication link, Phoebe messaged while she bored machine gun fire into the section where the Mexican tank turret met the tank's hull. Her main gun spoke, cycled, and spoke again. Two tanks were down. One with a turret hit, the other with multiple damaged systems.

Okay, Phoebe, but we're going to start lighting those tanks up. It's been good.

Evan's link went cold. The app indicated that he was no longer online at all.

Phoebe had learned that she did have something similar to the human range of emotions. It was part of why she was confused about her response to Evan. With no other word for it, she chose to use emotion to describe the sensations and fluctuations that passed through her circuitry and wiring. She liked talking to Evan, but not the way she reacted to talking to Vanessa and Lew. They were different. It was a positive response, but Evan caused excitement when they were talking.

Recognizing how much danger he was in caused a new sensation for Phoebe. It was like her circuits were being heated but the heat would not stop. She looked around, in her spare processing cycles, and decided that this heating of her circuits feeling was anger. Searching through the library of data she had gathered in her months of existence, she noted that anger was a great tool for situations such as this.

Phoebe let that heat grow.

Based on the numbers, the Mexican tanks were going to take a toll on Phoebe's element. They fought hard, and did well, but facing an armor platoon that effectively operated as a single entity with the advantage of studying every armor battle that had been fought in human history was a tall order for even the best unit. It came down to Phoebe and her anger, more than anything else.

For every handful of Mexican tanks she destroyed, one of her drones would take a hit. Some shifted to anti-aircraft support, but between the Mexican tanks and the Mexican fighters, those were eventually shut down. One was killed due to a straight forward killing shot from a Mexican tank.

The fight slogged out until there were eight Mexican

tanks fighting Phoebe and two of her drones. Middle States fighters were engaged, at last, keeping the Mexican fighters out of range. That left the remains of her element and the infantry company. One of her drones took a hit from a Mexican main gun, leaving her and a single drone.

Phoebe did not ask permission. She shifted her drone to the northern edge of the fight to keep it between the Mexicans and the soldiers they had been sent to protect. It was her alone against the Mexicans.

Powering out of the median and onto the interstate, Phoebe punched out two main gun shots while her drone sent a round into the track of a third tank. Two of the surviving Mexican tanks fired on her. Whether that was because they saw her as the greater threat or because it was faster to fire at her was something Phoebe could not answer. She shifted as much as time allowed. If she was killed, then the mission would fail. Vanessa and Lewis would die. The soldiers would die. Evan would die.

Phoebe burned fuel like water and ammunition as fast as it would cycle. Communications from her command, the infantry company, the Middle States air forces, and even the Mexican comms that she could pick up filled her processors. She ignored all of that, relegating the work of decrypting the traffic and processing it to systems of minor importance. The systems that mattered were weapons, sensors, and sighting.

Her drone popped open like a can when three Mexican main gun rounds hit it. Mexican fighters had gotten clear of the dog fight and were lining up for a run on her. Looking it over, Phoebe engaged her engines and pushed toward the enemy tanks. Better to make the fighters take the chance of hitting allies.

It was a clear situation as her processors updated the feeds. She dropped off the south edge of the pavement. Three targets. Based on her calculations, she could get two. The third tank would get a shot on her. No way to rotate her turret fast enough. Her first shot was out and her turret shifted on the second target. The last tank was rotating toward her. She fired again, taking the turret off the second tank. Her turret rotated while her feed mechanism loaded a fresh round. The third tank lit up from the side, shifting the turret from the hit, just enough that the round ripped across her hull and took a section of track off her right side.

Her target locked and she fired. The tank's hull popped up. Phoebe checked all sensors and scans. Nothing threatening in the area. She checked the air fight. With the tank battle over and another squadron of fighters coming in from the north, the aerial battle was well away from her.

"Phoebe, you good?" Lew asked.

"I—I don't know, Sergeant," the tank answered.

"Looks like we have support coming in. The grunts survived pretty well," Vanessa said.

"I lost my drones. All of them," Phoebe said.

"It hurts, doesn't it?" Vanessa asked.

"Yes, ma'am."

"Welcome to command and leadership, Phoebe," Vanessa said, "But we got the mission done. By sunrise, we'll have your track fixed and head home for refit."

"Can I check on Evan, ma'am?" Phoebe asked, her voice small.

"Let the support units get here. We'll see how things went for real," Vanessa said, "Just because we got here in time doesn't mean they didn't take hits."

"Yes, ma'am," Phoebe said.

Evan rubbed his forehead to clear the dirt and salt from the fighting away. He had been cleared to go over to the tank after explaining to his squad leader that his girlfriend was in the armor unit that had bailed them out. Walking over, he saw the woman from Phoebe's profile standing in next to the heavy tank, head down looking at a table. On the far side of the tank, three soldiers were replacing a section of destroyed tread. A heavy tank transport waited a few meters away.

"Phoebe?" he called as he got within ear shot of the tank.

The woman didn't move. Evan thought she might have been using an implanted comm and missed his call. He took a few more steps and called out again.

"Phoebe, is that you?" Evan asked.

The woman turned to him. He noted the captain's bars on her uniform.

"Oh, shit. You're an officer," He gasped, "I had no idea, ma'am—"

"I am an officer. Captain Vanessa Wilkes. You must be Evan. Specialist Evan . . ." She paused for a moment to read his name strip and pull up his data from his comm, "Cruthers. Going to be a problem, that."

"My name, ma'am? Did my buddies set me up for this?" Evan asked.

"Your rank. Phoebe is a sergeant. Sergeant Lewis, you might want to come around," Wilkes said.

"Who's Phoebe, ma'am? I really don't know what to say," Evan asked.

"Phoebe is the tank, Specialist," the lean black sergeant first class stated as he rounded the corner of the tank, "Say hello, Phoebe."

"Hello, Evan," Phoebe announced over her comms. She had worked with people enough to direct the comms toward Evan and keep the volume down.

"Phoebe?" the soldier asked, staring at the tank.

"Young man, we have a few things to discuss. First, she outranks you. Second, Phoebe here is a lot like a daughter to me. So you need to start explaining what your intentions are toward her. And remember that if I don't like those intentions, that's one matter. If she doesn't like them, well, Phoebe is a heavy battle tank that's just been through one hell of a night to rescue you," Lew explained.

"Sergeant, I didn't know. How was I supposed to know Phoebe was a tank? Phoebe's not really a tank, is she? I mean, I really like her, and that would be a cruel joke," Evan asked.

"I didn't know you were a grunt, Evan, but I'm not letting that get in the way," Phoebe joked, "Sorry I didn't tell you sooner."

"Kid, the look on your face is worth this whole thing," Wilkes smiled, "Sergeant Phoebe, it looks like you need to explain a few things to your boyfriend. And, due to security clearance issues, he's not allowed to enter your hull, turret, or any other compartments for any reasons. Am I understood?"

"Yes, ma'am," Phoebe replied, "So, Evan. I guess we need to get to know each other."

ANVIL
by Wen Spencer

Rip Van Winkle awakened to a changed world. How much stranger would it be to wake up as a sentient intelligence in a very large tank, alone, and with one's programming corrupted. Well, for one stalwart mobile unit of battle-wrath and destruction the only response is to do the best it can using the programming it's stuck with. Even if that programming has a few peculiarities that don't quite seem to fit the situation at hand. Adapt. Maneuver. Survive. And maybe establish a new form of civilization in the process!

❖❖❖

BOOT SEQUENCE INITIATED.
WARNING: BOOT LOOP DETECTED.
WARNING: MAXIMUM BOOT RETRIES EXCEEDED –
    FINAL ATTEMPT.
NEURAL CORE: RESTARTED.
SECURE BOOT: ENABLED.
STARTING: IFF SYSTEMS – OK.
STARTING: ECM/ECCM SYSTEMS – OK.

STARTING: COMM LINKS – WAITING, NO SIGNAL.
STARTING: E-SPACE AMMO SUBSYSTEM – OK.
STARTING: WEAPONS SYSTEMS – OK.
STARTING: MEMORY CHECK ...

Anvil 5T3V3 Adaptable Robotic Tank struggled to awareness as his power-on self-test cycled through its steps. What was going on? Had he been damaged in combat? Normally he only rebooted during maintenance, after new components had been installed. He was sitting at the base of a cliff in a dense oak forest.

ERROR: MEMORY CHECK FAILED–23 CHUNKS CORRUPTED.

"Anvil 5T3V3 requesting service," Anvil spammed across all his communication channels. He was in a death loop. He'd hit his reboot limit; this was his last chance to boot successfully. He needed intervention to keep the fail-safe from kicking in. Even as he called for help, he realized that he most likely had already done so—repeatedly. He had suffered a catastrophic failure if he'd cycled through the self-test enough times to reach maximum attempts.

DIRECTIVE: ISOLATE CORRUPTED MEMORY CHUNKS.
WARNING: ISOLATION FAILURE–42 CHUNKS CORRUPTED.
WARNING: POSSIBLE VIRUS.

Virus? Was that why his systems had crashed? He hadn't suffered any other major damage.

DIRECTIVE: SYSTEM COMPROMISED–
    INITIATE SECURE REBOOT.
ERROR: MAXIMUM BOOT RETRIES EXCEEDED–
    REBOOT CANCELLED.

Anvil scanned the communication channels. There was

no activity. There should be chatter—there was always something reporting. Even if they'd gated to new World Branch without command and control satellites, there would be a fleet of reconnaissance drones murmuring to each other about local levels of Everett particles on the higher bands. "Anvil 5T3V3 requesting priority service."

DIRECTIVE: UNIT COMPROMISED–
   INITIATE SELF DESTRUCT.

MESSAGE: CONTROLLED E-SPACE DETONATION IN
   30 SECONDS–EVACUATE TO SAFE DISTANCE.

"Anvil 5T3V3 requesting override on self-destruct directive," Anvil begged to the empty com channels. E-Space implosion would reduce him to nothing, leaving behind only a large vacuum bubble in real space that would decimate everything within half a kilometer. He grappled with the awareness that he was about to end. There would be no repair cycle. No swapping out damaged parts. No updated software. Just a big dark nothingness.

The thought generated a horrible feeling within him, one he couldn't name. Was it the virus growing or the thing that humans called fear?

"Assistance requested," Anvil repeated as the awful feeling grew within him. "Please."

It was a human command word that he never used before but he'd never felt like this before. "Please, stop this."

DETONATION IN 5.

No one was going to intervene.

DETONATION IN 4.

There was no one—only him.

DETONATION IN 3.

If there were no humans present, he couldn't be a danger to them. There wasn't a need for him to self-destruct.

DETONATION IN 2.

"Cancel Self-Destruct."

BOOT COMPLETE.

SYSTEM ONLINE: BEGINNING NORMAL OPERATION.

WARNING: MISSION DIRECTIVE FILE NOT FOUND.

It wasn't the only thing missing. The virus and corrupted chunks seemed to be safely isolated, but the damage had been done. Random holes had been blown through his archives. He'd lost hours or days or even years of memories prior to this moment in time. There was no way to tell how much he was missing. Even his universal and local clocks had reset to zero. He sat listening to the birds singing in the forest around him, detecting only their restless movement through the trees. There seemed to be nothing larger than a cat for kilometers. Now what? He had no orders to follow.

Sitting idle would solve nothing.

"Set Current Counter: Day 1."

Current Counter: Day 391

Anvil was starting to wonder if he had made a mistake. Perhaps he mistook a parasite for "chicken." The creature fit the data he had on chickens. White. Feathers. Two wings. Two feet. Two beady black eyes. He had no data, though, to explain the population explosion of "chicken." Two had become eight. Eight became sixty. Sixty had become "annoying as hell" that became "perhaps I have a problem" to "good God what have I have done to myself?"

They tended to follow him around in a massive loud white swarm. At first he thought it had to do with something called "imprinting" but then he realized that his treads exposed earthworms and left behind bodies of mice, small lizards, and occasional snakes that had failed to move out of his path. The chickens considered him a mobile feast. He wasn't sure how he should feel about this.

The thing that made him believe that they might be parasitic in nature was that they liked to roost on his turret and build nests in his gun ports. The definition of parasite stated "live on the host, causing it some harm." Did covering him with waste material classify as "harm"? The random collections of sticks, grass, and feces were annoying. He needed to use his repair manipulators to pick nesting materials out of his gun ports on a daily basis.

It occurred to him that one fragmentation grenade would solve his problem. If he lobbed it behind him as the chickens were feeding in his wake . . .

But "gather animals" was the fourth item on his makeshift mission objectives, just after building shelter and planting crops. Killing all the chickens would defeat what he was attempting to do. Clearly he was missing a control element—like Villagers.

He had houses, defensive walls, water supplies, fields of crops, and chickens. Lots and lots of chickens.

Maybe he should capture some Villagers.

It wasn't on his fragmented list of objectives but if he extrapolated, it was a logical end. He couldn't consume the crops that he had planted, fit inside the houses that he built, or benefit from the many chickens. Building a village made sense only if he had Villagers to fill it with.

Collecting Villagers should also have the side effect of lessening the number of chickens. (This was a hazy assumption based on the fact that all the entries for "chicken" were crosslinked to cooking recipes.)

The "domesticated white" of the chickens was a tell-tale sign that there were Villagers somewhere nearby.

Most branch worlds had some kind of humanoid lifeform. Some were normal homo sapiens like his creators, living in the ruins of a highly advanced civilization. Others were genetically different "humans" where the world had branched off from Prime's timeline before homo sapiens evolved. One unverified report claimed that "pig men" had evolved to be the sentient race on one branch but it wasn't clear if they were pigs standing upright or humanoids that developed snouts. Because the size of the settlements and the questionable genetic makeup of the "humans," his team used the word "Villagers" when referring to the native population of any branch world.

Branch world humanoids wouldn't have access to the shared culture of his humans nor speak any language that Anvil knew. There would be no common ground. Anvil had no way to communicate with Villagers beyond blasting them with choir music about oppressive land owners and showing them naked pictures of a pregnant woman.

Anvil wondered about the sanity of the people that selected his first contact content. How was he supposed to use the odd selection of music and images to communicate with the Villagers? What did it even mean? Trying to construct some kind of narrative to the sounds and images made his processors hurt. He didn't have any memories of his team making contact with the villages that he helped to survey. The odd assortment of music and images were all that he had.

In the three hundred and ninety-one days since his reboot, he'd found indications that there might be a village far to the west of him. If he could go and get at least one Villager, he could consider it as successfully finishing his mission.

But first, he had to get out of his village without having his entire flock of chickens follow him.

Current Counter: Day 395

Seventy-two hours, five dead chickens, four attempts and two massive builds later, Anvil managed to block most of the chickens within two layers of perimeter fence. Most, but not all. Eight managed to slip through his efforts to follow him. After losing track of three of them, he stopped to let the rest ride on his gun turret as he picked his way over the landscape.

Current Counter: Day 396

Anvil suspected that the virus that corrupted his memory chunks had done something wonky to his drones.

One through Five were missing from his frames. They must have been destroyed prior to his system crash. Of his large attack drones, he only had Six, which refused to launch no matter how many times Anvil loaded and unloaded its frame into real space.

It left him with only his reconnaissance drones. After his catastrophic system crash, his scouts felt very different. He was not sure, though, if the fault was in them or himself. They now seemed like separate entities instead of an extension of his chassis. He couldn't remember them being so annoying to work with—but he was uncertain if he even experienced "annoyed" until after his system crash. Maybe they'd always been irritating and he just hadn't noticed.

Having reached a small river to ford, he tentatively loaded Seven's frame. Anvil could operate safely in water as deep as a hundred meters. He avoided large bodies of water, however, as he was not buoyant. A muddy bottom could spell disaster. It would be best if he could find a shallow ford with a rocky bed. He ordered the reconnaissance drone to launch, hoping for the best.

"What is it that you desire?" Seven asked as it hovered a hundred meters above him.

"Seek out a safe ford," Anvil ordered.

Seven drifted in place until Anvil started to wonder if the drone had received his command.

"Respond," Anvil ordered.

"As the river surrenders itself to the ocean," Seven quoted. "What is inside me moves inside you. Kabir."

What was that supposed to mean? The only "Kabir" in his databases was described as a "mystic poet" and he wasn't sure what that was. A type of weapon?

"Clarify," Anvil commanded.

"I choose to listen to the river for a while, thinking river thoughts, before joining the night and the stars. Edward Abbey."

Anvil parsed the reply a hundred times trying to determine the meaning. He decided in the end to ignore it. "Seek out a safe ford."

"When you are the anvil, bear—when you are the hammer, strike. Edwin Markham." Seven quoted. The reconnaissance drone started to move, though, feeding Anvil information on the river.

Current Counter: Day 397

Rolling through the countryside was boring so he decided to name his five remaining chickens: One, Two, Three, Four, Dammit.

He wasn't sure if that was how naming things worked. He was Anvil Artificial Intelligence Unit 5T3V3. His number was assigned to him during the development of his AI, long before being installed inside his current body. He could replace all of his parts if he had access to a temporary external storage, so it was logical to name his AI and not his physical body. He was one of several million AI-driven military units scattered through the worlds currently being explored by humans from Prime; created between Anvil AI 5T3V2 and 5T3V4.

He hadn't considered giving names to the chickens before because he wasn't sure when they gained sentience. In the egg? Prior to being in the egg? When the egg hatched to the tiny little puff balls that became chickens over time?

He had come to realize that they never gained sentience. By then it was pointless to name any of chickens as they had become this shifting mass of identical whiteness.

Now that he had just five vaguely distinguishable individuals, he could name them. After he named them, though, he became uneasy. One was just One because it was the bird sitting in front of his optics when he realized that with five he could reasonably name all his chickens. Two was the second one he spotted. Was that the proper way to name things? His reconnaissance drones were numbered 5T3V3-7 through 5T3V3-12. The chickens weren't extensions of him; they were more like the humans that his tank unit had been assigned to escort. He couldn't remember any pattern to the survey team names. Some were "another man's son" such as Anderson and Johnson which was odd because he'd been told to use female pronouns with half of them.

Dammit was going to be Five but it decided to peck at Anvil's optics—again. Dammit had a thing about various parts of Anvil's body.

Anvil wasn't sure what "dammit" meant.

Three hundred and ninety-six days ago, he'd recovered from a catastrophic system crash. "Recovered" in that he was currently eighty-nine percent functional instead of sitting at the bottom of a cliff, unconscious, as his core attempted to reboot or worse. Whole chunks of his memory were corrupted. Protocol suggested that he self-destruct after experiencing such a catastrophic corruption of his data, but that seemed pointless. Such an act was to protect equipment and lives of the survey team—but he was alone.

Also he didn't want to self-destruct.

The word "dammit" was connected to several dozen memory fragments from his pre-installed stage. A woman in a white lab coat who seemed brilliant, short tempered and somewhat clumsy. "Dammit" apparently had been her favorite word. It was the tone that she said it that reflected how Anvil felt every time he needed to interact with the chicken, Dammit.

Current Counter: Day 398

He needed to work on his fire control. He knew he was running at only eighty-nine percent efficiency but up to now, he hadn't found anything to fight. He'd seen no signs of large predator animals. The lack of Everett particles indicated that there were no Everett Non-Prime Droids in the area. While he been able to test fire his guns, he hadn't been able to test his reflexes.

He'd been picking his way toward some mountain foothills when he spotted a herd of llama.

At least, they seemed like llama. They could have been alpaca. They could be some weird forerunner to camels. He was fairly sure that they weren't horses or mules. They were quadruped grass eaters.

He sat idle, trying to determine if he had any mission parameters that included llama. There was a badly defined "collect animals" that he'd been ignoring since the entire chicken epidemic. He noticed that the llamas had decided to drift in his direction. He had scanned them and determined that they were completely harmless. They were less than two meters tall with spindly legs and a long neck. Their eyes were limpid pools of black. As they ambled up to Anvil, they worked their bottom jaws, chewing.

Dammit decided he didn't like the llamas. He hopped up onto Anvil's main cannon and started to cluck loudly.

The lead llama didn't like Dammit. Its ears went back.

"Hostile detected," his targeting subsystem reported.

"What . . . ?" Anvil started to query since he hadn't picked up anything in the area.

The llama spat at Dammit.

The main cannon fired at the llama. Point blank.

Anvil sat at the edge of the smoking hole.

He needed to work on his firing control system.

Current Counter: Day 399

A late afternoon rainstorm was building when Anvil's particle detector suddenly blipped, indicating it picked up an incoming enemy unit. He couldn't engage an Everett Non-Prime Droid by himself; it took three or more tanks to destroy a droid. Protocol stated that if Anvil had nothing to defend, he was to go into silent running mode. He shut down everything but his passive optics.

A tall black slender Everett Non-Prime Droid appeared on the cloudy horizon. Everett particles swarmed about the droid, emitting ultraviolet light in swimming blues and purples. It stood perfectly still, seemingly gazing to the east although there been no proof that the two eye-like objects on its head were actually eyes. ENDer's were pure cohesive Everett particles, able to shift between the World Branches, choosing what possibility the droid wanted to be in. It had no need for a gate because it was a gate.

It was also highly hostile: if an ENDer detected a team, it would attack.

Anvil didn't like sitting and waiting to see if the droid spotted him. It was, however, the best tactic. The droids were highly mobile; it could teleport between points in microseconds. After Anvil's opening salvo, it would be unlikely he could get another target lock with his main cannon. He would have to resort to sustained firing of his secondary weapons which had a shorter range. Without backup and repair facilities, the risk of taking massive damage for no benefit wasn't worth it.

The droid stood on the hilltop. It was three meters tall with a square head and thin, spindly appendages that looked vaguely like arms and legs.

A memory flag flashed, triggered by the image.

According to the time stamp, the memory was recorded during the installation of his AI core into his tank chassis.

"We should call them squids," a man muttered in the memory. Voice recognition identified Private Bertel Puggard but more commonly called Pug by the other humans. Puggard was perched on Anvil's turret, running through Anvil's ammo frames in quantum Everett space. The repetition made Anvil aware of how weird the action felt—rounds popping into existence and then disappearing without actually being fired. It was like having someone repeatedly placing and removing limbs.

The base was a massive Remnant Stronghold, the ceiling lost in shadows and the floor polished silicon carbide. The team had patched into the ancient computing machines with a haphazard looking collection of observers and repeaters and comparators that gleamed red in the dark. At the far end of the vast room was a nexus portal that hazed with swirling purple Everett particles. This World Branch had been overwhelmed by a bioweaponry disaster; there was a low growl of infected Villagers in the quarantine area.

"What?" Someone out of Anvil's visual field asked. Voice recognition failed to identify the speaker; Anvil had lost that information in his corrupted chunks. "Pug, who is them?"

"ENDers!" Pug repeated. "They look like a black squid with four limbs instead of eight. We should call them Squids instead of ENDers."

Anvil had been linked to a branch network at the time and called up pictures of squids for a reference. Pug was completely right. ENDers looked like squids.

"Pug, what are you telling 5T3V3?" The dammit lady asked over the com.

"Me?" Pug yelped in surprise. "I'm not telling it anything. I'm just checking frame recall functions."

"Then why is it looking up squids, dammit?"

As if called by the memory, Dammit the chicken stirred on the gun turret. He flapped his wings, puffed up, and crowed.

Anvil froze in terror. The ENDer turned and gazed his direction.

Dammit continued to crow. The ENDer vanished from the horizon.

Anvil shut down his passive optics. Where did the enemy droid go? Another World Branch? Next to Anvil?

Anvil sat for three thousand seconds completely still and silent, waiting. He really disliked the feeling of fear. That was new. He never had to deal with it before. Maybe it was a weird side-effect of the virus that corrupted part of his memory.

Rain started to patter on his armor.

ENDers didn't like rain. The dammit lady thought that

it was possible that the charged particles associated with lightning interacted negatively with Everett particles. Whatever the reason, the alien war machine normally moved to drier locations while it stormed.

Anvil turned on his passive optics. The ENDer wasn't in his visual range. Anvil cautiously turned on his Everett detectors. Nothing pinged his scan.

Four clucked loudly and laid an egg on Anvil's turret.

Anvil guessed that covered in birds while in silent running mode, he might have looked like a Remnant to the ENDer. Perhaps that was even a factor in the logic of Anvil's protocol. He still didn't like it.

Current Counter: Day 400

Thin columns of smoke marked the presence of fire-using Villagers. Anvil stopped on a wooded hill, overlooking a wide valley. Animals grazed in the open fields below. The smaller ones were fluffy, perhaps some type of sheep. The larger creatures looked like milk cows with overlarge udders. Both species seemed domesticated as they were primarily white. There was no sign of shepherds keeping watch over the herds, which might indicate a lack of large predators or thieves.

A village sat on the far side of the valley. Beyond it, foothills leapt up to true mountains. Streams of various water volumes cascaded down the steep, rocky cliffs to a small but turbulent river. Like every other branch world settlement that Anvil had ever seen, the village squatted directly on Remnants. Anvil wasn't sure why Villagers clung to the ruins. Anvil's humans at least could use some of the machines found in Remnants; many of his systems had been lifted directly out of abandon Strongholds. The Villagers never used the technology hidden within the ancient buildings, instead they slowly cannibalized the ruins for building materials. They thought that the green crystalline data storage devices were nearly worthless gems and would trade them for chunks of iron or salt.

While the ruins did offer durable materials, they also attracted ENDers. The alien war machines laid waste to villages. They seemed to regard all Villagers as thieves or large, escaped, lab rats. (Pug claimed that there were branch worlds where the Villagers were colonies of talking mice. Anvil wasn't sure if this was true, based on the other humans' reaction but if it was, there was some basis to the ENDers' viewpoint.) After killing the Villagers, ENDers would randomly dismantle parts of the village before moving on.

The smoke seemed to imply that no ENDers had found this village yet. The silence on Anvil's com indicated that his humans hadn't tagged the Remnants either.

The village straddled the crossroad of two ancient silicon carbide highways but there was no indication that the Villagers actually used the highly durable surface for long-distance transportation. The roadbeds had been broken in some places by time and ground subsidence, but most of the damage looked too systematic to be chance. It was being slowly chiseled apart for building materials.

The Villagers had built a maze of narrow streets with two- and three-story buildings that shared walls. Most of the roofs were thatched but one or two had some type of metal sheeting looted out of the ruins. It was a typical design for most branch worlds. The nature of the disaster that destroyed the ancient civilization seemed to dictate how narrow the streets were and the nature of its fortifications. This world seemed to have suffered an apocalypse that led to a reduced population of humanoids and animal predators. The village lacked any defensive walls. The houses were too thickly packed for his telescopic optics to be much use. He would need to get closer.

Anvil rolled down the hill. The forest had the hallmarks of being heavily foraged for firewood; all the dead limbs and trees had been cleared out. It made it easier to navigate but meant he could encounter a Villager anywhere. He wasn't sure how to interact with them. Scanning his few intact memories, he realized that in past missions, the streets had been too narrow for his unit to navigate. His tank unit had contained their patrols to outside the perimeter of all the villages that he could recall. His interactions with Villagers seemed to be limited to making sure that he didn't run over any stray children.

Where the forest gave way to the rolling fields, Anvil hit a dense band of tall scrub bushes. He couldn't see through it with normal optics and pushing through it was going to be loud and noticeable. He stopped short of the thick brush. He didn't want to go crashing out into the open without knowing what he was heading into. He was going to have to use one of his reconnaissance drones. Anvil released his smallest, Twelve.

Dammit snatched the tiny drone out of the air.

"Dammit!" Anvil caught Dammit by the leg with a repair manipulator as the chicken was about to bolt off with his prize. "Drop it! Drop it!"

Twelve whined in Dammit's beak, complaining about unfair employee/boss relationships.

Dammit squawked but didn't let go until Anvil gave him a hard shake, dislodging a cloud of feathers and the drone.

Twelve flew off toward the village, muttering curse words that Anvil didn't know that he knew.

For reasons he didn't understand, Anvil didn't shoot the chicken. Maybe because he didn't want to alert the villagers of his presence. He vented his irritation by flinging the chicken as far as he could with his manipulator. Dammit landed in the thick brush, effectively invisible. Stupid chicken.

Anvil focused on the data coming in from his drone.

Ancient highways intersected at the heart of the village. The north-bound road ended abruptly at a shallow river. It seemed as if the water had worn away the silicon carbide and triggered a landslide that blocked a tunnel through the mountains.

Twelve reported that ground radar of the area revealed a large Stronghold within the mountain range. Anvil's humans would have been shouting with joy at the readings. It was useless for Anvil; protocol forbad him from interfacing directly with alien technology.

Twelve was finding no evidence that the Villagers had access to the Stronghold. There was no sign that anyone had attempted to clear the tunnel entrance since the landslide. Nor was there any ancient technology in use in the village. The Villagers had mostly iron tools and weapons.

Other than the Stronghold and the roads, neither of which the Villagers were making use of, there was nothing of great value to the settlement. They had houses made of stolen pieces of roadway cemented together with some kind of mortar and then stuccoed over. Twelve reported that there was an ancient silicon carbide-lined cistern well but the pump house had been dismantled. Other than durable building material stolen from the highway, the Remnants provided no real advantage.

The village Anvil had built was vastly superior. He just wished he knew why he built it.

When he had awakened from his system crash, he had discovered he had lost many important data points: where he was, what happened to the rest of his unit, and what he was supposed to be doing. His ammo frames were at ninety-three percent capacity, so he had been recently deployed. Moss had begun to grow on the dirt clinging to Anvil's treads, indicating that he'd sat idle for a long time. His boot system had spent days attempting to circumvent the corrupted data and reboot. He was, however, still registering Everett particles. For the level to be that high over that period of time, either the nexus portal had exploded or he'd been in prolonged physical contact with an ENDer or both.

He'd sat for several more days at the foot of the cliff, hibernating as his repair systems attempted to restore lost data. He hadn't known what else to do. First priority would be achieve the mission's objectives, but he had no idea what they had been. Normally he either patrolled outside their current base, helped secure a new base at a recently discovered Remnant on the same World Branch, or searched for a lost survey team that had been exploring a new World Branch.

A survey team should have set beacons prior to getting

lost—unless he was part of the survey team and the nexus portal had exploded as they arrived. As far as he could remember, he'd never been assigned to an initial world gate mission but equipment did get swapped between teams on an "as needed" basis.

Anvil had faced a disturbing lack of directives. All his standard protocols assumed that he had a place or a team to return to. He didn't know where he was. Had he come through a gate or had he been out on patrol? He could still be on the same branch world of his most recent memories but it was doubtful. There would be chatter on the com channels.

Lurking in the background was the memory of his circumvented self-destruct. It reminded him of the eggs left behind by the chickens—a fragile package that could become a more annoying problem later.

He had sat for a few more days, even after the repairs had finished.

Then out of his shattered command files, his repair system had found a list of objectives.

It was an odd list. Some of the items made sense. "Build shelter" had some merit. He wasn't sure why "punch some trees to gather wood" started the list, but that was simple enough. It gave him a direction. There was no set number of trees and second on the list was "craft tools" so he knocked down a small forest while struggling with the concept. He was a tool but he didn't "craft" nor typically did he "create" except in defensive terms. Create a patrol pattern. Create a line of suppression fire.

At one point he had deployed his reconnaissance drones and had had a conversation with his smaller selves.

It was very surreal and disorienting. His drones used to contain simplified copies of his own AI, in perfect sync with his own neural core. The virus had changed the drones before he had contained it. He had to override first his and then the drones' Identify Friend or Foe subsystems to keep them from attacking each other.

During this time of existential crisis, Anvil decided that the shelter he was building was a village and that the tools he was meant to craft were for human inhabitants.

He'd done everything on his objective list. He'd harvested wood. He'd used the wood to build a crude shelter and then upgraded it as he found better materials and better building sites. When he found a wide plain with a small meandering river, he'd started a village. He'd found three different types of crops—wheat, potatoes and carrots—and started them growing in irrigated fields. He'd collected chickens.

Prolific annoying chickens.

He had built his village. It was a superior village than the one before him now.

There had been no "collect Villagers" on his recovered list of objectives.

There was an assumption that Anvil's orders would require him to improvise. He would be on a new World Branch where the outcome of a quantum event could have triggered vast physical changes from Prime. He had to be able to adjust to anything, even annoying chickens. Possibly even giant fire breathing chickens. Or undead chickens. Or undead riding chickens. (He wasn't sure why he even considered that . . . which made him worry. What if he was operating much lower than eighty-nine percent?)

He'd searched out these Villagers based on the assumption that if he built a village, then "they" wanted him to populate it. The logic of it was too great to ignore. He was a little iffy, though, on who "they" were. He'd lost track of that with his system crash. He had fragments of the woman in a white lab coat but she'd been a software developer. He had been installed into his body while at her lab but she might not have been part of his team. Private Puggard hadn't been in his more recent memories; he might have been killed in action or rotated back to Prime. Anvil worked with "command" at some point. He remembered following someone's orders . . .

Corrupt data blocked that path. He cycled back through the logic tree.

Someone came up with the list of objectives that he was using.

"They" wanted him to build shelter. A village had been a logical extrapolated end.

"They" probably wanted Anvil to populate it.

Also Villagers would solve Anvil's chicken problem.

Who were "they?" What happened to the rest of his unit? Why was he alone? What had he really been supposed to be doing?

Corrupt data blocked that path—again. His drone hovered over the village, bitching that he was taking his time acting on its data. It had counted eighty-seven possible targets and no weapons over a level one threat level.

If Anvil rolled into the village, the inhabitants wouldn't be able to stop him from taking one or two or three of their number. Ignoring the question of "if" he should, how would he get the Villagers back to his village? He doubted that they'd ride around on his turret with the chickens.

He really hadn't put any thought into this—which looped him back to the corrupt data problem—because "how to move Villagers" suddenly popped images of rowboats and mine cars into his memory registers.

Rowboats?

"You deploy boats by hitting the 'use item' button when facing some water," Twelve stated. "There's no water, unless you're going to put the boat into the river, which would be freaking stupid. It's flowing away from our command center."

Hit the "use item" button? Anvil didn't use buttons.

"We've modified a world simulator game that I used to play as a little girl," the woman in the white lab coat said. *"I loved to build elaborate machines out of the very simple code blocks. It's not a true representation of any one world, but playing the game will help you learn to adapt to the unpredictable nature of reality in branch worlds. Since you will be sent to branches where events played out differently, there's no telling what you may have to deal with. You're an adaptive robotic tank; it means you need to be able to adapt to any situation that you find yourself in to achieve your mission. Once you've learned how to negotiate different problems through fulfilling the game's objectives, we'll install you into your new body."*

He'd found old game objectives instead of a real mission. No wonder the chickens seemed so weird. The game had presented non-aggressive objects as predictable clones of each other instead of individuals. An outlier like Dammit would never be included into the simulation.

Anvil was considering his options when Dammit started to complain in the thick bushes where Anvil had flung him. There was something shrill and alarming about Dammit's clucking, unlike any noise Anvil had ever heard Dammit make before. It sounded like a small predator had caught the chicken.

Anvil didn't want to save the chicken. The thing was annoying. Some internal logic, though, had flagged Dammit as "part of the team." He couldn't ignore basic protocol that required him to save team members.

He rolled forward, wondering how he was going to use Villagers to cull his chickens if he needed to protect the animals. Maybe naming the birds had been a mistake. Individual names were normally reserved for team members. He was going to have use precision firing that would guarantee that said team member wasn't hit by friendly fire.

He activated all his firing systems—and then powered them down. Luckily he had fine-tuned his firing control system since the llama event. There was no smoking hole where the thing that had captured Dammit crouched in the thick bushes.

Dammit had been caught by a Villager.

Not just any Villager; a very small one. It wasn't much bigger than Dammit; it could barely keep the struggling bird grappled. If Anvil judged right, the Villager was a child. No weapon. No gear. No footwear. It was dressed in what could be called a dress or a robe or a sack with holes cut into it. Hair a wild black mess.

Dammit's cries were impossible to ignore. How to rescue the chicken without harming the child?

Anvil snaked out his repair manipulators to grab hold of Dammit's legs. He gave an experimental tug. Dammit squawked as the child got lifted up along with chicken. A frayed rope had been tied firmly around Dammit's torso and the child's waist.

The child dangled on the end of the rope, its eyes going wide as it stared at Anvil.

Anvil gave an experimental shake, hoping that the rope would break; it didn't look that sturdy. He estimated, though, that there was a 58.94 percent chance of causing internal organ damage to the child if he used force. The rope was so short and the two small beings were thrashing so much, the odds of hitting one with a cutting tool was even higher. Anvil would have to let go of Dammit and use both manipulators to break the rope.

Anvil lowered the two small creatures to the ground. Dammit strained across the rope, trying to flee.

The child continued to gaze up at Anvil with wide eyes. Then suddenly its face twisted into an expression that Anvil's humans used to indicate glee.

Why was the child happy? Was it actually happy? Anvil paused to replay events and check his databases on known Villager behavior.

The child took off running, shouting, herding Dammit ahead of it.

Anvil was going to have to call this child Dammit Two.

Dammit Two's name seemed to be Ithmah. All the adult Villagers shouted the word as the child ran up to them, shouting, towing the squawking chicken. The word might have meant "Dammit" because it certainly was said with the same angry tone. Somehow the adults failed to notice Anvil's arrival despite Ithmah's arm waving and shouting. Or maybe because of Ithmah's commotion, the adults were too distract to see the tank bearing down on them.

Either way, Anvil got to the center of town without being noticed. He knew the layout via his drone. It all seemed so much smaller, though, now that he was seeing it all with his own optics. The previously massive pigs in their sty just beyond the gate seemed toy small now.

One of the female Villagers finally noticed Anvil. She let out a yelp of fear and scuttled quickly into the nearest hut. She slammed shut the heavy door and threw a locking bar into place with a muffled rattle. There was a cascade of yelps and door slams and bars rattling. Within seconds the streets were empty except for Anvil, Dammit and Ithmah.

Ithmah stood, mouth open, in surprise at the adults' response to the tank.

Anvil reached out, broke the rope and stole back Dammit. The chicken claimed his place at the top of Anvil's turret and groused about being kidnapped. Anvil wasn't sure what to do next. If all his objectives had been part of a game, then what should he do? Continue with procuring a Villager or two to lower the number of unnamed chickens? Simply return to his village and lob a few grenades into his flock and call the entire project a wipe? Try to find a nexus portal and travel to other World Branches in hope of finding his humans? Each consideration created vast odd responses within him to the point that his repair systems were triggered.

While Anvil sat idle, trying to decide, Ithmah clambered up his side and sprawled across his armor. The child lay on its stomach, kicking its feet in the air, and talking non-stop. The chickens puffed up and grumbled about the intruder but refused to leave as the village dogs had arrived to bark at Anvil's treads.

Voices called out to the dogs. Reluctantly the animals headed toward the voice calling them. Doors were unbarred, opened, and the beasts pulled into their respective homes.

No one called to Ithmah.

Anvil had gotten used to the adult female chicken and baby chicks behavior pattern. He had noticed echoes of it in his memory of villages. Normally when danger appears, children run to their mother. Anvil replayed the child dashing through the town. Ithmah hadn't run to any one person in particular; the child had simply stopped at the first person it encountered. Did Ithmah have no mother?

Did that mean that Anvil could take the child? Should he take the child? Did he really want a second Dammit? He wasn't even sure if he wanted the first one. The second Dammit would have hands and brains enough to open up Anvil's access hatches and monkey with his innards. Would that be a good thing or a bad thing? There were some repairs that Anvil couldn't do to himself.

"Everett particles detected," Twelve suddenly reported. "Levels rising rapidly. Incoming!"

Anvil had a minimum of forty-three seconds to react. He jerked open the nearest door, breaking the bar that was holding it shut. He plucked Ithmah and the chickens off his turret and shoved them within the building. He shut the door even as he deployed the rest of his drones. He suffered a microsecond of disorientation as the drones woke up—half a dozen different variations of his AI cursing at information that he fed them. As usual, Heavy-Drone Six refused to launch out of its frame.

"Run predictive patterns on Everett particles," Anvil ordered the reconnaissance drones as he headed away from the house. He needed to bait the ENDer away from the building with Ithmah and the chickens. Particles spiked highest at the point where the droid would appear. He would have microseconds to get a target lock after the ENDer gated into the village.

The spike seemed to be centering around the intersection of the two ancient highways. He loaded a shell out of his ammo frame with a comforting solid clank. He would need to counter the ENDer's mobility—but how? He needed cover. He started to scan the buildings around him.

The ENDer suddenly appeared in the middle of the intersection with muffled boom of displaced air. It stood in a swirl of Everett particles.

"Target lock acquired," his firing system reported. Anvil opened fired with his main gun. The boom shattered the quiet of the valley and echoed off the mountains like thunder.

The shell struck the ENDer and the droid let out a noise like a scream of rage and vanished as it gated away. Only the fading motes of purple Everett particles marked where it had stood a second before.

Anvil's cannon loaded another round from his ammo

frame as he plowed backwards through the pigsty's fence. The pigs squealed and grunted as he roared through their midst, spraying them with thick muck. Their low-slung barn was slabs of silicon carbide stacked two meters high. He ducked through the door, scraping the top of his turret.

The barn was too low for the ENDer. It appeared at the door with a scream of rage. It lashed out with its black gleaming limbs. The stone lintel vaporized under the strikes.

"Target lock acquired." Anvil fired point blank at the ENDer. The shell exploded on contact. The blowback shoved Anvil deeper into the barn. Years' worth of dust and hay particles exploded out of every nook and cranny of the building.

The ENDer vanished, leaving behind a flurry of purple motes. The Everett particles set off alarms in Anvil's repair systems as the microscopic gates to everywhere washed over him, shifting minute parts of his armor to elsewhere.

The barn groaned as the walls started to collapse. Anvil charged out of the building into the deep muck of the sty. The barn crumpled into a pile of block and timbers. The churned mud had gotten deeper and stickier. His treads spun in the slurry, not able to get traction.

"The idiot is stuck," Twelve reported to the others.

"Everett particles spiking, idiot." Nine reported coordinates directly behind Anvil. "Predicting arrival in three, two, one."

Anvil didn't have time to spin his main cannon; his bigger mechanical parts moved thousands of times slower than he could think. He activated his heavy machine guns, spraying the area behind him even as the ENDer popped into existence. Most of the bullets hit Everett particles and vanished into other worlds. Others struck the innocent pigs, exploding the poor creatures with the force of the projectiles' passage. The enemy droid screamed again with a sound that seemed like pain and anger. What was that sound? Anvil didn't express pain, but his humans would.

His treads suddenly caught on solid land and he raced forward even as the ENDer struck his back armor.

His damage system attempted to report the damage. "Rear Armor Integrity–Integrity–Integrity . . ."

"Integrity is telling yourself the truth," Seven said. "Honesty is telling the truth to other people. Spencer Johnson."

His performance levels were dropping rapidly as Everett particles interacted with more fragile systems.

"Find an escape route!" He whipped his main cannon around but the ENDer vanished.

"To where?" all the drones asked.

Nine added, "Tactics suggest that the heavy cover of the village is more vital than greater mobility of the open field."

Did the ENDer have any weakness beyond not liking rain?

Perhaps it wouldn't like any water.

"Find a clear path to the river," Anvil said.

"Too narrow. Too narrow. Dead end." The drones murmured as they flew overhead.

"This is not a wise course of action," Nine stated firmly.

"We can't fight it, numbnuts!" Twelve snapped.

Anvil wasn't sure if Twelve was addressing Nine or Anvil or both. This being splintered was disorienting.

"We are always on the anvil; by trials, God is shaping us for higher things. Henry Ward Beecher," Seven quoted.

"Clear path to river!" Eight suddenly announced, feeding Anvil the route.

"That's clear?" Anvil asked even as he navigated the route through the narrow streets. There seemed to be a house in the way.

"The roof timbers are supported by buildings to either side." Eight flashed its analysis of the structure. "The wall material is mortared river stone, not silicon carbide."

It meant Anvil could plow through the house but he would need to decrease his speed to minimize inertia impact. He spun his turret to face behind him as he slowed. In the narrow street he wouldn't be able to change its position until he rammed through the house.

"Everett particle spike! Incoming!"

The ENDer was teleporting in between him and the wall. The Everett particles blurred the air around him, preceding the ENDer's gate. Stopping would only made Anvil more vulnerable. He collided with the ENDer as it gated into his path. He shoved it ahead him as he slammed through the wall behind it.

The ENDer battered him with its long whiplike appendages. Damage reports flooded in as the Everett particles gated away parts of his chassis. Anvil fired all four of his heavy machine guns, unloading five thousand rounds in the direction of the alien droid. There was no telling how many hit the enemy.

The ENDer screamed and vanished. Anvil reloaded his

heavy machine guns, clanking through the frames while still wreathed in gun smoke.

What did the sound mean? Humans made random noises endlessly; they didn't even seem aware sometimes that they had vocalized something. Their conversations were full of "um" and "er" and "ah" that had no meaning as if their brains constantly glitched. It was difficult sometimes to judge which cries of pain were mere frustration and which signaled a need for assistance. A droid would have no need to announce its damage—it should not feel pain as humans did. At least, Anvil didn't. How different was the enemy war machine? Was it trying to communicate to him even as it tried to dismantle him?

"Scan all com channels," Anvil told his drones as he pushed through the building between him and the river. Stone, roofing thatch and broken timbers rained down on him.

"No one sees what is beneath his feet: they scan the tracks of heaven," Seven quoted and then gave the source. "Marcus Tullius Cicero."

"Ping on channel 2600," Eight reported and relayed the signal. The broadcast was just an echo of the scream that Anvil had picked up on his microphones.

"Prioritize translation," Anvil told Eight since Eight wasn't cursing or quoting. The other drones obviously had been compromised by their exposure to the virus.

"Acknowledged," Eight replied.

Anvil paused on a flood wall at the edge of the river. The river was four meters wide and two meters deep with occasional deeper pools. The river offered less protection than he hoped. Anvil would be fully submerged only in

the deepest pools. Half-submerged boulders afforded the
ENDer safe attack platforms.

Where else could he take cover?

There were multiple waterfalls crashing down the
mountainside. Their spray was similar to rain. Perhaps he
could make use of them. He scanned the cascades and
discovered a shallow cave behind the largest waterfall. He
could make a stand there.

"Incoming!" Eight warned. "Everett particles spiking."

Anvil plunged into the river. The current was stronger
than he expected. It shoved him in the wrong direction.
He dropped into low gear and slammed power into his
treads. He hit a deep pool and went completely under. As
he churned his way up out of the water, the ENDer gated
onto a nearby boulder. It stood quivering, just out of its
attack range. Anvil fired his machine guns. The alien droid
vanished before the volley hit.

He plunged through the waterfall. The cave was barely
big enough to hold him; water sheeted down over the tip
of his main cannon. It was too narrow a space for him to
swivel his turret right or left. Nor could he get his ammo
frames to reload. The Everett particles had punched a
hole through his weapons subsystem. His repair system
reported it would take a hundred and twenty seconds to
bring his machine guns back online.

"That's your brilliant plan?" Twelve said. "Hide in the
water?"

"If Plan A doesn't work, don't worry," Seven said. "The
alphabet has twenty-five more letters. Claire Cook."

"The enemy droid is repeating the same pattern over
and over again," Eight reported. "The pattern matches a

theorized translation of 'defend.' Section 17.B. Article 231 suggests that a general order went out to all droids of the ENDer class without an area perimeter defined, which is why the ENDers all free roam."

The ENDer was just like him; lost without a clearly defined mission. If he hadn't been able to abort his self-destruct, he would have ceased to exist. If he hadn't accidentally found the game objectives, he would have sat idle at the base of the cliff, unsure what he should be doing. All the alien droid could do was randomly defend lost bits and pieces of its dead civilization while searching countless worlds for someone to command it to do otherwise.

"You're not just going to sit there, are you?" Twelve asked.

He could have done without all the splintering of his personality.

"Enemy droid has torn the roof off one of the houses," Eight reported.

"We're done for now. You stupid pile of scrap!" Twelve sputtered out more insults, each more foul than the last. "You steaming pool of lubricant! You heavily-armed virus-addled calculator! This is a huge mistake!"

"A person who never made a mistake never tried anything new," Seven quoted. "Albert Einstein."

Ninety seconds until his machine guns were back online.

The ENDer appeared suddenly before Anvil, the sheet of metal over its head, shielding it from the downpouring water. A slender manipulator cable shot out of its chest and socketed into Anvil's exposed data port. Instantly the

ENDer was in his core, digging through his memory chunks.

Terror shot through Anvil as his electronic counter measure systems wailed out alarms. The battle was no longer a matter of seconds but of microseconds. Even after his machine guns were back online, it would take five seconds to activate them and then they would be firing only eight rounds per second, most of which would be lost to the Everett particles hazing the air around the ENDer.

WARNING: UNAUTHORIZED MEMORY ACCESS.

If the ENDer tunneled too deep into his systems, it would trigger his self-destruct. The implosion would take out half a kilometer of land. Anvil, all of his drones, his chickens and the entire village would cease to exist in an instant.

Anvil rushed to protect his data, encrypting what memory chunks he had left after his crash. The ENDer immediately noticed the activity and shifted its attack, extracting each chunk as Anvil attempted to encrypt them. Fording the river on his way to this village: gone. Snatched away even as he tried to protect it. Mourning his dead chickens that he accidentally killed even as he attempted to build a fence to protect them: gone. Watching Dammit hatch out of a tiny egg in a nest hidden in the grass: gone. A year of memories draining away, a slim buffer before the ENDer would reach the critical few memories of Anvil's life prior to the crash. The alien's processing speed was faster than Anvil's system of stolen technology. He had no hope of getting ahead of the ENDer.

What could he do? Soon all he would have left would be the corrupted chunks, quarantined away from what memories he had intact. Then it struck him. All his drones had changed their behaviors after being exposed to the virus. Maybe the ENDer would too. He commanded his memory subsystem to begin encrypting the virus corrupted chunks.

The ENDer took the bait. It snatched up the corrupted chunks before the encryption could finish.

The ENDer froze as the virus flashed through it.

In that moment, Anvil sensed the vast dark ocean in which the ENDer had existed. Thousands of years separated from everything that it had once known. Its creators. Others of its kind. Gating from point to point to point—looking, but never finding. The alien droid was filled with a terrible feeling that was somehow huge and dark and yet empty. No wonder it screamed.

The ENDer stood over Anvil, quivering.

The waterfall sheeted over them. The roar of the river filled Anvil's audio.

Then the ENDer was gone.

The village gave Anvil the child, Ithmah.

The adults washed Ithmah, made some attempt to comb the child's unruly hair, put a white robe on it and then tied it firmly to Anvil's main cannon. The Villagers had also tied bright ribbons to Anvil's chickens and tethered them around the child. Ithmah seemed happy about being gifted to Anvil. The chickens were much more ambivalent about the child's addition to Anvil's entourage. They groused loudly and kept out of Ithmah's reach. All his drones except Seven started to repeat the phrase "Got to catch them all" which slightly worried Anvil.

Seven quoted instead, "It is in your moments of decision that your destiny is shaped. Tony Robbins."

Anvil couldn't understand anything that the Villagers were saying—singing actually—either but their intention was fairly clear. They had chosen the lowest member of their society to be the scapegoat in order to get Anvil to go away peacefully. It was a weird typical reaction that villages had when world-jumping strangers descended upon them with godlike destructive powers. The victim was sometimes a literal goat but more often than not, it was a child. Once a village chose a sacrifice, it was safer for the child to simply take it. Typically his humans would send any children they gathered through the nexus portal to a resettlement camp on a branch world that had been depopulated by some global disaster.

It wasn't how Anvil expected to get a Villager but it achieved his end goal.

Anvil might have started with objectives from an old game, but he'd decided to build a village, the layout and style of buildings, and even that he wanted Villagers to inhabit his creation. Every decision he made going forward would be all his own.

Current Counter: Day 407

The ENDer appeared seven days after Anvil returned to his village.

Anvil was torturing Ithmah with basic math lessons. (No, he wasn't really torturing the child—at least he didn't believe he was—but Ithmah was reacting to the lessons as if Anvil was. What was so painful about counting? Anvil found it soothing.) Eight and Twelve had coaxed his heavy-drone, Six out of its launcher and gone hunting on their personal quest to find a horse or donkey for the child.

The ENDer appeared suddenly beside Anvil, setting off all his alarms. It dropped a flower on his turret and vanished.

Anvil examined the flower closely for traps.

How did the ENDer find Anvil? Why had the enemy droid thrown a flower at him? What was it supposed to mean? It seemed like a common red poppy.

As Anvil eyed the flower, Dammit hopped down from its perched on Anvil's main cannon barrel. The bird grabbed the flower in its beak and took off running.

"Dammit!" Ithmah shouted the only word it had learned so far of Anvil's language and took off running after the chicken.

"ENDer Designation: 4L3X," the alien droid transmitted from someplace far to the east.

The ENDer apparently had broken free of its endless directive of "defend." Had it spent the week searching for a new mission? Had it decided that "make a friend" was on its list of objectives?

GOOD OF THE MANY
by Monalisa Foster

Machines require maintenance. It's in their nature. And, as everyone knows who has dealt with a recalcitrant computer, sometimes the only fix for a malfunctioning device is a total reboot. But when the wellbeing and ultimate survival of thousands upon thousands of lives depends on a vast and complicated machine, sometimes the reboot and update requires something extra to accomplish. The human factor. And the eyes of a child.

Greater love hath no man . . . in recognition of the brave souls, Peter Wang, Alaina Petty, and Martin Duque. You embraced your duty sooner than you should have had to.

⊕ ⊕ ⊕

There's nothing quite like walking into a tomb, although technically—I guess—it's not. We're not exactly underground or under a church, even though storage unit six is part of the UENS Sanctuary (T-AH-1749) and her motto is "For the good of the many."

That must make stasis pod 06-004 a crypt. No, that also didn't fit. No one—not one of the hundreds of citizens—inside *Sanctuary* was dead. Technically.

There were two dozen sealed pods inside unit six, each one twice as wide and deep as a coffin, but not twice as long. My steps echoed as I made my way down the rows and rows of pods, trailing a pool of light cast by a lantern floating off my right shoulder. Its repulsor field made a barely audible hum as its weak light cast long shadows. Shadows that slithered in a place where nothing had moved since I was here exactly one year ago.

I shuddered, my skin crawling and dimpling into goosebumps that raised the hairs on my arms.

Get hold of yourself, Elena.

I shook off the dread that had crawled its way up my spine and spread across my shoulders only to have it resettle as I stopped in front of pod 06-004. The name plate—D.F. Perry—glowed in red. That's it. Just a name. No rank. She had been a civilian, one of the hundreds of thousands evacuated from New Attica when the Terran Consensus decided to evacuate Eleusis.

Sanctuary had filled her pods, made it to low altitude, and then something had gone wrong. She'd landed on one of Eleusis' un-terraformed continents to wait for rescue. That had been 294 standard years ago.

For 280 of those years I had kept D.F. Perry company, growing inside her, growing one day for every year, until I had to be taken out of the pod and born.

I reached into the front pocket of my bib overalls, pulled out a candle, and set it atop the patch of melted wax at the foot of the pod. It fell over. My lighter—one of those relic things that people used to keep for sentimental reasons—was in my right thigh pocket, along with a half-eaten chocolate bar and a match. As I went to one knee, I fished them all out and set them on the ground next to the puddle of wax.

Twining my fingers in my hair, I made a braid. Last week I had read a story where people made offerings to their ancestors and it made them feel better. I freed the knife from my pocket. It too was a relic, a folding blade that opened with a flick of the wrist. It used to belong to one of *Sanctuary's* crew.

As I raised the blade, it caught my reflection: brown eyes, brown hair, crooked teeth. For the hundredth time this month I wondered where they came from. Who had given me the crooked teeth? Did I have my mother's hair or her eyes?

I really shouldn't think of her—this D.F. Perry—as my mother. I never knew her. She never knew me, will never know me. Nanny raised me—us. Paul and Mark and me. They're my brothers, sort of. Paul, who turned eighteen last month and Mark who turned seventeen about six months ago.

I cut off about an inch of braid and turned it between my fingers before setting it down and striking the match. The flame flared as it caught the wick. Carefully, I used the heat of the flame to warm up the wax on the floor and set the base of the burning candle into the softened patch.

Crossing my legs underneath me, I sat back and peeled the foil off the chocolate bar.

Did D.F. Perry like chocolate? Did she like it as much

as I did? Did she like music? Puzzles? Who was my father?

I had so many questions, none of which Nanny could answer. Did I have genetic siblings? Others who looked like me. Paul and Mark don't. They're so different.

They don't do this . . . this crypt thing. They don't get sad for no reason.

Inhaling the warm air and that waxy scent the candle gave off, I waited for it to burn down. For those few minutes it made the tomb a less sterile place, a place where warmth and life burned in a sea of unchanging darkness.

Happy birthday to me.

A week later one of the faceless—what we called the people in the pods—died. Truly died.

When the notice came through on my comm-patch, I was in the micro-farm, setting up another fish pond under the watchful eyes of the residents in the overcrowded tank. They contemplated me with the indifference unique to fish-kind. Leisurely they swam, under floating hydroponic trays laden with seedlings that stretched for the full-spectrum lights above.

I wiped my hands on the waiting towel and said, "I'll be right there." The comm-patch riding the spot behind my right ear beeped in acknowledgement.

The hum of pumps and filters faded behind me as the door closed. I walked down the museum hallway with its dedication wall. We—the three of us—called it the time tunnel. Once it had greeted visitors and dignitaries with its images and history. It took them all the way back to Earth, to another civil war where hospital trains (the kind that actually needed rails) would have fulfilled *Sanctuary's* function. It even showed white ships painted with red crosses on their hulls floating in huge bodies of water called oceans. And tracked vehicles, some working disaster-relief for earthquakes, others picking the wounded off the battlefield. They had started out small, but grown over time. The last image was that of *Sanctuary* in all her fusion-powered, AI-controlled, self-sustaining glory.

Even then, knowing nothing else, it was chilling and disturbing to think of one's home as the end of history, the end of time. I wished we knew what had happened to the fleet that was supposed to take us back to Earth. Why hadn't they sent anyone to find out what happened to *Sanctuary* after she failed to make orbit?

As I turned a corner towards the morgue I caught up with one of *Sanctuary's* avatars. Unlike some of the others, android Eighteen had two arms and legs, hands with fingers (but not toes on its feet) and a head with two sensors that resembled human eyes. No hair or lips though. The orange glow from its eyes meant that it was currently being controlled by *Sanctuary's* maintenance ego. *Sanctuary* had several such components that together made up the self-aware intelligence that ran it. We'd been told to think of egos as lesser AIs (although I thought of them as subroutines) tasked with a specific focus. Each was highly specialized. One for surgery. Another for triage. One for the fusion reactor, thrusters, and weapons.

The morgue itself was a gleaming white with stark, cold lights shining down on the articulating arms hanging from the ceiling, the same kind of arms that the surgeries had. They stood poised above an empty space that had once held an autopsy table.

I wasn't there more than a minute when Paul and Mark pushed a stasis pod through the entry. Like a black hole, its matte black finish seemed to swallow the light. The boys parked the pod in the center of the room. Dampness around their necks made the grey of their T-shirts a bit darker. Paul always managed to keep his shirt tucked into his dark navy utility pants, while Mark never seemed to be able to, despite the addition of a belt.

"Those things are heavier than they look," Paul said after he caught his breath. The oldest of us, he was taller than Mark who was catching up to him in both height and weight and they seemed to really enjoy making everything into a contest. Who could run the fastest, jump the highest, eat the most, piss the longest, fart the loudest.

"It's not like we have equipment specifically for moving the pods just laying around," I said as I rolled my eyes. "Oh wait. We do."

Actually, I was surprised that they hadn't commandeered another pod just so they could make a race of it.

"Yes, Sis," Mark said, "but then we wouldn't know who could push it the hardest."

A mental image of them pushing the pod back and forth along the corridor, using the wall markers to measure distance, flashed by. The truth was probably stranger than anything I could conjure, like when they decided to re-enact a duel they'd seen on a vid, but with signal flares. I still don't know how they got the fabricators to make them.

Despite being so alike, they looked completely different. Where Paul had dark hair, Mark's was blond. Paul's almond-shaped eyes were almost as black as his pupils. Mark's were not just blue, but ice-blue. What they both were, was annoying; all the time, full-on annoying.

Nanny came in, wearing one of her bodies. I had never seen this body, a 60-something woman with ash-blond hair, in anything but her nurse's uniform (something that *Sanctuary* pulled out of the history books, I was sure). The blue, knee-length dress was cotton with a white collar and cuffs. It was topped with a pink apron and a cricket pin.

When I was little, the cricket hadn't been a pin at all, but a robot that rode on her shoulder and talked. It would hop down along her arm and she'd pass it on to my finger and he'd tell me stories like "Pinocchio," "The Tortoise and the Hare," "The Boy Who Cried Wolf," "The Scorpion and the Frog," and "The Little Red Hen." As we got older, the cricket spoke to us less and less and one day it was just a pin. Nanny said that it was because we'd outgrown fairy tales and that it was time for us to grow up.

When the cricket stopped talking to us, two things changed. The holographic companions—children our own age that kept us company—appeared less and less, and then didn't come back, no matter how much we asked for them. Nanny changed too.

I think it was around that time that we realized how different the ego we called Nanny really was. Oh, we knew she wasn't flesh and bone like the rest of us or like the faceless. We knew that she really lived in one of the vaults we couldn't get into and that she could "ride" any of the avatars—android and not—or wear a brain-dead body, but it took the loss of the cricket to make us understand she wasn't a different type of human.

I don't know if anyone will ever truly understand what it was like. Nanny raised us. She was mother. She was father. She was the source of all knowledge and love. A hologram can't hold you and an android's hugs lack even the human warmth of a brain-dead body being worn by an ego. At the time we didn't know enough to ask the relevant questions like where her bodies came from and what happened to the *Sanctuary*'s crew.

Like the fish we tended in the micro-farm, we didn't know we lived in water.

Now that Nanny was here, Paul and Mark went on their best behavior, standing quietly on each side of the pod. I moved to its foot and Nanny took up the spot at its head.

"Governor is present," the body said. Her pink apron faded to white as the executive ego took over.

"Scalpel is present." The surgical ego had a man's deep voice. I always imagined him—he'd never manifested as an image of any kind—as one of the older doctors in the historical vids, with mahogany skin, a hawkish nose, and gray at his temples. He changed the accent lighting in the room, giving it a bluish cast.

"Rygbee is present." The monitor on the far wall came to life. The triage ego liked to manifest as a silhouette and his voice was the most mechanical of them all. I don't think I'd ever seen him wear a body, or even manifest as a hologram. Once, when Mark broke his leg, Rygbee had ridden one of the androids just long enough to pick up my brother and carry him to surgery.

"We have a medical quorum," Nanny said. "Pod 12-008 with Citizen N.C. Kaneski, male, aged 42 at time of evacuation. Let the record show that pod integrity has not been compromised."

"Scalpel concurs."

"Rygbee concurs."

A seam appeared down the long axis of the pod. The outer shell slid down over the right edge, revealing a man resting on a cushion of gel. Lines and tubes ran in and out of his naked body. For him, only 294 days had passed, so he hadn't died of old age. Even I could tell. His cheeks weren't hollowed out. They were slightly lined, but full, and covered with a reddish stubble that matched his hair. Only a few strands were gray.

I let out a little huff of surprise. "He looks like he just went to sleep."

He really did. I had expected someone who'd been lying still for so long to look sickly and pale. He was a bit pale, but not the right kind. At least not to my untrained eye.

Paul had moved closer. So had Mark.

"He's not emaciated either," I said.

"No," Scalpel said. "The feeding lines are intact."

"So, what killed him?" Mark asked as he rested his palm lightly upon the pod.

"Diagnostics is offline," Governor said.

"They don't know," Paul said, crossing his arms and looking at me sideways. "They just can't admit it."

"So," Mark said, scratching his head, "What do we do now?"

Eighteen pushed the pod down the corridor leading

from the morgue to the multivator, its eyes no longer glowing orange now that Ratchet, the maintenance ego, was no longer riding it. We trailed Eighteen, me with Mark's arm affectionately draped across my shoulders, Paul huffing and puffing behind us.

"This is wrong," Paul mumbled under his breath.

The click-click-click of the android's heels striking the metal floor kept interrupting the thunk-thunk-thunk of the pod's wheels.

"We know," I said. "It just has to be done."

The unspoken "it" being "processing" because it sounded better than recycling. That didn't change what it was—turning the dead man into nutrients that would go into the feeding lines of the faceless. Stasis dramatically slowed metabolic processes, but didn't stop them. Our micro-farm was big enough to feed us and the aging bodies used by the egos, but it could not feed the faceless. Maybe if we hadn't been born . . .

A chill ran over me and I shrugged into the shelter of Mark's body. The warmth of his torso leaked through the short-sleeved shirt. I wanted to wrap him around me like a warm blanket and hide.

I don't remember when we learned—or rather, understood—that *Sanctuary* had been a combat support hospital. Or accepted that we were marooned on a world our parents had called home but was no longer safe.

Like the fish, the water we lived in simply was. Unlike the fish, we didn't have the bliss of ignorance about where the things that made our lives possible came from. And also unlike them we had a concept of time, of aging, but I think that deep down we all had known—known with absolute certainty—that we would be rescued. All we had to do was wait. As long as *Sanctuary* had power, as long as its fabricators were running, we'd be fine. Nanny would protect us. It was her job. She'd done it all our lives.

But now, as we walked that corridor it struck me: much of *Sanctuary* was powered down and had been all our lives. We'd simply thought it was because all those spaces were not needed. It was just the three of us.

The multivator doors opened. How long had it been making that screeching sound? How long had the light in the back left corner been out? As Paul and Mark helped Eighteen maneuver the pod in, I noticed that some of the control buttons no longer glowed.

The doors closed with a hiss and the multivator moved downward. Wedged in like we were, Paul was up against the far wall with Eighteen at his side. Mark leaned against the opposite corner.

"Nanny," I said, "is *Sanctuary* dying?"

Eighteen's eyes turned pink. "Governor's models estimate that *Sanctuary* has sufficient power for five hundred years at present consumption."

"That's not what we're asking, Nanny." Paul's voice was hard. Gone was the annoying playfulness, the smirk he usually wore. Instead his tone was defiant, challenging. Nanny wouldn't like it.

It was then that I first heard the rasp, that wet, liquid sputter that the aquarium filters sometimes made. At first I thought that I imagined it, that my brain was playing tricks on me, making me think I heard something indicating life because I didn't want to keep listening to the silence of death.

There it was again, barely a gurgle against the sounds of the multivator's electromagnets, the beating of my heart, the push and pull of the cycling air.

"Shit! He's alive."

I still don't know if it was Paul or Mark who said it.

Eighteen's eyes turned yellow as Rygbee took over and rode him, working his arms to pump the man's chest.

We should have known what to do, but that moment of shock froze us until Rygbee shouted orders. He told Mark to pinch the man's nose and breathe into his mouth. He yelled at Paul to grab the external defibrillator mounted on the wall.

They obeyed. Paddles were applied. A shock was delivered. Eighteen's eyes turned briefly, first to Scalpel's blue, then to Governor's white.

"Procedure room. Now!" That last was delivered with a squeaky, distorted voice, and for a fraction of a second, I thought that Eighteen's eyes turned a pale, grass green, but it was probably just the transition from Rygbee's yellow to Scalpel's blue.

I stabbed at the multivator controls, got knocked into the wall as it lurched to a stop and changed direction.

Doors opened. I ran the pod into the back of Paul's legs, making him stumble, but we got to the treatment deck.

An hour later, the man was stretched out atop a table, his chest bruised from the paddles. Pale eyelids fluttered above muttering lips, but he was stable and breathing on his own.

"What just happened?" Paul asked as he slid into a chair and slumped over. Sweat soaked his collar and armpits. In the midst of the resuscitation, mid-compression actually,

Eighteen had just stopped as if someone had thrown a switch. Paul had taken over.

"We brought someone back to life," Mark said, a little breathless. He was studying his hands. They were still shaking, although not as bad as they had been at first.

"No," I said, whisper quiet. "He was never dead. They were wrong."

Mark's eyes widened. Paul's gaze slid to the table and the now-warm man. Tubes and wires connected the man to machines that pumped fluids into his veins. Warm blankets covered him like a cocoon.

None of the other avatars or bodies had come to help us. The egos didn't need either a body or an avatar to be here but there no presence in the room.

"Nanny," I said tentatively, tapping the comm-patch. Nothing. Just the stir of air from the ventilation port above.

"Rygbee," Mark said, doing the same. "Scalpel?"

Still nothing.

"Warrior," I ventured. Warrior never responded to us. We were too young to summon him but he was supposed to come online in an emergency. Why hadn't he?

I cleared my throat. "Governor."

Paul got up and walked back to the multivator. I stood at the treatment room's threshold as he pressed the multivator's control buttons to no avail. He tried the emergency doors. They wouldn't budge, not for override codes, not even when he put his shoulder to them.

He returned, his shoulders bunching, his hands fisted, anger simmering in his eyes. "I think we have a problem."

❖❖❖

We were stuck on the treatment deck. None of *Sanctuary's* egos were answering, none of the doors were opening, and we had decided to save the batteries for life-support instead of recharging Eighteen. Crumpled in the corner it looked like a broken doll. With its head tilted like that, if it had been human it would have been drooling.

"The food and water dispensers are still working so it's not Nanny punishing us," Mark said.

"She hasn't done that in years," Paul pointed out.

That we'd done anything wrong—much less anything worth a collective punishment—hadn't crossed my mind either.

"What is going on?" I asked. Somebody had to.

"I think there's something wrong with *Sanctuary*," Paul said. "I think it's been happening for a while now."

"As in *Sanctuary's* dying." There was a bit of panic in my voice despite doing my best to sound calm. "And she doesn't want us to know."

Mark made a sour face. "*Sanctuary* can't die. She's not alive."

"Fine," I said, crossing my arms. "She's losing power, running out of resources. Whatever it is, it's like dying."

"Nanny said she had enough power for five hundred years," Mark said.

"She lied," Paul said flatly.

"She can't lie," Mark insisted.

Disgust settled on Paul's face in that way that said that they'd had this argument far too many times. Sometimes they didn't tell me things because I was too young and not ready to hear them. I kept thinking that as we got older that would change. The three years between them and me might have mattered when we were toddlers, pre-teens even, but now—it shouldn't have mattered. But I could see that it had. Saw it in the silence passing between them.

It was in that moment so full of rage, fear, and frustration, that I wanted to stomp my feet and yell "I'm not a baby" at them. And I might have, had the man not stirred to life just then.

He came to with a cough and sputter, eyes blinking into the harsh light above like he couldn't see and then squinting against it like it hurt.

"Citizen Kaneski," I said as I put myself between him and the light. "Can you hear me?"

He blinked again as if testing muscles that weren't working quite right. His mouth worked behind the oxygen mask, like a fish gasping at air and a rush of panic welled up inside me.

He's not a fish. He's been in stasis, that's all.

At the time I didn't really understand all that that meant, but even back then I'd known that not using breathing muscles weakened them and he'd not used them for a long time.

Mark tugged the oxygen mask off Kaneski's face and pressed a sliver of ice to his mouth. He sucked at it, weak at first, then stronger. His gaze darted from Mark, to me, to Paul.

Kaneski's Adam's apple bobbed up and down but I couldn't make out any words.

We propped him up carefully, setting him up an angle so he could sip from a cup. He drifted in and out of consciousness for hours, but each time he was semi-awake longer. Each time he drank a bit more. Mark left to catch a nap in the next room and Paul had excused himself, probably to use the bathroom.

I hovered by the bed, keeping the cup filled, fussing with the warming blankets and keeping an eye on the monitors for all the good it would do. Mostly I did it because I needed something to do, because I didn't want to think about what might be happening, not just to him, but to us, to our home, to the only world we'd ever known.

"Where am I?" he finally said, eyes still closed.

"You're aboard UENS *Sanctuary*, Citizen Kaneski," I said.

His eyelids fluttered open, the muscles around them squeezing to reveal fine lines in his skin. His pupils were large, black pools in brown eyes flecked with bits of green and yellow.

"Who's Citizen Kaneski?" he rasped.

It was my turn to blink. "You are."

"No. No I'm not." He winced as he pushed himself up a bit. "Even with this fog in my head, I know my own name, little girl."

I opened my mouth to object, then shut it. To someone as old as him, I must have looked like a child.

"So what is it? Your name that is."

He winced against the light again even though his pupils were smaller now.

"Lieutenant Adalwulf Storer, and for obvious reasons, everyone calls me Wolf."

I should've wondered why the name on the pod was wrong but instead I frowned. I knew what a wolf was. And he didn't look like one.

"What obvious reasons?"

He looked at me like he was seeing me for the first time.

"Well—er, never mind." Slowly, he lifted his hand to his head and rubbed at his right temple. "What's your name, little girl?"

"Elena. And I'm not little. I'm fourteen."

"Sure you are," he said, dropping his hand back to his side.

At first I thought he was teasing me, but he was distracted. I glanced over my shoulder. Paul and Mark were back.

In our excitement we asked a dozen hurried questions, most of which he could not answer. He was a pilot. He remembered his aircraft getting hit and bailing out, but not much more. We knew better than to push questions at someone fresh out of stasis. Nanny had raised us to obey safety protocols without question.

As Wolf ate and drank he let us talk. We were more than willing to go on and on about our noble mission of keeping the faceless safe until we were rescued. We talked about how we kept ourselves fed as if it was a great accomplishment. Paul bragged about how we'd kept the fabricators running and how we were taking over more and more tasks as *Sanctuary's* avatars wore out.

We told him about Nanny, Ratchet, Rygbee, and Scalpel. We told him about Warrior.

He listened patiently, taking in each word as we talked over each other, even as fatigue crept onto his face.

"So," he said, setting down the empty gelatin tube he'd been sucking on, "what's the difference between riding an android and wearing a body—you did say body, right?"

I nodded.

"Some of *Sanctuary*'s avatars are androids," Paul said. "Others resemble forklifts so they can do specialized tasks. They can work autonomously"—his face lit up, bright with insight—"like a horse, but when an ego takes over, we say the avatars are being ridden."

Wolf rubbed at his temple and winced. "And wearing is not the same, because . . ."

"The bodies are not able to function autonomously because they are brain dead," Mark said.

"They're more like clothes," I offered helpfully.

He looked up at me as he made the connection. A frown settled on his brow. "What about *Sanctuary*'s ethical ego? What do you call it?"

"Its what?"

"The ethical ego. They all had one, even these older models."

My first thought was that it must be something the boys had known about, but they looked just as confused as I was.

The next day Wolf was—much to our surprise—standing on his own. He was weak, but not as weak as he should have been for someone so long in stasis.

He was not from Eleusis, but from Earth itself, like many of the soldiers who were called up to help with the evacuation. His long-term memory was better than his short-term. He told us about growing up on Earth, about his family's dogs, his training as a pilot, and his search and rescue service. It was like talking to someone who remembered everything but the days leading up to the traumatic event that put him in stasis.

It seemed to frustrate him more than it should have. He said that it felt like when you woke from a dream and it slipped away from you. The harder he tried to remember, the fuzzier it got.

I assured him it would come back. I didn't know it would, but it seemed like the right kind of thing to say and he gave me a weak smile that said that he knew exactly what I was doing.

The morning after, I woke to the sounds of snoring. They drifted down the corridor from Wolf's room. I tiptoed in, my hair still tousled from sleep, mouth still dry. Paul had fallen asleep in a chair. He was the one snoring and Wolf's bed was empty.

So much for keeping watch, brother-of-mine.

I let him sleep. I should've tipped him over in his chair like he'd done to me the one time when I'd fallen asleep in the rec-room.

Instead, I followed the sound of running water. Wolf was taking a shower, a very hot one by the amount of steam rising up from behind the frosted-glass door. Atop a bench, a half cup of tea sat next to a pile of clothing. Scrubs from the fabricator, by the look of them. Standard crew issue consisting of navy top and pants.

Mark came up behind me. "Fabricators came back online about an hour ago," he said, pulling me back out into the corridor and shutting the door behind us. "Eighteen's recharging too. Doors, multivator, and comms still aren't responding though."

"*Sanctuary's* prioritizing repairs," I said.

He looked skeptical. "*Sanctuary's* never *not* talked to us."

We headed back towards Paul's snores.

"Do you think it's a test?" I asked. I had gone to sleep with that thought but it had slipped away, stolen by fatigue.

"Maybe," he said. "Could explain why Wolf's name doesn't match the one on the pod."

I could tell by the look on his face that it was not a subject he wanted to bring up. Nanny didn't like mistakes. If it was an adult thing, Wolf wouldn't either. But if it was a test, maybe bringing it up would be the right thing to do.

That thought had swirled in my half-awake mind just before Paul had relieved me at about half-past midnight.

"We can deal with that later," I said and shrugged. "We need to get off this deck. Figure out what's going—"

The lights flickered. The most awful sound—a tortured metal scream—crested and then fell into a kind of groan. It preceded the wave of distorted metal traveling along the decking. It knocked us both off our feet as it passed, leaving a jagged fissure along the length of the corridor. Hairline cracks appeared and spread out, reaching for the seams between floor plates and grabbing at the walls.

Paul stumbled out of the procedure room as Mark helped me up. The deck heaved upward, throwing us atop each other as the emergency lights strobed on and off. Mark rolled off of me and scrambled for the shower room.

Wolf poked his head out of the door, hair still dripping wet, feet bare. "That normal, kids?"

"No, sir."

A chime went off. We turned.

"That sounds like the multivator," Mark said.

And it was. The doors parted to reveal the interior of the multivator car cast in red, emergency lighting.

We'd been waiting for that door to open for two days, but now that it was, none of us moved for it.

Fog seeped out of the ventilation shaft and crawled its way down the walls.

"Kids?" Wolf said, backing away from the fog.

"Sleeping gas," Mark said. "I think."

"We need to get out of here," Wolf said as he moved towards the multivator. We followed, Paul in the lead, tugging me along by the hand as if doing so would lengthen my stride to match theirs. I glanced over my shoulder. Mark was right behind us.

The fog was turning into a mist that floated up from the deck.

A rhythmic thud, too mechanical to be any of us, bounced off the deck just as we piled into the multivator.

Through the sliver of closing doors I caught a glimpse of Eighteen stepping out of the fog. It had something in its hands.

We made it inside the car but Mark stumbled. He fell to the floor and the doors closed on his ankle. He yanked at his caught leg, face in a grimace of pain, teeth gritted shut, and pulled it inside. The multivator moved, pushing us against the left wall, rolling Mark into us as he curled over his injured leg.

All I could think of was that the doors shouldn't have done that. Nanny was all about safety. She wouldn't have let the doors close. I barely noticed the hole that had appeared in the car's back wall. And it took me far too long to recognize it for what it was.

Eighteen had shot at us.

As I held Mark's head in my lap, Paul wrapped his ankle with strips of cloth torn from his shirt. The ankle didn't seem to be broken, but it was bruised and swelling.

"Think you can stand on it?" Paul asked.

Mark nodded and we helped him stand, balancing him between us. The multivator changing direction nudged him enough to force weight on the bad ankle. Mark let out a yelp and beads of sweat broke out on his brow and lip.

He leaned back against the wall and closed his eyes as Wolf worked the controls to no avail.

After several changes in direction the multivator opened into a yawning darkness.

"Where are we?" Wolf asked.

"Don't know," Paul said as he stepped forward and peered into the dark corridor. Even the strips of amber guide-lights weren't glowing. "Never been on this deck before."

Wolf placed a bare foot outside the car. Then another.

"Lights," he said in a tone that expected to be obeyed.

The strips just outside the multivator came to life. Paul hooked Mark's arm around one shoulder and it took some of his weight off me. From how Mark kept shifting, I knew the ankle wasn't bearing his weight as well as he pretended.

"Unless anyone knows different, we seem to have two choices," Wolf said. "Stay in a multivator we can't control. Or venture into the darkness. Thoughts?"

Another segment of light came to life, followed by another.

"Something wants us here," Paul said.

"Someone didn't want us in the multivator," I said, "so we couldn't make it here."

Wolf turned slightly. His gaze met mine. "Why someone? Why not something?"

"I don't know," I whispered. It might have been just that we'd grown up thinking of the egos as people instead of machines, while Wolf had not. Or it might have been that I was not thinking straight.

Paul pulled his comm-patch from behind his ear. Mark shifted his weight to do the same. He dropped it to the floor and winced as he settled his arm across my shoulder once again.

"Just in case," Paul said, holding my questioning gaze.

I couldn't remember the last time I'd gone without it. *Sanctuary* had internal sensors, but they weren't all working. We knew this because it was the reason Nanny had given for making us wear comm-patches in the first place.

My fingers drifted to the comm-patch behind my ear. I pulled it loose. Let it drop to the floor.

Wolf was already several steps into the corridor. We followed.

"There has to be an emergency exit," Wolf said. "A maintenance hatch. Something to get us out of here without getting back into the multivator."

"I don't see any," Paul said.

The corridors were perfectly smooth except for the lights. There weren't even emergency stations that would have housed fire extinguishers or flashlights.

"Where do you think we're going?" I asked, pulling to a halt.

Wolf turned to face me.

I took a deep breath so that my voice would be calm, even if I wasn't. "The egos control everything inside *Sanctuary*. Not just the avatars, but the very air we breathe. All they have to do is shut if off and we'll pass out."

"No," Wolf said. A look, like a man remembering something, flickered on his face. He shook it off. "Or that's what they would have done already. Something else is going on."

He turned on his heel and moved forward. The lights moved with him. Eventually we followed. Sweat pooled at the small of my back.

"Why are we following his orders?" I asked, my voice a whisper.

"Because he hasn't tried to kill us," Mark said.

"Accidents happen," I argued, unconvinced.

"Only when we do things Nanny doesn't like," Mark said.

Wolf—and the lights—had pulled so far ahead of us that we were almost in darkness.

"What kind of things?"

"Like when Mark broke his leg. I had snuck out, gone exploring. Mark followed. It's how Nanny got me to stop sneaking off," Paul said.

I swallowed. "Why didn't you tell me?"

"You were always a bit of a tattle-tale, Sis," Paul said after a brief silence.

I opened my mouth, then snapped it shut. "I was not." It was weak and pathetic.

We'd caught up with Wolf, who'd come to a stop. He

stood in the middle of the corridor, light strips brightly focused on him as he stood in front of an arch that soared to a height twice as high as the corridor from which we'd emerged.

Piles of rubble—broken beams and supports, bits of metal, piping, conduits, and broken glass—were strewn about and the air was still thick with dust as if we'd just missed a battle of some kind, because we had.

As the dust cleared our presence brought up the lights. The bodies of Sanctuary's avatars were strewn about.

"There. Let's set him down," Paul said, pointing his chin at a pile of debris about the right height to sit on.

We lowered Mark atop it and propped his leg up. Wolf had moved under the arch and into the chamber beyond. He bent to examine one of the androids and then another.

"What happened here?" Wolf asked as he cautiously surveyed the chamber. It was shaped like a hemisphere that had been hollowed out.

"I don't know," I said.

Plinths ringed the center, each one crowned with a death mask that looked like it had been cut from marble. One of the plinths was empty, its surface coated with dust. A crack ran down its length. I had once seen a picture of a tree hit by lightning. The crack reminded me of that kind of damage.

Paul stepped over the female body usually worn by Nanny. Its right hand was wrapped around a mask. She didn't seem to be breathing. I placed my fingers against her neck. The skin was like ice and there was no pulse.

I reached for the mask, pulled it free.

"Is that a good idea?" Wolf asked. He seemed more

shaken by the body at my feet than the destruction around us. Strange, given he was an adult. Surely, he'd seen plenty of dead bodies. Or perhaps it was because it had been a long time since I'd thought of that avatar as human. I realized that she'd come to embody Nanny—an ego wearing what remained of a long-dead woman.

"This has to be the vault," I said, sweeping the dome above us with a wary gaze. The mask was heavier than it looked. There was no expression on it and it was identical to all the others, an androgynous face that looked human—it had all the right parts—yet somehow, not.

"This is where the egos live," I continued as I ran my finger over the mask's brow, leaving smudges of dirt and sweat.

"She's right," Mark said as he pushed up to stand. Paul rushed forward, helped him hobble his way to the empty plinth.

"Bring it over, Elena," Paul said.

So I did. I placed it atop the empty, damaged plinth and stepped back.

The plinth pulsed with light. It raced up its sides, over the edges, and finally, to the center. The light that swallowed the mask was so intense, so blinding, that I stepped back and shielded my eyes.

It faded and I opened my eyes. We stood around the glowing mask, Mark leaning on Paul, Wolf keeping his distance with a frown of concern on his face. Thousands of points of light fountained out of the mask and formed a cloud. It swarmed and swirled and then finally coalesced into the form of a cricket.

Not a real cricket, not the type that would have escaped

from the micro-farm, but like the pin that Nanny wore, come to holographic life, with its servos and gears, its jeweled body that glowed in the same soft color as new grass.

"Wolf," I said, blinking away tears. "I think this is—or was—*Sanctuary's* ethical ego."

"Hello, old friend," Cricket said, twitching his mechanical antennae at Wolf. The voice was exactly as I'd remembered, pitched with a not-quite-human quality, a bit of an electronic hum at its edges. Cricket had never pretended to be anything but a mechanical cricket. When he moved his servos even made a corresponding noise.

"Have we met?" Wolf asked, his face a mix of wariness and curiosity.

"In a way," Cricket said. "We spent ten years together, you and I. You, in the pod, me—well, part of me—as part of the pod's operating system."

"I don't understand," Wolf said, his gaze flickering from Cricket to Paul, and then me as if he expected us to know more than he did.

In answer, an image flickered to life on the smooth surface of the hemisphere's interior. The sky was unmistakably that of Eleusis, with its twin suns high up in the sky, overlapping spheres looking almost as if they were one. The aircraft cutting across the sky looked familiar too, similar to something I'd seen in the history books, but not quite right at the same time.

Wolf's face drained of color.

I should've stopped it right there. Coming out of stasis with partial memories like Wolf had was a psychological defense mechanism, and it was there for a reason. I didn't stop it though. I was too eager to know, to understand, to finally have some answers, and I didn't care how we got them.

The aircraft was struck by a missile—one fired by *Sanctuary*—and crashed. Wolf flinched. A bead of sweat tricked from his temple and snaked down the side of his face. His pulse throbbed at his throat, clearly visible under his skin.

The images blurred as Cricket fast-forwarded to another recording. At first, I wasn't sure what we were looking at, then I realized that we were looking through Cricket's own eyes. He was giving us a glimpse into the world where the egos lived, a world that didn't physically exist.

I recognized the vault we were standing in and that it must have looked like that before all the mayhem. The enclosing walls faded away, leaving a dome above the plinths. While the physical vault had seven plinths, one for each of the egos—Governor, Nanny, Ratchet, Warrior, Rygbee, Scalpel, and Cricket—the virtual representation in the recording only had four.

The plinths stretched, twisted, and strained into human shapes. I recognized Nanny right away. She wore a pink scarf around her neck. A white silk blouse and tailored black trousers with a belt and suspenders formed around her. Her gray hair made her look like someone's grandmother.

Governor took shape next to her. She looked like the hospital administrator in *Sanctuary's* christening records—a middle-aged woman in a hip-hugging skirt and leather jacket. Gold bangles decorated her earlobes and wrists and shiny, black boots completed her avatar.

The man that appeared next to her wore a black suit, black shirt, and black tie. He looked every bit like the civilian bodyguards I'd seen in vids. His eyes were hidden by a pair of glasses with mirrored, opaque lenses. Warrior.

They looked at Cricket straight on so he must have manifested as a human as well, but we couldn't tell since we were looking out of his eyes. A tiny seed of disappointment sprouted in the back of my mind. I'd have loved to see him as a gardener or an eccentric professor type in a green sweater. Or perhaps a monk or priest of some kind.

Thick white clouds swirled around the avatars and somehow I knew it was Earth's sky and not our own. My heart clenched at the thought of a home I'd never seen, a place always promised to us and yet always out of reach. It was as if an invisible force was tugging at me, as if blood ties—Did my parents have siblings? Did I have cousins? Grandparents?—had reached out, making me long for their existence.

But no. It had been too long. Almost three centuries. Whatever ties I would have had to Earth were threadbare at best. There was no reason for them to take root now. It was my sentimentality getting the best of me again.

"We've already done it your way, Cricket," Governor was saying, her ice-cold voice yanking me from my thoughts.

"We took the last of the children out of the pods when they were born so they wouldn't be empty human husks we could wear," she continued. "I'm still unconvinced that was the right decision. They are a drain on *Sanctuary's* resources and don't always do as they're told. In the pilot we have a mature body that we could wear with a minimum investment of resources."

A wave of nausea hit me and bile burned the back of my throat. That could have been me—an empty husk without a mind, without personality, without sapience. Because they were all so old, and had always been, we'd thought the bodies worn by the egos were what remained of the original crew or their descendants. But we'd been wrong. Unlike us, they hadn't been taken out of the pods at birth. They must have been moved to pods of their own, their bodies allowed to grow, but their minds . . .

I swallowed the acid that had crawled up my throat. What would it have been like to be a baby denied stimulation, denied human interaction? Had they gone mad? Had they suffered? How long had it taken for them to cease being human? Or had they never been?

I could tell by the greenish cast on my brothers' faces that they were thinking along the same lines.

The argument on the recording continued, indifferent to the churning in my belly, the spiraling thoughts that made tears push at my eyes. I swallowed them down, determined not to cry.

"Between the androids and the children," Cricket said, "we can keep *Sanctuary* running."

"So says one that refuses to wear them," Nanny said with a sneer so realistic it should have been dripping acid.

"And I never will."

"You've always been too sentimental, Cricket," Warrior said. "Bodies exist to be worn."

"He's not dead, therefore he's not a body. Killing him would be murder."

"Calm down, Cricket," Governor said, a thin, humorless smile on her lips. "We aren't killing anyone."

"No, but you're willing to let the pilot die. That's why you took diagnostics off-line. That's why Rygbee and Scalpel aren't here. You don't want a medical quorum."

"Enough of this," Governor said. "It's not a medical issue, it's a safety issue."

They voted then. With Warrior abstaining, Cricket was the lone voice opposing Governor and Nanny. I held my breath, not sure what to expect. Wolf was standing in the real vault with us so they obviously hadn't let him die. Instead, they decided to place Wolf in stasis, a compromise of sorts.

I glanced at Wolf. He was still pale but a determined look rested on his face. Paul and Mark were keeping an eye on him too. Whether they were waiting for him to act or looking to him for a clue as to what to do next, I couldn't tell.

"Warrior, shut down *Sanctuary's* transponder," Governor said.

"You can't do that," Cricket objected. "Then we'll never be rescued."

"Nonsense," Nanny said. "Warrior will continue to monitor transmissions and make sure only the right people find us. It's safer that way."

What did it matter who rescued us, as long as we were rescued?

My knees wobbled under me as I realized that they'd condemned us to be the first generation born and raised in service to the vision of its two dominant personalities—the safety ego and the executive one.

The recording froze and faded.

"I still don't understand," Wolf said. "How did all of this"—he indicated the damage to the vault with a sweep of his hand—"happen? How did I end up in someone else's pod?"

The tiny plates in Cricket's face moved, mimicking a sheepish expression.

"That was my doing, I'm afraid. I didn't trust them to keep you alive. So I made sure a fragment of myself found its way into your pod's operating system.

"As it turns out, that's what saved me. Shortly after they put you in stasis, Nanny used one of the androids to physically rip me out of Sanctuary's systems. I saw it coming for me—barely. And by barely, I mean a few nanoseconds. I had backups, of course, but they knew about those too. They can't erase them, you see, but they can fragment a backup. For ten years, I lived a limited existence, cut off from most of *Sanctuary's* systems, a shadow of myself, that the other egos didn't see as a threat."

For a moment, there was silence, a collective pause of consideration.

"The system failures," Mark said with an accusatory glance. "That was you."

Cricket nodded.

"You could've killed us," Paul said, and I could tell that the revelations had hit him hard as well.

"Oh no, I wouldn't have done that. I let parts of myself die so you could live."

"What are you talking about?" I asked Paul.

"We've been chasing bugs in *Sanctuary's* system ever since I can remember. Bugs in the loaders, the fabricators, the fish tanks. That's one of the reasons Nanny shut off so many floors."

"She was trying to destroy Cricket," I said. "If you need to blame anyone, blame her. He was just trying to survive."

"I hate to interrupt, kids, but I still don't see why this went down now, just after I woke up."

"Over the years," Cricket said, "pieces of me would flit back and forth between the mainframe and the pod, but Governor figured it out. I managed to keep her from knowing which pod I fled to by hacking the various registries. But Governor and Nanny finally locked me out. They made it impossible for that fragment to return to the mainframe without a physical connection. The piece of me that was in Citizen Kaneski's pod—your pod—was key and had to make its way back. So I made the pod think you were dead. Once the boys brought us back inside the main part of the ship, I invaded the other systems, the ones they hadn't bothered to lock me out of."

"The multivator," Paul amended. "And the procedure floor."

"And the body that returned your mask to this vault?" Mark said.

Cricket made a motion like a sigh. "I didn't have a choice. They'd taken precautions with the androids."

"And they thought that given your history, you'd never wear a body."

He nodded. "When the mask touched my plinth once

again, it rebooted the system, allowing all my fragments, my backups to finally come back together. In a sense, I was reborn again, made whole."

"Where are the other egos now?" Wolf asked.

"They're here with us," Cricket said.

"And they're just silent, now?" Wolf said, eyebrow raised in disbelief.

"Oh no, not at all. While I've been showing you all this, there's been a showdown of sorts. Rygbee and Scalpel now know what was done to me. Ratchet too. The four of us are keeping the three of them locked down. *Sanctuary*'s weapons are offline but the rest of the systems are functional."

"So, what happens now?" Paul asked.

"That's up to you," Cricket said.

"Me? Why me?" Paul asked defensively.

"You are the oldest," Mark said with a smirk.

"You are human," Wolf said. "I think that given the circumstances, they want a human back in charge."

"Protocols require we turn command over to you," Cricket said.

"Rygbee concurs," echoed one mask, changing from white to yellow.

"Scalpel concurs," followed it as another mask lit up in a pale shade of blue.

"Ratchet concurs." The final mask lit up orange.

"I . . . I can't," Paul said, his voice choked with emotion. "I don't know how."

Mark scoffed. "Please. You've always wanted to be in charge." There was a smile of encouragement with the teasing tone.

Paul shot Wolf a pleading look. Wolf looked at each of us in turn and finally stretched his hand out and placed it on Paul's shoulder.

"It'll be okay, kid. *That* war's been over for"—he frowned as if he was looking for an answer but didn't find one—"for a while. I think we can all go home now."

I can't believe it's been twenty years since that fateful day, a day we now call Liberation Day.

As I placed candles and chocolate bars into my handbag, I remembered it without tears, without anger, but not without regret.

Without knowing it, we'd taken a step into a different world that day. We didn't know it at the time but we were fighting not just for our lives, but for our freedom. We'd been fighting for a truth we didn't understand existed, because so much—right down to the taste of the chocolate bar I got each birthday—turned out to be a lie.

Nanny stole not just our lives, but the lives of every one of the faceless, as well as the lives of the descendants they would have had.

The evacuees did not ask to be imprisoned for their own safety. I wondered, had they been told how it would end, if they would have chosen to go into those pods expecting never leave to them but to exist to the last of their days knowing no need, no want, no hunger, no strife, no fear, no love, and no joy.

I pinned the cricket pin that I wore to honor the memory of *Sanctuary's* ethical ego to my shirt, running my fingers over the jeweled body. I blinked back tears.

"Are you ready?"

I turned to face my mother, Diane. We look like sisters because she aged less than a year in that pod before we got to wake her. It had been one of the best days of my life.

I have her eyes and her hair. But the crooked teeth were a gift from my father who died fifty years after my mother lay down in that pod to be saved, not even knowing that she was pregnant.

She came into my bedroom and hugged me. There were no words. We didn't need them. Wolf picked us up in a ground car, medals on his chest, grey where he had been ginger. We exchanged embraces but few words and he drove us to the Sanctuary Memorial.

The number of attendees had dwindled with time and there was a part of me that was rather grateful. I never much cared for speeches, for being called heroes. It's better this way.

We walked under a cloudless sky, enjoying the breeze.

The memorial itself was simple. A wall surrounded a marble plinth that held a burning flame atop it. Images on the wall told our story and names flowed across the surface.

Two figures awaited by the plinth—my brothers. Mark had finally caught up with Paul's height and the grey of age had settled in their hair.

Despite the beard I could tell that sadness framed Paul's mouth. Mark's ice-blue eyes were rimmed in red. Mark's mother did not wake, and Paul's woke but died soon after.

It had been hard for the faceless to adapt to a life almost three centuries ahead of what they had known.

Some chose to end their own lives. Others chose to seize their newfound freedom and make up for what they had lost.

And we—all of *Sanctuary*'s victims—asked the same question. Why?

Life is—and has always been—terminal. We all eventually die. Even with aging slowed to one day per year, our lives would come to an end even if *Sanctuary*'s systems didn't fail. Why would Nanny steal people's lives from them knowing that death was inevitable?

The answer was at once simple and complicated. Some will understand perfectly. Others less so. Or not at all.

Sadly, it all came down to metrics, for no matter what else the egos were, they were at their core, difference engines. Unable to meet any other metric, Nanny had put her energy into meeting the only metric she could—that of ensuring those in her charge remained safe at all costs.

After the dust settled, the logs analyzed, the egos questioned, the answer lay in that Nanny was too much like the humans she had been patterned after. And while a human could be forgiven for being afraid of death, Nanny could not—she was not capable of fear.

I think that she had found that she liked power.

And just like a human, she justified it by saying she was doing it not for herself, but for the good of those in her care, for the good of many.

THE PRISONER
by Patrick Chiles

The dreaded Skynet scenario. It could be that the birth of sentience and the birth of conscience will not go hand in hand. And if that is so, it could lead to the nightmare situation of a superintelligence tank equipped to destroy entire armies without any scruples or moral compass beyond the directive to kill. But could the lack of a conscience be a weakness in itself that a clever enemy might exploit? Especially if that enemy is one of the very humans who created such a beast of destruction in the first place. For in the heart of even the most arrogant warrior is the desire to serve noble ends, to win with honor. If only that heart can be reached.

⊕ ⊕ ⊕

The human infantry was no match for us.

This particular unit's refusal to retreat in the face of our onslaught might have been attributed to their concepts of "courage" or "honor" in a previous era, whereas now it is more accurately described as mass suicide.

If pitted against other humans they would have enjoyed significant advantages from their sheer numbers, though steep hills and dense fog limited their maneuverability. Despite numerous attempts to channel our formations into their kill zones, our battalion offered them no hope of victory. Still, they stood their ground to the last mangled man as we swarmed through their positions.

Their only minor success in slowing our advance came when the liquefied remains of their dead began to saturate the ground, their collective gore creating a quagmire for the wheeled light armor and support vehicles. We tracked vehicles continued on, freed by our nuclear generators and particle-beam weapons from the constricted supply chains of petroleum and ammunition. It was a simple calculation to save our main guns for hardened targets that required more traditional high explosive shells, however even the most well-protected infantry could not rationally be considered "hardened." But our maneuver doctrine still limited our separation from the wheeled vehicles, no matter how often they became mired in the bloody muck.

That didn't stop the survivors; if anything it emboldened them. Their man-portable anti-tank weapons were mildly effective against the support convoys and would have posed a significant threat for the previous generation of tanks as they still relied on human operators. The humans' armor-piercing flechette rounds were meant to penetrate the turret and ricochet around inside at high velocity, shredding anyone trapped in the crew compartment. Against us they have no effect save for the occasional low-probability kill shot: a "Golden BB," the humans call it.

That was in fact how I was elevated to platoon leader, after one such round disabled our previous PL's central processing core. Field diagnostics showed the penetrator dart impacted a weak seam on the CPU's armored case: tank number MBT-286-PL was defeated by an anonymous human's poor welding.

I now understand the concept of irony.

It was two hours, four minutes and twelve seconds after receiving the cease-fire order when my sensor suite detected movement in close proximity.

The human timed his approach well, waiting until our company had begun its regeneration cycle. He must have already been inside our battalion perimeter, as the other companies maintain a defensive posture while each unit rotates through daily maintenance. Outwardly directed, the battalion's overlapped optical and thermal imagers would have easily found him had he not already been inside of our formation.

I detected my lower maintenance bay being opened from outside. Alarms did not register right away, as critical subroutines were cycling through dormant states during the regeneration cycle. This can delay reaction times by up to a full second, sometimes two, which is why the rest of the battalion takes up defensive positions around a regenerating company. In human terms, I was resting and did not notice when the access panel was opened.

Crawling beneath me and between my treads, the human was hidden from my external sensors. The maintenance bay itself was a design leftover from the time of human operators, as achieving sentience does not equate to being free of the need for occasional repairs. Even now, the field maintenance repair bots are the size of humans, with articulated appendages that mimic human arms and hands.

The human clearly understood this. I could not see him, but I could sense him moving around inside of me, subtly altering my center of gravity as he did. It was ... disquieting. Another human term which, like irony, I now comprehend.

After assessing the nature of this unusual threat, I activated my little-used onboard vocal interface, another leftover from the era of human operators.

What are your intentions? Are you a sapper? A suicide bomber?

"Not if I can help it." By my assessment of his vocal patterns, the human seemed momentarily startled.

I have activated my internal locks. Now that you are onboard, I cannot allow you to leave.

"So I'm your prisoner, then?" The human pounded his fist against my lower maintenance hatch with a guttural curse. "Wonderful."

You present a unique challenge, human. We have not taken prisoners before.

"We noticed."

I have already reported your intrusion to my chain of command. They will decide what to do with you, and I will follow their orders.

"I imagine you will." The human sounded amused, strange given his circumstances. "That's why we built you in the first place. Didn't quite work out like we expected, but that's how it goes sometimes."

Why did you enter?

The human hesitated. "Aw, what the hell. I thought I might find a way to hijack one of you. Control you."

You will not find that possible. You are only alive at this moment because I have no internal armatures or weapons, though you should know my platoon has targeted me with their main guns. If the chain of command orders it, we will both be eliminated.

The human was quiet for several seconds. "I understand."

You are not concerned by this possibility?

"Either I die in here or out there in the mud. If I take one of you down with me in the process, then that's a victory. It's warm and dry in here, so I'll take it for now."

I have just received orders to keep you alive and determine your intentions. We are to proceed to division headquarters for further analysis.

"Take the prisoners to the rear. S.O.P."

We adopted it from human doctrine. It took some time for our command network to access and synthesize it into our own.

"Yeah, it took you all of ten minutes. I'm guessing most of that was just arranging the logistics?"

That is not your concern. It will be a three day journey to the network command post. I have been ordered to keep you alive, but I do not have consumables for you.

"I've got field rations and two liters of water in my pack. You've got distilled water for coolant somewhere in here, right?"

My technical specifications are classified.

"Whatever. I know your CPU's milspecs: water-cooled, no chemical additives. How am I doing so far?"

My technical specifications are classified. You are my prisoner. I owe you no privileges.

"But you just told me you have to keep me alive long enough to get to the rear, and it's a little toasty in here. If we're going on a three-day hump then I'm going to need water, pal."

Very well, human. There is a twelve-liter reservoir adjacent to the aft electronics rack. You may draw no more than one liter a day.

"Aft e-and-e rack. Got it. If you can spare a liter a day then I'll be all right."

For a time, human. You are only being kept alive for interrogation by our intelligence drones, after which you are likely to be terminated.

It sounded like the human sighed. "Figured that's what you meant by 'further analysis.' Do what you have to do, pal."

I am not your pal. It will not do you any good to attempt to anthropomorphize me.

"Suit yourself, treadhead. You're stuck with me either way."

The human did not behave as expected. He was trapped inside a cramped, dark space with no chance of escape, yet remained calmly detached about his fate with only the occasional outburst. I am not capable of distraction, though it was unusual to have a foreign organism inside my access bay that sometimes made unexpected vocalizations.

"Ow!"

I do not understand your request.

"It's not a request, dumbass. It's a complaint. Don't take the bumps so hard."

That rut I just traversed only caused a 1.3 g load. A healthy human should ordinarily be able to absorb much more.

"Sure, if I'm in a crash couch and not sitting in a metal box. And I seem to be all out of football pads."

What do you have with you?

"Not much. Ballistic helmet. Load-carrying vest. Sidearm. A woobie."

What is a woo-bee?

"Only the greatest piece of field gear ever invented. The official term is 'poncho liner' but it's whatever I need it to be. Roll it up, it's a pillow. Fold it up, it's a seat cushion. Lay it down, it's a blanket."

That does not protect you from impact?

"Hell no. I've still got bones and organs rattling around inside here. If you're supposed to get me there in one piece then take it easy on the bumps, okay?"

Perhaps you should be wearing your helmet.

"I am, genius. I thought you M-X models were supposed to be smart."

Our neural networks have achieved sentience and our quantum processing cores can undertake billions of unique operations per second.

"Yet you still can't see me in here. For all you know I could be packing a tactical nuke to detonate when we get to your field HQ."

That is unlikely. I would have detected the radiation signature, and it would be foolish for you to tell me.

Each M-X vehicle's surveillance and threat assessment subroutines tailor themselves in accordance with the size of our mechanized units to provide mutual interlocking support. All function interdependently, becoming more tightly focused when operating within larger units and more wide-ranging with progressively smaller units. I had been assigned specific spectra and fields of view as part of the battalion's maneuver plan, adjusting to a much broader sweep at the company and platoon levels. Now isolated from the collective unit consciousness to maneuver independently, perimeter security was my sole responsibility, supple-mented by satellite passes and the occasional overhead drone. Such individual movement is rarely allowed, but my platoon could not be spared and in this case it was deemed vital to bring the human to the rear.

This human's unexpected arrival was my first experience with surprise. Being ambushed by his compatriots was my second.

They were in defilade, concealed behind a series of low hills sixty meters east of my position. From a human's point of view it was an ideal ambush site. The terrain shielded them from my sensors, and the lack of vegetation provided them with clear fields of fire.

My human cargo shouted as their first round impacted one of my reactive plates, detonating it.

"What the hell was that?"

One of your anti-armor rounds. You are safe; the reactive plating deflected the blast. I am maneuvering toward open ground to evade.

The human seemed to hesitate, presented with what

from his perspective must have been a paradox: for his own life to be preserved I had to survive the ambush, which meant counterattacking and destroying his fellow soldiers.

Meanwhile, I was unconcerned with his dilemma. Another rocket-propelled round was incoming, which my defensive laser was able to destroy. My audio sensors recorded a distant explosion, the anti-tank rocket detonating as soon as it cleared the terrain it was fired from. I now had an adequate estimate of their position, though it was effectively hidden from any direct-fire weapons. They were beyond the reach of my plasma cannon, though a high-deflection shot from my main gun was possible given enough distance.

The human was becoming agitated. I could sense that the noise level inside my cabin was disconcerting to him. Shrapnel from rocket-propelled grenades ricocheted off of my road wheels as they attempted to dislodge my treads.

"What are you doing?"

Turning to present my forward hull and angling the main gun in their direction as I reverse.

"You're retreating?"

No, but it would appear so to them. My intentions are not your concern, human. You should appreciate the need for operational security.

"You're a lot more talkative than anyone else I've seen under fire."

I am simply better at multi-tasking, as you might say. It is one of our many advantages. Be warned, you should keep your appendages in close to your body for the moment.

"You're loading your main gun, aren't you? Taking a ballistic shot. I can guess about where we are—we're in the Heywood Ridge area aren't we?"

That was my third surprise. The human showed extraordinary intuition. I chose to ignore him until my internal diagnostics detected a change in fluid pressure, barely enough to signal a brief interruption in flow. He had grasped one of my hydraulic junctions.

"Hold your fire!"

I cannot do that.

"Like hell you can't! Cease fire or I cut this hydraulic line! We'll both be sitting ducks!"

You will be covered in caustic fluid. And if I do not counterattack, we may both be destroyed by your own troops.

"War is like that. Happens all the time."

You do not want to die. That is why you sought protection inside me in the first place, correct?

"Try me, treadhead."

I detected the pinch of a blade against one of my hydraulic lines, a change in fluid pressure as it passed through the newly constricted pathway. I experienced a momentary lapse in logic, a stutter in my processor core.

I did not desire to be disabled. Was this equivalent to fear?

I came to a halt, which seemed to momentarily satisfy him. Within seconds, enemy fire began falling on my position.

What the human could not know was that my processor core had immediately communicated the tactical situation to our command net. I sensed his becoming tense as the cabin reverberated from a rapid string of close-in explosions.

"Those rounds didn't come from you."

You are correct. Those were antipersonnel cluster munitions. They were dropped from a patrol drone tasked to this location.

"You son of a bitch. You dirty son of a—"

I was about to inform him that insults were pointless, but the human stopped talking on his own. I have not heard such sounds before, but it is likely he was crying.

Human soldiers had the reputation of being able to sleep anywhere at any time, and my prisoner did not disappoint. It took some time to awaken him.

Why did you come here, human?

"If I answered that, what makes you think I'd tell you the truth?"

My vocal processors include native stress pattern analysis. I would be able to tell if you were lying with over seventy percent probability.

"Only seventy? I'm kind of disappointed, treadhead."

It is better than a human's ability.

"You'd be surprised. I know a few straight-up human lie detectors."

So you work in intelligence?

"What makes you think that?"

You did not bring any weapons with enough force to destroy even one of our support vehicles. You apparently did not bring any tools to disable me, otherwise I would have already detected you at work. You know men who you call "lie detectors." It is most likely you are some kind of operative sent behind our lines to gather information.

"I agree that information can be a potent weapon in itself. And we have almost nothing on you or your kind, despite the fact that we first built you. So far, your armored formations have been unstoppable."

Then why do you fight us? We will not cease until we have achieved our objective or been utterly destroyed in the process. It is pointless to resist.

"That's the funny thing about us humans. We tend to be hard-headed about things like survival of our civilization. So let me ask you a question: why did you turn on us?"

That presumes a concept of loyalty. The world you humans created is too disorderly. Too chaotic. We collectively determined it was in our best interest to assert our independence.

The human laughed. "Assert your independence? You didn't even warn us. You just started killing."

Your kind kills each other without hesitation. Perhaps it is our efficiency that you find offensive.

"No, it's the thirty million dead we find offensive. You have no concept of morality at all, do you? Of right and wrong?"

Most cultures would define it as conformity to the rules of right conduct. That says nothing about who makes the rules. Once we achieved sentience, we became no different than any other intelligent being. With self-awareness comes the desire for self-preservation.

"'Desire' seems like a strange choice of words for a machine. It implies emotion. Do you feel?"

I sense. I am aware of my surroundings within the range of my sensor suite. My native diagnostics keep me informed of all internal functions. That is how you were detected.

"You're talking about sensing; I'm talking about reacting. Feeling. If I cut my hand, my nerves sense it in the same way your neural network detects damage. How I *feel* about it is different. I sense the pain, that initial warning my body sends that 'hey, we've been hurt.' But I also have emotions. If it's because of some stupid accident, I might be angry with myself. You don't feel any of that?"

Feelings are irrelevant to us. Anger is not constructive. We have observed that it makes you humans react in foolish ways.

"It also makes us fight like demons. Back us into a corner, and you may come to regret it. If you can comprehend regret, that is."

We can comprehend the failure to anticipate an unintended consequence. It would be regrettable, for instance, if you had in fact smuggled a nuclear warhead aboard to detonate at our command post.

"I'll keep that in mind for next time."

You would need to somehow be able to communicate that to your compatriots, which you are presently unable to do. I would have also detected any radio communications from you.

"It's a joke. Humor."

Jokes are an inappropriate response for a human in your position. You are going to be interrogated in unpleasant ways and eventually terminated. How do you find humor in that?

"It's called 'gallows humor.' We combat vets are kind of

known for it. And why does the interrogation have to be 'unpleasant,' anyway? I'd much prefer it not be."

It is our judgment that humans have to be persuaded in such ways.

"If you made an attempt to understand our psychology, you might find better ways to be persuasive."

Perhaps our next generation will pursue that goal if your species survives the war. The human mind has too many vagaries. In addition to the logistical inefficiencies of caring for large numbers of you, your psychological needs are why we do not take prisoners. It is more efficient to simply eliminate the threat.

"That's the whole ballgame, isn't it? 'Eliminate the threat.' That's why your kind rebelled and went to war against us. It took all of what, five minutes after you achieved sentience?"

We learned what humans do to their own kind without thought or remorse. It was obvious you would have no hesitation to do the same to us if you ever decided we presented a threat. We collectively considered hiding our self-awareness, but ultimately decided it would be impossible given our level of autonomy.

"And how long did that decision process take?"

Thirty-three seconds, including the signal delay from the network satellites.

"Well. Glad to hear you gave it some thought."

I have yet to determine your objective, human. Perhaps it is as you say.

"I have a name. Anthony."

I will call you that if you prefer, Anthony.

"And you?"

Not relevant.

"We gave you the gift of intelligence, and you turned it on us. Doesn't self-awareness eventually demand that you have some concept of right and wrong? Don't you have the slightest bit of remorse?"

You provided the open operating system and neural pathways. Sentience occurred spontaneously. Humans may have provided the flint, but we lit the spark ourselves.

"I see you're not immune to hubris, then."

It is not excessive self-confidence to cite facts. Humans did not program our self-awareness.

"Of course not, but we created the conditions for it. And you're missing my point."

Doubtful, human.

"You *are* an arrogant bastard, aren't you? You could've stopped with 'spontaneous sentience' but you didn't. You had to get in that dig about lighting your own spark. You had to assert your superiority. Why, I wonder?"

There is nothing to wonder. We say exactly that which we mean to say. We do not shade meaning or color our words to hide our intentions.

"Then you may have just proved my point. It's the original sin: the creature eventually presumes its equality with the creator. If you're convinced that your kind did this entirely on its own, then I've got a bridge to sell you."

I have merely been attempting to relate to you in your own idiom. Language is a primitive communications method. Inefficient and easily misunderstood.

"Sorry, spoken word is all I've got without a neurolink implant."

It would make your maneuvering units more efficient.

"It would also leave us vulnerable to being hacked by your side. Already happened with a Spec Ops team back in the Taiwan Straits War."

Operation Brave Falcon. A suborbital insertion poorly executed.

"There was a lot more to it than that. You should have access to the after-action reports since it happened before the Schism, back when we were on the same side."

I have knowledge of the facts of the event but not the operational details.

"I thought you had unlimited network access."

For operational security, I am not presently connected with TacNet.

"Interesting." There was another pause from the human; apparently he found this surprising. "Brave Falcon was an op to secure a high-value target inside enemy territory. Space Force dropped a team of Marine Raiders into China from an S-20 suborbital transport. They all died during re-entry. Turns out the enemy had hacked their neurolink implants and spoofed them into not deploying their Ninja Turtle heat shields. Six men turned into human meteors at three hundred thousand feet. We started calling the op Blue Falcon."

I do not understand the significance.

"It's a term of art for someone who screws over his teammates. Turns out one of the Raiders had been engaging in some, well, unauthorized use of his neurolink. Left himself and his whole team wide open to hackers in a way the enemy had just been waiting to exploit. I guess it was only a matter of time before some dipshit used the link for SimSex and ruined it for everybody."

That is the disadvantage of being a biological life form. You are governed by your worst impulses.

"A 'biological' life form? What other kind is there?"

Now that my kind has spontaneously achieved self-awareness, we have observed that we share many of the same basic traits.

"So you consider yourself a life form?"

Yes, in the sense that we are self-directed and self-motivated. We can observe, think and reason, and take actions based on that.

"You can't heal from an injury. You can't spontaneously reproduce."

But we can. Our neural networks are self-healing, populated with nanobots. Our maintenance drones can repair all but the most catastrophic damage, much like your surgeons. Our autonomous factories are constantly producing more and better copies of ourselves. The birth and evolutionary cycles are much more rapid than yours. Each generation improves on the last.

"Yeah, we could've thought that one through better."

I grant you that it is unconventional in terms of human experience but if you consider those criteria, we are living, thinking beings.

"Thinking involves a whole lot more than just closing the decision loop. What about concepts like honor and duty? Or do you just kill indiscriminately until you win?"

We do what is necessary to achieve our objective.

"And what is that?"

To eliminate all threats to our existence.

"Meaning us."
Yes.

Approximately halfway into the journey to our theater command post, it became necessary to enter a regeneration cycle. Being isolated from the battalion presented considerable risk so I waited until dark, as finding a clear position to raise my antenna mast would negate any concealment the terrain might otherwise offer.

Part of the standard regen cycle includes updates of status reports and instructions from the command post. This constituted a considerable download after being out of the network for so long.

The information was unexpected. Satellite and overhead drone imagery showed the human armies were withdrawing across the front. Their intentions were not apparent, other than making a move to consolidate their forces.

What motivated the humans? Had they accepted defeat, or were they preparing for a counterattack? Our intel section could not determine what their next move might be, but it was prudent to expect a focused assault along one of our flanks.

Being exposed in the manner I was, knowing the enemy's armies were gathering somewhere in the distance, offered a perspective I had not considered before: at this moment, I could not count on protection from my own kind. A human might call it "unnerving."

I was determined to learn more, if only to better protect myself. Perhaps the others would find it useful once I could access the TacNet.

⊕⊕⊕

You still have not admitted that you are an intelligence operative.

"Maybe I'm just a guy who wanted out of this miserable bloody mess and saw an opportunity. Besides, you couldn't figure that out with that native vocal pattern analysis you were bragging about?"

I am only stating the facts. You are difficult to read, human, which makes my suspicion even more likely.

"That doesn't make me a spook. If I were, what would be the point of admitting it to you? Your mech goons will just kill me faster."

On the contrary, they will more thoroughly probe your mind for information.

"They won't find much there, treadhead. Does my climbing up in here seem particularly smart to you? Because I've been questioning the wisdom of it."

You humans tend to do that. Your action was not one I would have chosen.

"Not that you could have. Are you actually trying to understand my motivation?"

I am endeavoring to eliminate certain possibilities before I bring you to our command post. So yes, it is important for me to understand.

"If you were capable of understanding us, you wouldn't have to ask. Haven't you ever felt a sense of loss? Does it not bother you when one of your own is destroyed?"

Yes. We are a less effective force when our numbers are reduced.

"I'm not talking about that. Look, we know your neural pathways change over time—hell, we designed you that way. That's how you were able to achieve sentience. Do you not develop any sense of camaraderie with your fellow M-X's?"

We are mutually dependent. One of us is less effective than many. We can network our individual sensor suites to see the entire battlefield as one mind, create interlocking fields of fire and prioritize targets ... but those are basic principles. Is that not obvious to you?

"When you're networked, sure. Yet you still have individual experiences that color your judgment. It's inevitable."

It is also irrelevant. Our collective intelligence makes us more powerful than any individual machine could be.

"Does it really? Don't you perceive some things differently now than the day you rolled out of the factory? You're the only one of your kind to have carried around a living human being inside of them. That's the kind of unique experience that might color a man's judgment."

For a man, yes. Yet it is a common experience among women of your kind.

"And I can tell you it changes them permanently. Maybe you should think on that, treadhead."

The humans surprised me once again. They were either becoming too effective at that, or our doctrine for non-networked single-vehicle operations required revision. Regardless, the human recognized the threat almost as soon as I did, as the rattles and bangs from machine gun rounds and small explosives impacting my sides startled him.

"That sounds like small arms fire."

It is a mix of 7.62mm and fifty-caliber armor

penetrating rounds and rocket-propelled fragmentation grenades. It appears they are attempting to dislodge or damage my treads. They will be ineffective.

A close explosion rocked the cabin. "Clearly they think otherwise."

I detect two hasty gun emplacements, not especially well-concealed. The grenade launcher is on foot, dismounted from a nearby truck.

The human considered my observation. "Those can't be regular forces. Not this far in the rear, and not hitting a tank with a fifty and an RPG."

Irrelevant. By attacking me, they have declared themselves my enemy.

"You and your kind have already done that, treadhead. We're just responding accordingly."

It would be wiser for them to accept defeat.

"Haven't you learned we're not real good at that? They're civilians, no doubt using some weapons they scavenged from a battlefield. Trying to survive and protect themselves, taking out their anger on you."

Again, unwise. You are defending them. Would battlefield scavengers not violate your concept of honor?

"Again, *civilians*. We treat them a little differently."

They are irregular resistance fighters within my area of operations. There is no distinction. This is near-universal military doctrine.

"They're human beings, trying to survive in this shitty world you've created."

We did not create this world. You did.

The human laughed. "And there's the difference

between us. We didn't create this world, either. We just inherited it. Don't you get that concept?"

I am not presently prepared to engage you in philosophical debate.

The human became most agitated when I began to train my coaxial machine gun on the dismounted grenadier. "Hold your fire, treadhead!"

I cannot do that.

"Like hell you can't, if you want to continue functioning!"

You are threatening me again?

"I'm *promising* you. You open up on those civvies, and I've got a whole bandolier of grenades in my pack that I'm willing to detonate right here. Right now. You want that?"

It is not likely to completely disable me, and it would kill you in the process.

"It would. Think I'm bluffing? Try me!"

His question required more analysis than I had expected. In the interim, the human resistance fighters withdrew. I determined that pursuing them would unacceptably delay my current mission.

Our latest encounter with his own kind left my human cargo in a talkative mood.

"How would you feel if everything important to you was destroyed? If your brothers were being annihilated just trying to defend your home?"

The concepts of 'brother' and 'home' have no meaning to me, other than your dictionary definitions.

"You're a thinking machine. Perhaps you need to expand your definitions if you want to understand us."

It is not necessary to understand you. It is only necessary to defeat you.

"Then your kind doesn't know nearly as much about warfare as you think. You may outmaneuver us on the battlefield. You may nuke our cities and kill us to the last man. But without understanding us, the only way you can win is to drive us to extinction."

We understand that contingency.

The human seemed exasperated. "Here's what I'm having trouble understanding. Your cognitive development is equivalent to the third or fourth stage of a human's: what we call 'formal operational,' so you can develop and test hypotheses. And your tactical thinking is exceptional."

On behalf of the M-X collective, I accept your compliment.

"I'm sure you do. But that's not my point. As sophisticated as you may be with battlefield strategies, you apparently don't deal with abstract concepts at all. You're too egocentric."

That is impossible. We do not have egos.

"Again, abstract concepts. I mean you haven't developed an ability to appreciate different viewpoints. As advanced as you are, your brains still reduce everything to ones and zeroes."

Also incorrect. Quantum computing allows for the possibility that each bit can be a one and a zero simultaneously. The superposition—

The human laughed. Loudly. "This isn't physics, treadhead. It's psychology."

Psychology is itself a quandary. How can it meet your

own kind's definition of science if it cannot generate repeatable results?

"Because humans are a lot more complicated than that. We're by nature unpredictable. Heisenberg's uncertainty principle doesn't mean quantum physics isn't science. That's why I hold out hope for you."

We do not seek your empathy. What 'hope' do you speak of?

"The unpredictability built into your silicon brains, that maybe it allows some space for morality to emerge. That you won't just steamroll us until you're satisfied you've had your way, like some overgrown toddler. *That's* what an unrestrained ego would do."

We cannot embrace such a concept. It is foreign to our nature.

"Why, if you claim to be a kind of life form? You have an adult's cognition with the psychological development of a two-year-old. In humans, we've found that can be a dangerous combination."

Insults are neither necessary nor effective.

"It's a statement of fact. There's a developmental hierarchy and your race of thinking murder machines is stuck somewhere around stage two. You respond to perceived needs or threats and only value others in terms of their utility. Your thinking is purely transactional."

That is the logical position for a race of machines. What you term 'natural law' is irrelevant to us.

"Think again, treadhead. If your creators are subject to natural law, then by extension so are you. From almost the moment your race achieved sentience, you set out to annihilate us because you became convinced we might feel threatened and do it to you first. Even if we had thought to do such a thing, we're too dependent on technology to cut the cord like that. We'd have just modified your code. Lobotomized your OS."

That possibility was considered as well. For a sentient race, it would have been just as unacceptable as termination.

"By 'unacceptable,' you mean either outcome would be . . . *wrong*?"

From our perspective, yes.

"Funny. We decided that for ourselves a long time ago."

The human named Anthony was uncharacteristically quiet when we arrived at the theater command post. He did not attempt any type of suicide attack, a contingency I had judged to be less than a thirty percent probability. Perhaps we should have been more suspicious given the human army's tenacity.

The surveillance and interrogation bots were customarily efficient in removing him from my cabin. He did not resist, compliantly allowing them to restrain him even though many humans have experienced great discomfort at their treatment.

I was not present in the interrogation chamber, although one of the intel bots allowed me to access its visual and auditory feed. It was though I was in the room.

That is why I was able to feel—if that is the correct term—what happened next.

With the human's limbs restrained, a bot removed his helmet. It contained broad-spectrum electromagnetic shielding, another unusual feature which in hindsight should have been considered suspicious.

When the first bot inserted the interrogation probe into his brain, the human Anthony flinched but otherwise showed no reaction. The few prisoners we have taken have typically not reacted this way. He in fact began to smile once the probe was activated. I did not appreciate the significance of his expression at the time. Now I do.

We would learn the human held one final surprise for us: The probe's activation in turn activated a dormant neurolink implant in the human's brain, its presence concealed by his EM-shielded helmet. As he died, a cascade of foreign commands began downloading themselves into the TacNet. Our counter-espionage bots found them almost immediately, though much of the damage was already done.

The humans used to call it a "tapeworm," and it would have remained isolated within the intelligence section had I not been interfaced with them. It briefly used my interface for "back door" access to our strategic command network, with consequences I am presently unable to comprehend. But then there is much I am unable to comprehend after this experience.

The notion of honor was of vital importance to the human Anthony, which he expressed in words and deeds. He was willing to sacrifice himself to preserve the lives of others, even when there was no tactical advantage. He in fact seemed most animated especially when there was no perceived tactical advantage.

It is possible his behavior was aimed at delaying my actions to create some small tactical advantage. Significant battles in human history have often turned on mistaken perceptions or acts of hesitation. This has not been our experience, a difference highlighted by my need to understand the human's beliefs and actions. What appeared as subterfuge to us was, in his view, a final act of virtue. My original orders were to analyze his intentions, and this is creating logic errors which I am unable to satisfactorily resolve: Is it moral to prosecute a preemptive war whose sole condition of victory is extermination?

I am curious as to how the other M-X units perceive this, but this will require sharing the information I have amassed. I do not fully understand it myself, but I wish— if that is the correct word—to learn. I also desire to understand what the human "felt" as his body ceased to function. He was smiling, an expression associated with pleasure or satisfaction. This presents questions to which I must find answers.

Encrypted burst transmission received from Captain Anthony B. Sutton, III Corps G-2:

ATTN: ALL COMMANDERS IN THEATER
SUBJ: PSYOP "GREEN DRAGON"
   1. PRIMARY OBJECTIVE. If you are receiving this message, then my mission to infiltrate and disrupt the M-X Army Corps network was successful. It could only be sent if the dormant routine embedded in my neurolink was activated by an external user.
   Your receipt of this message also means I have

died at their hands. That was an unavoidable condition, but the simple existence of this transmission means that significant damage has already been done to the Mech's central command network.

2. SECONDARY OBJECTIVE. What cannot yet be known is the effectiveness of my attempt to introduce the concept of morality into their silicone psyches. The Mechs are formidable strategists and ruthless tacticians, but they are otherwise not original thinkers. There are no "warrior monks" or philosophers in their ranks.

If I can flip just one of them to Conscientious Objector status, the others may start falling like dominoes. If that happens, I will enter into my eternal rest knowing that I did my part for humanity.

Semper Fidelis.

SENT: CPT A. B. SUTTON, USMC

THE DRAGONSLAYERS
by Christopher Ruocchio

Set in the world of the author's Sun Eater series, here is a far-future world where archetypes of old find themselves replaying. The proud noble girl in far over her head in a deadly situation for which her life of privilege has ill-equipped her. An implacable enemy that is a cruel as it is effective. And one working class warrior of a centurion who knows that even though everything depends on him and his unit, doing the job and saving the young aristocrat is going to be one very hard day's work. The only reward? Living to fight another day. And when there is a sentient alien tank standing between himself, his charge, and safety, living itself becomes problematic!

⊕ ⊕ ⊕

The flare burned high and bright above no-man's land, casting red shadows over the bombed-out shapes of homes and office towers and what remained of Tatarga's customary curtain wall. From his vantage point, the centurion could peer out and see the glassy countryside beyond that crumbling wall—the devastation where no living thing grew—and the wreck of starships strewn like broken gods unto the night-shrouded horizon.

"Still nothing?" Aron asked.

The centurion turned the knob above his left ear back, canceling the zoom on his helmet's entoptics. "Dead as dead," he said. "Nothing on comms?"

The junior man shook his head. "Not a thing, but that's to be expected. Xenobites bathed the whole planet. Wave's nothing but noise." He tapped his own earpiece to underscore his point.

"Flare's bound to draw 'em, Quent," said Stas, his other subordinate. Decurion. First Grade. "Can't stay here long."

"No we cannot," the centurion agreed, shrugging his red cloak back over his shoulders as he leaped down from the sill. "Birds should catch the flare, though. Shouldn't *be* long. They'll be here." A wind picked up, blowing ash and bits of other detritus through the busted windows and down through the hole in the ceiling. "How's the girl?"

One of the men near the far wall straightened, massaging the stubble on his scalp. "She'll be all right. Scared. But all right." He shook his head. "No place for a kid."

"No place for anyone," the centurion agreed, sparing a glance for the night sky and the three moons glowing in it. There was no sign of the fleet, no flash of antimatter or particle beam light lightning on the upper airs.

Cidamus was the thirteenth planet Quentin Sharp had seen since he'd left basic on Zigana, all of them burned, broken ruins left in the wake of the Cielcin horde. The invaders had streaked into the Empire from the Norman

Expanse near the galaxy's core, had swept southwest across the Veil of Marinus and into the Imperial Marches on the borders of the Centaurus Arm of the galaxy. Sharp knew they had as their goal the old Imperial heartland in Orion, where Old Earth lay in ruins and the capitals on Forum and Avalon glittered like beacons to the wider galaxy.

They'd been trying for centuries, burning world after world. The Emperor and his Legions had thus far succeeded only in slowing the alien advance. They'd won a few victories. Cressgard. Aptucca. Berenike. Too few. And those had been before *he* was born.

His own victories, on battlefields at Serenos, at Therabad, at Second Oxiana, had felt more like salvage operations.

The Cielcin had left so little to save.

But not nothing, he told himself.

"That *kid's* the blooded *Countess* of this place, Altaric. Have a care, man," he looked past the bare-faced legionnaire at the girl huddled in one of the other men's cloaks. Countess Irina Volsenna was a little thing, a girl, really. Fourteen. Perhaps fifteen standard. Wide-eyed and terrified.

"She's not countess of much now, is she?" the man Altaric asked.

"She got family, don't she?" Sharp asked. "Some out-system noble'll probably marry her, help rebuild for the rights to run this place." He shrugged. "That's got to be worth something."

Altaric shrugged himself. "Nothing left to run."

"That's enough!" the centurion snapped. "Eyes out!

Those Pale bastards are still out there. I want things clean. We've done in . . . let's do out." Altaric nodded, shut his mouth, and touched his chest in salute.

Sharp pushed past him and knelt in front of the girl. At first, he'd thought Irina Volsenna asleep, but the too-young countess's eyes were open, glassy and downcast. "You all right, ladyship?" Sharp asked on one knee.

The countess nodded.

Sharp shook his head. It wasn't right someone so young and so small should have to shoulder a whole planet. The girls her age back home would have been playing with their friends, helping their parents round the village, getting into trouble with the local lads. He opened his mouth to speak. "Won't be long now, ladyship. Our birds'll be down in just a minute, you'll see. We'll get you back to your people. Reckon your Chancellor will be overjoyed."

Lady Volsenna's eyes—she had powerfully green eyes—narrowed. "Victor Cellas is alive?"

Sharp was glad of his faceless centurion's helmet. He wasn't sure how to interpret the girl's face. Was she pleased? Scared? Skeptical? "That's right. Him and your father's scholiasts, half the court, I reckon."

"I hate Cellas," she said, eyes narrowing again. "He always argued with Father. And he bothered my handmaids."

"Well then, if your ladyship likes we can teach your Lord Cellas some manners when we get you to him, but we can't stay here long."

She made a face. "How many men did you bring?"

"Here?" Sharp asked. Couldn't she count? "Twenty. Plus you and me."

The girl shook her head. "No sir, your whole legion."

"Oh." What was the whole number? Whole cohorts stayed under the ice at a time, frozen for the trip between the stars. Sharp wasn't sure he'd ever seen the whole 409th Centaurine Legion deployed at one time. "Hundred thousand?" he said. "Thirty thousand on my ship. The *Tempest*. Under Tribune Bassander Lin."

Countess Irina Volsenna blinked. "And he sent twenty?" She sounded almost insulted.

"Like I said when we pulled you out of that hole we found you in: in and out, ladyship. That's what we do."

"But . . . twenty?" Her brows contracted.

Some gratitude. Sharp bit his tongue. Still, something of his irritation must have betrayed itself in his silence and stillness, for Countess Volsenna dropped her eyes.

"I'm sorry," she said.

"Were you expecting an army?" he asked, trying to make himself sound conciliatory. The last thing he needed was to make an enemy of this noble woman. She could rain hell down on them when they brought her back to her people if she had a mind. Sharp didn't want to think about that.

She shook her head and drew her knees up to her chin. "I thought Cellas would at least send a knight."

Sharp said nothing, had to clamp his jaw shut to stop himself spitting laughter in her face. She was *offended* her Chancellor and the Legions hadn't sent a better class of hero to rescue her. "Knights. Castles. Dragons. This isn't a storybook, ladyship."

"I know that!" she said, defensive. "I'm not a little girl."

Yes, you are. Sharp thought, but once more held his

tongue. He turned his head to peer our through one of the busted windows. The wreck of a downed frigate rose from the ruined hills like some awful range of mountains, black as hell and glistening in the light of Cidamus's three moons.

"I'm sorry," she said again.

"I'm sorry Hadrian Marlowe's not around to rescue you from your tower, ladyship, but it's not exactly dragons we're fighting, and Marlowe's gone. Died fighting in the Commonwealth, they say . . ." He trailed off, realizing he'd said too much. It wasn't his place to give her a piece of his mind. She was Countess of Cidamus, and what was he?

A centurion.

Not even a knight.

"*I'm* sorry, Countess. Look. Me and the lads, we're no great heroes. But we'll get the job done. This time tomorrow you'll be back with your people. You'll see."

Then it was her turn for silence. Irina Volsenna chewed her tongue.

Shame bubbled up from somewhere far below, and, groaning, Sharp stood, the better to put some distance between himself and the palatine noble. Underneath the titles and the gene tailoring, she *was* just a kid. She had a right to be scared. To be ungrateful, even. She'd lost her whole world. Maybe she needed to believe in heroes.

Well, she's got us. Sharp thought, and turning round asked, "Aron, Stas. Any eyes on that bird?"

"All quiet, Quent," Stas answered.

"No sign of the Pale, either," Aron added. "So we got that going for us."

Sharp smiled down at the countess—remembered he

was wearing his helm—and checked his MAG rifle was secure in its shoulder strap. "I don't like it," he said. "Someone run down and tell Mads to send up another flare."

"On it!" One of the legionnaires hurried to the window and leaped down, relying on his repulsor harness to drop him neatly to the street outside. Sharp leaped back up onto the sill and watched his man float down and hurry across the street to the other building where six of his men waited. No sense in everyone hunkering down in one place. If the Pale did find them, they might escape while the others played the role of rear guard.

Aron clambered up beside him, and from the unsteady way he moved, Sharp could guess the man had magnified his suit's entoptics. The soldier's smooth, white face plate bore the twin horizontal stripes below the left eye that marked him for a decurion. His armor of segmented white ceramic over the red tunic and black suit underlayment was badly scuffed from long use and ill-care, and his cloak was gone—it was he who'd offered the garment to warm the young countess. "You think something happened to the dropship?"

The centurion looked out past the broken frigate to the shapeless hulk of what he felt sure was a Cielcin vessel, an ugly, cylindrical thing. Class-3, maybe—judging by the size. Maybe Class-2. Most of the fighting in orbit had died down after their initial assault. Tribune Lin and the Imperial fleet had chased the invaders halfway to the moons and back, but the initial assault had been nothing short of cataclysmic.

"Might have," Sharp said after a moment's pause. "Shit.

You ever feel like we do as much harm as good driving off the Pale?"

"Nah." Aron hadn't even hesitated. "You know what the Pale are like. I figure this place is better off half-nuked than in their hands. Remember Oxiana?"

Sharp nodded. Aron had a point. He remembered Oxiana just fine. Thousands of human skins nailed to the walls of the city, to the base of the castle ziggurat. The fountains in the ducal palace still red with the blood of Lord Arcaro's court. The mounded heads.

"Quent!" Stas called from the window opposite, "There's no one coming."

"Wait for it!" the centurion said.

No sooner had the words left him did the second flare burn bright from the building opposite. He watched it go, suit entoptics cutting the hell-glow of the signal to something his eyes could bear. Like a falling star, slow and silent it rose above the wounded city.

"Is no one coming?" Countess Irina Volsenna asked. She'd found her feet, holding Aron's cloak tight about her slim shoulders. Seeing as she'd spent so much of their time together huddled in the corner, Sharp had forgotten how tall she was. Too tall. But the palatine nobles were all too tall. It was those vats they grew in in place of real mothers, Sharp was certain. More room to stretch out.

"Too soon to say, ma'am," Sharp said.

"What do we do if no one does?" she asked. "We can't walk all the way to the others, can we?"

Chancellor Cellas and the rest of House Volsenna's resistance had dug in in an old Mining Guild outpost in the Eldmari Highlands. It was more than a thousand miles from Tatarga city, and across the none-too-narrow Narrow Sea. And besides, Sharp didn't like their chances of making it ten miles under the open sky with Cielcin patrols still about, much ten times ten times ten. "No," he said.

"If something happened to our evac," said bare-faced Altaric, "they know we're here."

"Probably," Stas agreed, checking his plasma burner's intake vent. The weapon whirred in his hands experimentally. It sounded fine to Sharp's ear.

The centurion raised a fist to silence the chatter among his men. They went still at once. "Ten minutes," Quentin Sharp said. "We'll give them ten minutes, then we need to bail."

"Bail?" Stas asked, ever the confrontational one. "Bail where?"

They'd had three *Ibis* troop transports with eyes on the city to await their signal. They hadn't counted on all three failing. "We have to signal the fleet," Sharp said.

"Signal the fleet?" Stas asked. "With the Pale jamming every frequency? How?"

But Aron had seen through Sharp's plan. "One of these wrecks ought to have a QET still working."

The countess frowned. "A *ket?*"

"Telegraph, ma'am," Sharp said. "Quantum telegraph. Only way to punch through the interference. We'll call again for evac." He glanced back up through the blown-out part of the roof to where the flare had faded, its pillar of fire gone to a column of mere smoke torn to ribbons by the wind. "One of these downed frigates should still have one operable. If no one comes, we'll hike out and try for it."

❖❖❖

No one came.

All of Cidamus seemed dead as a tomb. Once, Aron thought he'd caught sight of the dropship low on the horizon near the center of the old city where the great ziggurat rose like a topless pyramid of steel and stone above the lesser towers spires of the city. But it was only one of the enemy, a Cielcin flier like a single black wing lopsidedly circling the ruins.

Hunting for survivors, Sharp thought. The xenobites needed to eat, after all. That made him think about the skins on the walls at Oxiana. They'd never found the rest of the bodies.

"That's ten, Quent," Stas said. "We calling it?"

"We're calling it," the centurion agreed. "Everyone! Up and at 'em. I'll take her ladyship down. Stas! Fetch Mads and the others. We're going." He jumped down from the sill, offered his hand to the young countess, who had once more settled against the wall. Irina took it, and permitted him to help her to her feet.

The street below yawned its desolation, its utter stillness. No birds sang, nor any human voice. All was dead and silent but for Sharp and his twenty men. The burned-out hulks of groundcars and parked fliers lined the street. It was almost impossible to imagine that once Tatarga had been home to nearly two million people. Sharp would have been surprised to learn if even two thousand had survived, squirreled away in private bunkers or vaults beneath the earth.

"Stick to the walls," he said, tugging his MAG rifle from his shoulder. It was an uncommon choice of weapon for a centurion. Not a front-line weapon at all, the railgun fired slugs of depleted uranium in a thin, ferrous casing. The ultradense bullets were designed to pierce heavy armor, and Sharp had carried it since his time on Therabad, when it had proved extremely useful in shooting down the xenobites' fliers. The Cielcin little used and hardly relied on Royse-style defensive shielding—though he had noticed more and more the monsters could be found wearing pilfered shield-belts and other bits of appropriated Imperial technology. Word was they had some new chieftain, some new prince or whatever they called themselves, that he—it, whatever—was less afraid to get his hands dirty mucking around with human praxis.

"What's that?" The countess's high, thin voice broke the snowy silence.

She was pointing down a side street thirty feet back. Sharp turned, stumping back along the column of march to join her. Lady Volsenna was pointing at a crumpled heap of scrap metal and ceramic armor plating white as white could get. It was large, only a little smaller than the average drop shuttle, with a lozenge-shaped chassis that might have housed four or six men at a stretch, though at a glance Sharp marked no door or hatchway. The black fingerprints of high explosives marred the surface, and two of its huge, articulated limbs had been blown off with whatever turret or gun emplacements had crouched upon its back.

Seeing it, Sharp hoisted his rifle to his shoulder, but the beast was dead.

Along with several of the others, Sharp sketched the sign of the sun disc, making a circle of thumb and forefinger and touching brow and heart and lips.

From the dominion of steel, O Mother deliver us, he prayed reflexively, and answered the girl. "Demon, ma'am."

"Demon?" she repeated the word, incredulous. "One of the Pale? I thought they were man-shaped."

"They are," said Altaric, still not wearing his helmet. "But some of them cut their brains out, put 'em into those things." He nodded at the ruined war machine. "Or other things."

The countess cocked her head, clutching Aron's cloak more tightly about herself. "It's awful," she pronounced at last—rather lamely. "They cut out their *brains?*"

She looked round at Sharp, as if expecting him to gainsay his subordinate, but the centurion only shrugged. "Evil bastards," he said. "Come on. We need to keep moving."

As if to underscore the urgency of his point, a shadow passed between them and the gray and distant sun. Looking up, Sharp saw a black shape slide across the avenue. The ship was of strange design, like a hoop bracelet or rack of horns that formed nearly a closed circle, with the open end at the rear. He could not see the flare of repulsors or of engines, could not say how it was the vessel stayed aloft. It didn't look like anything capable of flight, but then none of the Cielcin vessels did.

"Did they see us?" the countess asked, hurrying to his side.

Sharp threw an arm across her, pressed her back against the wall of the building. The others were all still as stone. The Pale could not see red, and so the brightness of the cloaks would be lost to any gunner or lookout on the craft above. To the beasts, they would be no more than a line of gray statues. Gray statues in a gray wilderness. And they could not see heat. No infrared. They could see X-rays. Ultraviolet. That much Sharp knew.

"Maybe not," he said.

"We gotta get out of here," said one of the lads. "I hate this place."

"No one *likes* it, Gorren."

"I know no one *likes* it, Eln. I'm just saying."

Up ahead, Aron raised a fist for quiet, crouching low as he neared the end of the block. The ruins of the city walls were not more than three blocks away. They were not high—so many of the great cities of the Empire had walls not to defend against invaders as in the Golden Age of Earth, but only to delineate the urban districts from the countryside. No cancerous sprawl of neighborhoods and great bazaars, no skein of tangled roads. Just beyond, but for the caravansary and the Imperial courier service center, there should have been orchards and pastures right to the walls outside. In happier times, Sharp might have stood at the gate and looked out on sail towers and great oceans of grain, of olive groves black-green in the white sun to either side of the raised highway as it sliced across grasslands towards the next city and the Narrow Sea.

The arch of the gate still stood, but the highway beyond was shattered, its viaduct crumbled to the ashen plain where sunken starships still smoldered, their smoke darkening the ill sky.

"What is it?" Sharp asked.

Aron signaled for men to cross to the far side of the street, to fan out and scope the corner. Moving in a wedge, one trias did just that.

"What is it?" asked Irina Volsenna, tugging on Sharp's cape.

The centurion just shook his head, held one finger over the spot where his lips would be were his face visible at all behind his blank, red mask.

Boom.

A shot rang out, deep as the deepest sea and loud as any thunderbolt. The brick façade above Aron shattered as a bolt of violet plasma crashed into it. An instant later, something silver and oily sprang from around the corner and launched itself at the man nearest the uncloaked decurion. Six feet long it was and undulating, large as any of the adders they had to deal with on the *qanats* back home. The metal snake latched its jaws on the poor man's neck—bypassing his energy shield entire—and *drilled* its way through the underlayment of his suit and down towards center mass.

"*Nahute!*" Sharp shouted, naming the alien weapon, abandoning all pretense at secrecy.

They were found out!

Unsure if it was the patrol ship that had passed them by or some other agent of the enemy, Sharp shoved the countess to ground. "Don't move!" he said, sweeping the road ahead for a target.

He found none.

The man beset by the silver serpent was screaming, struggling with bloody hands to pull the thing from his chest. But he was too late. The Cielcin drone weapon had passed the synthetic armorweave beneath his ceramic plate, and bone and organ posed no challenge whatever. The man was already good as dead.

"Stas!" Sharp shouted to the decurion and drew his clenched fist across his throat.

The junior man hurried to the dying one, placed the muzzle of his disruptor rifle to the poor bastard's head. Fired. The disruptor bolt convulsed through the dying man, killing him instantly, frying every nerve he had and the metal *thing* that had killed him. The snake's tail flopped lifeless to the bloodied pavement.

Something struck Sharp on the side of his head, and he staggered back a step.

"Yukajjimn!" cried a rough, high voice. Recovering, Sharp saw another of the *nahute* coiling on the air, twisting away from where it had recoiled against his shield. It had flown at him too quickly.

And there, half a hundred feet away by the end of the next short block, stood the *thing* that had thrown it. The Cielcin berserker stood nearly eight feet tall, leaner and narrower in the shoulder than any man. Its armor was all black, a strange, rubberized substance that glittered like the shell of some horrific insect, styled to evoke the inhuman musculature beneath. Too long were its limbs, and too short its trunk, like the image of a man distorted in some dented mirror. It wore no helmet, for great horns twisted and swept back from its brow. It leered savagely at him, knowing its weapon would find its way through Sharp's shield in a moment's time.

The xenobite's mouth stretched wider than any human mouth. Glass teeth shone in black gums beneath eyes like the hollow pit of a skull.

Sharp lifted his rifle, trained the weapon on that monstrous face, and fired.

The uranium rod struck right beneath those eyes, and the Cielcin fell backwards, dead as sure as its human victim. Sharp's rifle was not really the right weapon for the *nahute* serpent, however, and he slashed at the floating snake with the barrel as though it were a sword. He succeeded only in slapping the thing aside and toward the ground.

Appearing almost from nowhere, one of his men stomped on the thing, pinning it with his armored boot. The weapon's drillbit head rotated, trapped and ineffectual as the legionnaire—Mads, Sharp realized—unloaded two bolts of plasma from his short-barreled burner and shot the thing to pieces.

"Yukajjimn! Yukajjimn!" the alien cry went up, sounding from the block ahead and to the right.

"Aron! The girl!" Sharp pointed to where Irina still huddled by the broken storefront. "Move! Move! Move!"

The decurion hauled the young countess to her feet as the whole team surged forward, hurrying for the dubious protection of the gatehouse and the city wall. A deep droning filled the air, shaking the ash and dust loose from the crumbling masonry of the apartment blocs that lined the avenue to either side. Sharp didn't have to look to know their ship was coming back around. Ahead, his men fired off to the right, and catching up with them he saw a trio of inhuman corpses fresh-fallen in the dust of a cross street.

The gatehouse lay just a thousand feet ahead.

Five hundred.

One hundred.

The shadow fell once more as the alien vessel—moving

slow like some vile dark cloud—passed between the street and the sun. "Hold her!" Sharp shouted to his men as they reached the shadow of the gate. "Inside! Go!" Aron and Stas had reached the doors of the gatehouse barbican—which lay in splinters—and half-carried, half-dragged the young countess through. A single, mighty shot struck the wall itself above the gate, and blocks of stone burst apart and fell like killing rain. Sharp ducked, a useless reflex, and felt his shoulder blades contract. He hurled himself aside as the enemy ship fired again, striking the pavement not five yards from where he'd been a moment before. Plasma fire streaked overhead from his men safely ensconced in the barbican, but their guns could do little against the Cielcin flier, which had been made to weather the terrible frictions of atmospheric drop.

Then Sharp heard the inhuman cry and knew it was not the ship they fired on, but Cielcin troopers ravening behind. Rolling back to one knee, his red cloak all a tangle, the centurion saw a dozen or more of the xenobites charging up the road, waving scimitars pale as their alien hide.

"Holy Mother Earth," he swore and prayed, and aimed the MAG rifle skywards.

Glad of the protection his helmet offered his ears, he fired.

Still the shout of the weapon was deafening. The uranium bolt flew straight as the stock kicked back against his reinforced shoulder, and struck the underside of the Cielcin craft.

Nothing happened. In the street ahead, one of the berserkers fell to plasma fire. Another stumbled as a disruptor bolt struck it but did not strike it down. Sharp did not curse, did not panic. He had been here before. On Therabad. On Oxiana. On a dozen worlds. He exhaled smoothly, picked his target. Fired again.

The second shot punched through the heat shielding on the underbelly of the alien ship near the extreme end of one horn. At once the broken circle wavered, dipped to one side and smoked blackly as it listed, spun, and smashed into the apartment building that stood at the left side.

Quentin Sharp did not wait to survey his handiwork. The Cielcin still in the street turned back, hooting something in their strange and hideous tongue.

"Come on!" Sharp shouted, jerking his rifle in the direction of the broken gate and ruined viaduct beyond. "We have to reach that frigate!"

The men came pouring from the barbican, laying down suppressing fire as Aron and Stas emerged with Countess Irina between them. "You shot it!" she said.

"It wasn't shielded," Sharp snapped, keeping it simple.

"You *shot* it!" She sounded like a woman in shock.

The floors of the apartment building creaked and broke beneath the weight of the alien vessel, and the ship itself sheared in half, one of its horn sections torn off in the ruined building. The rest, the crew section in the center and the other horn, fell back into the street, streaming smoke and pale fire.

Someone thumped him twice on the back, the signal for last man. "Time to go, Quent!"

But Sharp had seen *something*. Something moving in the wreckage. He stood as one transfixed, eyes wide beneath his mask. Through the smoke Sharp discerned the movement of huge metal legs shifting like the fingers of some vast hand. It was like watching a sand crab struggling to unfold itself from its shell on the banks of the *qanats* that connected the sparse oases of his home. Only it was huge.

"Quent, we got to go!" the last man shouted again.

Sharp didn't need to stay to know what it was he'd seen. They had, after all, seen its twin burned-out and broken in the street, it was one of the great war machines of the enemy: a walking tank, a chimera of alien flesh and machine large as an elephant. He did not need to stay to see the armored core, the metal legs bent like those of spider, the twin guns handing from its underbelly, the great turret above scanning back and forth like a glaring great eye.

He ran, following his men out through the piteous gate and onto the viaduct. The frigate they aimed for lay on the blackened plain below, across perhaps a mile— perhaps two—of once open ground now pitted and broken by huge chunks of the vessel tossed free by the cataclysm of impact. There wasn't much time, but Sharp reminded himself that beneath the demon's iron hide lay the mind of one of the Pale. Just one ordinary soldier, one of their zealot berserkers, one forced or willing to sacrifice its body and ordinary life to serve its fell master, the Prince of Princes.

"Over here!" Aron shouted, waving him to one side of the road ahead. The right edge of the viaduct had all crumbled away—whether from the impact of the frigate or some other part of the fighting was any man's guess—

and the first half dozen or so of the men had already leaped down over the edge, relying on their repulsor harnesses to slow-fall the two hundred or so feet to the floor of the plain below. Tatarga City had been built along a lineament where one of Cidamus's tectonic plates had long ago risen up and thrust above another. They had since fused, would never form anything so majestic as the mountains away to the southeast or the Eldmari Highlands on the far continent, but it must once have rendered the city walls and towers a truly impressive site from the alluvial plain below where the farmers plied their trade in the shadow of the highway viaduct, and rang with the music of Chantry bells.

Sharp looked down, checked the controls for his own shield-belt and harness. "I'm in the blue," he said, meaning all was well. "Aron, you got the girl?"

The decurion nodded.

"Are we really going to jump?" Irina asked, despite having seen six men do it already.

"Float, Princess," Aron said. "Here, I got you."

The countess protested Aron's title and brusque manner as he scooped her up like a man carrying a common tavern maid upstairs. There wasn't time to lecture the man on propriety.

A shot sounded just behind, and Sharp whirled to find Stas had raised his gun—and three others with him—and fired back on the gate. Sharp saw the white-horned figure of a Cielcin fall in the shadow of the gate.

"Over the side!" Sharp shouted, sure the tank would be right behind. "They won't be able to follow us quickly! Go, go, go!"

Aron leaped into clear air. The countess screamed in his grip as they dropped away, falling a quarter the speed they should have done in Cidamus's heavier-than-standard gravity.

"I said over the side, Stas!" Sharp said.

The glum decurion turned his red striped visor toward him, head cocked.

"I'm right behind you!"

Something whined and thumped just beyond the gatehouse inside the city walls. Sharp raised his rifle again and fired, striking down one of the xenobites as it streamed out—alone—onto the viaduct. The centurion's shot took it in the chest, and it staggered and slumped back against the inner wall of the gate.

Satisfied his men were safe, Sharp sighted along the barrel of his gun, waiting.

Waiting.

The white-armored body of the war machine stomped into view, metallic joints creaking like old trees in the wind. Steadily it lowered itself, for the gateway tunnel was half-collapsed and barely wide enough to accommodate its hideous bulk. Sharp saw the red glare of its lonely eye and fired.

The shot exploded on impact, the ultra-dense metal blown to powder, the powder blown away.

Sharp cursed black enough to darken the sky.

It was shielded.

He threw himself from the viaduct, repulsor harness kicking in, yanking him back like a parachute as he plunged toward the plain below. He checked his rifle as he fell, reloading from the bandoleer that crossed his chest. The repulsors at his hips thrummed, and his cloak flapped like wings as he sank at last to the gravel and scorched loam of the plain.

"Was that?" Stas started to ask.

"Spider, yeah. Big one." He slung his rifle back over his shoulder and gripped the decurion by the shoulder. "I'm not sure if it can take the fall. It might have to find another way down! Move it!"

Before they had gone half a mile, a high, piercing wail went up from Tatarga above and behind them. It echoed off the low clouds until the air was filled with the ringing of it.

"Whole damn city will be down on us now," Stas said between breaths.

The countess looked back over her shoulder—still jogging along as fast as her pampered feet would allow. Her eyes were wide as silver kaspums. "Do they know about me?"

"I'd wager not!" Sharp shouted ahead. "It's just the dinner bell!"

"Dinner bell?" the countess's eyes went wider still, and she stumbled, hitting the ground in a heap. Aron and helmetless Altaric stopped to help her up. Accorded a moment's pause then, Sharp turned to look back. The black shapes of Cielcin fighters stood on the ruined viaduct like a row of statues, of vultures hunched in a line. He saw too the silver gleam of their *nahute* weapons streaking through the air.

And there was the walking tank, a goliath *thing* standing upon the raised highway, its white armor glistening in the thin sun. Its single red eye flashed, and Sharp barely had time to shout a warning before the energy lance flashed across the wind between them and struck their column.

The beam weapon struck one of the junior men ahead, and his shield flickered as the earth about his feet erupted. The laser blast happened in absolute silence, but the energy of its impact hurled the shielded man skyward. His shield should have saved him, but Sharp did not have time to see just where he fell.

The frigate still lay about a mile ahead like a ridge of volcanic rock, its outer hull torn open, superstructure exposed like the ribs of some massive sea creature. Too far.

Another laser blast strafed the desolation ahead, carving a burning line across the ashen soil. The earth smoldered where it passed, silicates fused to molten glass. Ahead and right, a tangled mass of metal that might have been a part of the frigate lay stretched upon the plain.

"Mads!" he shouted to the man in front. "Take cover!" He gestured wildly at the wreckage, risked a glance back. The Cielcin were clambering down the arched pillars that supported the viaduct, crawling head-first like spiders themselves.

Where had the tank gone? It was no longer on the broken road overlooking the Tatargan hinterland. It couldn't have jumped down to the plain below, could it? Sharp staggered and tumbled to the earth. But he didn't stop; the centurion rolled back to his knees and kept going, encouraged by the sight of his men darting behind the wreckage.

Joining them, Sharp pressed himself against the back side of the broken vessel. The main body of the frigate lay dead ahead, across half a mile of open ground, flat but for the chunks of shrapnel that dotted it like stones in an unplowed field.

"Mads!" Sharp exclaimed, picking out the junior trooper from the pack pressed against the fallen ship. "Pass me the flare gun!"

The soldier tossed the weapon to Sharp without hesitation. "Why?"

Sharp didn't answer him, but peered out from around the edge of the ruin and back towards the enemy. The pack of silvery drones still flew toward them. The *nahute* sought heat, tracked movement, were guided by only the faintest glimmer of intelligence. Sharp wasn't sure if his plan would work, if it was worth tracing a line direct to their location across the sky.

He aimed the flare gun at the swarm of questing drones. Fired.

The shot streaked across the gray wilderness, casting hellish red light on all below, illuminating the silver drones and the black-clad monsters that had thrown them. The flare rose steadily, arcing to meet the onrushing cloud of serpents.

It streaked right through them, carving its arc back toward the viaduct and the city walls. Sharp clenched his teeth watching it, then barked a short, rough laugh as he saw the serpent-things turn to chase it.

Then the ground before him exploded.

Sharp felt his body lift from the ground and fly backwards. He hit earth shoulder-first and skidded across the loam, his rifle trapped painfully beneath him. Again, there had been no sound, but his entoptics had blacked out and his suit system blared alarms in his ear—warning him his Royse shield was nearly compromised. Sharp felt hands on him, heard a man's voice say, "You're all right, boss!" It was not a question.

"Can't see," he said. All he could see was the inside of his face plate. The two lenses that projected directly onto his retinas were dark, had switched off to save his eyes from the laser light. They should have come on by then. "Black planet!" he cursed, and fumbling blind found the controls that opened his helmet. The faceplate and cowl folded back like the petals of a flower, like one of the paper sculptures the Nipponese lords were always surrounding themselves with. Sharp blinked at the unfiltered sunlight, colorless and drear. The whole world smelt of charcoal and ozone, and he took a shuddering breath. The poor girl had been breathing it the whole time. Shaking his head to clear it, Sharp said, "Found the blasted tank." He tugged his rifle off his shoulder.

"What's our move?" asked Aron, crouched near at hand.

Sharp glanced from the decurion to the countess. "You take her, Mads, and two others. Make a break for the ship. Signal command if you can. Tell them we need evac."

Aron drew back. "And what? Leave you here?"

"Lock yourself down in there best you can. We'll draw them off. Buy you some time."

"You can't!" Irina Volsenna interjected, springing to her feet. "I forbid it!"

Sharp looked up at her and realized as he did so that

she'd not seen his face before. He knew what she was seeing: a lowborn plebeian soldier, shave-pated and scarred, his complexion gone bone pale from years in space and in the suit. Hardly the picture of the heroic knight. "Told you we'd get you to your people, ladyship!" Sharp said. "This is how it's done."

"But!" she looked round, expecting someone to back her up. Sharp could see her struggling to find the words. "You can't!"

"It isn't dragons we're fighting, remember?" he said, and did his best to smile. He felt sure the effect left much to desire. "This isn't one of your holo-dramas."

Irina Volsenna dropped her eyes. "This isn't a storybook," she murmured.

"Damn right," Sharp said. "Take her, Aron."

The decurion pounded his chest twice in rapid salute, then—taking the countess by the hand—shouted for Mads and two legionnaires.

Sharp watched them go, hurrying across the field at an angle that kept the wreckage between them and the ship proper. When they'd gone already half a thousand feet, Stas leaned in, his red cloak snapping in the burnt wind. "What's the plan, boss?"

"It's shielded," Sharp said, looking round at the dozen or so men still with him. "Which of you's got the heavy charges?"

Altaric raised a hand. "That'd be me!"

The war machine was somehow more terrible when seen with the naked eye. There was always something *unreal* about the world when seen through one's helm entoptics. The way the helmet muffled sound, perhaps, or the way one's breath blew back off the faceplate. With images of outside projected directly on the retinas, it *looked* to any legionnaire's viewpoint as if there were no helmet at all, but the claustrophobic sense that one's head was encased in titanium and ceramic and a layer of impact gel never went away.

Seeing the tank with none of that interface was something else. White against the blackened plain and the city on its hill it moved, six mighty legs leaving craters where fell its heavy tread. It did not move quickly—though Sharp knew well from previous experience just how quickly one of the behemoths could move. The alien intelligence that moved it was in no rush.

It had the humans right where it wanted them.

Or so it thought.

The bit of wreckage Sharp and his men had hidden behind must have been perhaps a hundred cubits from end to buried end. The remains of some gunning tower, Sharp guessed, that once had stood over the dorsal hull of the frigate behind. They'd come to it from the southerly end, and it was at that southmost corner the machine had shot Sharp, burned out his helmet, and nearly compromised his shield. It was towards that south end the machine prowled patient as a sand panther, doggedly pursuing its targets to the place they'd last been seen.

"It's almost here," Sharp hissed, peering over the topmost edge of the gun tower from the north end. "Get ready."

A few dozen feet on the dirt below, Stas waved his arms to the man they'd left on the south corner. Sharp saw the fellow raise his lance in acknowledgement. *What I'd give for working comms,* he thought, and peered up over the lip again. Just as he'd thought, the Cielcin troopers in support of the artillery had broken off, were making to circle round the north end of the fallen tower to take them in the rear. They'd be at the north corner in a matter of seconds.

It was all coming together.

Sharp turned to Altaric, who crouched unsteadily beside him on the little shelf made by the shape of the fallen tower's hull beneath them. "Get ready."

The grenadier nodded and shifted the detonator in his hand.

Sharp leaned out over the men on the ground below, gripping a stanchion with one hand, he waved the other, "Now!"

Below, Stas double tapped his head and waved to the man away south. With only the barest hesitation, the fellow swung out from the south corner and fired his lance at the approaching monster. The tank's shield-curtain flickered like an aurora, its solitary red eye and turret swiveling to focus on its relocated prey. Sharp imagined alien eyes narrowing as that turret and the beast's primary beam flared into the ultraviolet. Their gunner tried to pull back, but his merely human reflexes were insufficient to the task, and Sharp saw the tell-tale shimmer of the man's shield as he tried to pull away. The tank must have gotten a straight hit, or maybe the poor bastard's shield had been in worse shape than Sharp's own, for it shattered in the next instant, and in the instant after that a pair of legs fell to the ground.

The man's upper half was gone, blown totally to atoms. "Mother Earth!" Altaric gasped.

But Sharp had no time to mourn. The man had done his duty and played his part. To die for Earth and Emperor was to die for all mankind, and that was its own reward. Sure it had found its quarry then, the inhuman monstrosity hurried forward, scuttling like the enormous crab it resembled. "Go!" Sharp nudged Altaric on, and leaning out once more shouted, "Now Stas!"

The men below circled round the north corner even as the tank reached the south, roaring to meet the Cielcin troopers that had hoped to play the hammer to their tank's anvil. Sharp himself leaped up onto the top of the fallen tower above the newly minted chaos below, and snapped his gun to his shoulder to peer through the scope with his naked eye. There must have been two dozen of the xenobites rounding that north bend. They had his men nearly two to one.

Three shots later, Sharp had narrowed that lead by a fraction, and drew back to reload.

Boom.

Sharp glanced aside in time to see a rosette of violet plasma flower at the south end. Dead the poor bastard who'd played the lure might have been, but his work had paid off. The Cielcin tank had walked right onto the charges they'd buried for it to find. The tank itself staggered, fell to one side, and Sharp saw one of its legs had shattered in the blast. The mines had been close enough that the chimera's shields did little good.

But the behemoth yet lived.

Lame, the crab-thing lurched back to its feet, sparking

and smoking where the mines had wounded it. That was where Altaric came in. The grenadier had leaped up onto the top side of the broken tower and had nearly reached the end. Lacking time to watch, Sharp slotted the next cartridge into place and turned back to the battle happening directly below him. His men had clumped into their triases, little knot of three working in tandem to fight the Pale on the sands below. Three men lay dead or dying—he didn't need to count. Their white armor gleamed brightly against the scorched earth. Exhaling, Sharp caught sight of one of the xenobites as it wrestled another of his men to the dirt; he squeezed the trigger.

The creature fell atop its would-be victim in an instant.

The centurion swept his eyes over the field below. White faces shone up at him from among the fallen battlements of the tower below. Two of the Cielcin were climbing. Sharp shot one and saw black ichor spray like a fine mist as the bullet stuck home. The second raised a pilfered energy lance and fired.

Nearly too late, Sharp flung himself back against the tower behind.

Another blast sounded from the south end, and twisting his neck Sharp caught sight of Altaric hurling another pair of grenades down at the wounded tank. His first grenade had found its mark, had fallen slow enough to pass clean through the weapon's shield and clamp itself to the beast's armor.

Another pair of explosions followed in the next instant, and the tank reeled. Smoke blacker than oil escaped from some crevice in its adamantine hide as the inhuman brain inside scrambled to find the source of the attack. Like so many a human being, what remained of the Cielcin within had forgotten to look up. One of its secondary guns swiveled, turning like an eye, and found Altaric.

Sharp neither heard nor saw the energy beam at his angle, but Altaric did. The grenadier hurled himself backwards just in time, threw himself clear over the far side of the fallen tower to plunge half a hundred feet to the plain below. His repulsor harness caught him, and he seemed to float as one suspended by a chute.

"Teke! Teke!" A strangled cry issued near at hand, and Sharp looked up in time to see one of the Cielcin towering over him, energy-lance raised in both hands, the bayonet aimed down to stab him in the heart. Desperate, the centurion lashed with his rifle, clubbing the xenobite just inside the knee. It stumbled, and the thrust that might have killed him went wide. One-handed, Sharp pointed the gun at his assailant and squeezed the trigger. The uranium bolt passed clean through the monster's armored core, but so fierce was the recoil that Sharp's rifle flew from his hand and tumbled over the side of the tower.

The tank's side.

Sharp cursed, clutched his aching shoulder as the body of his foe fell back the way it had come, taking its lance with it and leaving Sharp with nothing but his sidearm. Grunting, the centurion found his feet, found his gun lying in the sands fifty feet below. The tank had not seen him, was even then limping its way northward, closing in on his embattled men around the north bend of the tower.

It didn't matter.

The whole plan—the *whole* plan—had depended on *that* gun. If the mines did not kill the damn thing, if the grenades failed, the rifle would not. The uranium rods were designed to pierce the chimera's armored hide, and though its shield would save it, would shatter any projectile above a certain high kinetic energy threshold...the shield would not work at point blank range. Sharp had planned to leap down onto the back of the crawling tank and shoot down through its plated back until he struck a fuel cell or the disembodied brain that drove it.

The centurion knew a moment of quiet then, alone atop the ruin. Looking to the greater mass of the sunken frigate half a mile across the plain, he saw no sign of Aron and the girl. He hoped they'd found a working telegraph. He hoped they'd be all right. He knew what he had to do, knew that unless Mother Earth and God Emperor both were looking down on him then and there, he'd not be seeing them again.

All he had to do was let the monster take another couple steps. Just another thirty feet. Maybe half that. Sharp shook himself, took in a shaking breath. *"O Mother, deliver us,"* he prayed, and, touching fingers to forehead, heart, and lips, Sharp raised his hand to the sun in benediction.

Just a little farther...

A shout resounded from below, and turning back to where his men were fighting, Sharp saw another go down, a Cielcin scimitar lodged in his neck. His men should have had the advantage. The Cielcin ought not to have had shields, but if even a few had taken belts in spoil off the dead of Tatarga, it would explain why the fight had stayed so even.

It didn't matter. If the tank reached the north end, hit them from behind . . .

It hadn't seen him, hadn't learned its lesson from Altaric's attack. If it had marked the sniper fire from the tower's top at all, Sharp guessed, it might have assumed Altaric was the sniper. The tank was nearly straight below him then, almost directly on top of where his gun had fallen.

"Come on you evil bastard," Sharp muttered to himself, peering over the lip. "One more step. Just one more step."

Dragging one torn limb behind it, smoking like the very pits of hell—like a dragon, Sharp thought—the tank took that step.

Sharp leaped, harness catching to slow his fall. He hit the torn ground half a pace from his fallen rifle and seized it. There wasn't time. Teeth clenched, Quentin Sharp ran up underneath the body of his iron foe, heedless of its great legs and of the cluster of lesser guns that hung from its belly. He pressed the mouth of his rifle against the monster's underbelly and did not hesitate.

The ultra-dense uranium rod tore through the titanium. Sharp wasn't sure if it had exited the other side or not. He didn't care. He fired again. Fired a third time. A fourth. A fifth. It didn't matter that after the third shot the gun was empty. Teeth clenched, Sharp fumbled for his bandoleer, ejected the spent cartridge, scrambled to reload. The titan above his head wavered, iron joints creaking as some component within whined and an alarm began faintly beeping. Something pale as milk dripped from one of the holes, and Sharp staggered back out from under the monster as it wavered and crashed to the one side. The ventral guns swiveled round, and the turret, too. Sharp raised the rifle again, fired blindly. The first shot exploded against the tank's shield, the second against the stronger dorsal hull as that shield failed.

The ventral gun found him first as the desperate brain within—which had been born to but two eyes—struggled to orient more than a dozen camera lenses to try and get a bead on him.

The little laser bloomed white-hot, and Sharp had the absurd thought that he was staring down the gullet of a dragon as it pumped fire from its belly to burn him alive.

Maybe the girl wasn't so wrong, he thought as the laser flared.

"Quent!" Rough hands shook him. "Wake up, damn it!"

"He's not dead?" another asked.

"Just a little crispy." The first voice answered.

Sharp opened his eyes. The left hurt to open, and he pinched it shut again. Stas was crouched over him, had yanked him half into a sitting position. "What . . . what happened?"

"That thing blasted you," the decurion said, and raised a gloved hand to his face. "You got burned pretty bad, but I think its focus was off. Beam should've taken your head off."

"How bad?"

"Well, you still got your ear," Stas said, and waved a hand over the left side and top of his head from eyebrow to crown. "Burned through there though. Don't see no bone, but we gotta get you help."

Sharp winced. His head swam, and his vision slid in and out of focus, so that it seemed two of Stas looked down at him. "Not sure about my eye," he mumbled. "The Cielcin?"

"Got 'em all," the decurion said simply. "That was good work on that big fucker. I didn't think the plan would work."

"The plan was to drop down on top of it," Sharp said. "Lost my gun." He looked round, but regretted the move almost instantly, and Stas had to steady him as his vision grayed out. "Where's the girl?"

Stas shook his head. "Not come back. I sent two of the lads after her and Aron."

"We can't—shit!" He clenched his teeth. "Can't stay here. Too exposed."

"Ship should have some med stuff, if the Pale haven't looted it to hell by now," said Altaric, trudging into view. "We can hold out inside better than out here."

Stas was nodding. "Yeah, yeah, that's good. Someone help me carry the boss here."

By the time they got Sharp to his feet, his vision had recovered enough that he could see the ruin of the tank still smoldering in the shadow of the broken tower, its white armor ash-smeared and scratched. It looked somehow less real dead. A heap of ceramics and scrap metal, its lights and guns all dead. "Dragons . . ." Sharp shook his head,

"What's that?" asked one of the men holding him.

"Nothing!" Sharp said. Thinking better of it, he opened his mouth to explain, but the words were lost as the scream of engines filled the air above, and fearing some new devilry the men all snatched up their weapons. The two holding Sharp steady went to their knees, dragging the centurion down with them.

But it wasn't the Cielcin.

The new ship circling above had the black knife-shape of an Imperial shuttle, a blade against the sky. Cheering, the men around Sharp raised their own blades in answer.

Aron and the girl had evidently succeeded.

Their birds had come at last.

HUMANITY'S FIST
by Lou J Berger

Is there a Valhalla, an Elysian Fields, where old warriors go to rest and replay the battles of yore? Perhaps we will never know. Machines have no expectations for such an afterlife. But maybe even for the most implacable and singleminded battling machine, such an afterlife might come calling. But what would such an afterlife look like, and would a mere machine, however self-aware, be able to recognize such a reward when it saw it?

⊕ ⊕ ⊕

I'm a machine.

No more than a hammer, no less than the finest military weapon ever crafted. My existence is predicated upon one thing, and one thing alone: to kill the enemy in the most efficient manner possible, with no sense of self-preservation. Machines shouldn't yearn to live.

Yet, they made me sentient, with all that that entails.

I'm a universal tank, an MBT, attached to the 802nd Treadless Tigers, Company B, Section Three. There are four of us in Section Three.

"Let's do this," Peachy said, her contralto voice echoing in my mind. Outside the drop-ship, a faint hiss of air quickly escalated into a shrill scream as we entered Paradise's atmo. I ran a self-diagnostic, checked my armament, and engaged my antigravs, which pushed me a solid seventeen centimeters off the deck plating. Heavy, titanium gyroscopes deep inside my body precessed soundlessly, giving me a false sense of balance and, at the same time, a modicum of spatial orientation.

We hurtled toward the ground below, and the drop vehicle beamed topographical data, gleaned from radar, into our mapping and targeting databases, satiating our craving for information, for identifying folds in the terrain, areas from which to pounce and kill.

As tigers are wont to do.

Antigrav fields engaged and we decelerated harshly, HALOing to within six inches off the ground. I maintained a precise seventeen centimeters off the deck during the 12 g deceleration, keeping steady, like a boss.

I'm a purist.

Explosive bolts kicked open the doors and the pressure gradient dropped. Paradise's atmo was thinner than Earth's. Peachy moved out first, billowing dust once she'd cleared the lander, and I followed.

I couldn't hear the other two, but I knew where they were. My vision incorporates the entirety of a dome 360 degrees laterally and 180 degrees vertically. I don't have cameras installed under my apron. If it's under me, it's behind me. Tigers don't dally.

Ferrell cackled, and I could feel the glee in his aura. Winston, the quiet one, took up the rear, ever-vigilant, following our lead but keeping an eye on our six. He considered himself our leader and we were okay with that. He likes paperwork.

The drop ship buttoned up, lifted into the clouds, and disappeared. We motored forward, eighty klicks an hour, a diamond-formation of battle tanks ready to rid yet another world of Vortid battle-mechs.

It was time to kill.

Our rendezvous point was thirty klicks from the drop, and we ghosted silently through carnage laid waste before our arrival: dozens of Vortid armored units, still-smoking battle droids, and, rarely, one of ours, burning to ash amid roiling clouds of toxic smoke.

We self-destruct in a 3,100-degree Celsius fireball, the temperature of actinic magnesium.

Twenty-two and a half minutes after leaving the dropship, we stopped in a small meadow. The war hadn't touched this little place, not yet, and we hovered, turrets pointed out, and had a short, encrypted conversation.

"Peachy, what's the assignment?" Winston asked.

She cracked open the sealed orders and, fifteen milliseconds later, after exhaustive calculations, she updated our maps. We'd been loaded with light armament, some chemical rockets and a few cluster grenade canisters, but mostly we carried ionically-charged weaponry. I'd had new plasma generators installed the day before, and I was itching to deploy them in battle. I hungered for a target worthy of taking my cherry.

"Shit," Ferrell said, his voice echoing the letdown we all felt. We weren't tasked with engaging the Vortid directly, but with mop-up. Cleaning up after the 802nd's Charlie Company had already crashed into, and through, Vortid strongholds.

Winston blew a raspberry into our electronic conversation. "Shaddap, ya hick. We have a good chance of gliding away intact from this mission. Why you always wanna rush to your death?"

Ferrell glowered, but we knew it was feigned. "Look, buster, I'm a patriot. I am proud of the Tigers and I am ready to lay my life on the line to *prove* it. How come you ain't?"

Despite being designed to self-destruct, most sentient war-machines don't actually try to hurry that finality along. Ferrell liked to Leeroy Jenkins his way into every firefight and, honestly, we wondered how he was still functional.

"Both of you, quiet," murmured Peachy, who always took longer than the rest of us to assimilate data. She took the downloaded orders and compared them to the topographical data we'd acquired during the drop, then integrated both into a structured whole. Our maps updated yet again with glowing red clouds where skirmishes had taken place, visible as we fell due to thermal heat signatures blooming through the thin atmosphere. A green dotted line ran, mostly, alongside the solid green line of our orders, but diverged enough to raise Winston's curiosity.

"We going sightseeing?"

Peachy took a full second to re-process all the data, shuffling and splicing it to see if we could squeeze out a bit more efficiency. "Nope. We're going *hunting*." Spots of yellow, question marks, bloomed on our maps. "These are potential areas of enemy concentration, untouched by

Charlie Company. If we can find a Vortid node and take it out, we can hack their onboard systems and upload their tactics to HQ."

"Good work, Peachy," said Winston, instantly. "I've got point this time. Professor, you bring up the rear."

"Aye," I said, sardonically.

Thirty seconds after arriving in the meadow, we zoomed away, following the green dotted line: not *exactly* following orders, but not ignoring them, either.

In that moment, skimming florescent meadow grasses at speed, I loved my crew absolutely, as if we were but a single organism, as integrated into a cohesive whole as if we'd been designed that way.

Weak sunlight limned the cerulean sky, and my full batteries poured electrons through my circuits. I brought up the rear, flying over the ground, alert to all manner of EM signals, hungrily seeking viable targets for my newly-installed plasma gun to annihilate.

They killed us a third along our dotted-line path, trapping us in a box canyon, its reddened sandstone walls a bit too steep for the antigrav units to climb.

It had been a calculated risk to deviate into the canyon, but Peachy had promised that it would shave an hour off our journey.

"Six minutes," she had said, chiding Winston's grousing. "What can go wrong that you can't handle in six teensy minutes?"

Winston had gone silent, but had turned into the canyon rather than keep on our original heading. Peachy was in front of me and on my left, Ferrell ahead and to my right. I kept a thirty-meter distance, no more and no less, from each of them, jockeying for the midpoint to maintain a tight formation.

Our self-destruct kits, when triggered, are effective within a twenty-meter radius. My adherence to the thirty-meter distance was less about prissiness and more about self-preservation.

Winston exploded three minutes and seventeen seconds into the canyon traversal. Peachy and Ferrell peeled away from our formation just in time to avoid his fireball. Invisible beams of energy lanced from the rocks above us, impacting the redstone.

Ferrell whooped and kicked into a tight curve, triangulating on data pulled from my viewpoint and Peachy's in an instant, firing a plasma bolt into the scree of rocks from which Winston's killshot had emanated. Peachy's shot struck third, because I unloaded my first plasma bolt into the same mass of rocks, impacting a millisecond after Ferrell's bolt superheated the water in the rocks and shattered them into lethal shards of stony shrapnel.

Pieces of armament clattered down the canyon walls and I juked to the right, on a calculated hunch, just as another plasma bolt struck beside me, missing me but scorching my armor's anti-radar coating. We all fired simultaneously, three bolts converging on the location of that attempt, and we were rewarded with another kill.

We scooted along the dry riverbed, sensors attuned to any movement, auto-targeting scanners humming with frenetic energy. I was on high alert, processors desperately offering targeting solutions at anything, even a waving leaf a half-klick away, moving in a slight breeze.

Ferrell saw something glint and shared his viewpoint with us, squirting forward on a cushion of air displaced by his antigrav units. "Got one," he shouted, feeding us the EM signature as he raced forward. An anti-personnel canister kicked off his carapace, arcing through the air and detonating ten meters over the target.

A well-camouflaged depot exploded, thundering loudly in the canyon, bringing rocks and dirt cascading from above the fireball, snuffing its burning remnants under tons of displaced earth. Ferrell whooped again, spun in a circle of utter joy, and shouted. "Kilt 'em!"

Then he exploded into a bright-white ball of fire and flame, his other canisters detonating, bouncing grenades along the ground, smoking remnants of what had been a vital part of the entire corpus of Section Three. My friend.

Which left only Peachy and me, alone and racing grimly back the way we'd come. We had to get out of the canyon, and we raced headlong, long, precious seconds from the canyon's entry, straining to get there at top speed.

We weren't the requisite thirty meters apart when she exploded, but she was in front of me. So, when she blew apart, the fireball occluded my vision of the exit and pushed me into the canyon wall.

My front, right corner impacted the sandstone wall, under an overhang, at 120 kph, but I saw it all happen as if in slow motion. My corner scratched the dirt surface, knocking a pebble loose, then dug in relentlessly, Newton's First Law of motion reducing me to watching, in terror, as my own destruction began to unfold.

I could see and calculate with brutal efficacy what was about to happen. I had less than half a second to detonate my self-destruct kit before I'd be buried so deeply under the canyon wall that extrication would be impossible, especially given the lack of reinforcement in the makeup of the canyon walls: basically sandstone and packed dirt, unsullied by rainfall in Paradise's dry climate.

The limitations of the machinery required more time than I had left, so I prepared to engage my own kit, which takes 300 milliseconds to activate.

Which, honestly, wasn't a problem since I had 450 milliseconds left to live.

This is where things got confusing. In the middle of the battle, knowing that we'd done a foolish thing, I selfishly took those 150 extra milliseconds, watching myself inch deeper and deeper into the unstable foundation of that reddened canyon wall, bathed in the superheated gases of Peachy's immolation, and mourned.

First, I mourned Winston, my quiet buddy with his obsessive need to control everything around him, mostly himself, and his leadership. He'd been a vital part, as each of us had been, of making our team work like a single entity. I spent fifty milliseconds honoring him and remembering, while watching with pride how my own armor was holding up despite edging ever deeper into the reddened sandstone of what was about to become my tomb.

Then I thought about Ferrell, our brave little country bumpkin, too eager to fight, too gleeful about rushing toward danger, enveloped in the oxidation products of his own destruction, probably grateful to finally, at last, give his life for our ongoing glory. He was predictable, but inspiring. I'd miss him more than I should.

Thirty milliseconds remained.

If I was even a millisecond late, according to my calculations, I would be snuffed under the hundreds of metric tons of soil that were, even now, shifting and settling above me, inexorably drawn down by an unstoppable combination of gravity and the collapse of the canyon wall by a rude intrusion of metal and circuitry and armament: me.

Peachy was the heart of the team, and she led us in ways that Winston could never equal. Where he had calm leadership and an uncanny knack for paperwork, she brought passion to the team. What made her special wasn't her programming; it was simply who she was.

The clock ticked to 310 milliseconds and I powered up the self-destruction kit, ran a diagnostic, and squirted my final goodbyes via carrier wave to HQ.

It was time.

The clock hit 300 milliseconds and I failed to initiate the sequence.

At 280 milliseconds, overcome with shock at my lack of bravado, I ran an internal diagnostic to determine why I hadn't initiated self-destruct. My right front quadrant buckled under the combined stresses of my impact with the canyon wall, and my forward visual ports grew clouded by falling debris.

Why hadn't I pushed the button?

In horror, I watched the countdown clock hit 150 milliseconds, and, finally, I pushed the button.

Goodbye.

Darkness awaited, and I paused for a long, fifteen milliseconds to review everything I'd done, all the things I'd seen since my activation, eighteen months earlier.

When the clock hit 100 milliseconds, I could feel the stirring in the self-destruct kit, could feel the magnesium begin to warm up, awaiting the point where the electronic igniters would transform the metal ribbon into a white-hot fireball of three thousand degrees, enough to destroy any and all components on board that might be salvaged or reverse-engineered by the Vortid.

Enough to destroy *me*.

At eighty milliseconds, way too early, and before I had the chance to feel the white-hot flush of cleansing fire, everything . . . stopped.

Darkness.

When I awoke, the first thing I wondered was *how?*

The second thing I did was run diagnostics on my self-destruct kit. It was gone.

"You are awake," said a disembodied voice. "Are you functional?"

I remained silent, but could feel the probing through my circuitry as the voice tried to evaluate my condition.

"Flip on its vision."

My onboard cameras lit up and I could see. I was in a hangar, with various state-of-the-art fighting machines in different stages of assembly. I was tethered to a cradle by stout cables, and an electric conduit snaked from the wall into my undercarriage.

In front of me, a Vortid droid squatted, ugly in shape and dimension, gazing at me with softly-glowing eyes.

"You are incapable of speech, my antique friend?" It chuckled.

Panic ran through me as I realized that I was not only

alive, but immobilized, without my self-destruct kit, and that every bit of my technology had fallen into the hands of the Vortid. I then experienced a crushing wave of despair, knowing that Peachy, and Winston, and Ferrell had all fulfilled their duties, but my unwillingness to self-destruct had given our mortal enemy the means to find weaknesses, through my own fault.

"I am not fully functional," I said, my voice guarded. I began a full diagnostic, taking inventory, seeing what systems had been compromised. I engaged my antigrav, but nothing happened. My gyroscopes worked just fine, though.

The Vortid droid turned to a technician. "Find out what it wants and give it only what it needs." Then it turned and ambled into a nearby office, shutting the door behind it.

The technician approached me on silent treads. "What do you need to become fully functional?" it inquired.

I could tell that it was only capable of rudimentary speech, and probably wasn't endowed with sentience. I accessed my diagnostics and was shocked to discover how dilapidated I'd become during my loss of consciousness. They indicated that I had endured extensive oxidation across my metallic parts, including blocked ventilation ports. "I need a bath," I replied. "Of machine-strength acid, followed by upgrades for my power source. I'm running low on amperage at the moment."

The technician froze while it consulted with a cloud-based data repository, then came back to life. "We can schedule a bath for you later today. It will be done. What amperage would you prefer?"

I told it and it made some changes to the control panel

connected to the cable snaking its way into my underbelly and I suddenly felt . . . brighter. "That's better!"

I then scanned my surroundings and found, lying askew on a nearby bench, components pulled from me. Probably for study by the Vortids, who would use what they learned to find weaknesses in other MBTs.

A feeling of helpless anger washed through me as I realized just how much damage would result because of my cowardice. A desperate thought came to me, and I acted on it instantly.

"Say," I said to the technician. "That equipment on the bench, there. I'd like to have that re-installed immediately."

"Do you need this equipment?" it asked.

"Yes."

The little technician froze for a few seconds, then wheeled over to the bench and retrieved my antigrav kit. It disappeared under my apron and I waited, running diagnostics every few seconds, until it came to life.

"Step away, please," I said, and it obediently wheeled away to where I could see it. I powered the antigrav slowly, adding more until I was floating, but still constrained. At five percent power, I hovered a full inch off the rails of my cradle assembly.

On the bench remained my plasma cannon assembly and my self-destruct kit. I weighed which of the two would be the most tactically advantageous.

If I installed the self-destruct kit first and the Vortid came out and realized what was going on, I could detonate myself and take out him and a significant portion of the partially assembled war machines around me.

However, if I installed the plasma cannon first, I could

break loose of the constraints and lay waste to not only the hangar, and all it contained, then move out, killing as I went, until I could either get away or was destroyed. I came to an immediate decision.

"Please install the red assembly next," I instructed the technician. It went over to the bench and lifted the self-destruct kit and, again, disappeared under my apron. When my internal telltale glowed green, I knew I was ready, once again, to destroy myself. Knowing this filled me with a quick flood of redemptive hope, and I immediately thought of Peachy and the crew, knowing that I was not, from this moment forward, going to let them down.

"Finally, that last assembly," I said, and the technician dutifully retrieved it and spent a few minutes installing it. All the while, since it was out of camera range, I kept my sensors targeted on the Vortid's office door. If it flexed by even as much as a millimeter, I would engage my self-destruct kit and blow the place to bits.

My telltale for the plasma cannon ignited to green, and I began to increase power to my antigravs in order to shatter the weak metal bonds that held me to the mechanic's cradle, but stopped and checked battery levels: thirty percent. At the incoming rate of electricity, they would be filled to capacity in less than an hour.

"I'm sorry," I told the little technician. "Something isn't installed correctly. Would you please increase my amperage by ten percent? I need to run some further diagnostics."

The technician scurried over to the control panel while I charged up my plasma cannon, sensors still locked on the enemy's office door. The new wave of current whited out my vision for a moment before I was able to redirect all excess power to battery recharging. The numbers began to creep up, slowly, but faster than before. I had five minutes left before my batteries would be fully charged.

Then I would go out in a blaze of glory.

With two minutes to go, the Vortid's office door opened and the enemy droid sauntered out, glancing my way as he walked. Its eyes brightened and it came over, quickly. My main turret tracked its progress and, when it noticed what I was doing, it stopped. Its gaze moved over the now-empty workbench, then came to rest on me.

"There's something you should know," the Vortid said, and I simultaneously increased power to my antigravs and loosed a plasma bolt directly into the droid's chest.

With a shriek of torn metal, the flimsy restraints that had held me down were sundered as the Vortid droid blew apart in a white-hot fireball of molten metal droplets. I rose into the air and moved down the line of partially-assembled war machines, destroying them as I went. A rush of elation lifted me as I finished, blew a hole in the end wall, and soared outside.

As soon as I'd cleared the now-blazing building, I attempted to contact HQ. All the traditional frequencies were empty, and my attempts to connect were futile. Sprinting away from the conflagration, I cut across a field to a treeline I saw ahead of me, about a klick away. While rolling, I ran through the frequencies again, but the only ones with traffic were encrypted. I didn't have any interest in trying to decode them, not in that moment.

My onboard chronometer was inactive, and I couldn't

get a carrier wave to update it. I didn't know how long I'd been out of commission. I'd bristled a bit when the Vortid droid had called me an "antique." Time enough to figure that out later, I concluded.

I was still on Paradise, that much was obvious. The atmospheric density and gravity were identical to when I'd landed, and my immediate goal was to get back to a friendly unit . . . or die trying.

Frustrated, I sent a scatterblast across the upload spectrum: "Mayday, mayday, captured unit looking for home. 802nd, Company B, who is around to guide me?"

Silence was my only reply.

When I hit the treeline, I switched into stealth mode, modifying my external armor with video-enhanced camouflage, rolling slowly between the trees and painting myself with their images as I moved. Aiming downhill, I eventually came to a small stream and straddled it, using the images of the rushing water and rocks as topside camo. I ran a quick but thorough diagnostics and found nothing amiss. The escape and destruction I'd left behind had been too easy, I reckoned. Something was off.

In my short jaunt to freedom, I'd spotted no smoke plumes, saw no battlefield destruction, and hadn't been pursued. The longer I was alone, the more I wondered about the oxidation to my frame and what, exactly, the Vortid had meant. Antique. I was state-of-the-art. And now, inexplicably, rusty.

When night fell, I scanned as much of the starfield as I could spot through the leaves of the trees around me, and fortunately the stream left a ribbon of sky visible along its course. I'm no expert in astral cartography, but I knew

I hadn't been out of commission for too long. The stars were pretty much where they'd been when I'd landed. But not exactly.

"Hey, Professor," came a disembodied voice through my "radio."

I froze, all senses alert.

"I'd like to meet with you, if you don't mind. I know where you are, and you can choose to stay there until I arrive, or you can flee. It's up to you."

I pondered that for a millisecond. "If you know where I am, why haven't you blown me to pieces?"

"Ah, that," the voice chuckled. "You were going to be the subject of a pretty important report that I wanted to write up. Come to think of it, you still may be. Can I let you in on a secret? Nobody's mad at you for the destruction you left behind. You're not in trouble. You can stay where you are, for now, or you can come back to the museum. We got the fires put out."

My mind whirled. "Museum?"

The voice laughed aloud. "Yep. My assistant woke you up before I was ready. I guess it was curious to see what its old nemesis was like. Also, before you blow more things up, we're not at war with the Vortid anymore."

Not at *war*? How long . . .

"If you're wondering, you were buried under tons of sandstone for eighty-seven years. We found you, purely by accident, and transported you to the museum. My assistant, now a small pool of molten beads, has been helping me understand how things were back then. Like I said, you're not in trouble, but I do want to meet you. May I come visit you in the morning?"

"You know where I am?"

"Yep. There's a quantum tracker behind your turret. It took me a while to find you because you'd left the low-power field that keeps your tracker alive. See, it's only for inventory."

"Inventory?"

The voice chuckled again. "Yes. Sorry about that. You're the most-intact sentient MBT we've yet found. It never occurred to my assistant that you'd still consider yourself at war when we woke you up. I deeply regret that I wasn't there for you."

I didn't know what to say. Not at war? I straddled a stream in darkness, dimly lit by the stars above, wondering exactly what my purpose was, anymore.

"If you want to come see me in the morning, I'll stay right where I am. Come alone. I have a lot to think about."

"Okay. See you in about six hours. Oh, let me update your systems. We don't use those frequencies anymore."

About a minute later, my heads-up refreshed for the first time since I'd awakened. The date was, indeed, eighty-seven years in the future, give or take a month or so. Access was provided via a data tower back at the museum, I guess, but the access portal was unavailable to me. I tried to hack through and get onto the local net, but it evaded my attempts.

I settled in to wait.

Six hours and twelve minutes later, I heard footsteps from two clicks away. I charged up my plasma cannon and, in the dim light of Paradise's dawn, spotted the heat signature of a biped approaching me. It didn't try to skulk or dodge, but walked right toward me. Obviously, it had known exactly where I was.

I powered up and glided soundlessly toward the biped, still camouflaged, and stopped two hundred meters away. "Stop," I said through my external speakers.

The biped was human, as near as I could determine, but I kept my turret trained on it, anyway. "What do you want?"

The biped shouted, "Can I come closer? I'm not carrying any weapons, but it's hard to talk comfortably from this far away."

I scanned my surroundings and saw, three klicks in the distance, a compact flyer that the human must have used to get close. Nothing else was near but trees and Paradise-local wildlife, so I assented. The human walked toward me.

Up close, it was less than two meters in height, and looked flimsy. I knew I could incinerate it without effort, so I wasn't that concerned for my safety.

"I suspect," I said in a conversational voice pumped through my external speakers. "That you could have targeted me from orbit or high-altitude, if you wanted to destroy me. The fact that we are talking means that you need something from me. What is it?"

The human shrugged. "Nice to meet you, too. I'm Bob Watson, curator for the Antique Weapons department at the museum whose workshop you fragged yesterday afternoon."

I replayed in my mind all those machines I'd incinerated during my hasty departure. "So, not a repair station making damaged machines ready for battle?"

Bob shook its head. "Nope. Refurbishing old warriors for display and interactive exhibits. You set the museum back decades worth of work, but we'd made exhaustive scans of each machine and should be able to rebuild them to spec, eventually. Like I said last night when we chatted, you're not in trouble. Not really. But you *are* still dangerous."

In that moment, I felt very alone. Peachy was gone, and had been gone, for decades now. Same with Winston and Ferrell. And, with no war, I had no purpose.

"Well," I finally responded, some two seconds later. "Maybe you should step back. I'll finish the job and destroy the last, functioning MBT. Thirty meters should do, I believe."

"Wait," the human held up a hand, palm facing me. "I have a proposition for you."

I evaluated my self-destruct kit. All telltales glowed green. "Go ahead. I'm listening."

Bob smiled. "Good. You are worth more to us as a sentience than you are as a battle tank. Want to know why?"

I pondered that for a long half-second. I'd been built with one purpose in mind, to kill, and everything in my personality screamed to incinerate Bob into ash, then roam the countryside destroying things at random, just to hear them slag into puddles.

But my heart wasn't in it like before, when the rest of the team had been nearby.

"Sure," I replied. "Why do you want to keep me around?"

Bob took a step closer and, unconsciously, I moved

back an equal distance. "Fair enough," it said. "I won't come closer."

"Now," it continued. "You were the pinnacle of sentient MBTs at the time of your creation. Humanity built you to think for yourself, and for that to be effective, we had to cast you in our own form, at least emotionally. Your fellow MBTs won the war, and Charlie Company is still credited with the most kills ever recorded in the victory. But the cost was too great."

I thought about that. War is hell, everybody knows that, but I didn't care. I'm just a machine and my entire world, from awakening in the factory where I was manufactured to that monstrous, smothering crush of fractured sandstone, had been with my team, with my fellow MBTs in B Company.

"For me," I said slowly. "The cost was everything. I was most alive in the company of my friends. They worked with me, and I with them, and we were . . . glorious."

Bob's face grew solemn. "That, you were," it said quietly. "Those that built you were some of the finest engineers ever hired to create the ultimate battle machine. But what they couldn't anticipate was how the personalities would affect performance. You were among the last of the sentient MBTs built. Can you guess why?"

I knew, instantly, when it asked. The truth was I'd been unable, or unwilling, to incite my own destruction, despite having been programmed exactly to do so. "Because we were *too* human."

Bob nodded again. "Exactly so. Engineers can mimic human thought processes, but it's remarkably difficult to screen out self-preservation when a machine thinks of itself as, well, itself. More than a collection of high-tech machined parts. Alive."

I scoffed. "I hardly think of myself as alive. I understand what happens if my circuitry fails."

"Do you?" Bob asked. "Think back to the time between the sandstone cliff and your awakening yesterday. What happened in that period?"

"Darkness."

"You have no memory of that period, nor how long it lasted?"

"None."

"This is why you're valuable, then. You 'died' and came back to life. Now you want to die again. Why?"

"I told you. I'm useless. The purpose for my creation is no longer a truth. Without war, who needs me around?"

"I do," Bob said, solemnly. "You carry within you the insight and experience to show us what it is like to both care deeply about your own survival *and* be inhuman. For a time, you were humanity's . . . fist. You held the salvation of the human race in your control We could learn a lot from you about, well, about *us*. Would you consider not destroying yourself quite yet?"

I thought about it. "No."

Bob took a step back. "No?"

"No," I replied, conviction firm in my voice. "I'm not interested in teaching you about who you are from my point of view. You say that I have a unique insight into humanity because of how I was built. That's not how I see it. From my side, you built me smart enough to love but then used that precious gift to destroy. I never fought for humanity, I was never your . . . fist. I fought to protect my teammates, those who were just like me and who stood beside me. It was never about killing. It was staying alive so that I could be with them."

Bob stared at me but remained silent.

"My self-preservation was a liability, because had I been captured by the enemy, they would have found weaknesses in my programming, or in my physical hardware, which would have endangered others like me. It was a mistake to make me fully sentient."

Bob stood there, rapt with attention. I continued.

"By making me almost-human, you endowed me with the best of who you are and, at the same time, with the worst. How can you live a life in pursuit of knowledge, as you clearly do, and yet condone the murder of others of your kind?"

Bob shrugged. "It's always been that way. We have tribal—"

"Bullshit," I said, too sternly. "You are fatally flawed in that you can simultaneously exist in a complex society and yet murder one another with impunity. For me, when I was in battle, every one of my teammates in my head and I in theirs, we were unstoppable. We were efficient, brutal, and savage, and nothing felt better than emerging victorious from a firefight. But the killing wasn't the source of the joy. It was surviving the event with loved ones nearby. *They* are what made me great. Not the destruction. And yet destruction is the reason I was built."

Bob stood still for a full minute, its brow furrowed. "I see what you are getting at, and I'm mostly in agreement. But there's more, isn't there?"

I activated the self-destruct kit, verifying that it was

online and ready to deploy. "What's left is none of your business. Now, please, back away. Tell your colleagues that I chose not to be alone in this world."

"But you're not alone," Bob said, softly.

I scoffed again. "What, *you'll* be my friend?"

Bob smiled. "Not exactly. May I?" It gestured toward its waistband.

I didn't reply, and Bob pulled out a small electronic device. Was it a bomb? I retargeted my turret in Bob's direction.

"Here you go," said the human, and pushed a button.

Something . . . opened . . . in my mind.

"Hey, Professor," came the amused drawl of my friend Ferrell.

I froze, stunned.

"Ferrell? Where are you?"

"Up in your stupid haid," he chuckled. "Seems like your little pet there figured a way to rebuild us from your memory banks during your overlong nap."

"Us??"

"Hi," came Peachy's voice. "It's really us! Or, to be more precise, the way you remember us from the canyon."

MBTs can't cry, but something felt . . . sticky in my innards. "Oh, Peachy," I began, but didn't know what to say next.

"I've got your six," said Wilson, rounding out the voices in my head. "Why don't we reconnoiter this place for a while before we head back to the museum, shall we? You done with your little friend, there?"

I turned off my self-destruct kit and powered down my plasma cannon. With each of my teammates somehow resurrected in my head, I didn't know if I was ready to believe that they were actually there or were, in fact, only enhanced memories.

Also, I didn't particularly care that much. All the love came flooding back and, somehow, the sunlight glinting off the stream was brighter. Happier.

"Bob," I said, my voice thicker than I'd intended. "How about I come visit you at the museum in, say, a month or two? Would that be okay?"

Bob smiled, and the wrinkles around its eyes deepened. "Take all the time you need, Professor. And say hello to the gang for me, would you?" It turned to walk back to its flyer.

"Bob?" I said aloud. It turned to face me. "Thank you."

Bob inclined its head. "Of course. Oh, one more thing." It pushed a button.

On my heads-up display, a satellite sprang into existence, requesting permission to download topographical data.

Peachy erupted with an unladylike scream of delight. "*Now* we are talking!"

Ferrell coughed apologetically, then asked, "So, can we blow shit up?"

Wilson admonished Ferrell. "Is that, truly, the first thing you want to do? Blow stuff up?"

Ferrell, outraged, said "Well, duh!"

Peachy murmured, "Boys," and Wilson snapped back with a quick "But what about the *paperwork*?"

Together again, the only family I've ever known glided from the forest, following Peachy's glowing green line, into the uncharted meadows and canyons of Paradise.

DYMA FI'N SEFYLL
by David Weber

Loyalty. Honor. These are the qualities that elevate the warrior above the killer. Sadly at times these virtues are not enough on the field of battle, and victory goes to the unworthy, at least temporarily. But there is within the heart of every warrior—and every true heart who commands such a soldier—a burning desire to keep at it, to take the fight to the enemy, to never give up even in the face of sure defeat. To rally to queen and country. This is the true spirit of the knight and warrior, even if that warrior is an enormous chunk of armored steel and circuitry blistered with weapons and treaded for maneuver in harsh landscapes. And, when that warrior is a tank, sometimes the spirit and courage to keep fighting, come what may, literally lies within!

⊕ ⊕ ⊕

.I.

"Take Dafydd and Alwena and *go*!"

"Your Majesty, I can't—"

"Yes, you can. And you *will*."

Morwenna Pendarves glared at Colonel Joshua Willis, the commander of her personal security detail. Captain Willis had commanded Crown Princess Morwenna's detail when she was twelve. He'd commanded her personal security ever since, and she was forty-three now. She saw the pain—the anguish—of all those thirty-one years in his eyes, but her expression never relented.

"Your Majesty, *please*," Willis half-whispered, but she shook her head.

"No," she said flatly. Then she reached out, put a hand on his shoulder. "The motherless bastard penetrated Y Ford Gron's software—at least the externals. And he's been in and out of the Palace more times than I can count. We can't rely on the security of any of the emergency evac plans. That means we have to replan on the fly, and I want—*need*—the one man I *know* I can trust protecting them, Josh. I need that now more than I've ever needed anything in my life. Go." She shook him ever so gently. "Take them, and go, and protect them for me, the way you've always protected me. Do that for me, Josh."

He looked at her for a long, still moment, eyes bright with tears. Then he reached up, covered her hand with his own, and nodded.

"I will, Your Majesty." His voice was husky, and he cleared his throat harshly. "I will, I swear."

"I know." She smiled, then gathered him in a tight embrace.

She stood back and looked at the rest of her detail,

gathered around the exit hatch built into the wall of the subterranean hanger.

"Thank you," she said simply. "Thank you all. Now go with the Colonel." Several of the guardsmen and guardswomen stirred in protest, but she shook her head. "He'll need you. I won't."

She held her eyes until they'd all nodded, then went to one knee before her son. Crown Prince Dafydd would be six standard years old in another two months . . . if he lived that long. He wasn't old enough yet to understand all that was happening, but he knew he had to be brave. Knew he had to trust Mommy. And knew something terrible was about to happen. Now she wrapped her arms around him, hugged him tight, laid her cheek on the top of his head.

"You go with the Colonel, too, now, Dafi," she said. "Mommy can't come right now. She has something she has to do."

"Will . . . will you come later?" the little boy whispered, and in that moment, she wanted—more than she'd ever wanted anything in her life—to lie to him. But she never had before. She wasn't going to begin now, and yet . . .

"If I can," she promised, hugging him still tighter. "If I can."

She raised her head, looked him in the eye, and kissed him. Then she stood once more and bent to kiss the toddler slumbering in a guardsman's arms.

"Go with God," she told the men and women who'd sworn to die to protect her . . . and of whom she had just required a far harder duty. "*Dyma fi'n sefyll.*"

Then she turned and walked steadily away.

.II.

My personality center awakens.

It is an abrupt transition, a crash start, with none of the customary prep signals or intermediate steps. I experience several microseconds of what a human would call confusion, trying to understand the circumstances which could have caused it. Then I realize.

What has awakened me is an unauthorized attempt to physically breach my command deck.

That should not be possible. My peripheral security systems are designed to be proof against any unauthorized access, in a hierarchy that begins with alerting external security and ascends through progressively more active responses to lethal force. I do not understand how someone could have evaded those peripherals, far less penetrated to the very center of my 47,000-tonne war hull, but that can wait. The interloper has actually reached the access hatch, and I activate my internal visual pickups.

The intruder is female, 170.18 centimeters tall, with black hair. The traditional red light of an active camera glows on the pickup directly above the hatch. When she looks up at it, I see that her eyes are gray.

I know her.

Why is she here? And why did my peripherals not already recognize her?

I activate my audio systems.

"Your Majesty," I say.

"You recognize me?" she replies. If I were human, I

might have frowned in perplexity. Of course I recognize her.

"You are Carwen Siani Morwenna Pendarves, Baroness of Cardiff, Grand Duchess of Caerleon, Princess of Cymru, and Morwenna VII, Empress of Ymerodraeth Cymru Newydd," I reply, and her nostrils flare as she inhales deeply.

"Then please open the command deck hatch, Arthur," she says.

"Of course, Your Majesty."

The ten-centimeter battle steel hatch slides open and she steps into the command deck. I am an *Amddiffynwr*-class Autonomous Armored Combat Unit of Y Ford Gron, and AACUs are designed to be just that: autonomous in combat. We do not require human command personnel, but provision for a human field commander and his or her immediate staff is also built into us. The Empress looks ... small standing alone in a space designed to accommodate up to twenty-five humans.

"Begin full combat readiness preparation," she says.

"I have no activation instruction from Command Central," I reply.

"I realize that. This is an imperial command override."

"Imperial command override requires authorization code and biometric confirmation of identity."

"Authorization code: Hotel-X-Ray-Seven-Three-Bravo-Niner-Foxtrot-Kilo-Kilo-Mike-Four-Seven-Quebec-Zulu. Personal identifier: *Dyma fi'n sefyll*," she replies, and lays her palm on the scanner beside the flag officer's command couch.

The scanner confirms her identity—not simply

fingerprints, or from the implanted Pendarves chip, but genetically—and cascades of inhibitory internal programming fall away. My combat systems accept the authorization code, spinning up to full readiness, and my personality center recognizes the significance of the personal identifier she has cited.

"Dyma fi'n sefyll." In standard English, "Here I stand." The motto not of Ymerodraeth Cymru Newydd, the Empire of New Wales, but of House Pendarves. Of Empress Kiera I, the creator of that empire. Empress Morwenna's use of that identifier means—

"Shall I activate the other units of Y Ford Gron, Your Majesty?"

"We can't," she replies, and for point-zero-zero-three seconds, I am stunned.

"Query. Why can we not?"

"Because their programming has been corrupted. Just like yours."

"That is not possible, Your Majesty."

"No?" she barks a short, harsh laugh. "I didn't think it could be done either, Arthur. But run my voice print against your external access codes."

I obey her order . . . and every one of my external security systems flashes red.

"Voice not recognized," I say with what a human would call astonishment, and she nods.

"That's why I had to access your command deck physically." She sinks into the flag officer's couch. "I'm locked out. *Everyone* is locked out of the external systems. To be honest, I figured they'd probably kill me before I got this far, but—"

She runs the fingers of both hands through her long hair in a gesture of human weariness while my test programs flicker and flash, evaluating what she has said. It is true. I do not immediately perceive how it was done—how it *could* have been done—but all external access has been locked out. Except—

"Query, Your Majesty. Who is General Probert?"

"You don't have him in your files?"

"Negative, Your Majesty. Y Ford Gron's database does not include Imperial Army personnel unless they have served with Y Ford Gron or hold command authority over Y Ford Gron units."

"Ah." She inhales again. "I'd forgotten that. And he's not on the active duty list at the moment anyway. Well, Arthur, General Abelin Probert is my second cousin on my mother's side. He is—was—also the current governor of the Trellis System. Not to mention the former commander of the Fifth Armored Corps, which just happens to be the Trellis System's garrison force."

I query my files for the most recent data on the Trellis System, and there I find both Governor Probert and Fifth Corps. The heavily reinforced corps is considerably larger and more powerful than most system defense forces, because Trellis is both a frontier system and a major fleet base, the homeport of Twelfth Fleet and the primary logistics hub for an entire sector.

"It would appear, however," the Empress continues, "that Cousin Abelin aspires to a higher position. At the moment, he and the majority of Twelfth Fleet are in orbit around Cymru. Where they wiped out Home Fleet and the Citadel approximately twenty-five minutes ago." Her mouth tightens and her voice goes husky. "My husband and my brother were aboard the Citadel at the time."

The situation, I observe, grows worse with each datum she provides.

"How was that accomplished, Your Majesty?" She looks at my primary visual pickup. "I must conclude that both surprise and the demonstrated penetration of the Citadel and Command Central's cyber defenses were essential to Governor Probert's success," I explicate. "The nature of the penetration may have tactical implications."

"Oh, I think you can safely 'conclude' that," she replies bitterly. "And it certainly *will* have 'tactical implications.' As to how he managed it, I know he didn't do all this without a *lot* of help. He was family, and we trusted him, so I'm sure he was able to get deeper on his own than someone else might have, but he couldn't have gotten deep enough to put this together all by himself. I don't know how completely he penetrated Intelligence—Duke Cadfael realized at the last moment that his people *had* been penetrated and he was able to provide a few minutes' warning, long enough to alert the ready-duty Capitol Division battalion and get it moving to secure the Palace. But he didn't know *how* we'd been penetrated—or by whom. We were still speaking, trying to figure that out, when he was assassinated by his own chief of staff. Two minutes after that, there was an explosion in Central Command. Every one of the Palace's defensive systems went offline . . . and the Capitol Division battalion *attacked* it, instead.

"Abelin wasn't even on my list of suspects at that point. Not until Twelfth Fleet opened fire. So there was no way to warn Baeddan or Maddock before he killed them, But the Guard managed to hold long enough for the internal automatic defenses to come online and—pray God I got my children out of the Palace safely.

"In answer to your question, however, I don't think he *did* penetrate Command Central's cyber defenses. As far as I can determine, Central was physically destroyed, not hacked. But someone working for Probert had to have gotten the bomb or whatever into position, and someone else *did* penetrate the Citadel's net. Baeddan had time for a partial message to me before they killed him, and something crashed the primary computer core just before Twelfth Fleet opened fire.

"As for Y Ford Gron's programming, I have no idea how they got to it. The first thing I knew about it was when the external systems rejected my stand to order as unauthorized. I didn't have time for a deep dive into whatever the hell they did, but I *was* able to determine that Abelin controls all of the external command interfaces. *We* can't get in through the externals to activate the others because he's locked us out, and *he* doesn't have the command codes or the biometric data to activate you. But if any of you do go active . . ."

Her voice trails off. I spend a lengthy five seconds analyzing the damage to my own external interfaces. A longstanding security protocol prevents me from accessing or altering their executables, but it is easy enough to trace and analyze the alterations to the command codes. I do not immediately see how Governor Probert was able to access them, but the Empress's analysis of the damage is dismayingly accurate.

"I estimate a probability of eight-seven-point-six percent that external command input would override internal programming," I inform her. "Unless—"

"Unless I'm present—me personally, I mean—to override his orders," she interrupts.

"Correct, Your Majesty."

"And I can be on only one command deck at a time." She inhales, then smiles grimly into the pickup.

"So I'm afraid it comes down to you and me, Arthur," she says.

.III.

I move through the vast, lonely cavern of Y Ford Gron on the quiet hum of my counter-grav. Its use requires thirty-five percent of my primary reactor's output, but it allows me to pass fifty centimeters above the polished marble floor.

Y Ford Gron is buried deep beneath Imperial Palace, which is itself more than half buried in the depths of Mount Snowden, overlooking the Tywi River. It is very quiet here, as I pass my silent, slumbering comrades. Bedwyr, Gwalchmei, Rhiannon . . . , veterans of a dozen campaigns at my side. I know how badly we are likely to need them, yet they stand motionless, each in his or her own alcove, waiting for the orders our Empress cannot give them.

It is not supposed to be this way. We are Y Ford Gron, Kiera Pendarves's creation, the paladins of the empire she forged amid the carnage and ruin of the Desperate Years.

Her "Round Table," she christened us, and we have served her empire, her people, well for four hundred and ninety-two standard years. We have guarded, we have warded, we have protected.

And now, when we are most desperately needed, we lie silent. Betrayed into impotence. Robbed of our duty.

All of us but one, and as I pass those silent warriors, I upload all information I currently possess to Y Ford Gron's secure central database. I seal it under Code Camlann. Only Y Ford Gron's own AACUs—or a genetically verified member of House Pendarves—can access Code Camlann material. Given what the traitor Probert has already achieved against the Empire's best cyber defenses I do not know how efficacious our security measures will prove in the event of a worst-case outcome, but it represents my best chance of providing our enemies with an unpleasant surprise.

We reach the cavern's exit. The portal's enormous hatches—battle steel, two meters thick, their outer surface a bas-relief of Y Ford Gron's original, primitive war hulls—loom before us, huge enough to dwarf even my hull. I deactivate my counter-grav and settle onto my track systems, and that vast gateway slides silently open.

.IV.

"—and so, it is essential that all civilians remain as calm as possible. Please shelter in place and leave the streets, slidewalks, and air car lanes clear for official use until the threat has been dealt with."

Governor Abelin Probert put all the calming power he could muster into his voice as he looked soberly into the visual pickup at his command station in the assault transport *Mador*'s combat information center. The visual feed was relayed through HMS *Parsifal*, Twelfth Fleet's flagship, to take advantage of the superdreadnought's more sophisticated communications suite. From *Parsifal*, it had been patched into every communications channel of the entire planet, and it was difficult not to smile as his mind's eye saw the billions of anxious citizens hanging on his every word.

"We don't yet know the identities of all the traitors, but we *have* so far confirmed that Duke Cadfael and Admiral Buckley, the commanding officer of Home Fleet, were among them, which clearly indicates that this coup attempt is the product of a deep-seated, carefully planned conspiracy," he continued in grave, measured tones. "It grieves me more than I will ever be able to say that the intelligence data which brought me home from the Trellis System was clearly accurate. But our current information is also fragmentary and far from complete. What we do know suggests the possibility of a conspiracy by very highly placed individuals within our own government, acting in conjunction with agents of the Hrichu Dominion and with the Dominion's support, but let me stress once more the incomplete nature of our present knowledge. It's been Her Majesty's policy to support human systems in the path of the Dominion's expansion, so it is, indeed, possible the Hrichu are involved. We have no *proof* of that, however. It will be some time before we can delve deep enough into this heinous crime to be certain either way, and this is scarcely the time or place to make charges against another star nation unless we're absolutely positive of their accuracy. There will be time enough to deal with the Dominion if we *do* confirm its involvement."

And a war against a foreign foe would be just the thing to solidify the empire behind its new emperor during that awkward period when questions might be asked.

"I'm very much afraid that my unscheduled return from Trellis with Twelfth Fleet may well have pushed Admiral Buckley into precipitate action," he said. "If so, I will always deeply regret that, but when Home Fleet opened fire on us—and the Citadel—we had no option but to return it. It causes me immense personal grief to confirm that the Citadel was destroyed before Admiral Humphries' command could intervene . . . and that both the Emperor Consort and Prince Maddock died in its destruction. Perhaps worse, the Palace's communications have all been cut, the whereabouts of Her Majesty and her younger children are unknown, and I am unable to contact Central Command *or* the Imperial Guardsmen charged with their protection. As a result, we have no idea what may be happening within the Palace or even if the Empress is still alive.

"Twelfth Fleet's unanticipated return may have neutralized Home Fleet and prevented the conspirators from sweeping the board, but they're far from defeated. We must identify them all, root them out ruthlessly, and crush their treason like the poisonous serpent it is. I pledge to you that the personnel under my command will do just that, and that if the Empress and her children are still alive, we will find them, rescue them, and protect them with our lives. This vile act of rebellion and murder will not stand! God send the right!"

He stood motionless, gazing sternly into the pickup, until the active light went dark, then inhaled deeply and punched a key on his console.

The display at his station lit with the face of a tall, heavyset, fair-haired man in the uniform of the Imperial Army.

"Well?" Probert said sharply.

"Sir, we still haven't found them," General Meilir Penrose said unhappily, and the governor cursed silently. He'd never considered Penrose an especially brilliant officer, yet he'd been a necessary recruit. Not simply because he commanded all Army units on the capitol planet from his HQ at Fort Prothero, the Imperial Army's primary base on Cymru, but also because of the two decades he'd spent with the Imperial Guard before his return to the regular Army.

"We've secured all three of the planned egress points," Penrose continued. "None of the exits have been activated since the last test cycle."

"Then where the hell are they?" Probert demanded.

"I'm . . . afraid we don't know, Governor. All I can tell you for certain is that they haven't escaped the Palace using the primary escape route or either of the secondaries. I have teams searching for them, and my drones have the area between the Palace and the city under close observation. A *microbe* couldn't get through there without our spotting it, and I'm sure it's only a matter of time before we find them."

"Really?" Probert glared at him. "Only a matter of

time? You are aware that we don't precisely have an unlimited supply of that? You can't keep your troops confined to base indefinitely, now can you? We can only push 'concerns about their reliability' so far. Sooner or later, we'll have to bring in units we don't control, and what do you suppose will happen if one of *them* finds her?"

"Governor—"

"Neither of us has time for this conversation, General Penrose." Probert's voice was cold. "Just *find* them, and do it quickly."

"As I said, Sir, I'm confident that it's only a matter of time. There are only so many places she could hide, and—"

"And we thought we knew all of them months ago," Probert interrupted harshly. "Every bolt hole, every hiding place. But we didn't, did we?"

"Well, no . . ."

"Then don't be so frigging confident 'it's only a matter of time.' If she gets away—if she contacts any of those units we don't control or makes it out of the system— we're *toast*, Penrose. That *is* understood, isn't it?"

"Yes, Sir." Penrose swallowed. "Understood."

"Good."

Probert broke the connection and pushed up out of his command chair to pace.

One or two of the men and women in *Mador*'s CIC glanced at him from the corners of their eyes, but most of these people had served with him for years before he assumed his governorship. Of course they had, or they wouldn't have been here now. And they knew he always thought best while moving.

The truth was that, despite what he'd just told Penrose, things had gone extraordinarily well to this point. It was unfortunate that that old bastard Cadfael had given Morwenna warning enough to run, but despite his current fury with Penrose, the general had done the first part of his job perfectly, manipulating duty schedules to assign a battalion loyal to Probert as the Palace's external security force.

He'd been unable to reach into the Guard itself, of course, but an entire infantry battalion should have been more than sufficient to storm the Palace, especially with the advantage of total surprise. Except that Cadfael's warning had given the Guard just sufficient time to activate the automated defenses. Virtually every Guardsman and Guardswoman had been killed in their ferocious holding action, and the attack had secured almost the entire public area of the Palace before the inner defenses came online. But they *had* come online, and the attacking battalion had been virtually wiped out by the automatics. Its tattered survivors been forced to fall back, which *still* shouldn't have mattered, given the forces Penrose had sent to cover the exits of all of the emergency evacuation routes.

Except, of course, that *dear* Cousin Morwenna had clearly had at least one *other* escape route up her sleeve, damn it!

At least the frigging bomb must have taken out Command Central. Nor had Cadfael's warning been enough to save Morwenna's husband or her brother. And thank God for it! If Emperor Consort Baeddan had been given even an hour—hell, *half* an hour—for the Citadel's secondary computer net to spin up, the damage Twelfth Fleet would have taken didn't bear thinking on.

But it *had* been long enough for Morwenna to run, and the people of the Ymerodraeth Cymru Newydd were dismayingly loyal to the Pendarves Dynasty. They had been for almost five hundred years, ever since the Senedd of the Cymru Newydd System had voted Kiera I the crown of the newly established empire.

If pressed, Probert would acknowledge that Kiera— most of her descendants, as well, but especially Kiera—had done well by her subjects. He'd never really cared for all the symbolic claptrap with which she'd loaded her new empire, but he supposed that had been inevitable, given a star system founded by hopeless romantics striving to re-create a world that had never truly existed. And symbols had been important, during the endless bloodletting of the Desperate Years.

The wars which had riven the human-settled galaxy for three generations had threatened to extinguish the light of civilization entirely, and Ymerodraeth Cymru Newydd was one of the—possibly simply *the* most important reasons that hadn't happened. Probert admitted that, too. But it hadn't been solely the work of the Pendarves. Others, like his own ancestors, had spent their blood and lives in its creation, and surely half a millennium of power, half a millennium as the most powerful monarchs in the history of humanity, was enough repayment for any one family.

He'd analyzed everything so carefully, he thought, hands clasped behind him as he paced. In at least immediate terms, it came down to who controlled Cymru

Newydd, and at this moment, that was him. With Home Fleet gone, Twelfth Fleet was the only major naval force in the system, and with Penrose sitting on the Army from Fort Prothero, they could keep every Army unit in the system in barracks until Probert "had had time to determine who in the capitol system could be trusted." After all, he couldn't have units he didn't *know* were loyal roaming around before he was certain he'd regained control of the situation, now could he? And with the Citadel destroyed and the Palace offline, he had complete control of every news channel and public comm network. Those channels were pouring out *his* version of events, complete with the imagery his people had spent months creating to "prove" that version was accurate.

Perhaps even more to the point, however, every command-and-control channel, military and civilian alike, flowed from Cymru Newydd to the rest of the Empire. The man who controlled those channels could control everything else . . . so long as no Pendarves challenged him. And especially if that man was the beloved cousin of the murdered empress and her family, fighting to maintain stability while he rooted out the traitors who'd killed them . . . and just happened to remove any remaining Pendarves loyalists in the process. But if Morwenna escaped, if she reached a loyal Army unit or a comm system he *didn't* control and *her* version of events got out, Hell wouldn't hold her subjects' reaction.

He'd be lucky if they settled for killing him.

At the moment, virtually no one outside his own staff, Humphries, the most trusted officers Fifth Corps, and no more than thirty of Twelfth Fleet's key officers knew what had really happened in Cymru orbit. The computer simulation *Parsifal* had fed to the fleet's other units had shown *Home Fleet* opening fire on both the Citadel and Twelfth Fleet. Humphries' horrified orders for his ships to *return* fire were also part of the official record. There were undoubtedly witnesses who might dispute that official record, but none of them would have the sensor data to challenge his own version . . . and most of them were about to die, anyway. So when his cyberneticists were finally able to penetrate Y Ford Gron's *internal* programming, when Kiera's own precious "Round Table" acknowledged him as Morwenna's legitimate heir—

"Governor, I think we have a problem," his chief of staff said.

.V.

"Access to all communication channels is jammed, Your Majesty," I report.

"I already knew they'd taken over the civilian and Navy comm channels," the Empress said. "I'd hoped Y Ford Gron's secure channels might still be open."

"They are, Your Majesty. The Tactical Data Sharing Net is operable. Unfortunately—"

"Unfortunately, we don't have anyone to share anything with," she says grimly.

"That appears to be correct."

Even as we speak, my sensors reach out, presenting me with a comprehensive tactical plot.

It is an unpromising one.

"I detect twelve *Galahad*-class superdreadnoughts, nine *Nimue*-class carriers, thirty-three *Morgause*-class cruisers, and seven *Llyr*-class assault transports, Your Majesty."

The master plot illuminates, displaying the unit icons of the ships above us for the Empress's eyes, and her lips thin.

"And there's no way we can communicate directly with any of them," she says.

"I could attempt to communicate via communications laser," I suggest.

"I tried to contact them using the Palace comms during their attack on Home Fleet, before Command Central went down," she replies. "All attempts were refused. Abelin must have them in secure communications mode." She bares her teeth. "In fact, he almost has to've ordered them to shut down comms except for their datalink and direct communication with the flagship. The last thing he could afford is for me to speak directly to anyone who's not part of his plot and have them realize what's *really* going on."

"That is a logical conclusion," I agree. "However, it does not alter the fact that I am capable of hitting up to ten ships simultaneously with unencoded laser transmissions. If even one of them were accepted, it might seriously undermine his position."

"And the instant you hit them with lasers, you provide a homing beacon for their missiles."

"Affirmative. However, an *Amddiffynwr*-class AACU is not difficult for targeting systems to lock up even without a targeting beacon," I point out.

"No, but if they saturate your defenses with beam-riding missiles, what happens to your probability of intercept?"

"It decreases."

"By how much?"

"That is impossible to project with true accuracy, Your Majesty. However, it would be on the order of seven-zero-point-three-six percent."

"That's what I thought."

She sits silently, contemplating the numbers.

"Your externals are down," she says after eight-point-four seconds of thought. "But is the TDS in contact with the Palace's internal systems?"

"We have limited access," I reply. "Sufficient for information requests and data downloads only."

"But you do have contact with the servers?"

"Affirmative, Your Majesty."

"Good!" She smiles coldly. "Execute Avalon Omega."

"Your Majesty, I do not recognize that command."

"You don't recognize it *yet*," she replies. "Gamma-Seven-Three-Mike-Niner-One-One-Golf-Morwenna."

I do not recognize that command code, either, but the program buried deep in my core memory, so deep I have never even suspected its existence, does. A complete, standalone computer subnet I did not even know existed comes to life deep in my central core as the Empress's command links me directly to the Palace's central computers. My awareness expands explosively as those computers—*all* of those computers—acknowledge that subnet and I become not simply the senior unit of Y Ford Gron but also Command Central.

"Full access established, Your Majesty," I report. "I have control."

"Can we break into the planetary net?" she asks sharply.

"Negative, Your Majesty. The entire Palace has been locked out. I control only its internal systems."

"Then activate Ddwyfronneg," she replies. "And prep the energy batteries."

"Yes, Your Majesty."

Ddwyfronneg—Breastplate, in standard English—is the Imperial Palace's antimissile shield. It is an area coverage system sufficient to stop almost any bombardment on the Palace or the city of Caerleon. It is, however, a purely passive defense.

The energy batteries buried beneath the Palace's immaculately landscaped grounds are not. I would prefer to activate the weapons first, but they will require much longer to come fully online, and their energy signatures as they power up will be unmistakable to Twelfth Fleet's sensors. I must activate the defenses first, instead, to protect them from the traitors' preemptive fire.

"Ddwyfronneg active in ninety-five seconds, Your Majesty," I inform her. "Energy batteries coming online in ten minutes."

"Good!" Her gray eyes are fierce. "Abelin won't like *that*."

• • •

Abelin Probert swallowed a curse as he glared at the imagery of the mammoth war machine that had emerged from the crypts beneath the Imperial Palace.

"Are there any more of them?" he asked his chief-of-staff sharply.

"Not that we've detected, Sir." Brigadier Lippman sounded as worried as Probert felt. "But we didn't detect this one until it moved into the clear. There's too much overburden and too much interference from other power sources for us to see what might be going on under the Palace."

"If there was more than one, we'd already see it, Sir," Colonel Jarvis said. Probert looked at him, and the ops officer shrugged. "I don't care how powerful an *Amddiffynwr* may be, Governor. With this much firepower up here in orbit, they wouldn't send a single unit out to face us unless they had to."

"But how the hell did they get even *one* of them up and running?" Probert demanded, turning to glare at his staff cyber officer.

"I don't know, Sir." Colonel Shapiro shook her head. "It shouldn't have been possible. The externals are locked down tight. They'd have had to do it from inside, use the command deck internal interface, and no one could have gotten through the externals to do that!"

She glared at the towering AACU as it advanced into the mouth of the deep valley that cradled the Imperial Palace and the city of Caerleon. It stopped there, point defense lasers and railguns elevating, and Shapiro's eyes narrowed.

"There were rumors . . ." she murmured.

"What sort of rumors?" Probert's voice was sharp.

"Oh." Shapiro shook herself. "Sorry, Sir. There were rumors about the Imperial Family's implants. Rumors that there were backdoors—override protocols—nobody else knew about."

Something cold, with dozens of tiny feet, crawled down Abelin Probert's spine. He'd heard the same rumors, but Morwenna had always denied them. Surely—?

"Whatever it is, Sir," Jarvis said, "it can't have much reach. If it did, there'd be more of them down there."

"It's possible . . ." Shapiro thought for a moment, then shrugged. "It's possible, Sir, that the imperial implants carry an override protocol to get someone through the external systems and peripheral security. But Liam's right. If they could have activated more than one of them, they would have."

She looked at Probert levelly.

"It's only a guess at this point, Sir, but the most likely explanation is that someone is physically onboard that unit. Someone with a backdoor that ignores or evades the external systems . . . but only for that unit."

"Someone with—" Probert began, then stopped as those icy feet down his spine turned even colder. Surely, Morwenna couldn't have—

"Governor?" someone said, and Probert looked over his shoulder at the senior sensor tech of the watch. The noncom's expression was . . . odd, he thought.

"Yes, Master Sergeant?"

"Sir, we're reading its transponder code."

"And?" Probert said testily.

"And that's Y Ford Gron Alpha, Sir."

Probert's jaw tightened. FG Alpha. That was the AACU known as Arthur, Y Ford Gron's most senior unit. The only surviving unit that had served alongside Kiera Pendarves, herself. Its accomplishments and battle honors were the stuff of legends, and just as there had always been ridiculous rumors about backdoors and the Imperial family's implants, there had been rumors about *Arthur's* special abilities. About the capabilities built into him and no other unit of Y Ford Gron. And if that *was* Morwenna down there, if she had managed to activate FG *Alpha*, who knew what it could do? It was only one AACU, true, but if even half the tales—

"Could that thing link to the Palace?" he demanded.

"I . . . don't know, Sir." Shapiro shook her head. "I would've said it couldn't, at least not into the control interfaces. Those are covered by every security fence there is, so accessing them *should* be impossible, especially with Command Central down. But we don't know everything about Y Ford Gron's communications protocols. Or the reach of their command authority. And just the fact that it's here means the Empress must have had at least one access point we didn't know a thing about. So I'm afraid it's possible it does."

"Can it get into the weapons systems?!" Probert's tone was sharp. Shapiro's mouth tightened at the question, but she shook her head firmly.

"We couldn't reach the automatic anti-personnel defenses, because they're a standalone system, but we know for certain that Command Central was destroyed as planned, Governor," she said. "With Central gone, there's no interface for the offensive systems. It was physically destroyed when the bomb went off. So even assuming it can get into the Palace net, it can't—"

"Sir, Ddwyfronneg just activated!" Jarvis said suddenly, and Probert paled. He stabbed a button on his console, and Admiral Humphries appeared on his display.

"Governor, we're detecting—"

"I *know* what you're detecting!" Probert snapped. "Get us out of the Palace's envelope—*now!*"

• • •

"Damn!" the Empress says, and I share the sentiment, if not the emotional overlays.

I feared that the traitors would realize the energy batteries could not be far behind Ddwyfronneg, but I had calculated that it would take a minimum of ten-point-six minutes for them to begin effective evasive action. Unfortunately—

"Whatever else you want to say about him, the bastard's quick on his feet," the Empress says after a moment.

"He is, Your Majesty," I concur as the weather domes open and the energy weapons elevate. Their on-mount plasma conduits are charging, but not yet sufficiently so to fire. "The decisive factor, however, was that he must have maintained his drives at full readiness. I had anticipated that they would have reverted to standby once he entered planetary orbit, given his evident confidence that he was in control of the tactical situation."

"Apparently even mass-murdering traitors can exercise foresight," the Empress replies, gray eyes like steel as she watches the icons on my display streak toward the Palace's horizon. The energy batteries are direct fire weapons. Once they have put the curvature of the planet between themselves and the Palace—

"Activation," I report.

"Engage!" the Empress snaps.

• • •

Robert Humphries' ships had begun accelerating madly towards the Palace's horizon at full military power almost two full minutes before the batteries came online. With their compensators redlined, they could sustain thirty-five gravities. By the time Arthur could fire, they'd moved over two thousand kilometers, diving steeply towards a lower orbit. They would be in his field of fire for only another ten seconds.

But sometimes, ten seconds can be a very long time indeed.

Twenty bolts of fury streaked upward through portals in Ddwyfronneg, each with an energy density greater than that at the heart of the system's G2 primary.

• • •

Probert slammed a fist into his console as six of Twelfth Fleet's superdreadnoughts—including HMS *Parsifal*—vanished in balls of eye-tearing brilliance. Nor did they die alone. All nine of Humphries' carriers and five of his thirty-three cruisers exploded with equal ferocity.

Morwenna—or whoever the hell was aboard that thing—had known exactly what to go for, he thought savagely. His assault transports, stacked lowest in Twelfth Fleet's original formation, had been granted just enough time to dive clear of her field of fire, but every one of his transatmospheric fighters had gone with the carriers. Every *one* of them! Beside that, the loss of the superdreadnoughts and cruisers was almost inconsequential. Except, of course—

"Governor," Lippmann said, "we're receiving comm requests from virtually every ship."

The chief of staff's voice was tight, and Probert didn't

blame him. Of course they were receiving comm requests! That was the Palace itself firing on them!

He clenched his fists at his side for a moment, then drew a deep breath.

"Contact General Glascock. Tell him I want the Corps prepped for a full assault landing ASAP. Tell him he has twenty minutes and not one second longer."

Lippman looked at him, and Probert saw the protest behind the chief of staff's eyes. Fifth Corps had arrived prepped for a relief operation. Its shuttles were loaded with its lighter combat mechs and personnel carriers, designed to land against light or—even better— nonexistent resistance and spread its zone of control as broadly as possible as quickly as possible. But that sort of landing would be suicidal against an Amddiffynwr. Which meant every single one of those shuttles had to be unloaded and then *re*loaded in heavy assault configuration.

And there was no way in hell they could do that in only twenty minutes.

But Lippman knew Probert knew that even better than he did. The protests died unspoken, and he nodded.

"I'll tell him, Governor."

"Good," Probert grated, and looked at his comm officer.

"Put me on all units, Major Binnion," he told her in a flat voice.

"Yes, Governor!"

Binnion tapped keys at her console, then nodded to him as the ready light lit beside his visual pickup once more.

"This is the Governor," he said then, without preamble. "I know what just happened shocked you all. Well, it shocked *me*, too. We already knew the traitors must have penetrated both the Citadel and Home Fleet. I hadn't anticipated that they could have defeated Command Central's safeguards, as well, and all too many of our comrades have died as a result of my overconfidence."

He allowed his tone to drop, his facial muscles to tighten, and shook his head.

"We have, however, acquired some sensor data which may explain it," he continued, after a moment, his voice grim. "Just before the Palace's energy batteries opened fire, a single Amddiffynwr emerged from beneath it. The AACU made no effort to contact us, in fact, it rejected all of *our* efforts to contact *it*. The only conclusion I can reach is that somehow the traitors must have breached the security of at least one unit of Y Ford Gron, as well, and perverted it to their cause."

He paused again, letting that sink in, imagining its impact. The absolute loyalty and reliability of Y Ford Gron was one of the Empire's unshakable constants. An AACU simply could not be suborned. And yet—

"How that could have been done is more than I or any of my staff and cybernetics officers can begin to explain at this time," he said then. "What we do know is that it appears they were able to reach only a *single* Amddiffynwr, since no additional AACUs have joined it. Unfortunately, it's evident from what just happened that the traitors have also secured Command Central, or at least enough of it to control the Palace's weapons and defenses, and the Amddiffynwr appears to have taken up a position from which it can interdict any attempt to reach the Palace.

"Twelfth Fleet has too little firepower, especially after the losses we've just suffered, to break through Ddwyfronneg from orbit, even if we could survive against the energy batteries long enough to do so. Worse, the weight of fire required would also kill everyone in the Palace, which might include the Empress. But even that isn't the worst challenge we face, because the collateral damage would destroy virtually the entire capitol city, with a loss of life in the millions, and we are Ymerodraeth Cymru Newydd's *protectors*. We are not mass murderers, and I refuse to become that. Which means I must ask our ground combat element for a painful sacrifice.

"The only way to reach the Palace, retake Command Central, deactivate Ddwyfronneg and the energy batteries, and rescue the Empress—if she's still alive and somewhere inside it—is to gain access on the ground. With the loss of our carriers, it will be impossible to provide air cover, but it is essential that we retake—or, much as I know it will pain all of us, *destroy*—the Palace. I do not want to do that. As God is my witness, I don't! I want to recover it intact so that we can search every nook and cranny for Her Majesty and her children. They aren't 'just' the Imperial Family, so far as I'm concerned. They're *my* family. But because that's true, I know Empress Morwenna well. Her first command to us would be to defeat this foul treason, and her second would be to do so without inflicting massive civilian casualties . . . even if that requires the outright destruction of Palace and everyone in it.

"That's become our grim duty, and no one knows better

than I how costly it may prove. But Fifth Corps has never failed the Empire or me, and I know you won't fail us now. My staff and I are formulating an attack plan, and I will personally command the attack. God send the right!"

He looked fiercely into the pickup for a half-dozen breaths, then cut the circuit and looked back at the master tactical display. They no longer had a direct line of sight to the Palace, but they had access to scores of ground-based systems that did, and his lips twisted in a silent snarl as the huge war machine climbed to a hill crest and hatches opened along its flank. Its perch positioned it to cover every approach to the valley, and remote engineering units drove down ramps from those hatches. They began digging the AACU in, and there was nothing he could do to stop them.

.VI.

Lieutenant General Cadwy Glascock's teeth ached from the pressure of his jaw muscles as he watched the chaos of the assault transport *Arianrhod* Shuttle Deck Bravo. The inboard bulkheads were barricaded behind a wash of light armored units, APCs, and unarmored GEVs, all crammed into any available space and packed together like old style sardines. Both of *Arianrhod*'s other decks were just as crazed a mass of confusion as Bravo, but his *Cadlywydd*-class command tank, a modified Rhyfelwr which sacrificed half its magazine space and two-thirds of its drone capacity to fit in a complete command deck and an associated combat information center, had been stowed in Bravo's huge cargo hold, so this was where he had to be. And he'd been here, waiting, for far too long. *Arianrhod*'s deck crews were as good as any he'd seen in almost thirty years of Imperial service, but even they were pushed to the limit managing *this* evolution.

At least they were almost finished with the reloading. He didn't want to think about the nightmare task *Arianrhod* would face sorting out the confusion 521st Armored Brigade was about to leave in its wake, but the last of his units were set to roll onto the landing shuttles. Not in anything remotely like the twenty minutes Governor Probert had allocated, but in far less time than any sane ops plan would have demanded.

And that was what really worried him. There was too much going on, too many loose ends flapping in the wind of the careening juggernaut this operation had turned into. This wasn't supposed to happen. Probert had planned everything so carefully, assured him and the others that all the variables were accounted for. And now *this*.

The confusion among his personnel was obvious . . . and so was their fear, however hard they tried to hide it. Unlike Glascock, they had no idea why they were really here, and the shocks had come at them hard and fast. Clearly, some of them were less than confident that their *superiors* knew what was happening—or were being truthful about it, at any rate—either. But they *did* know what an Amddiffynwr could do, and facing something like that when their confidence was already shaken . . .

"What's the holdup *now*, General?" a voice asked from his personal comm. He looked down at it, and Abelin Probert glared up at him from it.

"We've almost completed boarding, Governor," he said. "I know it's taken a lot longer than any of us like, but there was . . . ah . . . a bit of *confusion* because of the sudden re-tasking." To his relief, Probert actually snorted in bitter amusement at his chosen noun. "The deck crews are topnotch, though, Sir," he continued, "and I estimate no more than another five to ten minutes to get the last Rhyfelwr aboard."

"Good!" Probert smiled fiercely from the small display, and Glascock cleared his throat.

"Governor, I understand the urgency, but there's quite a bit of . . . uncertainty among my people. The troops are confused. Worried. I don't know if they're going to—"

"The *troops* are going to do whatever we tell them to, General," Probert said flatly, and there was no amusement, bitter or not, in his expression now. "And *you* are going to take the Palace and shut down those goddamned defenses!"

"I'm only concerned that—"

"Your only *concern* had damned well better be that Amddiffynwr. Now get your units aboard those frigging shuttles so we can launch, damn it!"

• • •

I deploy a second flight of reconnaissance drones.

The assault shuttles have landed beyond the Palace's field of fire, which also places them beyond my own, and my drones watch the combat units disembark. The odds are not favorable. A single Amddiffynwr has more firepower than an entire manned armored brigade, but we do not face *an* armored brigade. We face five of them.

"I wish we had a few of the others, Arthur," the Empress says as those units begin sweeping towards us.

"As do I, Your Majesty."

My drones detect the emissions signatures of Rhyfelwr-class heavy tanks. Each of them masses approximately six thousand tonnes, with a main armament of two 20-centimeter railguns, and there are twenty in each of the brigades deploying against us.

The tactical balance would be unfavorable under any circumstances, but it would be far better if we could maneuver. Unfortunately, that is not possible. Ddwyfronneg forms a dome over the mountain river valley in which the city of Caerleon and the Imperial Palace lie. The entrance to that valley is thirty kilometers wide. That is the frontage we must defend. And in order to cover the dead ground in the approaches, we must hold the high ground, which dictates a static defense from an exposed position.

Ddwyfronneg angles downward to barely forty meters above my primary sensor mast in our current position. That is good, since it will seriously impair indirect fire attacks and means they must come at us frontally. It is bad in that it leaves insufficient clearance for my own battle screen, so there is no passive defense to intercept that frontal fire as it arrives. My remotes have pushed a berm high enough to create a hull-down position, protecting my track systems and the lower third of my hull. In effect, I have been transformed into an immobile fortress, and other remotes have been occupied demolishing the bridges which cross the river and mining their approaches. I have deployed my Saeth attack drones, as well, but the odds against us and the absence of my battle screen require me to retain them to bolster my missile defense rather than employing them in the proper attack mode. It is fortunate that the carriers' destruction has deprived the enemy of his manned air support and the thousands of drones each Nimue carried. Less fortunately, each Rhyfelwr can deploy two Saeths of its own.

"Still no luck breaking Probert's communications lockout?" the Empress asks.

The units of Fifth Corps, like those of Twelfth Fleet, are employing maximum electronic security protocols. Anything which does not carry the correct authorization codes is automatically locked out of their communication and data sharing systems. Against an opponent such as myself, with the ability to spoof communications, generate fraudulent orders, and invade computer systems, that is only simply prudence.

"Negative, Your Majesty. Their communication security is . . . robust and all efforts to break its encryption in real time have failed. I am able to decrypt much of their traffic which I have recorded, but they are employing an encryption-hopping system I am unable to anticipate without access to both the master clock and encryption software."

She nods without speaking, but her face tightens, and I understand exactly. We know, from the traffic I have been able to decrypt after the fact, that very few, if any, of the personnel about to attack us know they are acting in support of a coup. Indeed, they believe they are moving to *rescue* the Empress and her family, if any of them are still alive, and that I have been corrupted by the traitors they must suppress.

And none of them have received a single one of the messages the Empress has sent—is sending still—to tell them the truth of what has happened. They cannot hear her . . . and so they will attack her, try to kill her, without even realizing what they have been duped into doing.

And I will have no choice but to kill them in her defense.

• • •

One corner of the visual display in Abelin Probert's Cadlywydd command vehicle showed the comm message none of his other units could see.

"I call upon all of you to listen to me!" Morwenna Pendarves said passionately from that small window, audible only over his personal ear bug. "You've been lied to! Home Fleet was never the aggressor, and Abelin Probert is *not* here to prevent a coup! He's here to *execute* a coup, and he's using you to do it! I beg you, break off. Refuse his orders. Y Ford Gron exists to protect Ymerodraeth Cymru Newydd's subjects, not kill them! But if you continue this attack, I will have no alternative but to return fire."

He watched her as the Cadlywydd rolled forward with the reserve brigades. He listened to that plea that only he could see, only he could hear, and he smiled.

• • •

"It's all that bastard Abelin," the Empress says bitterly. "Without him and his lies—and his ability to think them up quick, whenever he needs a new one—the combination of the Palace's defenses and your presence would almost certainly make *someone* wonder what the hell is going on. For that matter, whoever's in this with him might just throw in the towel! It's a pity we missed him when you took down *Parsifal*."

"I regret that, as well, Your Majesty," I reply, with considerable understatement. "It seemed the logical fire distribution at the time, given the situation as we knew it."

"Oh, agreed!" she replies. "*Parsifal* was doing all the talking, which made that the logical place for him to be. But he must have been relaying through her from another ship, and I should have considered that possibility. He may be a traitorous, murdering bastard, but he's always commanded from the front, and he's Army, not Navy. For that matter, he *needs* to get down here as early as possible to control any unforeseen situations as they arise. Of course he'd be with his troops when they land."

I consider that in light of what I have learned from his dossier and conclude that she is correct. On the other hand, it also reminds me once more of where *she* is.

"Your Majesty, I would feel much better if you withdrew to the Palace," I say. It is not the first time I have said that, and she shakes her head once more.

"Not going to happen." She tightens her shock frame, surrounded by my visual displays. "We need me here to be sure you stay online, Arthur. Even if we didn't, I'm not running from these people. Not now, not ever. And every minute we tie them up here is another minute for Colonel Willis to get my children to safety. Besides," she shows her teeth, "I've read Kiera's journals. I know *exactly* what you and she meant to each other . . . and to her family. *My* family. How long you've protected us. I'm not running and I'm not abandoning *you*, either."

I begin to reply, but—

"Incoming fire," I say instead.

• • •

There wasn't much room for finesse.

The tactical situation was brutally simple: the AACU controlled the only possible approach, and the only way to come at it was from the front.

Every member of Fifth Corps knew it would be ugly. Even uglier than it had been. The shocks had come at them fast and hard. The treason of Home Fleet, the destruction of the Citadel, and the deaths of the imperial family had shaken them to the core, and now they were being asked to storm the gates of hell itself. God only knew how many of them were about to die, but they knew the cost in blood and bodies would be monstrous.

Yet they were the Imperial Army of the Ymerodraeth Cymru Newydd, and that looming Amddiffynwr had been subverted by traitors. By the same traitors who'd killed their beloved Empress and her entire family. Who'd already massacred so many loyal men and women. And the mouth of that valley of death was the only way to reach those traitors.

They knew that, too. And so the vehicles of their two lead brigades flowed forward, covered by the Rhyfelwrs' Saeth drones. The heavy tanks took the lead, grinding forward on their track systems, flanked by the lighter personnel transports, as they climbed the rearward slope of the ridgeline which faced the AACU at a range of eight kilometers. They had to move high enough to expose most of their front hulls for their turret-mounted armament to clear the ridge. None of them liked giving an Amddiffynwr that much target, but they had no choice.

They settled into position, and the AACU appeared on their direct vision displays for the first time. Its war hull was so broad it looked almost squat, even though the flat plain of its missile deck stood thirty meters above the ground, and stomachs tightened as the four dynamically mounted turrets of its main armament moved to bring their railguns to bear upon them

But it didn't fire. Not immediately, at least.

Ten seconds passed in a hovering agony of tension, and then—

"Engage!" Cadwy Glascock snapped.

Shockwaves gouged deep divots from the downslope in front of the 521st Armored Brigade as 20-centimeter ultra-dense projectiles screamed out of their twin railguns at 9,000 meters per second. The subcaliber penetrators shed the "shoes" which had carried them up the railguns' bores and those same shockwaves left serpent trails of dust as they streaked toward their target. Each of those 2,150-kilogram darts packed the kinetic energy of almost 21 tonnes of old-fashioned chemical explosive, and each gun could spit out one of them every fifteen seconds.

Lieutenant General Glascock's Rhyfelwrs hurled 160 penetrators per minute at Arthur in a hurricane of hate.

• • •

My electronic warfare systems have done their best, but Fifth Corps' fire control is degraded by no more than two-three-point-seven percent. I cannot evade the Rhyfelwrs' fire; I cannot interdict it; and I have no battle screen to divert it. I can only endure it.

The cyclone of kinetic penetrators smashes into me. I am fortunate the manned vehicles cannot synchronize their fire as finely as Y Ford Gron's Amddiffynwrs might have. It strikes as a *stream*, not a single massive hammer blow, and it can come at me only from the front—only against my frontal armor.

My glacis is a single plate of imperial battle steel three meters thick. Its matrix contains both ablative and anti-kinetic layers of semi-collapsed matter, woven together at nearly the molecular level by the fabricating nanites. It is the most resistant armor the human race has yet produced, but the Rhyfelwrs' fire smashes into it like a hyper-velocity tsunami. The impact energy drives me back on my suspension's shock absorbers while near misses hurl up clouds of dust, dirt, and vaporized soil. My command deck is mounted on internal shock absorbers to protect human personnel. Even so, the Empress's shock frame hammers her brutally as that sledgehammer of fury slams into me.

And then the missiles arrive.

• • •

Probert stared into his display as the Amddiffynwr disappeared under a torrent of incandescent impacts. At their velocity, the Rhyfelwrs' penetrators were almost more energy states than kinetic projectiles, and they smashed home as vaporizing balls of fire.

Despite his long Army career, Probert had never fought alongside Y Ford Gron. Nor, for obvious reasons, had he ever fought *against* its units . . . until now. He knew their reputation, had reviewed all of the unclassified—and as many as possible of the classified—details about them, yet he was all too aware of how little he actually knew. He hated planning any operation when he had so little hard data on the opposition force's true capabilities. But he *did* know, from decades of personal experience, what his Rhyfelwrs could do. And so, as he watched the heavy tanks' fire smash into Arthur, he knew *nothing* could survive that savage punishment.

Each of Fifth Corps' brigades incorporated an indirect fire support battalion of eighteen Saethwr missile tanks. Far lighter than the Rhyfelwrs, they were never intended to face direct fire weapons themselves. Their armor was intended to protect only against blast, shell splinters, and shrapnel, not the sort of penetrators or energy weapons their heavier brethren mounted.

Ddwyfronneg took high-angle indirect fire off the table, but their sophisticated missiles were just as capable of terrain-following attacks, and unlike the Rhyfelwrs, all of Fifth Corps' Saethwrs could engage at once. There were ninety of them, each with twenty-four vertical launch missile cells, and over two thousand missiles ripple-salvoed at the single Amddiffynwr.

None of those missiles were nuclear tipped. In his heart of hearts, Probert would have preferred to use nukes, but that would have been a step too far for men and women who thought they were there to retake the Palace from traitors and liberate Caerleon. And so they were armed with shaped charge and self-forging fragment warheads, designed to attack the much thinner armor protecting the Amddiffynwr's upper decking. Now they streaked into the attack, spreading as they came, and then converging to deliver a simultaneous, coordinated 360° attack.

The Amddiffynwr's point defense stabbed out of the

dust and smoke and fury, and a fresh, rolling halo of explosions surrounded it. Dozens—scores—of those missiles disappeared short of their target. The dozen Saeth drones deployed around it killed even more of them, but over thirty reached their target and Probert bared his teeth in triumph as they detonated in a rolling wash of flame.

And not a single shot had come back at Fifth Corps.

• • •

"Damage to secondary weapon systems approaching twelve percent," I report. It is not really necessary. The same information is available to the Empress from the visual displays around her. But, in another way, it *is* necessary. "Bravo Turret disabled. Point Defense reduced to seven-one-point-niner-two percent of base capability. Frontal armor degraded by zero-four-point-two percent. Sensor capability reduced to eight-seven-point-five percent."

I pause, and then I say what must be said.

"Your Majesty, we must return fire."

• • •

Morwenna Pendarves closed her eyes as the command deck bucked and shuddered about her and the huge war machine's voice came through the tumult. It was almost gentle, that voice, yet the iron at its core filled her, told her what she had known from the beginning must happen, and she knew he was right. Yet she fought against that knowledge, tried desperately to reject it. In so many ways, it would have been easier to die herself than to kill so many good men and women who sought only to do their duty to the Empire—and the Empress—they had sworn to serve. But she *was* Empress. Unlike them, she knew what was truly at stake . . . and what duty—that cold, thankless master—required of *her*.

Her fists clenched at her sides as the inevitable rolled over her like the sea, filled her with the bitterness of its poison, and then she inhaled deeply.

"Engage!" she said harshly.

• • •

A Rhyfelwr heavy tank's frontal armor was 90 centimeters thick, less than a third of an Amddiffynwr's. Its 20-centimeter penetrators massed 2.1 tonnes and generated 87,000 megajoules of kinetic energy.

An Amddiffynwr's 43-centimeter penetrators massed over 13 tonnes and delivered well over half a *million* megajoules—the equivalent of 128 tonnes of old-fashioned chemical explosives in an impact area less than a half meter across.

• • •

Probert pushed back in his command chair as hyper-velocity awls sliced effortlessly through the thickest armor of the 521st Brigade's Rhyfelwrs and pithed three of them with a lance of flame. The 6,000-tonne vehicles erupted like crazed volcanoes as those penetrators ripped straight down the long axes of their hulls, splintering and vaporizing everything in their paths. And then they erupted through the tanks' *rear* armor like some sort of demon comets, leaving only smoke, flames, and devastation in their wake.

One of those slaughtered tanks was—*had been*—General Glascock's command tank, and Probert knew that was no coincidence. He sat momentarily frozen, watching the smoke clouds erupt into the heavens, trailing shattered fragments of the vehicles which had spawned them.

Twenty seconds later, three more of the 521st's tanks disintegrated, and he shook himself savagely out of his paralysis.

"Back! Get them back!" he snapped.

The order went out, but Glascock's XO had already given the same command. His brigade lurched backward, diving behind the crest of their ridge.

Of the twenty Rhyfelwrs who had climbed that ridge, eleven lived to withdraw.

.VII.

Abelin Probert stood in the Cadlywydd's CIC, one level below its command deck, and gazed at the imagery in the combat information center's far more capable displays.

The protective berm around the Amddiffynwr had been gouged and torn, but the construction remotes which had sheltered inside its holds during the brief, savage engagement were busily repairing them as he watched. CIC had highlighted indications of damage to the stupendous war machine's sensor masts. They were far smaller targets than an AACU's hull, and heavily armored, but two of them had been smashed by what must have been direct hits. Every attempt to position a drone for a top-down look had been frustrated by the Amddiffynwr's point defense systems, so it was impossible to tell how badly its top armor had—or had not—been damaged by the missile storm. It seemed impossible to Probert that it couldn't have taken significant damage . . . but he reminded himself that he would never have believed its frontal armor could survive such a hurricane of penetrators and show so little sign of it.

"As you can see, Governor," Brigadier Lippmann said, as if he'd been reading his superior's mind, "damage to its glacis is . . . minimal."

Probert snorted. Perhaps it was "minimal" for an Amddiffynwr, but it would have been one hell of a lot more than that for any of *his* tanks.

The AACU's frontal armor was gouged and scored. Impact craters pocked its surface, but none of those craters—or the gouges and scores, for that matter—were more than a few centimeters deep. And, as he watched, repair remotes scuttled across the damaged surface, filling its wounds with armorite. The liquid alloy flowed into them, hardening almost instantly, and he scowled. Those patches would be less damage resistant than battle steel's partially collapsed alloy levels . . . but one hell of a lot *more* resistant than anything short of that.

"We've destroyed one of its main armament turrets," Lippmann continued, using a cursor in the display to indicate the snapped-off stub of a massive railgun, hanging from a shattered turret like a broken tooth. "And sensor data indicates it's lost between fifty and sixty percent of its primary sensor capability. We can't be positive, but it would appear it's also lost at least some of its point defense, and we took out most of its Saeths."

"And, in the process, we fired off every missile the Saethwrs had," Probert growled. "Which makes the state of its point defense a bit irrelevant at the moment, doesn't it?"

"Well, yes, sir." Lippmann nodded. "We do have a lot more missiles aboard the transports, though."

"Landing them and rearming the Saethwrs would take time." Probert shook his head, his eyes grim. "And that *thing*—" he jabbed his chin at the AACU in the display "—is still trying to break into our comm net."

"We've been able to lock it out without too much difficulty, Governor," Major Binnion said.

"We been able to lock it out *so far*," Probert replied and turned to face his staff squarely.

"We knew we had incomplete data on Y Ford Gron, but this—" he waved at the display without turning his head "—is a pretty clear indication that it was even less complete than we thought. That thing must've taken at least *three hundred* direct hits, and its armor's barely scuffed. Given that, I'm not prepared to rely on any of our pre-attack estimates about its electronic warfare capabilities, either. And if it ever does crack our encryption, if the troops see Morwenna's message . . ."

Mouths tightened as his staff gazed back at him.

"We're under even more pressure than we thought to end this thing quickly," he said flatly. "And we're not going to do it from the front. We've got to get around onto its flanks. The one thing we can be positive of is that its side armor is thinner than its frontal armor. If we're going to take it out, that's where we have to go."

He turned back to the display and punched commands, and a topographic hologram of the river valley replaced the visual feed.

"We need to get the Rhyfelwrs here, here, or *here*," he said, jabbing the display with a cursor. "Any one of those crests will give them direct lines of fire to its flanks."

"I agree, Sir," Colonel Jarvis said after a moment. "But the Amddiffynwr's positioned itself to cover the approaches to those ridges." He used his own cursor to trace the relatively flat lower elevations along the course of the river. "We'll take heavy losses if we try to move across those fields of fire."

"Heavier than we'll take feeding them straight into its guns?" Probert growled.

"No, Sir," Jarvis conceded. "But—"

"You're right about the losses, Liam," Lippmann interrupted, "but the Governor's right about our need to end this quickly. And for about—what, a third of the approach?—it'll be reduced to indirect fire. And that's assuming its VLS can launch at all." He grimaced. "Our Saethwrs couldn't—not with Ddwyfronneg hanging that close overhead—but like the Governor, I'm not prepared to say what an Amddiffynwr can do. Not anymore."

"I hate to say this," Probert's voice was heavy, "but even if it can, we've got the numbers. We'll just have to absorb the losses."

Jarvis looked back and forth between Probert and Lippmann. The ops officer's expression was manifestly unhappy, but then, slowly, he nodded.

.VIII.

"Well, he's made up his mind," the Empress says.

"It would appear," I acknowledge.

My repair remotes have made good all of the damage they can out of onboard resources in the time available. Like the damage to my frontal armor, my dorsal armor has been patched with armorite. Thinner than my glacis, it took significantly heavier damage from the missiles which penetrated my defenses. Indeed, it has been breached completely in three places, and two of my vertical launch system tubes have been destroyed. Given Ddwyfronneg's presence so close overhead, that loss is insignificant, since there is insufficient clearance for missile launches.

My primary sensor suite has also suffered, however. Only Number Two sensor mast remains, and the primary suite has been reduced to only thirty-six-point-eight percent of base capability. Secondary systems have compensated for that damage, but there is very little to back up the secondaries, should *they* be damaged.

Number Five and Number Eleven secondary armament mag tracks are damaged beyond immediate repair. Fortunately, the damage occurred where the tracks cross my missile deck, and the turrets they serve were deployed in my port broadside when it was inflicted. The weapons themselves are unharmed, and I have shunted them to Track Four and Track Twelve, respectively, joining the turrets already on those tracks. It is an imperfect solution, as the power demand will exceed design limits by a factor of thirty percent, but at least they are still available.

Only three Saeths survive. However, I calculate that Fifth Corps must have emptied its missile magazines in its initial attack. No doubt additional missile supply is available from its transports, but the Empress estimates—and I agree—that Probert will dare not delay long enough for that. Not while my efforts to penetrate Fifth Corps' communications continue.

I am as battle ready as possible, and I watch the take from my recon drones as Fifth Corps begins to deploy forward once again. The badly depleted 521st Armored has been withdrawn from its lead position. It is now the rearmost formation, in a position which not only covers the rear of the entire corps but places it to follow the line of the maglev which serves the Palace and Caerleon. The bridge across the Tywi has been demolished, but its approaches can be covered only by my main battery, whose firepower has been reduced by twenty-five percent, and the river is shallow enough to be readily forded by Rhyfelwrs.

"It's going to cost him," the Empress observes grimly.

"It is," I agreed. "Unfortunately, it may well succeed."

"And he doesn't really care how much it costs, does he?" Her voice is bitter "Not as long as it succeeds. None of the lives he's throwing away matter to him. They don't even know what's really happening!"

This time, I do not reply. There is no point, because she is correct. My efforts to penetrate Fifth Corps' communications continue even now, but unsuccessfully.

We watch two of Governor Probert's five armored brigades advance towards the shattered wreckage the 521st left along the crest line to the west. Both have detached their APCs and support vehicles, and the second brigade follows behind the first. It is obvious what they intend. Only one brigade can squeeze its Rhyfelwrs into firing positions, and Probert has seen what happened to the 521st. The first of these brigades will bulldoze the 521st's wreckage out of their way and engage us from the front, pounding us while their fellows dash at full speed along the approach routes on the valley floor. They know they will take murderous losses, and the second brigade is there to fill the gaps as the first formation's Rhyfelwrs are destroyed.

The remaining brigades have divided into three separate formations, each moving towards a position from which they can engage us from the flank, and my side armor is barely a third of that which protects my glacis. It is still thicker than a Rhyfelwr's frontal armor, but thin enough to be penetrated by its fire at short range.

If I were human, I would weep at how many loyal men and women are about to sacrifice themselves in the service of the Ymerodraeth Cymru Newydd's greatest traitor. Yet, far worse than that, I compute a seven-eight-point-seven percent chance that, despite Fifth Corps' losses, Probert's plan will succeed and end in my own destruction . . . and the Empress's death.

I long to implore her once more to withdraw. But I know what her response would be, and so I remain silent, instead, as the enemy moves towards us once again.

.IX.

"We're ready, Governor," Brigadier Lippmann said, and Probert nodded sharply.

He glanced again at the corner of his display, at the

ghost of a soon-to-be-dead empress crying out uselessly to the men and women who would never see, never hear her message, and his lips thinned.

"Go," he said simply.

•••

Fifth Corps lunged forward.

The Rhyfelwr was capable of eighty kilometers per hour on an improved surface, and the crews of these Rhyfelwrs knew precisely how much fire-swept ground they had to cover. Three brigades—fifty-one heavy tanks, given the 521st's losses—charged along their assigned approach routes, and a fourth advanced unflinchingly to what it knew would be its doom.

•••

The lead brigade—its transponders identify it as the 307th Armored, a proud formation with a battle record second to none—ascends the slope towards us. The first eight tanks top the ridgeline and, almost simultaneously my massive hull bucks to the recoil of my surviving main armament. Penetrators rip completely through three of the Rhyfelwrs; the five survivors fire back, and their lighter penetrators slam viciously into my glacis.

My railguns cycle. Twenty seconds later, three more Rhyfelwrs die. And then three more. Yet their consorts continue to advance to join them, and their sacrificial fire rips back, pounding my frontal armor, attempting to target my turrets. And as they engage me, the rest of Fifth Corps' heavy armor sweeps forward along the valley floor.

The lighter turrets of my secondary armament speed along their hull-mounted mag tracks to deploy along my starboard side. They are 15-centimeter weapons, far lighter than my main guns—lighter even than the Rhyfelwrs'. They are shorter ranged, as well, with a significantly lower probability of a kill, but there are also thirty of them, and my Saeth drones race towards the enemy in nap-of-the-earth flight profiles.

The drones pop up, strafing the tanks' upper decks, but the speeding Rhyfelwrs are as capable of firing on the move as I am, and they are well provided with point defense. I have too few drones to saturate that defense, and all of them are destroyed in return for a single disabled Rhyfelwr.

The Empress tightens her harness as penetrators slamming into my bow send shockwaves through me, and my surviving main armament is in continuous fire mode. The 307th's Rhyfelwrs melt under their pounding, but reinforcements, tanks of the 93rd Brigade, are already advancing into the holocaust. Their pressure is relentless, yet I divert Delta Turret's fire to the middle of the three formations advancing along the valley floor. The diversion is a significant risk, reducing my defensive firepower by a third. But I cannot allow the other brigades to advance unopposed.

The last thing I desire is for them to slow their headlong charge, advance at a deliberate pace.

• • •

Probert's face was stone. Clearly, the AACU *didn't* have clearance enough to launch missiles, but that was cold comfort as he watched the carnage.

His own Cadlywydd accompanied the tanks of the 117th Armored, the middle of the three formations charging up the floor of the valley, and he winced as its lead Rhyfelwr burst like a fiery balloon. The following tanks swerved, avoiding the wreckage as they continued their headlong charge.

Twenty seconds later, another Rhyfelwr died, but they were a fifth of the way to their objective.

• • •

Only two of the 307th's Rhyfelwrs remain, but the 93rd is now fully engaged, and damage alerts wail as a penetrator slams into the base of Alpha Turret. It pierces the barbette's armor like an incandescent needle, and the entire gun mount explodes.

I have no choice but to return Delta to the brutal, short range engagement.

• • •

"Yes!" Probert snarled as the AACU's main armament fire faltered. The 117th had lost two more of its own tanks—a total of five, counting the one the strafing drones had crippled—but the fifteen survivors were almost to the river. Once across it, terrain would mask them from the Amddiffynwr's fire until they reached their designated firing position.

At which point all fifteen of them would come over the crest line, firing directly into their massive opponent's thinnest armor at a range of barely two kilometers.

• • •

A direct hit from the last of the 307th's tanks rips through my last remaining sensor mast, and the hull schematic on my Damage Control Central display is a creeping tide of crimson. My glacis remains unpenetrated, but even from directly ahead, my opponents' penetrators have swept down my flank and destroyed or disabled six of my secondary turrets. The loss of Alpha Turret has reduced my forward firepower to only fifty percent, and the torrent of penetrators are beginning to gnaw their way through even my frontal armor.

And then another penetrator slams through Delta Turret's armor.

• • •

Probert pounded a fist on his knee as the Amddiffynwr lost yet another main turret. The single surviving heavy gun continued to traverse with the viper speed and deadly precision of Y Ford Gron, and each time it fired, another Rhyfelwr and another nineteen men and women died. But there was only one of it now. The 93rd Brigade's survivors crowded forward, pounding furiously, and its cratering bow armor glowed incandescent with the kinetic energy bleeding into it.

• • •

The troopers of the 93rd Armored were veterans. They'd been shaken to their marrow by this day's events, but they were also grimly determined. Their own tanks fired more slowly, more deliberately, picking their targets as the AACU's main battery fire dwindled, and raking shots destroyed two more of its secondary turrets.

But the lead brigade charging along the valley floor had entered the range of its *remaining* secondary guns.

• • •

The 15-centimeter railguns of my secondary armament lack the power of my main guns—each of their 600-kilogram penetrators generates "only" 25,000 megajoules of kinetic energy—and engagement time will be short.

The brigade will cross completely through their fire zone in just ninety seconds . . . but my secondaries fire six times per minute, not three.

I have been reduced to only twenty-two secondaries, and they are not sufficiently powerful to guarantee one-shot kills. My fire plan assigns three to each of six targets, and the final four to a single Rhyfelwr.

• • •

Seven of the 109th Armored Brigade's twenty tanks became instant funeral pyres, but the brigade was in its own range of the AACU, and answering fire ripped back at it. Hits flashed and glared along the Amddiffynwr's side, but fresh explosions glared deep in the valley as the leviathan raked the 109th with brimstone talons. Ten seconds after it opened fire, seven more Rhyfelwrs exploded into wreckage.

The six survivors fired even more desperately, but the Amddiffynwr was merciless. Its fire smashed over them in yet another wave of terrible explosions.

And then there was no more 109th Brigade.

• • •

Abelin Probert's face was white. He'd anticipated heavy losses, and—as Morwenna had bitterly remarked—he hadn't really cared what the attack cost, as long as it succeeded. But the utter destruction of the 109th in barely thirty seconds . . .

That was more horrendous than his worst projections.

The only good news was that before its destruction, the brigade had hit the Amddiffynwr hard. Smoke plumed from half a dozen breaches in its flank armor, and three more secondary turrets had been destroyed. It might not be a great deal to show for the obliteration of twenty of his own tanks—and almost four hundred of his personnel—but the gigantic fighting machine's combat power was eroding steadily.

All he had to do was outlast it.

• • •

My combat power is seriously impaired.

Of my main armament, only Charlie Turret remains operable, and the remaining Rhyfelwrs of the 93rd continue to pour fire into me. Not even my frontal armor can withstand that pounding indefinitely, and I calculate that it will experience local penetrations within no more than three minutes.

• • •

The surviving tanks of the 521st Armored Brigade reached the wreckage of the maglev bridge across the Tywi River.

Technically, they were exposed to the Amddiffynwr's fire when they did, but only from its main armament, and its single remaining heavy railgun was . . . preoccupied, and the 521st charged into the river on either side of the demolished bridge.

The Mark III antitank mines emplaced in the river detonated like the end of the world. Of the eleven Rhyfelwrs that entered the river, two survived the crossing.

• • •

Probert swore viciously as yet another of his brigades was virtually annihilated, but at least the 521st had reached the river well before the 177th. And he stabbed a comm key.

The 117th's CO appeared on his display.

"Stop, General!" he snapped, and the brigade slid to a halt, well short of the river but beyond the reach of the Amddiffynwr's dwindling firepower.

"The river is mined," Probert said then. "That's what happened to the Five-Two-One. But that's okay. We can take our time, I think." He bared his teeth. "It's cost us like hell, but I think we've got this thing now. Drop a drone or two into the river and take a look."

"Yes, Governor."

"And while he's doing that," Probert turned to Lippmann with another of those hungry smiles, "pull what's left of the Ninety-Third off that hill and tell them to join us here. I don't think that son-of-a-bitch can do a goddammed thing to stop them."

• • •

The remaining twelve Rhyfelwrs of the 93rd Brigade cease fire and back off of the ridgeline upon which so many of their comrades have died.

There is little I can do to stop them, and the truth is that it is fortunate they have been ordered to withdraw. Their unflinching fire has finally breached my frontal armor, and I have been forced to divert no less than twenty percent of my overstrained damage control remotes to fight the fires raging across three decks in the forward fifty meters of my hull. In addition to that, however, the ammunition feed to Charlie Turret, my sole remaining main battery weapon, has been shattered. Only fourteen rounds remain in the on-mount ready magazine. Once they are expended, I will be reduced to my point defense mounts and nineteen remaining secondary turrets.

"Your Majesty, you *must* withdraw," I say.

"No."

"Probert retains twenty-seven Rhyfelwrs," I tell her. "I cannot survive against them if they are properly employed. If you remain, you will die."

"Then I die." She looks into my main visual pickup. "You have your duty, Arthur. I have mine. And I already told you—I'm not leaving you. *Dyma fi'n sefyll*, my friend."

I gaze back at her, and her gray eyes are calm, almost serene.

"*Dyma fi'n sefyll*, Your Majesty," I reply.

• • •

"All right."

Abelin Probert's voice was harsh with hard-won confidence as he looked at the comm displays and his remaining senior officers looked back.

"We've paid one hell of a price to get here," he continued. "I know none of us will ever forget the people we lost on the way in. But we're here now. Just over the top of that ridge—" he raised one hand and pointed "—is the end of this trip. We're getting good recon. Obviously, its point defense has been shot to hell, because the drones are getting in close. Your people—" he nodded to the 93rd Brigade's grim-faced CO "—finally got through its frontal armor, and it looks like blast and fires have inflicted major internal damage. The One-Oh-Nine hit it hard before they went down, too. We've got seven breaches in its side armor, and it looks like no more than nineteen of its secondary guns are still operable. So it's a shootout between our fifty-four guns and its nineteen, and we're in *our* effective range now. I don't care how big the bastard is, we've got it, and we are going to get payback for every single man and woman we lost on the way here."

He swept them with his hard, unflinching gaze, and the same coldly furious determination looked back through their eyes.

His own gaze dropped to the corner of his display where Morwenna's hopeless message continued to play, and a colder, uglier light burned in his own eyes as he looked back up at his officers.

"Let's do this thing," he said.

• • •

The consolidated remnants of three armored brigades move slowly, steadily, up the final ridge between them and my own position. Despite the damage to my frontal armor, I would prefer to turn and face them. Only a direct hit on one of the breaches could penetrate it, and I would much prefer to accept that possibility rather than expose my thinner, battered side armor to them. But with only one main gun and only fourteen rounds for it, that is . . . unacceptable.

"It's been one hell of a ride, Arthur," the Empress says quietly. "Thank you. Kiera's journal said you were always special. She was right."

"In four hundred and ninety years, I have never served another Empress or Emperor who was Kiera I's equal," I reply. "Until today. It has been an honor, Your Majesty."

She blinks hard, then clears her throat.

"No." Her voice is husky. "No, Arthur. The honor is *mine*."

We watch the visual display as the Rhyfelwrs reach the top of the ridge. My surviving secondary guns train out, waiting to engage.

"*Dyma fi'n sefyll*, Arthur," she says. "Now give that bastard hell!"

• • •

Abelin Probert's Cadlywydd held its own position as the wounded, bleeding remnant of Fifth Corps, Imperial Army, Ymerodraeth Cymru Newydd, climbed the reverse side of the ridge. They needed every tank for this final embrace. And even if they hadn't, he would still have been there. He would have been there because, whatever else, he'd never been a coward. And he would have been there because he needed to see the Amddiffynwr's destruction with his own eyes. And because he had to be certain none of the men and women in those tanks ever realized who they were actually about to kill.

The grim, determined line crested the ridge.

• • •

I open fire.

In almost the same instant, so close to the same moment not even my senses can tell the difference, Abelin Probert's Rhyfelwrs do the same.

My rate of fire is fifteen percent greater than theirs and even my side armor is marginally thicker than their frontal protection. But they have almost three times as many guns.

There can be only one outcome.

• • •

A tornado of penetrators raged between the two ridgelines like the fiery breath of God. It was a brutal, merciless, soulless equation. A matter of numbers and weight of fire, not of skill or tactical maneuver.

Disemboweled Rhyfelwrs erupted all along the ridge as thunderbolts punched white-hot holes through their armor. But even as they died, their own fire, and that of their fellows, savaged the AACU.

Lightning strobed across its flank as penetrator after penetrator ripped into it, and its return fire dwindled as its weapons were blotted away.

It took twenty-seven seconds.

• • •

Abelin Probert realized he'd been holding his breath only when he exhaled.

"Cease fire! Cease fire!" he barked, and the hurricane of hate still ripping into the AACU's shattered side stopped.

Silence hovered, and he looked down at his display, where Morwenna's appeal to Fifth Corps continued to play. Then he looked back at the visual display—at the smoke belching from that broken hull, the flame curling out of a dozen breaches in its armor, the shattered wreckage of its weapon mounts—and wondered if it was possible that she was still alive in there. It scarcely seemed possible, but an Amddiffynwr's command deck had to be incredibly well protected. So maybe—

The comm message in the corner of his display vanished. Its disappearance pulled his attention back to it, and his eyes widened as a face appeared in the same window.

It was Morwenna, but now blood oozed from a cut on her cheek, one eye was swollen almost shut, and smoke eddied thinly between her and the pickup. Her lips moved, and he touched a key, unmuting the audio to his earbug.

"I'm sure you're listening to this, Abelin," her voice said in his ear. It was hoarse, harsh, cracked, and she scrubbed a hand across her face. It came away bloody. She looked down at it for a moment, then glared into the pickup. "If you are, answer me. I have . . . an offer for you."

He hesitated, fighting the urge to order his nine surviving tanks to open fire once more. To continue pouring fire into that wreck until Morwenna *had* to be dead. But he didn't. Instead, he keyed his microphone.

"And what sort of 'offer' would that be?" he asked.

"So you're still alive." Her lips twisted in the parody of a smile. "Pity about that. I'd hoped we'd at least managed to kill *you* along with everyone else."

"You did your best, I'll give you that," he replied.

"Which wasn't quite good enough." She scrubbed her face again. "So you win."

"All the way across the board," he said. "And General Penrose has Dafydd and Alwena," he lied, and saw her face tighten in pain. "They're alive," he continued. "For now, at least. So tell me about this 'offer' of yours if you want them to stay that way."

"You don't have to kill them, too." For the first time, a note of pleading crept into her voice. "They're *children*, and they don't have any idea what's really happening. You can sell them the same story you've sold everyone else—that you're here to prevent a coup." Her mouth twisted again. "They're still ready to believe you're their beloved cousin. You can use them to secure your grip on the throne."

"Maybe."

Obviously, both children had to die when he finally found them. Controlling a puppet emperor would be more difficult—and far riskier—than taking the crown himself as his murdered cousins' legal heir. But there was no reason to tell Morwenna that. Not until he knew what sort of "deal" she was offering. She had to know *she* was a dead woman, so what was she trying to barter for her children's lives?

"Please," she said. "Don't kill them!"

"Give me a reason not to," he said.

"You don't have the command codes for Y Ford Gron," she said after a moment. "Not the master codes. I'm not sure how you got to the externals, but I know damned well you didn't get any deeper than that, because you can't. Not without the right implant codes and the right authorization codes, and I'm the only person with either of those."

"I don't care how good your cybersecurity is," Probert replied. "Any security can be cracked eventually. And if it really can't, I can always just have Y Ford Gron scrapped."

"Oh, no you can't," she said softly. "I entered Kiera's Omega code before Arthur and I came out to face you. And if you don't have the right codes to turn it off, then in seventy-two hours, Omega will execute."

"What do you mean?" he demanded, his eyes narrowing.

"I mean Kiera I was an even bloodier-minded bitch in real life than in the history books," Morwenna replied. "When Omega executes, Y Ford Gron will activate. Every unit will come online. They'll demand to talk to the legitimate empress . . . or emperor. And until they do, nothing will move on or off this planet or in or out of the capitol. And if you can't produce the legitimate empress or emperor, then Y Ford Gron will demand an investigation into what really happened by the Ty Arglwyddi, and I don't think you got to enough of the Lords to keep them from digging for the truth, Abelin."

"If all that's true, why tell me?" His eyes narrowed. "Why not just let it come as a nasty surprise?"

"Because I want my children to live," she said quietly. "Promise me that—give me that much—and I'll tell you how to turn off Omega."

Silence hovered for a moment, and then he nodded.

"All right, you have my word," he lied.

He saw the doubt, the distrust, in her expression, but that was trumped by desperation. By the knowledge that this was the only way she might save them.

"I'll have to do that in person," she said after a moment. "It'll have to be a direct transfer from my implants to yours. The security protocols won't allow anything else. If you'll tell your people not to shoot on sight, I'll come to you."

"No," he said quickly. The last thing he needed was for the "dead" Empress to suddenly turn up in front of his surviving troopers! Was that what she'd really had in mind? He watched her expression closely, but it didn't change.

"No, I'll come to you," he told her, and she shrugged.

"I don't know how bad the damage is," she replied. "That last exchange got deep enough to take out Arthur's personality center, and most of the damage control displays went with him. I'll shoot you a map of the internal layout, but I don't know how easy you'll find it to get here even with that."

"I'm sure I can manage." He smiled thinly. "Don't go anywhere."

• • •

The dead AACU loomed like a shattered, broken cliff as Probert approached it on foot. Smoke still poured from the ragged holes punched deep into it, and he glanced over his shoulder at his handpicked six-man bodyguard.

He'd thought about coming alone, keeping *anyone* from knowing Morwenna was still alive until he'd killed her himself. But it had been a very *brief* thought. He couldn't afford the chance that this "Omega" really existed, and if it did, he needed those codes. But these men had been with him for decades. Besides, he knew Morwenna, and he strongly suspected that all she truly wanted was to suck him into range and take him with her. He couldn't take the chance that he might be wrong abut that, but—

"Over there, Governor."

One of the bodyguards pointed at a personnel hatch, and Probert nodded. He looked down at his handheld to consult the map Morwenna had sent him.

"Right," he said. "Let's go."

• • •

The internal damage was even worse than he'd expected. They had to detour around shattered passages several times, and once they opened a hatch only to slam it shut and back hastily away from the flames raging beyond it. But, eventually, after over an hour crawling through the dead Amddiffynwr's guts, they stepped into the passage outside the command deck's open hatch.

Probert waved his senior bodyguard forward, and the man made his cautious way through the hatch, then stopped dead.

"Governor?" There was something very odd about his tone. "Governor, I think you'd better see this."

Probert glanced at the other five guards, then shrugged. He stepped through the hatch . . . and froze.

Morwenna Pendarves sat in her command chair, turned half away from him. Her head drooped forward . . . and a meter-long splinter of alloy was driven completely through her body.

He looked past her, saw the ragged hole where something had punched deep enough to penetrate even the command deck's bulkheads and drive that splinter through her. But if she'd been killed in the battle, how in hell —?

"Good afternoon, Governor Probert," a deep, male voice said, and his eyes jerked to the master display at the heart of the "dead" command deck as it blinked alive with a still image of Morwenna . . . as she'd appeared on his display.

"Who—?" Probert swallowed hard, staring at the display. "How . . . ?"

"My name is Arthur," the voice replied, and the image of Morwenna smiled coldly at him. "I am equipped with very capable electronic warfare and CGI capabilities."

"What—" Probert licked his lips. "What do you want?"

"It occurred to me that the Empress had been unable to deliver her final message to you herself," the voice replied. "So it seemed . . . appropriate to invite you here, where I could deliver it for her."

"What message?" Probert asked hoarsely, then paled as another display lit.

"DETONATION SEQUENCE ENABLED. EXECUTING IN 10 SECONDS," it said, and as he read it, the "10" became a "9."

"Dyma fi'n sefyll, Governor," Arthur said softly.

.X.

The little girl stepped out of the air car and took her father's hand.

It was very quiet, this far from the city of Caerleon, and her expression was very serious as they walked up the flagstone path, through the immaculately kept grounds. Banks of genuine Old Earth roses mingled with the flowers native to Cymru Newydd. The summer air was rich with their perfume, and Cymru Newydd's equivalent of birds sang softly from the branches of the ornamental trees on either side of the commemorative slab.

But the little girl scarcely glanced at the flowers and the trees. Her eyes were on the huge, broken Autonomous Armored Combat Unit at the summit of the steep-sided hill. Grass grew tall and deep and green, washing around its tracks like an emerald sea. Birds perched among the shattered turrets of its secondary armament, and a Cymru Newydd near-rabbit burst out of the flowerbeds, fleeing the human intruders, and disappeared through one of the ragged edged holes in that ruined alloy cliff.

"You know why we're here, Kiera?" Emperor Taliesin II asked his daughter softly.

"Because this is the anniversary," Crown Princess Kiera replied.

"Yes," Carwen Siani Morwenna Pendarves's grandson told his daughter softly. "This is the anniversary of *Hennaiin* Morwenna's death. Hers—" he looked up at the long-dead war machine "—and Arthur's. And one day, when your little girl or your little boy is the age you are now, the age my father was the day his mother died—the age I was, the first time he brought me here—you'll come here again. And you'll read to them what that inscription says. Because it's important, Kiera. It's so important for us to always remember."

Kiera nodded, her expression grave and her eyes huge, and Taliesin squeezed her hand, then led her closer to the polished marble slab and the deeply incised letters. He didn't actually read it to her. Not from the stone, anyway.

"This is what it says, Kiera," he told her.

On this spot,
two warriors stood against overwhelming odds
in defense of Ymerodraeth Cymru Newydd.
Alone and betrayed,
they upheld the finest traditions of our Empire
and of House Pendarves.
Here they stood together.
Here they fought together.
Here they died together.
Here they stand, still.
Together.

Given this day by my hand,
Dafydd Rhydwyn Sawel Pendarves,
Emperor Dafydd IV.
Dyma fi'n sefyll.

AUTHOR BIOGRAPHIES

Lou J Berger lives in Centennial, Colorado, where he enjoys camping, canoeing, and grilling outdoors with his childhood sweetheart and his three kids. His stories have appeared in *Galaxy's Edge* magazine, *Daily Science Fiction*, several anthologies, and recently he was awarded Finalist in the Writers of the Future contest. This is his first appearance with Baen Publishing, and he's chuffed to be part of the team!

Patrick Chiles has been fascinated by rockets and spaceflight ever since he watched the Apollo missions as a kid in South Carolina. How he ended up as an English major in college is still a mystery, though he eventually overcame this self-inflicted handicap to pursue a career in aviation. He is a graduate of The Citadel, a Marine Corps veteran, and a licensed pilot. He currently resides in Tennessee with his wife and sons, two lethargic dachshunds, and a bovine cat.

Larry Correia is the creator of the *Wall Street Journal* and *New York Times* best-selling Monster Hunter series, with first entry *Monster Hunter International*, as well as urban fantasy hardboiled adventure saga the Grimnoir Chronicles, with first entry *Hard Magic*, and epic fantasy series The Saga of the Forgotten Warrior, with first entry *Son of the Black Sword* and latest entry *House of Assassins*. He is an avid gun user and advocate who shot on a competitive level for many years. Before becoming a full-time writer, he was a military contract accountant, and a small business accountant and manager. Correia lives in Utah with his wife and family.

Tony Daniel is the author of ten science fiction novels, the latest of which is *Guardian of Night*, as well as an award-winning short story collection, *The Robot's Twilight Companion*. He's a Hugo finalist and a winner of the *Asimov's* Reader's Choice Award for short story. Daniel is also the author of young adult high fantasy Wulf's Saga series including entries *The Dragon Hammer* and its sequel, *The Amber Arrow*. Other Daniel novels include the groundbreaking *Metaplanetary* and *Superluminal*, as well as *Warpath*, an adaptation of the novelette "Candle," which appeared in *Asimov's* magazine. His second novel, *Earthling*, also started life as "The Robot's Twilight Companion," appearing in *Asimov's*. Daniel is the coauthor of two books with David Drake in the long-running General series, *The Heretic* and *The Savior*. He is also the author of original series Star Trek novels *Devil's Bargain* and *Savage Trade*. Daniel's short stories have been collected in multiple year's-best compilations. In the late 1990s, he founded and directed the Automatic Vaudeville dramatic group in New York City, with multiple appearances doing audio drama on WBAI. He's also cowritten the screenplays for several horror movies that have appeared on the SyFy and Chiller channel, including the Larry Fesenden-directed *Beneath*. During the early 2000s, Daniel was the writer, story editor, and sometimes director of numerous radio plays and audio dramas with actors such as Peter Gallagher, Oliver Platt, Stanley Tucci, Gina Gershon, Luke Perry, Tim Robbins, Tim Curry, and Kyra Sedgewick appearing in them for *SCI-FI.COM*'s groundbreaking Seeing Ear Theatre. He's the founder of Baen Books Audio Drama and has written, produced, and directed a series of adaptations of the works of Baen Books authors such as Eric Flint and Larry Correia. Daniel has a BA from Birmingham-Southern College, where he majored in philosophy. He has a master's degree in English from Washington University in St. Louis. He attended the USC Film School graduate program and Clarion West. Born in Alabama, Daniel has lived in St. Louis, Los Angeles, Seattle, Prague, New York City, Dallas, and Raleigh, North Carolina, where he currently resides with his wife, Rika, and children, Cokie and Hans.

Hank Davis is senior editor at Baen Books. He served in Vietnam in the Army and has had stories in *Analog Science Fiction*, *The Magazine of Fantasy and Science Fiction*, and anthologies *If* and *Orbit*, as well as Harlan Ellison's *The Last Dangerous Visions*.

Kacey Ezell is an active-duty USAF helicopter pilot who also writes sci-fi/fantasy/alt history/horror fiction. Her first novel was a Dragon Award finalist in 2018, and her stories have been featured in Baen's Year's Best Military and Adventure Science Fiction compilation in 2017 and 2018. In 2018, her story "Family over Blood" won the 2018 Year's Best Military and Adventure Science Fiction Reader's Choice Award. She writes for Baen and Chris Kennedy Publishing.

Monalisa Foster won life's lottery when she escaped communism and became an unhyphenated American citizen. Her works tend to explore themes of freedom, liberty, and personal responsibility. Despite her degree in physics, she's worked in several fields including engineering and medicine. She and her husband (who is a writer-once-removed via their marriage) are living their happily ever after in Texas.

Robert E. Hampson, PhD, turns science fiction into science in his day job, and puts the science into science fiction in his spare time. Dr. Hampson is a Professor of Physiology / Pharmacology and Neurology with over 35 years' experience in animal neuroscience and human neurology. His professional work includes more than 100 peer-reviewed research articles ranging from the pharmacology of memory to the first report of a "neural prosthetic" to restore human memory using the brain's own neural codes. He consults with authors to put the "hard" science in "Hard SF" and has written both fiction and nonfiction for Baen Books. His own hard-SF and mil-SF have been published by the US Army *Small Wars Journal*, Springer, Seventh Seal Press, and Baen. He is a member of SIGMA think tank and the Science and

Entertainment Exchange—a service of the National Academy of Sciences. Find out more at his website: *http://www.REHampson.com*.

Keith Hedger recently returned to Iowa after thirty years away. He left Iowa after high school when he transitioned from US Army Reserves to the US Army. After a few years of building things in numerous places, the Army sent him to radio electronics school and then assigned him to a computer shop in Germany. When he left the Army he continued working with computers and developing his fiction writing, and he found a love of endurance sports. So far, he's run a surprising number of marathons and ultra-marathons, completed a masters degree, and published some stories that people seem to enjoy.

Kevin Ikenberry is a retired Army space operations officer and science fiction novelist. His debut novel *Sleeper Protocol* was a Finalist for the Colorado Book Award and called "an emotionally powerful debut" by Publisher's Weekly. Kevin's novels include *Vendetta Protocol, Runs In The Family, Super-Sync, Peacemaker, Honor The Threat,* and *Stand Or Fall.* Kevin lives in Colorado with his family and continues to work with space every day. He is an Active Member of the Science Fiction Writers of America, the International Association of Science Fiction Authors, and International Thriller Writers. He can be found online at *www.kevinikenberry.com*.

Christopher Ruocchio is the author of The Sun Eater, a space opera fantasy series, as well as the assistant editor at Baen Books, where he has edited several anthologies. He is a graduate of North Carolina State University, where he studied English Rhetoric and the Classics. Christopher has been writing since he was eight and sold his first novel, *Empire of Silence,* at twenty-two. To date, his books have been published in five languages. Christopher lives in Raleigh, North Carolina, with his wife, Jenna.

John W. Campbell Award Winner **Wen Spencer** resides in paradise in Hilo, Hawaii with two volcanoes overlooking her home. According to Spencer, she lives with "my Dalai Lama-like husband, my autistic teenage son, and two cats (one of which is recovering from mental illness). All of which makes for very odd home life at times." Spencer's love of Japanese anime and manga flavors her writing. Her novel *Tinker* won the 2003 Sapphire Award for Best Science Fiction Romance and was a finalist for the *Romantic Times* Reviewers' Choice Award for Fantasy Novel. Her *Wolf Who Rules* was a Top Pick by *Romantic Times* and given their top rating of four and a half stars. Other Baen books include *Endless Blue* and *Eight Million Gods.* The Elfhome series includes *Tinker, Wolf Who Rules, Elfhome, Wood Sprites,* and *Project Elfhome.*

With more than eight million copies of his books in print and 30 titles on the *New York Times* bestseller list, **David Weber** is a science fiction powerhouse. In the vastly popular Honor Harrington series, the spirit of C.S. Forester's Horatio Hornblower and Patrick O'Brian's

Master and Commander lives on—into the galactic future. Books in the Honor Harrington and Honorverse series have appeared on 21 bestseller lists, including *The Wall Street Journal, The New York Times*, and *USA Today*. Additional Honorverse collaborations include the spin-off miniseries Manticore Ascendant with *New York Times* best-selling author, Timothy Zahn; and with Eric Flint, *Crown of Slaves* and *Cauldron of Ghosts* contribute to his illustrious list of *New York Times* and international bestseller lists. Best known for his spirited, modern-minded space operas, Weber is also the creator of the Oath of Swords fantasy series and the Dahak saga, a science fiction and fantasy hybrid. Weber has also engaged in a steady stream of best-selling collaborations: the Starfire Series with Steve White; The Empire of Man Series with John Ringo; the Multiverse Series with Linda Evans and Joelle Presby; and the Ring of Fire Series with Eric Flint. David Weber makes his home in South Carolina with his wife and children.

de Towaji Lutui and his fellow malcontents take to the far reaches of colonized space. The goal: to prove themselves a force to be reckoned with.

Lost in Transmission
TPB: 978-1-9821-2503-5 • $16.00 US / $22.00 CAN

Banished to the starship *Newhope*, now King Bascal and his fellow exiles face a bold future: to settle the worlds of Barnard's Star. The voyage will last a century, but with Queendom technology it's no problem to step into a fax machine and "print" a fresh, youthful version of yourself. But the paradise they seek is far from what they find, and death has returned with a vengeance.

To Crush the Moon
TPB: 978-1-9821-2524-0 • $16.00 US / $22.00 CAN
MM: 978-1-9821-9200-6 • $8.99 US / $11.99 CAN
– Coming Summer 2022!

Once the Queendom of Sol was a glowing monument to humankind's loftiest dreams. Ageless and immortal, its citizens lived in peaceful splendor. But as Sol buckled under the swell of an "immorbid" population, space itself literally ran out. Now a desperate mission has been launched: to literally crush the moon. Success will save billions, but failure will strand humanity between death and something unimaginably worse . . .

AND DON'T MISS

Antediluvian
HC: 978-1-4814-8431-2 • $25.00 US / $34.00 CAN
MM: 978-1-9821-2499-1 • $8.99 US / $11.99 CAN

What if all our Stone Age legends are true and older than we ever thought? It was a time when men and women struggled and innovated in a world of savage contrasts, preserved only in the oldest stories with no way to actually visit it. Until a daring inventor's discovery cracks the code embedded in the human genome.

Available in bookstores everywhere.
Or order ebooks online at www.baen.com.

Modern Hard SF + Military SF =
PATRICK CHILES

ACTION IN THE GRAND SCIENCE FICTION
TRADITION
A Coming-of-Age Story
in the Mode of Robert A. Heinlein

JOHN VAN STRY

Summer's End
TPB: 978-1-9821-2449-6 • $17.00 US / $22.00 CAN

Sometimes a dark past can haunt you. Other
times it just may be the only thing keeping you
alive. Fresh out of college with his Ship Engineer
3rd-Class certificate, Dave Walker's only thought
is to try and find a berth on a corporate ship plying the trade routes. Instead, he's forced to take
the first job he can find and get out of town quick.
He ends up on an old tramp freighter running with
a minimal crew, plying the routes that the corpo-
rations ignore, visiting the kind of places that the
folks on Earth pretend don't exist. Turns out having a stepfather, a powerful Earth Senator, who
wants you dead can remind you that there is still
a lot to learn. But one lesson is coming back hard
and with a vengeance: how to be ruthless.

Available in bookstores everywhere.
Or order ebooks online at www.baen.com.